Chapter One.

Morning broke under an insulting d stole much of the morning light before its r̶a̶ with little distinction between it and the wea chirped with praise for newfound morning – or rather in distaste of the weather it brought with it. Streets burst to life with the sleep deprived. And finally, the toll of the bell, at a distance it was a pleasant chime, but those unfortunate to be in closer proximity the sound rattled bones and roused the dead.

No church stood for seven miles, so the sound wasn't burdened with the purpose of explaining the hour nor calling the faithful to service. For the unknowing, the young and occasionally the willingly naïve, the sound served a fairly tedious, unassuming purpose, a warning that the night's accumulated petty criminals had served their sentence. Most were willing to think that the only purpose, ignoring the truth lingering in the shadows of their home.

For the bell took residence in an unkind part of town, capable of being kindly described as a pigsty. A small stone building with a smell that curdled milk and walls that writhed with fleas, was the habitat of the despairing, the disorderly and the drunken. The chiming bell to rouse the guards to free the prisoners, left fleeing with promises of a path set straight.

Whilst that was a fine enough purpose, a far better and infinitely more efficient option than posting a man at the door to spend ten minutes yelling 'Run for your lives,' on the off chance someone's straight path took an unexpected bend. There was a second purpose to the rattling bell so hated for its regular theft of a sleep in.

As the small town of Cresvy was resident to evil incarnate.

For in that little borough, monsters didn't hide under beds nor creep in the shadows. Rather the towns primary source of nightmares outside of a criminal lack of hygiene took the form of a man not yet above 25. The epitome of a wolf in sheep clothing, his curse was beyond dashing good looks and the occasional case of butterfingers. Lycanthropy had been thrust upon him from a young age, the experiences that followed rendered said descriptor an accurate one.

Said evil incarnate, currently dozed peacefully propped against a cold stone wall. Dreaming of playing with his niece and nephews, devouring his favourite meal, and being just about anywhere else but that cramped, dirty cell.

Given the cell was a regular habitat by now, the chime was little more bother than the howling winds. Rather what roused evil incarnate that morning, was the departure of warmth from his knees.

Blinking pale blue eyes apart in time to spot his night's companion, a fluffy cat dubbed as Whiskey departing through the bars of the cell. After all, evil incarnate was a friend to all forms of non-delicious wildlife, largely because he half counted himself amid them.

The young man stretched as best as his restraints permitted but found his feet at risk of removing the teeth of a nearby dozer. Someone seemingly either hadn't heard the warnings, didn't believe the warnings, or had elected to risk his luck at the chance of a decent night's sleep.

Either they hadn't notice the chains restraining his every limb, or they believed an adequate method of restraint for evil incarnate. The young man was increasingly sure he could spread rumours his hair had super strength and they would find a way to bind that in silver too.

Silver, among other rarer materials offered something in the way of a weakness to the murderous 6-foot tall pile of vile, seething hate, and had been sewn into his very clothes.

Whilst frustrating, he considered it a reasonable compromise in return for having a roof over his head rather than the woods surrounding the little town. Particularly during times where everything seemed to be plagued by the damned weather.

And it was not a one-way deal either. As being placed face to face with the jaws of death offered something in the way of an incentive to stay on the other side of the cell's silver bars. Though whether he was an effective deterrent came under some debate as it never felt like the population of their rotting cell decreased.

At least it gave the young man entertainment, and everyone needed a hobby.

The chiming bells in practice should have been the signal of freedom, but in practicality it usually took about ten minutes further. What was offered in excuse was that it provided a chance to evacuate the area, but more accurately the guards were not morning people. Or any time of the day people, really, but mornings seemed to bring out their crueller colours.

Heavy footsteps accompanied by a thud/drag pace caught his attention, a familiar sound. Though most sounds were familiar by now, from the scuttle of rat feet to the dripping of leaking roofs.

He wouldn't have gone as far as to associate the sound with a friend, but at the very least not an enemy, and given the present surroundings he was willing to accept such as a victory.

This particular 'barely friend,' was someone the wolf didn't know by name. A general rule of thumb meant that outside of these cell walls he was avoided, and within these walls he wasn't worth the time of day.

His eyes burned as the door flung open, light flooding the room like a bursting dam. The young wolf didn't move to wipe them, or rather he didn't move at all. A statue against the cold stone, only his eyes moved as they followed his den's trespasser.

Beneath the stench of ale and poor bodily hygiene there was nothing but the usual smell of damp. Occasionally when income permitted, his mother would offer the guards a bribe to bring him breakfast. Part of him pondered if she always did, but the result was more dependent on the guard's willingness to comply. Today he smelled nothing.

Around him, cellmates scattered to the bars, trapped rats lunging for a suddenly opened barn door.

Evil incarnate on the other hand took a more leisurely approach, lifting himself to his feet. The young man leant against the cold damp wall, less in an attempt to seem relaxed and more in an attempt to reveal the pressure from his aching limbs. The chance to appear nonchalant happened to be a happy side effect.

The rattling sound of greasy fingers fumbling with metallic keys as Mead casually searched for the correct implement of freedom. Either unaware or uncaring of the desperation of his wards to get the hell out of here. After a moment he found success and the mighty door was shoved open and the guard entered in silence.

Most of Cresvy still regarded the wolf fearfully even after all these years, in spite of the evidence that in his chained state he was about as threatening as the average lamb, and the guards' deviation from the norm left him respectful of the daring. Most of the guards he had come across found themselves somewhere between hatred and boredom in regard to him, this one bordered somewhere in the middle. A happy medium as far as he was concerned.

His night companions didn't take their chances at the guard changing his mind hurtling out without a goodbye. Leaving Silas and his sole comrade in their dust in the effort to be free of the cell walls.

"Morning," the wolf offered as way of a greeting. His line of sight remained at the guard's muddied boots and didn't lift when he continued into the cell. Whilst evil incarnate was yet to see someone utilise any of his various weapons, he didn't doubt that he would should the need arise.

Electing not to dignify the wolf's greeting with a response, The Guard knelt. Yanking the wolf's wrist upright and unlocking the chains in a swift movement. Now he was somewhat more elegant, a striking snake rather than an ungainly tortoise.

"Thanks," the wolf stood fully now; stretching, his gaze following the guard as he departed at a hurried pace. The wolf was kind enough to allow him some distance, waiting a beat to try and work some warmth and feeling back into his aching legs, before following suit.

Within moments he found himself in the outside world once more, the terrain underfoot torn up and muddied but it felt like freedom all the same. His eyes travelled across the street, nostrils flaring as he enjoyed what little in the way of fresh air Cresvy offered.

"You took your time, Silas," a voice sounded to the right but didn't take him off guard.

"Unfortunately, I don't think the guards are open for criticism, at this time, and the last man to add to the suggestions box lost an arm," the wolf's response was easy and nonchalant as he turned to greet the speaker. "Do check back tomorrow, though. The guards are lovely fellows always looking to improve their services." He said with crossed arms.

Despite a stoic exterior, his friend's lips parted to release a chuckle. "Careful, they might hear you and take you back," her tone was that of a scolding mother – the condescending shake of her head sent red hair flying with the efforts of her over emphasis.

In spite of his best efforts to look unperturbed, he found it difficult to contain his excitement as seeing his friend again. "What time did the cat drag you in this morning, it looks like you were hauled home by the ankles." He scoffed playfully.

"We got in last night," she added electing to ignore the latter part of his question for his sake. "And you try looking beautiful when you shower by a shared bucket each day."

Struggling to stifle the chuckle that threatened to tug free of his lips, he shook his head with amusement. He gave in to his attempts at restraint, launching forward he greeted his companion with a firm hug before she had the chance to reply. "I've missed you Flick."

Pulling free of his embrace. "I'm glad, and I've missed you too Silas. Glad to see you were able to keep yourself in one piece whilst I've been gone."

The wannabe pirate had been gone for the better part of a fortnight, travelling east with her father trading. She had leapt at the chance to be free of the town's rotten air and smoky streets, but Silas had missed her more than he had imagined he would. His life wasn't littered with an overabundance of friends, and her departure however short had been a bitter shock to his system.

It was an experience Silas would have given his left arm for but had known better than even try to ask if he might accompany. The seas were rough enough, and he doubted a captain would be willing to accept a wolf onboard even in the depths of a rum stupor. Despite himself, he couldn't help but begrudge his best friend a little of the fact that she had been able to go without him. Even a little more considering she hadn't even stopped to wonder what might happen to him whilst she was gone, gallivanting on the high sea whilst he was left there to rot.

"I'm not so inept that I can't keep myself alive for a fortnight." He scoffed in what he considered a reasonable attempt at offence.

"I beg to differ, last time I left you alone for more than half an hour you came back with a new coat and sharp teeth."

He grimaced at the poor attempt at a joke, the growl that tugged free of his chest a playful one for the most part. "Don't make me regret saying I've missed you, or I'll find you a ship and make sure you never come back."

Flick seemed unaffected by the growl that would have sent most scattering for the hills. Though after 6 years of friendship, Silas was of the increasing opinion a bomb would be incapable of surprising her. "You wouldn't know what to do without me, just admit it."

"Perhaps, anyway you'd likely bug them too much they'd bring you back within the hour.

"Well I managed to remain at sea for two weeks without being shoved overboard, perhaps you're just overly sensitive, Sy." Seemingly bored of the conversation, Flick's change of topic was as subtle as the average bull in a china shop. "Anything happen whilst I was gone?" But the burning gaze of excitement left Silas assuming there was some ulterior motive to her choice of subject.

"Not that I'm aware of, unless there's been a murder overnight," Silas returned with a shrug. "Despite my requests, they don't bring newspapers to the cells." Content to leave her hanging, he continued at a lazy pace, before adding with a grin. "Why, what have you heard?"

Grasping the chance before it could be snatched cruelly away once more, "Not from here," the words spilled from her like water cascading down the rocks, stopping in her tracks and spinning on the heel to face him once more. "Word is the King is set to return today!"

Halting on the spot to prevent smacking shoulder to shoulder, he set her with a gaze similar to how one might regard an over dramatic child, a not entirely unfair description for his best friend. Silas was unsure as to the source of her excitement, the King's departure from the lands had been well publicised but its purpose was nothing overly exciting nor reason to believe he might not come back. "So, he's been gone long enough. Even a king can't go on vacation forever Flick, he was bound to come back at some point."

Her head shook so violently he was rendered surprised it wasn't dislocated in the action. "You miss my meaning dumbass," she grumbled. "He's returning, and he's using the Littledusk wharf as his first port of call."

He was man enough to admit that wasn't what he'd expected, for a moment he watched her carefully. Searching for signs she might be pranking him, "I'm not lying," and as far as the wolf could tell she wasn't. Turning once more, she set off again with a huff. All of it dramatics, Silas knew his friend well enough to spot that from a mile off. Entertaining her excitement, he caught up to and maintained pace with the shorter woman in less than two strides.

"Why here of all places?" An eyebrow arched with uncertainty, "He's aware there are nicer docks, right?" Silas added with a snort, "Hell, pointed rocks probably offer a nicer port of call."

"Next time I'll be sure to offer him a few better options," Flick's tone was unamused, but her spirit wasn't easily dampened. "I can't believe it, a member of the royal family, in our little town!" Her gait was all but a skip, Silas watched her through narrowed eyes trying to remember if he could taste rum on the air around her. He knew it was the pirating stereotype, but she'd only been gone a fortnight and couldn't quite imagine her becoming an alcoholic that quickly.

Though not entirely understanding of why she was so excited, "I never pictured you to be the romantic type, Flick." No doubt he would present his face for all of three seconds maybe throw a handful of pennies to passing children, and then be off on his merry way. The excitement would linger for a couple of days and then be gone like a distant wind.

"It's not my fault you're as exciting as the average brick, Sy."

He understood the sentiment enough not to take offence. "A side effect of spending one's nights in a cell rather than out on the town," he replied with a shrug of his shoulders. Harbouring a wolf didn't exactly leave much opportunity in the way of socialising.

"You must be a little excited," Flick continued, making a sharp right as they began up the paths into the main part of Cresvy, leaving the heavy stench of the slums in their wake. "Getting to meet the King, how many people get to say they've done that in their lifetime?"

If meeting him means seeing him from a distance I imagine quite a few, he considered but kept it to himself to avoid a smack across the shoulder. "Sorry, Flick. But you've lost me I've got to be honest."

"At the very least I hear his sons are quite attractive," it seemed she accepted defeat at last that Silas wasn't about to leap for joy at her news.

"Thrilling," he nodded patiently. As though there were any chance either of them could get with a prince. "You're about as likely to marry an elf as you are a prince, Flick."

He dodged her right hook by the skin of a whisker, and only chuckled lightly when her left hand glanced harmlessly from his hip. "Ouch," he said for her sake. "What time are their royal highnesses meant to be getting into port anyway? If not as a wife, maybe I can convince one of them to take you away as a chamber maid, or perhaps a stable hand."

Seemingly deciding against wasting her energy on useless blows, she merely frowned. "Just before sunset." She cast her gaze skyward, "Not that that's much of a help, I don't think the sun's coming out to play today."

This time Silas ducked, taking shelter behind an upturned table nearby. He lifted his head above it to say a single phrase as quickly and quietly as he was able, "I've bad news for you, Flick." Sculpting his voice in an only half joking attempt to sound scared.

Once more she turned on her heel, hands on her hips and a frown etched so deep into her expression it might as well have been tattooed. "What?" Her voice was the storm and her gaze were the flame.

"You're at work."

She guffawed, "We'll be done at the docks before the sun has even reached midsky, don't be ridiculous." She would let nothing get in the way of her dream date at a hundred metres with a man she'd never met let alone knew she existed.

Despite not wanting to crush his best friend's dreams of marrying some handsome prince, being whisked away from their town, Silas knew avoiding the truth would be good for neither of them.

He shook his head. "Its Market day," he'd entirely forgotten she'd have no idea. Before she could open her mouth to say something further, he continued against his better judgement. "After the paddy the mayor threw when it was put off last month due to the rain, he decided it would be a good idea to bring it forward a week this month."

Flick looked like she'd been punched in the face. "You've got to be kidding me." Defeat left her shoulders sagging, the disappointment burning in her gaze made Silas feel guilty. As though he would have risked a prank at her expense just for the fun of it, knowing it would have shattered her heart like a dropped glass. "I mean no one will come to market if the King's here!"

"Tell him that." He offered but knew it would be of no help. "He practically had a heart attack when he was told he couldn't collect taxes that day. He probably can't afford the 27 butlers if he waits another week." His attempt at sarcasm fell flat on Flick's frustrated face.

"I'm going to kill him."

Silas shook his head, "If you do that the market will still be on and you'd be in the prisons so it's not exactly like you'd get to meet him."

"I'm going to kill you."

"Similar problem there, unfortunately," he retorted without missing a beat.

Flick turned to punch a wall, electing that was more easily bruised than her compatriot. All the same Silas pushed forward and blocked her before she had the chance, electing she'd be more annoyed by a broken hand than missing the King. "Please don't be an idiot," his tone was soft as he caught the blow before she could realise, he had moved to stop her.

However, his comrade merely shook his head. "Come on, we should be getting to the docks." She had barely allowed the 'k' to sound before she had turned once more and pushed onwards down the cobblestone-hill.

Silas parted his lips to offer something – anything in the way of further comfort but found himself lacking. Whilst he knew there was as much chance of her marrying a god as there was some prince, he disliked watching her frustrated. Particularly after her absence for a prolonged period of time, he wanted this to have been a happy reunion – not one that ended in frustration. But then it appeared there was little he could do in the way of fixing the situation. Merely offering something in the way of humour to lighten the dark circumstances she returned to.

Whilst not being able to be in the presence of a king for a few fleeting seconds would likely not be the death of her, he couldn't imagine returning to this foul town being the most exciting place to come home to after a fortnight of freedom on the wild sea. Freedom would only ever be a step away from his best friend, but the best he could ever achieve was being freed from his little damp cell. Where he was just as hated outside of as he was inside.

Silas swallowed hard and followed his best friend down the narrow streets wordlessly. His shoulders drooping and the skip to his step all but depleted.

Chapter Two.

Only when the sharp salt scent at last overwhelmed the damp and mould stenches of the streets surrounding the small port did the tension begin to melt. Not once did Flick offer something to break the silence that had developed between the two friends.

In fairness Silas had misspoken when he had implied that the Littledusk port was the worst dock anywhere had to offer. In fact, it wasn't even the worst in town, that was reserved for his workplace. But in truth there wasn't too much of a lie behind it; this dock wasn't exactly a place for stopping. Even the lowliest sailor didn't wait here for longer than necessary – they slowed their ships long enough to hurl various shipments to the docks below and then were gone on their merry way once more.

As a result, there was almost nothing nice about the Littledawn port; an attempt at amusement on the part of the workers given that as far as they were aware it had no official name. It was infested with rats to the point where Silas was grateful for the overwhelming smells produced by the sea.

The Littledawn port was little more than an over glorified parking lot. Slabs of metal, wood and concrete was all that separated it from the crashing waves bellow and was suspended above it by the height of an average man. It was vulnerable to any element nature could throw at it, and home to two upright buildings only.

The first of which was a squat hut of sorts, allegedly meant for the portmaster to use as his quarters, but in his three years of employment here he had never seen it go to much use.

He watched as his friend departed toward the second of two upright buildings on the lot – a lean too originally intended as a temporary site that had never been upgraded. Silas found himself a place to settle, legs dangling over the pier, watching the crash of waves beneath them, occasionally battered by a light spray.

Whilst there were no strict rules against his entrance into the office, it was something the wolf aimed to avoid where possible. One of few silver linings offered by his lycan traits – the docks weren't a place for the weak or feeble, and his heightened strength offered an advantage few others could envy. It had taken much convincing and ended in a trial day in which he had managed the work of three people in the space of half an hour to be accepted. But it was something, and it was something that paid at the very least. As measly as the work might have been, that was one huge positive in its favour.

Something silver caught his attention in the crashing waters below, the splashes of silver in the depths of the murky blue that made his stomach rumble. A reminder of his hunger previously forgotten in the happiness of reuniting with his friend; as short lived as it might have lasted.

He shifted on the spot, searching the dockside for the various equipment that was usually haphazardly scattered across the metal and wood surfaces. But what he found disappointed him. Some lazy soul had failed to put them away properly.

Around him sat a graveyard, the remnants of various fishing poles, a couple of tridents and even a fishing net were in ruins. Rendered tattered, snapped and broken by the storms that had overtaken much of the last couple of days, along with rubbish brought in by the tide.

Silas nose wrinkled in disgust and for a brief moment he considered pausing to attempt to tidy up. Maybe even see if there was anything worth bringing back with the hopes of salvaging it. But the sound of footsteps sounding above the howling winds drew his attention, and he looked back to spot Flick making her way over once more.

"What's the plan of the day?" Silas asked with an arched eyebrow, an attempt at peace making after their brief shared silence.

Flick scowled at him as though he were dirt trodden upon a newly laid rug, *mission failed*, "You'll never guess."

"We're sacked?"

"Worse," she took a seat at his side. "Due in about half an hour; a king's ship." But from her tone of voice he could guess that didn't bring as much joy as it could have done, that and the fact he could hardly picture the King of the Realm jumping from the high sides of the cargo ships that stopped here. "His cargo ship, bringing the rewards of his new friendships no doubt," she picked up a discarded stone and hurled it, he knew her grievances wasn't against the sea nor him.

Despite his best efforts, the wolf grinned with amusement at this revelation. "Do you think the King realises his valuables are to be delivered by… air mail?" He lacked a better descriptor, but the hesitation did little to ruin his fun.

Whilst he pretended to know nothing of the inner workings of someone so pure as a king's mind, he couldn't imagine he would be happy to learn that his valuables were to be hurled at speed from the sides of a dock. *Maybe Littledusk would be the better option.*

Yet there had to be a reason the King had elected to go a more private route for the delivery of his valuables. As far as Silas was aware the point of this sort of thing was to show off just how well he had done on his conquests, keeping it hidden seemed to be against the point. It was something Silas pondered for a heartbeat but came out with little in the way of an answer, or at least not a likely one.

But Flick's lack of amusement and apparent contemplation of murder left him stumbling on his words briefly, he paused. Trying to decide what the best course of action next would be to avoid a knife to the shoulder blade.

Making a risky decision, "Maybe not a prince but you might see a royal courtier?" He offered to receive a slap to the shoulder that failed in quietening him. "You might even be lucky enough to spot the King's ship from the distance, at least?" He offered a little more genuinely. Whilst hardly an amazing view, the docks would offer a much less crowded condition under which to see the King, and likely from a similar distance to what could be achieved in the centre of town.

"Hardly the sa-," she never had the chance to finish before being interrupted.

"I'm surprised you even dare say that name, Sy," despite the familiar nickname it was far from a friendly voice. "Does it not burn your very tongue?" Uninvited a figure slumped beside them on the dock the newcomer carried himself as though he owned the docks and the town, as though even the sea cowered at his command.

Alex, a man with a bite to rival the wolf's and a grin just as lupine, he was one of few folks daring enough to threaten – or at least bully someone who could have snapped him in half with a single bite.

But Silas wasn't about to risk it all for the sake of an idiot with too much free time. And he wasn't about to put to waste years of garnering what good reputation he could manage just to retort to someone who was little better than a bully. He took it on the chin as best as he could and wasn't below letting Flick get in the odd shot or two for his sake.

And as with most things – even in the sourest of moods, Flick came to bat for her best friend.

"Pray tell, Al," she lifted a hand to wipe the dirt from beneath her nails; an overly dramatic pose of confidence. "Why would you think that?" For now, she restrained from her barrage of insults though she treat him with more distain than she might have a stray dog found excreting on her front step.

"Even the sight of silver makes him flinch," had Alex owned anything of the sort Silas imagined he would have been toting it round like a flag. "Forgive me for assuming anything above his stature was like poison to him."

It took some effort for him not to snort at this. The logic was flawed to the point of hilarity, but if that had been the first thing on his mind Silas doubted they'd ever have exchanged a word in the entire time they'd been acquainted, by now his insults were so worn bare that they resonated with little offence.

But in an astonishing turn of events, Alex seemed to have second thoughts. "But then," he considered rubbing his chin. "He seems to tread across the dirt – hell even in dog's dirt without flinching. So, I suppose I was wrong." His cruel smile bared yellow teeth.

When neither target replied or as much as looked at him, he added. "What business do you have defending a mutt, anyway? Can't your boyfriend speak up for himself, does the cat have his tongue?" Every time Silas was certain the smile couldn't widen anymore he was proven wrong, he pondered briefly if the effort was painful.

Only then did he speak up, "Don't be so rude," he scoffed but likely not in response to what the idiot was hoping. "She's got far better standards then having me as a boyfriend."

Flick stiffened, not with annoyance but likely more with an attempt to stifle a laugh.

Alex looked far from amused, but Silas spoke up before he could offer more of his riveting insights about life, the universe and Silas' love life.

"As thrilling as our little chats always are," he stood up quicker than was necessary, but found some exhilaration in watching Alex flinch with surprise at the sudden burst of speed. "But either the ocean has caught fire, or the ship is on its way."

With the forceful expression of someone trying to maintain his cool, Alex stood upright. With the forceful expression of someone trying to contain a fit of laughter, Flick did as well.

Indeed, the sky seemed to have found a new blanket in the pale whites and greys of a burning ship fire. But the sight hadn't been what first caught the young wolf's attention, rather the scent of smoke underlying the salty sea that caught his attention. It caught at his lungs and left them feeling as though the very smell had singed them.

A handful of companions soon made their entrance, having spotted the skyward harbinger.

The approaching beast dwarfed the docks it ported at, it could have crushed them by the slightest wrong turn or breath of wind, but its course remained true in a show of astonishing expertise. Its size left him with a sensation of powerlessness that he found strangely enjoyable. Even when contained in threads of silver, Silas usually found himself the strongest man in the room, but his tininess in the wake of the hulking ship was humbling.

A soft rumble of sounded as the anchor plummeted from the ship's high walls into the ocean bellow, dragging the ship into a halt.

Not even a heartbeat had passed before the gangway was launched from the peaks of the ships side, an unwieldy arm sprouting without warning from the great beast of a ship and plummeting towards the dock.

Silas lunged, grasping it as best as he could as a pair of companions moved to aid him in securing it as best as they could. All they had were the wooden poles intended for far smaller ships, but it was the best they could manage, thus began hurriedly roping it into place. Hoping to offer something in the way of security for those who would soon be descending.

It was only a matter of heartbeats before a figure appeared at the top of the gangway, and they descended from it as though it were little more than a staircase worth a few steps. Silas didn't need to know this stranger personally to be able to guess that this would be the captain. The captain of the King's navy.

About him the crew began scrambling, trying to appear even mildly educated in terms of etiquette, but the wolf merely stood and watched. Never one to put too much importance on titles.

The captain was a tall man, coming from Silas that was quite the compliment for there weren't many he considered towers. Muscled and worn, he was an older gentleman with eyes as dark as the night sky, a captain's hat sat proud atop his head. And he regarded the dockworkers as one might the average sewer rat.

"We have seventeen packages and you will be careful with every one of them," he began with the abruptness of an explosion and a tone just as threatening. "Get to the top of the gangway and follow the corridors starboard, once you reach the double doors enter and you will receive further instructions from there." He did an about turn and returned up the gangway, only shouting over his shoulder once more. "You are to speak of this to nobody, and if I find out you have you will wake up on the ocean floor."

Silas had no reason to doubt a word of it, and accordingly, promptly complied.

Inside the vessel the air was stale and rendered unnaturally hot by the work of the engines, the darkness was only intermittently broken by the occasional flicking flame but otherwise they delved through the black following only the directions of the captain. For all any of them knew they could well have been walking towards their deaths, and it was one of few times any of his companions accepted Silas taking the lead.

Garnering something in the way of an advantage due to his sharpened eyesight, he kept his pace steady and careful all the same.

At last light flooded the corridor a little more, revealing the promised double doors through which he quickly pushed and entered the promised hall. Small and unassuming, it was more a storage room than anything overly grand that such a large ship might have otherwise indicated.

Silas had little chance to take in any of his surroundings before he came under attack.

Something was hurled at him, and the wolf scrambled to act. It reached inches before his face before he caught it, finding his opponent to be a large package wrapped in a thin almost parchment like fabric.

"We've come to port?" A melodic woman's voice sounded from somewhere beyond the package that now took up much of the wolf's vision. Silas nodded uselessly and Flick's voice sounded from beside him to offer something in the way of affirmation. "Grand, take those down; and for your sake, be careful as you do it."

Taking heed of what had been said, he took a moment to readjust. Fortunately, this package was not an overly heavy one, but it was wide meaning finding decent purchase was not an easy task but one he quickly succeeded in, and he retreated once more.

With the path somewhat familiarised and with certainty that death likely didn't wait for them on the other side, Silas now found some small confidence in the return journey. Weaving carefully through the corridors, stopping only to shift his box occasionally.

The roar of the ocean below caught Silas' attention once more, and soon he was out in the open air. Here it felt like he could breathe again, but now there was an entirely new obstacle to tackle. The journey back.

Now the skinny gangway felt more like a dead tree branch vulnerable to every wrong step.

Whilst the height wasn't such that it would have killed Silas to fall from it, it would cause injuries he didn't care to sustain.

He moved with the concentration of a hawk spying prey. Every footfall colliding cautiously to metal, every unexpected breath of wind rendered him froze, but after a handful of steps he began to gain confidence. Until after a few heart stopping moments, he returned to the dockside once more, depositing the box with a thud, he took a moment to catch his breath. Whilst not usually easily winded, the first true panic he'd known in a long while his heart was racing more than he cared to admit.

Looking back for the first time, he spotted the first of his colleagues making their descent as well. He stood up once more and took the chance once the gangway was free of use to make his way up the ship once more, his own body hating him for returning despite all of his best instincts.

By the time he returned to the hall, there were only a handful of boxes left. One or two were larger and he considered it for a moment before moving to pick it up from the floor. But he was interrupted in his efforts, pushed aside. He looked up to find Alex staring down at him with an amused expression,

"If you're going to be so clumsy might as well let me take that one."

Whilst for a moment he doubted the man's capacity to carry something so large by himself, Silas wasn't about to argue if it meant he might get the chance to see his companion make an utter fool of himself, so instead he simply nodded. "Please, ladies first."

Either he hadn't heard or wasn't overly caring, Alex leant down and grasped package, straining only just visibly, he departed as quickly as his legs could take him. Silas watched with a grin, but quickly set about following suit.

Allowing Alex to take the lead to avoid further arguments, now his movements carried more ease. More certain of where he placed his feet now, he could actually see the land in front of him, though obscured by the back of the bully, the pair made their careful descent. As confident as the man might have been when confronting the wolf, even he wasn't so stupid as to make jest when faced with the genuinely fatal fall that a mishap might create.

However, before they'd reached half-way down the ramp – still a couple of dozen feet towering between themselves and the ocean waters. The winds picked up into an almighty howl that could have left the trees shaken from their roots.

Instinctually Silas took a knee, inhaling sharply as though the very release of breath might have sent him tumbling, and he saw Alex do the same half a beat later. The wind continued to howl and batter, and the metal ramp beneath them seemed to strain with the effort, as though it wouldn't have taken much greater strength for the winds to rip the very ship from the oceans.

"We've got to get moving, its only getting worse." he knew the feeling of an oncoming storm, and if the ones that had plagued the last few days were anything to go by; being somewhere high the last place they wanted to be.

At first Silas wasn't sure the man had even heard him, he remained unmoving. Then slowly but surely stood upright once more, even the wolf could see how the man's legs shook as he did so. All facades of bravery drained from the bully's frame as genuine terror seeped through the man's every crevice.

Shaking visible; he took his first uneasy step.

The process was slow, painstakingly and agonisingly so, and for a brief and beautiful second, it almost felt like they might just get out of this dry and more importantly alive.

But by the time the three-quarter point was passed, a sudden gust of wind howled so loud it stole all sense of hearing from Silas. He stiffened, dropping once more to his knees so swiftly it left them tingling from the impact. Until a splash came to his senses accompanied by a distant scream. It took him a beat longer to realise the space in front of him was now empty, and the shriek had come from the shore.

With more hesitation than he cared to admit, he realised what had occurred and that the wind had stolen his companion from the gangway and was likely not far from doing the same to him.

At first, he acted on little more than instinct, pulling the heavier jacket from his shoulders and dumping it to the side of the gangway and then further stripped his thin shirt from his frame. Revealing the heavily scarred muscled form beneath. But as he moved to launch himself from the gangway, only to stop just before the leap.

He's already dead, he tried to convince himself but failed. *By the time you get there he will be*, still little victory. *He wouldn't do the same for you if he was offered all the money in Cresvy.*

Only heartbeats had past, but he still found himself hesitant and unmoving. The looming sea waters as appetising as the average sewer. But Silas was all too aware the choice was never going to be his and his alone.

Cringing when he realised there was only really one option left and forcing himself to action before he could convince himself just how stupid of an idea this was. Before taking a deep breath and plunging into the cold waters of the Cresvy sea.

Chapter Three.

Pain shot through him, enough to make him think briefly that he had collided with a brick wall. But the second sensation, that of bitter and all-consuming cold was kind enough to clarify. The shock of the impact stole all intelligence from him – in turn becoming something more feral and had it not been for the silver lacing his remaining clothes he would have likely shifted in those frozen waters.

Losing all sense of humanity to something far crueller, driven only by the need to survive – prove to the townsfolk that when it came down to it, Silas was exactly the monster they feared him to be.

Even with some humanity lingering in his line of thoughts, his first instinct was to lunge for the surface once more – forgetting any facades of heroism in a desperate and last-ditch attempt at saving his own life.

Go back, save yourself. Something entirely wild at the back of his head screamed at him, and with each passing heartbeat of desperate flailing; the he was more tempted.

He had all but accepted defeat, when a shadowed shape appeared through the murk.

Surging forward, his heart pounded so hard he was sure it could be heard at the surface. But he knew if he resurfaced now there would be almost no chance in finding the form once more, and if the wolf was struggling to hold his breath, his colleague stood no chance.

Thrashing about with the elegance of a bull in a china shop, at last his fingers collided with the sodden cloths of his companion's shirt and forced his grip about them. Dragging the form close, now he was left to pray he hadn't been so unfortunate as to find a different body in the dock's waters – far from an unheard-of prospect.

Kicking furiously once more, his legs aching with the effort and his lungs close to exploding.

When he breached the surface, he drew in air desperately. Coughing as water splashed his face in his efforts, the light stung his eyes till they watered. But he maintained enough vision to confirm that the creature he had brought to the surface was in fact Alex and found some gratitude to that extent.

As he came close to the shores, electing to aim for the beach rather than the port despite its further distance. Attempting to drag the soaked gentleman up the stairs would be like trying to lift a tree with the pinkie fingers.

Shadowed figures stood on the beach, and it took him a minute to realise that they too were entering the water and surging towards him.

Grateful as his burden was lifted, by no means was he the finest swimmer in the first place, he found his efforts beginning to falter, until finally sand replaced the surging waters underfoot.

In his concentrated state, he all but face planted onto the beach, but he elected not to worry too much about that, slumping to the dirt. He fought to catch his breath, inhaling with short sharp bursts.

Once the sensation of slow incineration departed his lungs, he breathed steadier. Sitting amid the sands, taking note of the aches and pains that now tugged at his every part. He grimaced; it would last a few days but nothing that would kill him.

It took him moments longer than it probably should have to realise that not all of them were stood catching their breaths, and that instead the one he had done all of this for was failing to.

Coming to his senses as best as he could, he stumbled to his feet to find others had been quicker to the matter than he. Rubbing his eyes insistently, he gained enough vision to see the bluing face of Alex, his arm bent at an angle so harsh it was impossible for either a man or a wolf.

They might have been out of the water, but they were far from out of the woods.

"We need to get him to a hospital," the words were muffled behind the amount of water in his ears. Silas shook himself thoroughly in a lupine gesture he usually would refrain from, the action sent water droplets slinging across the shore.

"The nearest hospital is too far," though no doctor, but he knew death well enough to see the signs in those close to crossing its borders. "And a month's wages from all of us wouldn't be able to afford as much as meeting a doctor for half an hour, he'll die long before we can get him there." He trembled as he spoke, the wind only adding insult to injury as he stood shivering.

"And what exactly do you propose instead?" It was the portmaster now, who had dragged himself from his office for the first time since Silas had met him. "I'm not going to leave a man to die on my port." Silas couldn't help but imagine that was because of all the bad reputation that might cause, rather than the pain from a loss of life.

"I know someone… my mum, my mum can help him." He explained breathlessly. "She's a doctor," he added rather uselessly.

Eyes turned on him, and Flick interrupted a little more solidly this time in an aim to aid her friend. "He's telling the truth," she too was drenched telling Silas she'd helped in the saving efforts. "She might be able to save him."

Silas had doubts the Gods could have helped at that point, but instead he nodded meekly.

"A hospital will sur-" but Silas didn't give him the chance to finish.

"We don't have time discuss; he's going to die." Silas interrupted with frustration; he could hear how slow his companion's heart was growing.

People exchanged looks of uncertainty, but at last they nodded. Understanding the urgency of the situation beyond the need to remain careful in the presence of the wolf.

Taking the non-verbal acceptance as the best he was going to get, he stepped forward. He knelt to take hold of Alex with a firm grip. He paused only to adjust slightly – this burden much more important than the packages he'd dragged from the ship. And took off at the fastest sprint his already over-exerted legs would permit him.

Though the strange stares were far from new, now there was an inkling of pity in the gaze of onlookers for the poor man in his arms. Silas was grateful for the fact both looked like drowned rats, for that would hopefully dismiss any concerns that it was the wolf who had done this, though might not entirely rid them of the idea this might have been some sort of drowning gone terribly wrong.

A mixture of the cobblestones accompanied by the heavy weight made his pace unsteady, but soon the paths became familiar and at last he found himself in the doorway of home.

Whilst the door was locked, he took no time to attempt opening it and instead went through it backwards; allowing his efforts to simply break the door. The broken hinges would be fixed easily enough, and he knew his mother would have little qualms if that had been the obstacle between life and death.

He tilted his head back and yelled as loudly as his aching throat could manage. "Mum, I need help."

Not waiting for an answer, he moved for the kitchen.

He rested Alex daintily across the tabletop, the man was too tall to fit, long legs dangling off the one end.

He hadn't even seen his mother that morning and knew this would be a strange first meeting.

The face that appeared, however, was not that of his mother but instead one of his three nieces. Peering wide-eyed at the stranger laying where she usually ate toast.

"Rosie, where's your grandmother?" He asked as calmly as he could manage between harsh panting breaths. It took the ten-year-old a moment to realise she'd been spoken too, she looked to her uncle through wide eyes. "Rosie!" He repeated a little louder now, hating himself for taking a harsher tone with the youngster but knowing she'd get over it soon enough with enough bribes.

"The neighbour is having her baby!" She replied as quickly as she could manage, and Silas grimaced. Hardly ideal circumstances, tearing his mother between one needy person and another.

"How long has she been gone?" He pressed.

"She left before midnight I think," Rosie was in a state of panic, and Silas hated himself for not having the time to ease her woes. "I'm sorry, I'm not sure." Her voice shook.

"I'll be right back," he knew which house the neighbours was, unless there was another pregnant woman he'd not heard of. "If he wakes…" he didn't want to be too hopeful, "Do what you can to keep him in place, I'll be back as soon as I can." He promised and was gone through the front door before she could offer much in the way of further questioning.

Launching across the street, he hammered on the wooden door of number 56 without thinking, but as the door swung open neither the familiar smiling features of his mother nor the rounded expression of the pregnant neighbour. But rather her husband, known for his distaste of the wolf he shared a street with.

The parted door flooded Silas' senses with the metallic tastes of blood mingling with fear and stress. Making him hate himself all the more for pulling his mother away; could he keep a man alive long enough for her to finish up here – he had no idea.

His neighbour visibly recoiled. "What do you want?" A normally timid man rendered defensive over his threshold. Silas was careful to keep himself away from the border – not wishing to trespass on an already volatile man's

"I was told my mum's…the neighbourhood doctor, Catrina is here?" Silas half explained half questioned, aiming to find a balance between urgency and calmness, but was struck with a belief he was likely failing drastically in both regards. "A man has been injured at the docks – I don't think he has much time left. Is she here?"

The gentleman shadowed in the doorway frowned and appeared torn. But before he could say a word a different sound broke the silence, the distinct and cry of a small baby. Something closer to a meek grimace than it was a smile, but it was the best he could manage given the pain in his veins and the urgency in his blood. "I think congratulations might be in order?" He asked, an arched eyebrow.

Something odd softened in the stranger, though slight the wolf's heightened senses caught even the slightest shifts. What would usually allow him to dodge a sideways blow was less useful then, but it allowed him some degree of relaxation.

"Belated," his tone remained steely, but the joys of a new father weren't something easily replaced or broken. "She was born earlier, they're just finishing up," he said with the confidence of a man who knew exactly nothing about anything his wife had just been through and was happy to keep it that way.

As much as he wanted to sound sincere, "Please, my mum." He was all too aware he sounded like a timid toddler but now he knew her services were freed he found more bravery in what he needed.

The neighbour turned, hesitated and added over his shoulder. "Wait here," Silas hoped it was his drenched nature that made him an unwanted guest but knew there were likely other factors. "I'll go get Catrina."

For what felt like an eternity he was left to wait, every passing second was torturous in the knowledge just next door a man might well be on his death bed, or rather… death table.

A thudding of footsteps and a long sweeping coat announced her arrival, the usually jovial features of his mother replaced in favour of concern. "Sy what's going on?" She didn't offer much in the way of greeting but Silas didn't take offence to that. She didn't stop her momentum, pushing through the door and letting it swing shut behind them, she continued at speed towards their home and Silas followed, easily keeping pace.

"One of the dockworkers took a fall from a gangway," he explained as fast as the words would come.

"And the door was a further causality of the day?" she asked stepping across the doorway where the oak entrance struggled to remain standing on its broken hinges.

Silas shrugged, a 'need's must' sort of gesture that he hoped would suffice. His mother merely nodded, and she strode for the kitchen without another word. Gratitude shot through him like a bolt of lightning when he heard the struggling but distinct sounds of breathing coming from the patient strewn across the table. "I did my best," he said sheepishly.

Catrina looked up from where she had set down the cloth bag to the side and smiled. "You did well," said teaching was minimal but Silas was thankful to know he had done something right in all the chaos.

Her movements were as efficient and practiced as water trickling down the slope and exuded a similar calmness. Whereas Silas' heart thundered, and his hands shook, his mothers were steady in both respects.

As he watched his mother work, a presence distracted him. Rosie.

"I did my best," she mirrored his earlier words, bringing a meek smile to his own features.

"You did great, kiddo." He promised and there was something genuine to his tone, "I'm sorry I had to make you wait with him."

Rosie scoffed in a gesture very like her own mothers, something that made Silas' heart ache. "Better than Oscar or Jess, he'd have stood no chance with them." A competitive streak that could have outlasted time itself.

"Of course," Silas nod was solemn, but he was once more distracted by a groan from the tabletop. He hesitated, "Is there anything I can do for you, mum?" He asked, desperate to have something, anything that might keep his hands steady and mind occupied. A nudge to the ribs by a pointed elbow from Rosie made him correct himself, "Is there anything we can do to help."

Catrina continued working, not acknowledging that Silas had spoken at all. But the wolf knew better than to try and speak again, press further. She finished what her efforts had been concentrated on and answered at last. "Dampen a towel in some drinking water," she explained moving once more – this time to study the broken arm, its angle harsh and inhuman. "Give that to Rosie, who can dab his head, keep him cool and keep an eye on his vitals" the way she trailed off made Silas assume there was an unending list of things that might steal Alex from the breathing.

But he obeyed and at speed, whipping around the kitchen like a mildly organised tornado as he sought out a clean towel and dowsed it in water. He offered it to Rosie who took it tentatively and did as her mother told her, though the colour flooded from her face, she remained a statue in her duty.

"And me?" The way his mother eyed the broken arm left him uncomfortable, but there was little room to back out now.

Catrina looked at him with an uncharacteristic grimace on her expression, "The break isn't clean," she explained smoothly. "I don't think he'll ever regain full function," that was a death sentence in itself – or at least surety that the man wouldn't find work again. "But if it heals like this it will only cause him pain for the rest of his life, maybe even infection." She over explained, and Silas knew his mother well enough to know that she was trying to convince herself that this was the right choice to make.

Her training was minimal; mostly what she had learned as a younger woman as a battlefield nurse, but Silas trusted the bones of her. He nodded trustingly, knowing any input from him at that point would have been as useful as a chocolate teapot.

Finding a position at his mother's side, he took grip on his colleagues' arm. Its limpness was bizarre, as though all life had been drained from the limb despite the warmth still exuding from it.

However, a sound jerked him from his position of concentration as someone cluttered through the door. He lifted upright, a protective spurt jolting through his system as he was taken off guard. But the face was a friendly one, Flick.

"Sorry I'm late," she panted evidentially having run as fast as her legs would take her in order to get here. "They wouldn't let any of us leave until the packages had been dealt with, the portmaster insisted that he would be fine in your mum's hands, not that I doubt that of course," she added quickly as though fearing a slap his mother would never deliver. "But I still wanted to be here, help…" She spoke like it was slowly dawning on her just how ridiculous her words were.

But Catrina shook her head, smiling despite everything. "You've come at the perfect time; I need someone to hold bandages for me whilst I work; but be warned it won't be pretty." She added, Silas was used to this – the average Wednesday, but Flick was less accustomed to the dirt, grime and blood of the little makeshift hospital.

"I'm from Cresvy, I can only hope there's nothing worse than what I've already seen."

That seemed fine enough an answer to Catrina.

Utilising a chair to brace himself, he kept his grip on the arm and kept himself steady as his mother worked. No matter how stomach churning the sound of cracking was, nor the moans of pain from the patient that made his eyes water, nor how Flick looked on the brink of vomiting in spite of her attempts at bravery before.

By the time their work was done, the limb had been rebandaged into a position somewhat more human. And Alex lay quiet, almost oddly peaceful

"You were all brilliant," little else that could be done now.

"All in a day's work," Silas said quietly.

"Unfortunately, the day is far from over," Catrina continued, lifting herself from her position at the tableside for the first time in a couple of hours, to cast her gaze skyward. To where the sun sat at the peak in the sky. "And I think I need to ask more of you before the day is over.

Silas turned his gaze back to his mother, an eyebrow arched but an exhausted part of him knew what was coming, and furthermore that he couldn't say no even if he wanted to.

"The market, I can't leave this man just yet, I don't think that's a safe idea." She explained firmly, "Can you go in my place?"

The aches and pains of a night in a police cell, a mornings work at the docks a sudden fall and dragging a man home made him want to refuse. Be selfish and take a well-deserved nap that would last at least a week, but Silas knew that he would hate himself for it.

Yet his second reason to offer a no was a little less selfish. He couldn't imagine having a lycan vendor would do much to entice potential buyers to the stall. But he knew his mother was more than aware of any excuse that he could possibly come up with.

"Okay," his own voice sounded exhausted and unfamiliar to his ears, the sound was a croaky rasp from a deep place in his ribs. More lupine than he was used to himself sounding, but in the context of close friends he knew himself safe to that extent.

"I can go grandma," Rosie attempted to interrupt in all her ten-year-old courage. "I've been with you before."

"Don't worry I'm not letting you out of this, I'm sure you'll both do a fine job of keeping the other out of trouble," Catrina replied taking the time to wipe a bead of sweat from her brow. "At least I brought the bags to the stall yesterday in preparation, so that's one job off your shoulders." It wasn't much of a comfort, but the prospect of lugging goods back and forth could dampen the mood of the most optimistic saint.

His mother fished in her apron pocket, sourcing and pulling free a small key which she handed to Rosie

Flick, seemingly much more willing to work at the market than she had been earlier that day, nodded her head. "We should probably get going, I'll be skinned if I'm too late." She added with some tone of worry.

Catrina nodded understandingly, "Of course. I'll hold up fort here, do your best." Catrina made meaningful eye contact with her son on that note, to which the best response he could find was an attempted smile of assuredness.

The trio, with as much bravado as a beaten dog and a similarly bouncy pace turned to make their way out of the house. And Silas had all but stepped across the threshold when a voice caught his attention.

"Sy, thank you," Catrina moved to hug her son for the first time that morning, and he was grateful for the touch. "You really did brilliantly today, no doubt that man wouldn't have gotten out of the waters without you."

His returning grin was perhaps forcefully sincere, "Ever at your service, Mum." He turned and was gone from their little home once more into the cold bitter air of Cresvy long before he'd hoped he would be again.

Chapter Four.

With all the enthusiasm of prisoners led to the gallows, departed for the markets. The earlier buzz of life was largely drained now, the wolf was grateful for the peace of the streets, knowing the chaos of the marketplace would soon be consuming.

Soon cobblestone streets turned to muddied fields, the heavy rains that seemed to have plagued the town for the better part of an eternity had rendered it more a swamp than a field. By virtue of well-placed trees and scraps of cardboard alone did the marketplace remain.

The only place offering solidity aside from on cardboard scraps was on the small stone square at the very heart of the marketplace, by no means an attractive place but it offered some sort of solidity to the sodden fields. The wood was half rotten, the place on any other day of the month stank; its very floors writhed with rats.

But on the last Saturday of every month, or in today's case on the third given the impatience of the mayor. It transformed into about the nicest place Cresvy had to offer, rotten woods were covered in colourful cloths and rats were replaced with people.

And even on the day of the royal arrival, it buzzed with life.

Silas found himself following an unfamiliar path, the marketplace wasn't a regular habitat for the young wolf. The sounds and smells were overwhelming, it felt impossible to concentrate on a single thing at once when his attention was constantly dragged away by a shout elsewhere.

Flick on the other hand, was such an adept hand Silas considered himself a fool in her shadow. She wove through the packed streets like a needle through fine cloth, the chaos which rendered Silas unwieldly seemed to be of little bother to her and Rosie.

The trio reached their stall without difficulty, everyone present more concerned with negotiation or roping in a purchaser that they paid almost no attention to the lycan, his niece and best friend.

The market stall was older than Rosie, a family heirloom of sorts. An invention of his father's, it was something between a desk and a suitcase. Its top folded upright, a large compartment beneath capable of being locked. Meaning the necessities of market life could be kept on site, making the life of his mother much easier.

Unlocking the stall, he set to work pulling the bags from their resting point and onto the cardboard under foot. Pulling out the tablecloth, he beat it in an effort to free it of the dust accumulated overnight, and spread it across the surface in a single swift movement. Doing what he could to ignore the aches and pains of his every crevice, he concentrated on setting out his mother's efforts. Shirts, trousers and dresses, as well as unused fabric soon covered the stall's every inch.

By the time he thought to look up, he found his niece and best friend watching him at a leisurely pace, seemingly amused by his over enthusiasm for the task at hand. "Please, don't feel like you need to step in." He narrowed a glare at the two but feared the amused glint to his gaze likely gave away the fact that he lacked in menace. "And don't you have somewhere to be, Flick?

"You seemed to be enjoying yourself, and it's not our fault your oh so much stronger than either of us." Flick retorted easily the teasing to her voice provided some menace, whilst playful. "And no need to go to so much effort to be rid of me, I'll get going."

"You'll be very missed," Silas promised without an ounce of sincerity, but she retreated without offering anything in the way of response. The wolf turned his gaze to Rosie, arching an eyebrow. "You're not much better, Ro; grinning like a lucky thief."

"It's not my fault your so much stronger," Rosie blinked about as innocently.

"I've got to stop letting Flick come around so much," Silas scoffed shaking his head. Working to straighten a rebellious shirt, attempting to batter out a crease or two from its fabric as he did. "She's clearly a terrible influence, and I don't need two of you around," he shuddered at the very thought.

In turn Rosie groaned, moulding her expression into one of near genuine disgust. "Please don't, she's loads more fun. I don't think I'd last a week before dying of boredom," she frowned. "Let alone you, I don't think you'd last ten minutes," she added with a more characteristic smirk.

Whilst he wouldn't have told his niece as much, he couldn't help but agree. Rather than announcing such, he responded with a roll of his eyes and a soft growl of playful warning. "I'm surprised you lasted a week as it is kid, let alone ten years." A little gentler the second time, he added "Anyway, I don't think I could convince Flick to stay away if I tried. I imagine she'd take it more as a challenge, really." He considered.

Gesturing for his niece to move forward, "Come on, Ro; I'm not exactly the selling point here," though they were yet to catch much in the way of attention he hoped that would change soon enough. "You're much cuter than me, anyway."

"I'm less fluffy though," Rosie replied, giggling - a little too proud of herself.

"I'm not a dog Ro," Silas scoffed watching passerbys in silence. "They only call me Mutt because its catchier than lycan, don't go around expecting belly rubs," he warned. A quick glance about their surroundings confirmed his assumptions; not many dared come close to their little stall.

The wolf ducked down, avoiding slamming his head onto the top of the wooden stall by the breadth of a hair, allowing the tablecloth to cloak his presence, but was still able to peer through where it parted.

Out of sight, out of mind and people had children to feed and he'd rather not rob a neighbour of a dime, however inadvertently.

A customer approached, and Silas watched with little more than mild disinterest. His post was not to sell or negotiate, but rather ensure the stall wasn't robbed in his mother's absence. An over glorified guard dog but he was efficient as his job, a man would have had to be insane to dare approach a lycan's den; even a chained. Silas would quite happily teach them a lesson without shedding his silver bonds nor human skin.

A smile sparked on his expression as he heard the exchange, compromise and resultant sale, money traded and quickly pocketed. A rather dashing shirt offered in return.

Similar trades continued, with little more than the odd raised voice in between, and after a short while of argument Silas lifted his gaze from where he had been settled. His gaze narrowed a shade, tensed on the off-chance things turned sour in the middle of the Cresvy marketplace.

Fortunately, he soon deemed intervention unnecessary. Rosie maintained a calmness her mother would have been proud of, even around an older and slightly disgruntled gentleman. And after fierce negotiation and slight compromise, the stranger departed.

"You did a good job there," he complimented, "I thought he wasn't going to go any higher."

"I didn't either," the ten-year-old admitted with some pride to her tone. "Though he looked like he could barely stand when he spotted you, I wonder if he thought you'd come after him if he didn't buy something?" She considered.

He scoffed, "If that was the case you should have asked for at least double what you got."

"I should have, you might just prove to have some use finally!" She turned back to her uncle with a victorious tone. "Can you not look a little more threatening, like you might eat some children in their sleep if they don't pay double the asking price?" More characteristically Rosie now, and he was thankful to see it. "Earn your keep once in a while, you eat like ten times the amount any of us do!" Her tone was moulded masterfully into that of a scolding and tired mother.

But he was distracted before he could think to offer much in the way of retort, as an almighty rumble came from deep within his stomach. Even Rosie looking startled, but quickly composed after she realised the source of the sound, "Point proven, I think."

"Unfortunately, the cells don't provide a dining service," now things were calming down it felt like his stomach was devouring itself from the inside out. "So, forgive me if I'm a little peckish."

"I'm pretty sure you're hungry immediately after you eat," Rosie retorted, leaning against the table. Continuing to concentrate on potential passerbys but considered Silas with the occasional glance. "Your version of heaven is just being constantly fed non-stop."

"Well you and your siblings could get full on air," it was the best he could come up with, "So of course I need to eat more. That and mum eats about as much as a mouse, so of course what I eat seems gargantuan compared to you four."

"You could devour enough to feed the King's army and navy in a single sitting," Silas wasn't sure if it was an entirely inaccurate over exaggeration.

Before Rosie could reply, Silas flared his nostrils. A tantalising scent danced across his tastebuds, leaving them watering lightly, so he withdrew from his makeshift den and sat upright.

"Well you're welcome to remain here on your high horse, Miss Normal Appetite," he decided, pulling himself to his feet and stretching. His legs howled in distress at being forced into movement once more. "I'm going to see if I can find something that will shut my stomach up," he accompanied his words with a rasp of his tongue across dry lips. "Of course, you won't want anything, given how rude you've been about my diet choices." He added with a contemplative expression.

"I wouldn't say no if you found some chicken wings," Rosie replied sheepishly, bringing a grin to Silas' expression. But then the youngster's gaze darkened with something more sincere, "Is that a good idea? I don't mind running on ahead, I won't take long."

Silas considered it briefly but shook his head. "You're the selling point here, Ro. Don't worry too much, I can manage to get something to eat without being shanked I think."

"Last time we left you alone too long you came back with a new coat and sharp teeth," she reasoned.

"You really need to stop hanging around Flick," he returned but shook his head. For a moment he fished through his pockets but found them lacking, "Lend me some cash and I'll get you the wings. I'll pay mum back when I get my wages on Wednesday, but it can be my treat." He knew his mother wouldn't mind if it meant they had full bellies, and they'd been working hard enough that day. She would hardly begrudge the pair a meal after the day they'd been subjected to.

Rosie complied and passed him a few coins which he took gratefully. Pocketing it, he pitied the fool who tried to rob a wolf but didn't necessarily put it against anyone, that and knowing his tendency towards butter fingers. "And I wouldn't be entirely against chips if there were any on offer." She added just as Silas turned to depart.

And she has the nerve to scold me for eating too much, but he kept the thought to himself. The only indication was the slight chuckle he stifled poorly. "Whatever you say, your majesty," but was gone before Rosie could offer a smart response.

The wolf wove fairly seamlessly through the crowds, keeping his head down and appropriating as inconspicuous a pose as he could manage.

The scents of the marketplace were overwhelming, and the infinite sounds left him drowning, but he was becoming accustomed to it and didn't find it quite as off-putting. Rather than following his eyes – rendered practically useless amid the writhing masses of people surrounding him, he followed his nose almost solely. Allowing the tantalising scents to draw him in the right direction. Though in typical manner, his heart lead more than his brain in the pursuit of food.

The crowds parted a little as he reached the more food orientated district of the marketplace. Most didn't bother paying for food here, or rather didn't tend to be able to afford it. The stalls were sparse but there were a handful of loyal customers even during the more money tight months.

Silas held back for a moment, allowing them to spot him first as not to take anyone aback, he only approached the stall when he was quite sure he had been spotted and wouldn't be stabbed in retaliation to asking for breakfast.

In the stalls shadow a woman sat beside a fire, slowly rotating an impaled bird above the licking flames.

It was not the woman who acknowledged him, but a younger boy probably only a couple of years older than Rosie. He regarded the wolf with something that bordered on either terror or curiosity, Silas couldn't quite tell. Either way he regarded the youngster with his best attempt at a charming smile and asked softly. "Two portions of wings, please."

Seemingly surprised that he wasn't asked to hand over his internal organs, the boy nodded so hard Silas worried he might suffer from whiplash and turned to look at the woman by the fire who stood too, moving towards a smaller cauldron to the side of the fire and fishing through its contents where she withdrew a handful of older product and placed it in a small scrap of newspaper.

"Oh, and chips as well if that's alright?" He added, remembering his niece's latter request at the last minute, the lady merely nodded.

"That'll be 17 shillings, please," the boy asked with a quiet voice.

Silas might have attempted to negotiate had it not been for the fear the effort would give the child a heart attack. So, he steadily lifted a hand to his breast pocket, moving with a steadiness that allowed his companion the chance to see what was happening and that the movement wasn't done with the intent to threaten. So for now he ignored the fact that the price stood at just under a quarter of what he earned after a full day's work and nodded his head in agreement. He found the coins and counted them out onto his palm carefully and offered them to the youngster once again.

But the child didn't take it, studying the extended hand carefully and looking back up at Silas. "Are you really a wolf?" It was a question Silas hadn't expected, most weren't upfront especially not those who looked on the brink of pissing their pants.

"I am," he replied, lying pointless.

When his response found nothing in the way of reply, he arched a questioning eyebrow. "Why?"

The expression the child's face contorted into told Silas even he wasn't sure as to why he'd asked and seemed to be increasingly regretting the decision to do so. "I didn't think wolves would eat chicken," he admitted sheepishly looking at his feet.

"Don't go about losing customers, Oscar," the voice that sounded was hoarse and raspy as the woman approached with a pair of newspaper cones. Silas' nostrils flared, inadvertently excited as food came into view and he shifted on the spot. She handed the cones over and took the pennies from his uplifted palm.

"Uncle Jasper says wolves eat children and brick."

Silas could only hope that was a saying the kid had been told to keep him well behaved and not something he'd been missing all these years. He crinkled his nostrils in an over exaggerated manner, "Well brick does go down well with chips," he said lifting the cone and licking his lips dramatically. "I find chicken tastes much better than small children; meatier you see," Silas hoped his attempt at a joke wouldn't be taken too much to heart, he'd already saved one life that morning he didn't feel like doing it a second time. He wasn't sure his legs could take another run.

"Well next month I'll be sure to stock up on bricks," the woman seemed to have become aware of the fact that customers were avoiding the stall like the plague now a wolf had taken centre point. "Please, do come again," her expression was blank, and Silas couldn't find any tone of sincerity to her voice, but he wasn't about to stick around to argue.

"Thanks again," he said and turned on his heels; departing the little stall without complaint.

Fishing a couple of chips out of the cone he dubbed would be Rosie's. He began a swift return journey, carrying the food close to his chest. A robber might not attempt thieving cash, but even a hungry child might attempt stealing something despite the wolf deliveryman.

However, he hadn't yet turned the corner when the edge of a conversation caught his attention and left him paused in place for a brief moment.

"Are you sure he's a reliable source?"

"I don't see exactly why he'd lie," a feminine voice returned, excitement bubbled through her tones, and Silas turned himself just enough that he could watch them from the corner of his eye. Attempting to look casual, as though awaiting a friend rather than eavesdropping. "The King at our little marketplace, can you picture it?"

"That's exactly why I ask, I can't picture it," the deeper voice retorted. "The journey between here and the palace isn't that long, what could they possibly need to buy so bad that they need to stop in the market? I'm half surprised they didn't demolish Cresvy to make it prettier for the King's arrival, let alone allowing him to stay here longer than necessary."

"Don't look a gift horse in the mouth, Jess, be happy that we're to be graced with the presence of the king," it was a tone as sarcastic as Silas' own, and it caused a slight grin to quirk at the edges of his lips, and that was his mistake.

Lips parted but no sound came free, as a pair of eyes landed on the wolf. "We're being listened to," it wasn't necessarily anger in the softer spoken one's voice, more something in the way of offence. As though how dare Silas have ears capable of listening to her voice.

"Forgive me," he said with some honesty having genuinely not meant to upset. "I can hear what's going on at the other side of the market, it wasn't my intention to be rude. You merely caught my curiosity," he said with a shrug of his shoulders. "If you wouldn't mind taking a moment to satisfy it, what's happening?" He was taking his chances but couldn't see the worst-case scenario going beyond a slap to the face and him being left answerless.

For a heartbeat Silas tensed, expecting the worst-case scenario when the strangers tensed contemplatively, but then relaxed in a mirror image of the women. "The King is on his way from Littledusk, he isn't going straight for the palace, but is choosing to stop at the market for a little while."

"Or at least that's what she was told," the friend added with a roll of her eyes. "I think it's about as likely as a leprechaun granting us wishes."

"Do you know what he might be wanting?" Silas asked trying not to sound too hopeful. If the King came to the stall they could surely convince him to buy even a single item, and someone so rich probably wouldn't have minded throwing out far more money at something than it was worth. To the King it would likely have barely made a dint in his finances.

"Food I think, doubt he'd want much else from Cresvy, he'd probably be concerned about fleas."

Silas did his best not to take too much offence at that, knowing for a fact nothing his mother had ever made had as much been in the same room as a flea before it was sold. But he couldn't help but deflate when he discovered the chance wouldn't be his. But the response of food did surprise him to some extent, of all the packages he'd pulled from the ship he was surprised not one of them contained something that might be eaten.

"Darn, I fancied myself becoming monger to the King, of all the finest wears." He admitted with only mild exaggeration, knowing such would have been a once in a lifetime opportunity. "But still, it might be worth going to check out, if nothing else but for the fun of it."

The feminine woman scoffed, "Good luck, I don't much see the point in getting so excited about being within a hundred foot of a king."

Whilst part of Silas couldn't help but agree, he couldn't push past the idea it might be worth investigating all the same. If nothing else aside for a little bit of entertainment, he nodded his head gratefully.

"Thanks for letting me know, I'll get out of your hair now." The last syllable had only just fled from his lips when he turned away and began making his way back to the stall. Thoughts of hunger once again fleeing from his frame, in favour of letting his excitable niece know what was going on.

The wooden stall came into view once again, his niece posed behind its wooden form, he could sense her anticipation on the air around her. And Rosie's gaze lit up when she spotted her uncle approaching with the cones gripped close to his chest.

"Finally! I thought I was going to starve, Silas offered it to her with a grin.

"Apologies, Ro, but I think I could have been moving at the speed of light and you'd still complain I took too long," he reasoned, and Rosie only nodded for her cheeks were already puffed with food now wedged into it, and Silas soon followed suit.

When she was halfway through her second bite, and Silas just finishing her third, did Rosie seemingly remember her manners. "Thanks! It's delicious," the gratitude all but flooded from the youngster, and Silas only nodded his head.

Now the hunger wasn't quite as bitter or brutal did the young wolf speak again. "Have you heard what's happening?" He questioned.

Rosie lifted her gaze from where it was all but transfixed to the greasy paper in her fingers. "About the King in the market?" She replied privier to the average gossip than Silas would ever be, even with heightened senses. "I've heard it mentioned, do you believe a word of it?" Uncertainty underlined her tone and laced her words, but there was a burning flicker of excitement all the same.

"I don't know," he admitted with a glance across the marketplace, slowly draining of life. "Do you think it's worth checking?" He added between chews.

A hopeful spark lit her dark gaze, but then dimmed a beat. "I don't know, wont mum be annoyed we left the stall this early?"

"How much did we earn?" He queried; the stall now looked notably less occupied.

"Err…" she concentrated for a moment, "About 320 shillings I think." She fished through the coins and notes compiled in their little metal box.

"That'll be fine, anyone remaining is hardly going to be sticking around to shop they'll be watching the procession," Silas reasoned easily, watching as his niece relaxed somewhat under his reassurances. "We won't make any money anyway, mum'll know that."

"Are you sure?" She looked as though seeking any reason that might confirm it would be fine no matter how slight, like a hungered cat she would preparing to pounce on the mouse, but first she had to see the tantalising tail being offered to her.

"Let's be honest, Ro," Silas reasoned with a good-natured sigh. "If anyone's going to get a hiding it'll be me for letting you go." His logic was sound, but still the youngster seemed to consider arguing further.

For a heartbeat the child seemed to contemplate, using the brief moment to shovel a further handful of chips into her mouth. Swallowing, she finally replied. "Okay, but if Grandma asks it was all your idea, and I only came to make sure you don't get yourself killed, okay?" She asked, eyebrows furrowed she offered a hand as way of making a deal.

"Careful Ro, keeping me alive is Flick's job, she'll be annoyed if you get her fired from it." Silas scolded, not moving to take her hand.

The child's expression didn't change except to grow sterner, as close to an intimidating facial feature as she was able to muster, which naturally was about as frightening as the average newborn kitten.

Silas sighed, lifting his hand to shake hers limply. "Fine, I promise," he swore with a playful solemnness to his tone.

Rosie immediately lit up, finishing the scraps of chips at the bottom of the cone and leaping to her feet with an almost lupine elegance. Excitement gifting her a supernatural speed, it would seem – that or the shopkeeper had accidentally sprinkled sugar rather than salt onto their breakfast.

Thankful to have a companion, he stood up beside her in a show of true lupine speed, partly playfully so he could grab her from the ground and chuck her over his head and onto his muscled shoulders. Ignoring the white flare of pain from the sudden exertion of aching limbs, but he disregarded it contently. "Come on kiddo, your legs are far too slow, and we have a King to meet!"

Or catch a glimpse of from a distance! But for the sake of his niece he kept that to himself, as he pushed past the stall an began making for the centre of the market. Rosie's delighted laughter backtracking his movements.

Chapter Five.

Every sense he had available to him was in overdrive as he made his way for the heart of the marketplace. The chorus of chatter surrounding him on every side left him regularly distracted, but he was grateful for Rosie's proximity to his ears, when she noticed him startled she would speak; by no means anything out of the norm for the youngster but he was thankful for it all the same.

The market's stenches were all consuming, the scents of people, sweat and mud all melded together into something that turned his stomach, no one's fault in particular though Cresvy wasn't known for its personal hygiene records. Even the sight, usually a more mundane capacity was dazzling. The colours and constant movement left him dizzy.

The journey was by no means a difficult one on the average day, but now the same streets were crowded, the thick mass of people had the gravitas of a tide. Anyone trying to fight against it had little to no chance, thus Silas was quite happy to go with the flow without complaint.

At least with Rosie on her throne atop his shoulders, he could relax in the knowledge she was pretty much the safest place she could have possibly been. Keeping himself safe was almost a piece of cake compared to keeping his eye on his pint-sized niece, it was like trying to keep track of a single ant amid a muddy patch of garden grass.

"Gentle on the hair Ro, it might grow back quick, but it still hurts when you yank it out by the fistful," Silas warned softly as he continued moving. Lifting a hand to scratch a newly balding part of his scalp.

"Slow down, I've met pigs easier to sit on!" Rosie replied, gripping with bony knees around his neck, though it would have taken about eight of her to come close to strangling him, small shoes against his Adam's apple was never going to feel great.

"Your welcome to walk," he lied.

Whilst she didn't reply, he felt her grip on his head loosen somewhat, though her sausage fingers remained a reminder of his precious cargo at the back of his head. He continued with the crowd, making careful attempts to push through towards the front of the gathering group, it wasn't long before Rosie said to him.

"I can see the square!" She declared with sudden delight. "But unless his carriage looks suspiciously like some kids playing kickball, I don't think he's here yet."

"I don't know the things spies can do these days will astonish you," Silas reasoned in turn, but he too soon felt the solidity of stone replace mud and grass, indicating that they were at least here, even if the King was being more leisurely in the pace he chose.

But he could go no further, as soon the wall of people soon made further progression impossible. "What's happening Ro?"

For a moment she concentrated, fingers gripping onto his head briefly as she straightened a little atop his shoulders. Leaning forward, "The royal colours are grey and purple right?" She queried and Silas nodded. "Good, it was that or we're about to be ambushed," she attempted to joke. "There's like twenty guards, they've cordoned off the square?" She sounded uncertain herself as she tried to explain what she alone could see. "And either they weren't spies, or spies are being chased off with swords and language that would make grandma blush," she added.

It made enough sense, not that the actions of a King would ever made a lot of sense to the wolf.. The hundred metre distance would be enforced rather than assumed. "Sy, how is he going to get to a food stall if he can't get through all this?"

Silas grinned, admittedly in his excitement it hadn't quite been something he'd thought about. "It's the King Ro, I doubt he's going to need to go within a foot of his carriage before he has food of every kind hurled at his feet." It was a lot of guessing, but he assumed there was some common sense backing up what he had said. The guards would hardly have allowed the King to go strolling the marketplace of Cresvy, picking out plums and gnawing down on chicken.

If wolves aren't meant to eat just chicken, I wonder what Kings are meant to eat?

Unfortunately given the size of the crowd and how far they were away from the frontline, it didn't seem like he would get the chance to ask the King face to face.

"Congrats, Ro, I think you're the only person who's going to be able to see a damned thing." Silas' grumble lacked any menace, "I can't wait till your older so you can return the favour no doubt," his teasing left him on the receiving end of a kick to the chin.

"You'd break every bone in my body," she retorted but her tone was distracted, she watched the ongoings with the carefulness of a hungry hawk circling a dying hare. "I still can't see anything, if this was all for nothing…" she trailed off, crossing her arms and resting them atop Silas' head. Utilising it as a resting place, the young wolf rolled his eyes.

"Don't worry, I'll find him myself if he doesn't show up. He doesn't get my niece's hopes up just to leave her disappointed," he shook a rueful fist.

"I don't think even you could get past all these guards, Sy," Rosie replied with genuine uncertainty lacing the words. "Why so many just for Cresvy, the worst we could throw at them is dung and a few rabid dogs," despite the joking use of phrasing there was a confusion to them as well.

"I assume it's the same everywhere, you can never be too careful." The wolf reasoned, "Though if they knew a lycan lived in this town, I think they'd have rather sprouted wings and flown over it than go through Cresvy."

That drew a laugh from his companion. "That would be a sight enough to draw this kind of crowd, a king sprouting wings?" The giggle shook Rosie's slender frame.

He parted his lips to reply, when a familiar voice broke through the chorus of conversation around them. He swung his head cautiously, and spotted a familiar figure approaching them through the crowd – fortunately a familiar one. "Flick! You made it."

"After all that I'd have thrown myself off the docks before missing it," Flick replied coming to stand before her best friend. "But the view from here is terrible," she finished with a grumble.

"Can't imagine it would have been that much better for anyone else, unless you fancy trying to fight through all that?" He asked, gesturing towards the mass of backs that blocked the way any further forward.

"Maybe not from here," Flick replied with a grin, "But I do have an idea if you're willing to comply?"

It was typical of his best friend to always have some sort of plan brewing, and he regarded her with an uncertain look. "And what exactly would that be?"

Flick shook her head, "It'll be easier to show you than it will be to explain," she said and turned away promptly, clearly expecting her companions to follow her without much further complaint.

Silas rolled his eyes, surprised he'd expected anything else. "What do you think Ro?" He asked, "How long do you think it will take until she actually notices that we aren't following?"

"I dunno," the youngster replied drawling out the latter vowels. "Is it a good idea to lose our place here?"

Silas permitted himself a quite careful shrug, "Well we're not really going to see much here. Though you might be able to spot the tops of carriages. Either we see little to nothing here, or we see little to nothing there, or if Flick has a few more braincells than I generally assume, a lot of things there."

Hesitation left silence for a brief heartbeat, before Rosie seemed to come to a decision. "Let's follow, Flick." She elected.

With orders delivered from his rider, the loyal steed departed from his spot and began to follow his best friend through the crowds.

Now that their momentum had stopped being with the crowd, more people were willing to part the way for the wolf.

It wasn't long before Flick pulled to a halt. In a crescent shape on the left-hand side of the square gathered a handful of stone buildings, usually used for richer marketplace users to store goods, and a couple were outright homes. They were tall, well-built and for now largely abandoned, anyone who usually inhabited them out in the market or watching the King's procession. They were alone. But in quite reasonable proximity to where the King would soon be travelling through the square from.

And it was quite apparent why, the steep, vertical climb required to get anywhere useful.

Silas grinned meekly, whilst it took him a moment to pick up on her meaning and once he did he elicited a grumbling sigh. "If you're thinking what I think you're thinking, your even thicker than you look, Flick."

"Hey," she warned giving him a glower. "You're just jealous you didn't think of it first, and you should be grateful that I let you in on my idea. You couldn't see a thing back there except for the backs of heads."

"Well unless you've been keeping your ability to turn into a mountain goat from me, from the looks of it you wouldn't be able to have done anything without me," Silas reasoned in turn.

In all of her ingenuity, Flick's idea walked a fine line between brilliant and idiocy. She didn't want to watch the procession from ground level, but instead take to higher ground – or rather higher roofs and watch from there.

The one downside was the incredibly tall and incredible steep walls that one had to manoeuvre around in order to reach the roof tops. Something Silas could have managed with reasonable ease, but he doubted either his friend or his niece could get to as much as the windowsill without finding it impossible to get any further. Any footholds provided by uneven bricks were few and far between, and incredibly narrow from what he could see.

"You underestimate me," Flick scoffed.

"I learned that was a lethal past time a long time ago," Silas retorted. "But please do explain your no doubt incredible plan."

"Well after this morning's brilliant show of carrying Alex like he was little more than a bag of flour, this should be almost nothing. Just pulling little old me and Rosie onto the roof after you," she reasoned with a smile. "Unless, of course that's too much for your old bones?"

"You underestimate me," Silas mimicked with a dark voice.

"I learned that was an incredibly fun past time long ago," Flick returned, but then looked to him with genuine hope to her voice. "Do you think you can manage it?" The playfulness was gone from her tone now, replaced with anticipation.

Lifting his niece from her throne atop his shoulders, he gently rested her beside his best friend and approached the stone hut. It was easily twice his height if not more, with the window settled a good third way up the wall. He paused, tensing every muscle, before lunging with all the power and momentum he could gather.

He caught hold of the window ledge and dragged himself upright, the glass offering a border from which not to fall forward, but it took some effort to ensure he didn't topple over backwards. He used the ledge as a resting point, and began looking immediately for his next foothold, bouncing on the tips of his toes.

Again, he surged upward and caught hold of the rooftop and scrambled to maintain his purchase.

Fortunately he wouldn't need to learn just how nasty a blow a fall onto stone would be to his ribs, as his fingertips remained gripped tightly to the damp rooftop. With a deep breath and a firm kick of his legs he was able to land on the rooftop with a metallic thump.

Catching his breath for a moment, he looked back with a smile. "What was that about underestimating me?" He queried, smiling more smugly than he cared to admit.

"Still a very fun pastime," Flick responded. "But I'll admit you do have your uses occasionally."

Before he could response, the bleat of a distant trumpet caught his attention and he straightened briefly, narrowing his eyes – the monarch and his procession were still not in view, but he could hear the thunder of hooves that demonstrated it likely wasn't far off. "Now let's get you two up, or I'm watching this all by myself, do you reckon you can push Rosie onto that windowsill, Flick?" Dropping to his stomach and peering over the side with a grin.

"Have you eaten recently?" Flick sounded uncertain but mostly playful and didn't give Rosie the chance to take her question literally as she knelt down. "Give us your leg, Ro."

At first hesitant, she kicked a leg back and Flick grabbed at it and pushed upright. Launching the youngster up onto the window ledge. Rosie seemed to stumble for a heartbeat, but Silas didn't let her move more than a millimetre before he launched himself down. Grasping his niece by the collar, he pulled upwards his second hand joining the fray before he inadvertently strangled the child – tugging her breathlessly onto the rooftop with minimal elegance to the action.

"I shouldn't have let you have those chips," he growled but with laughter glistening in his moon-kissed gaze.

Settling his niece beside him on the rooftop, he peered back down in time to call. "Thanks for your help, you can go back to the rest of the crowds now!" Before sitting back up and out of sight from the ground.

Flick's tone of voice was borderline as dangerous as any growl Silas had ever emitted. "You get your butt back to the edge of that roof this instant, Sy, or so help me I'll burn that hut down."

Not entirely sure that she wouldn't, Silas was quick to do as he was told.

Now there was no leverage from which to launch herself onto the windowsill, he leant down contemplatively. Trying to suss out how far he could push himself from the rooftop without losing his balance and breaking various body parts. He narrowed his eyes, "Do you think you can get yourself onto t-"

He wasn't allowed the chance to finish as Flick jumped as high as she could. Whereas Silas' movements had been accompanied by a lupine elegance, everything about his best friend was annoyingly human in that moment. She scrambled to keep her grip, kicking with her legs to launch herself further once she'd grasped with her fingertips. The process was arduous and lengthy, but after a few moments of squirming like a newborn pup, she'd found her purchase and was atop the windowsill with a frustrated grunt.

Trying to find his grip, it was trickier now and he grimaced. "Do me a favour and sit on my back, Ro?" He asked embarrassment glinting in his gaze. A little too eager at the chance to utilise her uncle as a throne once more, the youngster did as she was told.

Now with something in the way of surety that he wouldn't lose his grip and fall several metres onto hard stone – one near lethal topple from a great height per day was more than enough for the young wolf. He turned his attention back to his precarious friend, now with both hands freed, he launched down and grasped at Flick's shoulders, grabbing her beneath the armpits he lifted upright. Until the red head too sat beside him on the rooftop, out of breath and seemingly surprised she'd made it to the heights alive.

"I don't know why your breathless," Silas teased, but in truth was grateful they had all made it up alive and in one peace. "Now be quiet, I don't need anyone thinking I'm offering a lifting service, two is enough for one day." In truth he didn't want others to spot what they had done, and for someone to attempt to repeat his actions. "You can move now, Ro," he added looking back to where his niece had made herself quite content.

"You're comfortable," she complained but complied all the same before Silas could roll over and knock her off anyway.

"I might be, but you squishing my kidneys is not," he retorted straightening into a more comfortable position. Looking across the square for the first time, taking in what had been hidden from him amid the crowds.

The first thing he noted were the guards marked with grey and purple, their proud flags fluttered in the wind boasting the roses and sword banners that marked the King's arrival. There were a good couple of dozens of them as Rosie had mentioned, but seeing it was a lot more than hearing it described. It somehow made it all feel a lot realer to the young wolf, and it sent a shiver running down his back at the sight.

He was no longer the most powerful player in Cresvy.

But what he found even more worrying was that the people who had usurped his position were more than happy to use that power to their advantage.

Strapped to almost every guard he was able to see from his vantage point was a rarity in Cresvy – something he had only seen a handful of times in his lifetime. *Guns*.

And he was struck with the realisation it wouldn't take too much to see these trigger-happy guards use them.

Chapter Six.

In the midst of his concentration it took Silas a moment longer than it should have to realise he had been spoken to. "Sy, what's got your tongue?" Flick broke him from the depths of his thoughts, and Silas looked to them with mild confusion. "I asked if you could hear whether they were any closer," Flick cleared his confusion without too much concern, but her gaze was watchful and worried. "But you were clearly in your own little world, what's up?"

For a moment he contemplated lying, keeping his realisation to himself but stopped when he reasoned that it was obvious enough. "Guns." To add to his point, he gestured to the guard in the closest proximity to the trio. The silver object shining upon the guard's hip, for the world to see and more importantly be terrified of.

"Do you really think they'd have had the aforethought to load silver bullets?" Flick didn't see certain, and when Silas shook his head in response she added with a shrug of her shoulders. "Then what are you so worried about?"

"It's not me I'm worried about," he admitted lowly.

Flick shook her head, unworried and unperturbed by the presence of armed guards in her little home. "No one around here would be stupid enough to try and start anything," her reassurances were welcomed but in vain. "And if they are, frankly, they probably deserve what's coming to them, you've got to be pretty thick to attack the King."

Silas wasn't as certain as his best friend, but he could only hope she was right. For there was little chance to discuss the topic further, as atop the horizon, the King's procession had finally broken into the line of sight.

Accompanied by trumpeting harbingers, the purple and grey colours stained the skies overhead as flags soared high above the carriage. A proud boast of who was arriving. A further ten men sat upon horseback, armed to the teeth and ever watchful.

Even if it did send fear ricocheting through the system, the wolf was man enough to admit that it was all quite beautiful. Colours everywhere, the very carriage seemed to glow it was so meticulously cleaned as opposed to the mud stained everything of Cresvy.

Finally, his gaze set on the King himself. Hesitant at first – as though everything he'd been told in his life might turn out to be true, that setting his eyes on something so far above himself would cause pain to the eyes. Naturally it didn't, but the wolf felt the instinct to look just about anywhere else he could.

Despite himself, he continued to watch. Torn between feeling wrong to look at it and wanting to watch nothing else.

The King in his very nature demanded attention, he was marked with long thick hair that reached just below the shoulder line, much like every other part of the royal man it was neat and precise with a beard on equal form. Dressed in robes so thick it could have kept three families quite warm during the coldest of winters, a half blind man could have spotted the gold dressing his neck, fingers and just about every other inch of bared skin.

Despite the bizarreness of the procession, the King carried himself as though he had been through Cresvy every day of his life. An easy smile lit his features, as though the crowd weren't there or maybe that it was made up of only his closest friends, it was odd to watch the King act as though he owned the very dirt his carriage drove on.

But then, of course, the King very much did own the dirt, and the grass, the houses, even the people. It was all his.

Of course, he acted as though nothing could hurt him – this was a man almost as infallible as Silas if not ten times more so, and the thing that rendered him truly scared was the fact that he had no idea what this man's silver might be.

At his side in the carriage were three further armed men, a strange contrast to the ease and casualness that the King carried, they were stiff and watchful.

To the will of a signal that Silas couldn't spot, the procession came to an elegant and near synchronised stop as it reached the bare part of the stone square.

Shouts went up and the guards stood at attention with a thunderous stomp of boots. A man approached the carriage, opened its door and the King graced Cresvy with his feet, around him the carriage guards didn't bother using the exit and elected to leap over the sides of the carriage instead, coming to stand at attention beside their king too.

It was quite a sight there was no doubt about that, and it had one purpose alone. A performance of sheer power and Silas had no doubt that he would be little more than a mouse to these people, wolf or not, silver bindings or otherwise.

From amid the now parting crowd, the mayor became visible. The man Silas had once begrudgingly admitted being a powerful creature was rendered a mouse before the lion now. The wolf might have found it amusing, had there not been a thousand different signs that he should be terrified.

The mayor greeted the King like an old friend, and to his credit the King returned with an amicable smile as though they had known each other their whole lives. Silas doubted they'd been in the same room more than trice, and even more that they'd ever held much in the way of a conversation.

"William," the King greeted with a booming voice that echoed across the stones of the little marketplace's square. "It's good to see you again, I trust all is well?"

Silas was embarrassed to admit before then he had no idea what the mayor's name was, it was such an elusive figure that the need had never arisen. For the man didn't even appear when it came to the collection of taxes, hiring lackeys to go about the dirtier work. He held power only to a decorative extent.

Beside the King, Silas felt idiotic that this was a man he had ever been scared of.

"All the better now you are here," the mayor sounded about as sincere as a child who had been forced for hurting a sibling. "Welcome to Cresvy, your Majesty, I trust the seas were kind to you?" William was a man who had lived his entire life in this town; but he carried himself so stiff and terrified it was as though he was certain that the very ground underfoot might turn to lava without notice.

The mayor's voice was far quitter in comparison and commanded nowhere near the same amount of respect. The consensus seemed that the entire crowd wanted him to shut up, for that voice was fairly familiar, and instead for the King to continue. A man who usually controlled every aspect of this town was rendered little more than a commoner, again it might have been funny.

"Rough but nothing we hadn't prepared for," there was a defensiveness, a snappiness that he hadn't expected, but gone so quickly he doubted its presence in the first place. "I'm simply happy to be on my own terrain, and headed home," his voice was calmer that time. Silas assumed he'd merely misheard or misunderstood. "Just quite famished as I'm sure you can understand, and no doubt your wonderful markets will have plenty to offer to keep us full on our journey."

He regarded the crowd as though he had expected a cheer to go up, but the silence was deafening. Much of the town were either starving or had known starvation and the insinuation that this large man had known a day of hunger seemed like a cruel jest.

"We will be compensated for that, of course." Ezekiel clarified nervously. The money hungry mayor expected to profit from the king's visit as much as anyone else.

Admittedly the King seemed taken aback by this, he regarded the mayor for a moment as though trying to figure out if it was some crudely made joke. *Nothing in this town comes for free*, Silas stifled a chuckle.

"Yes, anyone who provides anything to my procession will be duly compensated for their efforts."

That brought forward more willing people, as various vendors began trying to push through the crowds, guards began raising shouts of warning as they struggled to find some remnant of control over the crowd, all of it quite boring.

Beside him began the sounds of rustling that dragged his attention from the ongoing for the first time, and he looked sideways to find Rosie shifting restlessly in her spot. "Not quite as entertaining as you were hoping?" He asked with a chuckle.

The youngster nodded with a frown, "It's all too polite," she replied. "I was hoping for a fight or something, not for such niceties."

He wasn't quite sure in what version of reality that Mayor would ever have enough confidence to dare threaten the king. "I'll make sure I leave him with some notes, a few suggestions as to what to do next time he graces Cresvy with his presence." Silas promised with an exaggerated solemn tone.

Rosie grumbled, she lifted herself up to her knees and stretched. "Next time ask him to do it somewhere where we might put a chair – or maybe even warn us in advance. Rooftops don't make comfy places to sit," she complained, and Silas understood. Even his own rear end was growing numb from sitting in the same position for the prolonged period of time.

"I'll bring some cushions, next time, I promise."

Pausing, he moved and pulled his jacket from his shoulders, bundled it up and threw it to her, "Here, try and sit on that it might be a bit comfier." He offered, thankful the day was warming up a little and he had donned a long-sleeved shirt that morning.

She grabbed it and settled in it, nodding "Thanks, Sy," she said appreciatively.

"Not as comfortable as my back, I imagine, but hopefully it will work," the wolf replied, allowing his gaze to flick back to the procession occasionally. A small queue had formed, showing their offerings for the king to enjoy and peruse at his will. Many were desperate to get close to the King, anything for a chance to sell him even a single chip.

"If you're offering?" The child queried hopefully but was silenced by Silas' firm shake of his head.

"I think any more pressure and my arms are actually going to break off," Silas replied, the aches were admittedly beginning to fade already but he wasn't about to risk it.

Flick, who had been transfixed on even the more mundane procedures of the procession below looked down for the first time, scoffing. "So selfish, Sy, it's not like it wouldn't heal!"

Silas frowned, genuinely uncertain. "I don't think I could heal something as big as a limb falling off," only to quickly add. "And I'm not in the mood to experiment before you ask."

"Boring," Flick complained but pried no further, returning her attention to the King's parade.

"We can always go riding around on your back, see how much fun you think it is?" Silas offered, but his prompting drew no responses – either his best friend couldn't think of a clever means of response, or she had already become transfixed once more in the procession below.

But amid the crowd Silas spotted something that brought a grin to his expression, it seemed that the trio weren't the only bored ones. A figure beside the King's guard – casual clothes contrasting against the uniform of the King's guard making him stand out like a sore thumb was a man about Silas' age. Looking like he would rather be just about anywhere else.

Part of Silas almost pitied the man – but his position even within a few feet of the King put him above just about anyone in the town of Cresvy unless they were a servant; and even a King didn't have servants as well dressed and proud looking as that.

That was no servant or even a baron, it was a Prince. And a very bored one.

Observant as ever, Rosie piped in. "What hope do the rest of us have if even a prince is bored by listening to his father's nonsense?" She queried, seemingly have spotted where her uncle's line of sight had fallen.

Silas looked to his niece, shrugging his shoulders. "He's probably heard this a thousand times over the last couple of weeks, his ears are probably about to fall off," he reasoned. In theory travelling with a King should have been a riveting, but if all of it went down like the procession today Silas struggled to imagine anything worse.

"He looks like he's about to fall over," Rosie grinned – a lean notable to the prince's features as he struggled to remain conscious despite sleep tugging at his senses. "His guards might need to start propping him up."

A soft chuckle was all Silas had to offer in return.

"How dare we be complaining about steel rooftops to sit on, when our poor, unfortunate prince doesn't even have a chair to sit on," Flick returned to the conversation at her own will. "Come, dear friends we must submit ourselves as furniture to allow our prince some comfort!" She beat the air with a tensed fist, her rallying cry brought little from Rosie and Silas outside of fits of laughter.

"You're an..." but he never had the chance to finish, as the sharp and thunderous crack of gunfire split the air.

His first reaction was to lunge forward, grabbing his niece and pulling her to the metal of the rooftops and hopefully out of view of any shooter. The movement had been made on feral instinct, before his brain had truly comprehended what the sound was; and as a second thought he grabbed at Flick and pulled her down beside him.

Below them the world had descended into chaos.

The hundreds who had made up the crowded streets below were now a desperate mass, desperately trying to manoeuvre wherever they might. But the packed proximity left them sitting ducks, Silas, his niece and best friend forming a macabre gallery left with little to do but watch in horror at what unfolded in their wake.

"Sy, what do we do?" Rosie's words were laced with panic, a sound that mirrored the thunder of his own heart. He didn't know and hated to admit it, but there was one thing they knew for sure. Up here they were little better than sitting ducks.

Now it was impossible to deduce where the shot had come from, or even if the trigger finger had been among the King's own guards. Silas sat up as much as he dared to; for the sound of gunshot continued in meticulous but irregular bangs. The guards seemed as confused as anyone else but would do anything to protect their king.

And Silas would do anything to protect his niece.

"We can't stay here," Flick interrupted when the wolf's silence carried on a beat too long for her patience.

Now the masses had turned from the procession, darting through the fields in a desperate attempt to get out of the line of fire. The guards cared not as to what targets met their bullets it seemed, and whoever was returning fire seemed to have even less regard.

Silas watched as the strangers wove through the houses, the handful fortunate enough to have been at the back of the crowd to avoid the initial tirade of bullets managing to find freedom in the fields beyond. Disregarding the safety of the King they had been revering mere moments prior, the stone below them now disappeared beneath a mass of running people.

The trio had to choices. To stay here and be rendered to little better than sitting ducks if things went wrong; or join the fray but with the chance of departing the battlefield.

Swallowing hard – the wolf could only hope he made the right choice.

Pushing himself upright onto shaking arms, he aimed to find a balance between keeping as low as possible and moving at a reasonable speed. "Come on, we've got to try and get down there." He decided was the best option, their window was narrowing.

Whilst the fire was not concentrated on the trio atop the rooftops, depending on how the firefight went it might soon be.

Silas launched himself from the rooftop, slamming against the stone floor with a sickening thud but he was on his feet again in an instant. Dazed from the impact but fine, "Jump," he shouted, and Rosie quickly complied, he caught her with ease and did the same to his best friend.

For a moment they cowered in the shadow of their little house, not daring to step out from the safety and shelter it provided but knowing it would be inevitable.

The initial cascade of people had been reduced to a trickle, as the streams thinned out now more people had managed to escape the battlefield. But the sounds of gunfire continued, and unless his ears were playing tricks on him it sounded like it was getting ever closer.

A glance over his shoulder – either a great idea or the worst decision he had ever made, determined his thoughts to be true. Now the flash of a gun muzzle was visible amid the long grass, Silas inhaled meekly. The window had closed in that direction, and now the stragglers unfortunate enough to be left behind were trapped between the Kings Guard and the opponent.

"If we can get behind the Kings Guard," Silas reasoned between panting breaths, "That's going to be our best bet, we're already cornered."

Flick and Rosie regarded him with something between terror and confusion but listened to him all the same. Nodding hurriedly, as haphazard and knocked together as it was they had something in the way of a plan.

Silas surged out of the buildings shadow and moved through the stone square, it was now littered with the bodies of the fallen, and those unfortunate enough to have not been killed by the initial shot; now lay bleeding out against the grey marketplace.

Flick hesitated, a cry tugging free of her lips that shattered even Silas' heart, but he knew there was no time for any of this. "Come on!" He warned his niece and best friend with a low growl, "It doesn't matter we have to move," with a not too gentle push in order to pull Flick out of her dazed and panicked state.

He would apologise for roughness later but first they had to get out of this chaos alive and intact.

It took her a moment, but she did as she was told without protest for the first time in her life.

The trio took the long way around, dodging behind stalls, foliage, even upturned stones in attempts to take cover. Silas felt as though he were stumbling over his own feet, every movement uncertain and panicked but they had very few options left. And from the darting shadows at the edge of his vision he knew his friends weren't the only ones attempting this feat. For now, he kept his gaze only on his own companions, he didn't need distracting by strangers or those who hated him. His own heart was too riddled with moral, and for now he let his brain take the lead.

Sooner than he'd hoped, the no man's land that divided the King's Guard from themselves came upon them. The carriages abandoned with horses still tied in place to their burdens – acting as further shield to the one proud king's procession, cowering in its shadow.

The great stone structures of the marketplace's square blocked attack from behind but otherwise they were cornered, the long grasses of the fields beyond only just visible from this place.

Wishing he had something white on his person, he resorted to waving like a mad man. Desperate to get the attention of a single member of the King's Guard and beg them to stop shooting even for a heartbeat.

If they did spot him amid the carnage, they didn't acknowledge it. And the firing continued.

Silas didn't know whether to be disappointed or unsurprised, but right now all those inklings of emotion were drowned out by the panic that took over everything else.

"Let's go," he whispered.

"They're not stopping," Rosie interrupted, a naïve desperation that they might only need a minute.

"And they're not going to," he replied pointing to the long grass left in their wake. "But we need to move," he didn't give her the chance to respond. Grabbing her and pulling her to his chest, he nudged his best friend in the ribs to follow, which she did wordlessly.

Moving as a leaf battered about by the wind, his bursts of running were erratic in an attempt to minimise the chances of being hit. His arms ached and his legs felt as though they were ablaze, but adrenaline drove him like a forceful tornado. Blood rushed in his ears, and even with his unnatural speed it felt as though he were running at a snail's pace.

A scream dragged free of his lips as the fierce burst of pain ricocheted through every crevice, the metallic scent of blood that followed told him that his best efforts had been betrayed by a sharpshooter. And a wet sensation against his shoulder told him where, his vision blurred by the pain that now took its mantle place beside fear. Still he pressed on.

Until his efforts in the first victory of the afternoon came to fruition, and he stumbled across the line of fire and into the wake of the King's guard. Collapsing against the ground, he coughed hard – doing what he could to remain calm.

Not the grazing wound he had hoped, fortunately the bullet hadn't penetrated anything essential, but more importantly no silver.

"Sy, you're bleeding!" Rosie's voice was panicked, now they were out of the line of fire she had the chance to truly take in what had just gone on.

Releasing Rosie with a grunt, "Trust me, Ro, I'm quite aware," he sat up as best as he could.

He looked up in time to see someone approaching, and the wolf tensed. Instinctually trying to disguise the extent to which his injuries were hurting him, a feral piece of him aware that showing weakness might be the death of him.

But the face he was greeted with was a kind one, a man knelt before him considering him not with the hatred Silas was used to, but when he took in the features of the newcomer he realised why. This was no

Cresvy native, nor one of the Kings Guard. It was their bored Prince from before.

"Guards, we need help here," the Prince seemed to decide after briefly considering the injured wolf for a moment.

Silas in one of his larger moments of idiocy shook his head. Partly because of the pain attempting to manoeuvre his head brought him, and partly because it might have prevented someone from stopping him bleeding out.

To say he wasn't quite present would have been a kind understatement.

"I can wait," Silas managed, his voice shaking with the effort. "A little bleeding won't kill me, your guards have other things to concentrate on," a moment of his naturally self-deprecating nature becoming a more dominant feature, taking over much of his more logical parts.

But there was fair reason to what he said. A distraction to the guard might well left them to be overtaken by the oncoming opponent.

"You're going to bleed out," the Prince's words were matter of fact, though he looked at the wolf as though he had recently sprouted a pair of fine antlers. "Some of the guards have medical training, they might be able to help you!" His words were incredulous, as though Silas had gone to all that effort to get his loved ones across the battlefield to give up at the last moment.

Silas parted his lips, but the words were stolen from him as all he could manage to elicit was a whimper of pain, stealing his train of thought from him before he could compose anything in the way of a logical sentence.

Flick – ever the loyal friend, spoke up for him. "He's a lycanthrope," she explained on a shaky voice, the panic in her eyes renewed when she realised this revelation might well be what threw them out onto no man's land once again. But Silas didn't dare look at the Prince's facial features at this, something he wouldn't normally have been so gung-ho in revealing. "But he has a point, Sy, we need to get that bullet out of you," she warned looking down at him.

"I'm f-" again the attempt at response was stolen from him before it could fully form.

"Point proven," Flick responded with a guttural growl that could have envied Silas' own but her temper wasn't the one they needed to consider right now.

She turned her attention to the guard with a grimace, "He has a point, your guards are kind of needed where they are right now."

Inhaling sharply, he managed to speak through the pain a little more comprehensively than before. "If you have something we can wad up and apply pressure with, I can manage with that until we get out of here."

If we get out of here, even in his pained state he had the common sense to keep that part silent.

The prince responded immediately, though not quite in the way Silas might have expected as he tore the shirt from his own body and offered it to the trio. "It might not be the cleanest, but good luck trying to get one off the guards," his attempt at humour fell flat.

Flick took the garment thankfully all the same, scrunched it up and looked to Silas contemplatively. "Sorry bud, I think we're going to need to get this off," she gestured his own shirt. Her voice portrayed a calmness now, though a somewhat forceful one. Now they were out of the line of fire she could concentrate on doing what she could to help her friend, particularly the one she likely wouldn't have been alive without right now.

Grimacing, Silas did as he was told though not without help. Shaking as he lifted his arms in an effort to remove the sleeves from him, revealing the fiercely scarred skin covered by the cloth. But right now, was not the opportunity to be self-conscious.

Flick, with little more than a few hours of medical experience from helping Catrina, applied as much pressure as she could apply to his bleeding shoulder. Silas grimaced under her touch but didn't say a word. "You guys are going to get me killed one of these days," the words he elicited were stronger now the bleeding was being eased somewhat. He still trembled a little from the loss, but he could hold his head upright with less effort now, and his vision was clearing a little.

"But thank you for your help," Silas managed as more of an afterthought, the statement targeted to all of those present, and his gratitude sincere.

"Oh yeah, it was a real inconvenience," Flick retorted, despite the fear and exhaustion of the day still finding the energy to be sarcastic, naturally. "It's not as if you are the only reason me and Ro are alive," she scolded, but Silas ignored her. Looking for his niece for a beat, who was being uncharacteristically quiet.

Rosie, who'd seemingly witnessed enough medical procedures for the day had turned away. Watching the no man's land in silence, the gunfire had lessened now. Far less regular and seemingly more precise when it did occur, Silas moved to warn her to get away. Not wanting her to see more of the carnage than she needed to, but before he could his niece spoke up.

"There's someone out there," Her voice was hopeful, enough death had been seen today that the sight of movement lit her up like a firework. "Someone needs help!" She panted.

Silas parted his lips to interrupt her, they'd been through enough today that further offers of help seemed to be testing the fates. Enough close encounters that he would rather sneak back to bed and never see the light of day again. He'd heard stories from veterans in the town that enemies would send hostages onto the battlefield pleading for help, and when those driven by a higher moral compass would go to offer help would be shot down for their efforts.

But he had barely parted his lips when he saw Rosie lunge forward from the barriers of the King's procession, once more onto No Man's Land before Silas could fully comprehend what he had seen.

Silas lurched upright, almost tackling through Flick had she not also turned to see what Rosie was attempting. "For the love of," but Silas didn't stick around to hear how she finished.

What proceeded managed to find somewhere between occurring in slow motion and ultra-speed.

A stray bullet shot across the battlefield, even Silas' vision couldn't track it, but the reaction was enough to say what it had hit. Not Rosie, thank the Gods, but one of the horses still tied to the carriages, and it set the animal in motion at a full charge. A fierce whinny accompanied by the thunder of hooves sounded, and in a blur of wood and wheels the carriage was gone like a firework.

Silas screamed his warning, the sound rough and accompanied by him hurling himself forward once more, regardless of the pain his desperation to react was immediate and desperate. He thundered onto the battlefield but felt almost crippled by the exhaustion of his legs and pain in his arms, his stumbling pace infuriatingly useless.

But still he forced himself onward, all but forgetting about the bullets that riddled the air even more so now there was a pair of visible targets to take aim at. But he might well have been shot through the head, but in his desperate concentration to get to his niece he wouldn't have noticed a bomb going off.

In his wake bullets continued flying, but this time a handful were directed for this horse and carriage. Desperate attempts to down the animal or do anything that might have stopped its momentum, but even as muzzles flared behind him he ran on, desperate.

His speed was enough to get him close but not enough to prevent what occurred next.

Rosie screamed as she saw what was coming for her, but that was all of a reaction she could produce as the carriage barrelled through her path in a blurred motion that Silas could barely process as he lunged for her half a beat later. Only to hear the cry that was dragged from her be cut horrendously short.

But all his efforts rewarded him was an already broken body.

Chapter Seven.

The scent of death was near immediate, a foul odour that made him despise his heightened senses as it only bestowed upon him with terror. It was a bitter, cruel scent that seemed to embody the concept of fear and hate into a scent, rot and ash and blood now replaced all everything she had once been.

But it wasn't the scent that was the most horrifying sensation, for that was one of the remaining senses that he could pin to the youngster. Rosie was rendered still, her golden skin bloodied, the sound of her voice silenced permanently. Everything that had made his niece his niece, gone in an instant.

Silas could barely breathe as the gravity of the situation set on his shoulders.

It took the wolf a heartbeat to hear the shouts of his name above the ricochet of gunfire. He lifted his head, dazed and hurting. For a moment he didn't move, forgetting everything as grief became all his brain could comprehend. But slowly he pulled himself onto staggering feet, lifting the still body of his niece into his arms and stumbling back towards the King's Guard. On autopilot, he didn't remember sending his body the order but from instinct alone his legs began momentum, as he stumbled across the border once more. Collapsing against the ground, every inch of his muscled frame trembling.

The sensation of a hand against his shoulder jarred him, he lifted dull eyes to greet Flick's tearful ones. "Sy, Sy, let go, let me help her." Her voice was desperate, and the wolf complied shakily, despite the fact he knew there was nothing left to help.

"No, no, please no." She begged someone who was no longer there to listen, shaking hands pressed against Rosie's lifeless chest, desperately trying to return breath to the youngster's lungs. Silas watched, wordless and broken.

After a few moments of fruitless efforts, Flick slumped back and against Silas' shaking form. Sobs shook her entire frame, whereas Silas was silent and unmoving except for the sudden inhalation at random, as though he had to force himself to remember to breathe. "Sy, I'm so sorry." She stammered, but he didn't have it in him to respond.

Thousands of questions ran through his head, and the lack of answers left him a broken creature. What if he hadn't convinced her to come to see the procession? What if he hadn't decided leaving the sanctuary of the rooftop? What if he had done any single variable that might have changed the outcome that might have meant his niece was still with them, as far back and as stupid as what if he hadn't dove after Alex or not received a bullet wound. If he'd been able to run faster might he still have a breathing, safe niece.

Hours might well have passed, Silas left in his grieving state he could barely process moments in a logical manner. He didn't realise the ricochet of bullets cease, nor the sudden presence of the prince once more.

When he looked up again, eyes blurred this time by tears, he hadn't even realised his shoulder wound had been reopened. The pain a dull reminder in the back of his head that he barely comprehended, he stared wordless at the newcomer.

"It's safe to move again," the words were directed at Flick, quiet and polite though those were hardly things he took into account, it didn't even cross Silas' mind to query as to what and how all this nonsense had happened. "Does the child have a mother who needs to be notified?"

Realising Silas wasn't in much of a place to respond, Flick offered with a hoarse voice. "Her parents work east of here; they aren't due back for a couple of weeks yet." She replied, the words shaking hard. "But she has a grandmother who'll need to know."

That did something to jar Silas out of his numbed state as he offered weakly. "I'll take her home," it seemed like the absolute least he could do. Take his niece home one last time seemed like some measly offering but he was insistent.

Both the stranger and his best friend seemed to contemplate refusal, but Silas would have fought tooth and nail to maintain that right. With or without the help of his more feral abilities, there was nothing left to be reasoned with in that moment. He would have happily become the monster most feared he might be if it meant he could keep this right for the sake of his niece.

"Okay, Sy," Flick's defeated tone echoed through the wolf's very bones. "Do you need a hand or are you okay?" She queried, managing to keep her voice even enough that every other word didn't shake as much as it had, but her cheeks were red and eyes puffy.

He managed to shake his head, though with everything else shaking that was not an easy feat to accomplish. Without a word he forced himself upright, legs threatening to buckle beneath the effort, but he remained straight through sheer power of will.

On stumbling legs and with little comprehension of politeness as he departed, Silas moved onward. Somewhere in his wake he heard his friend mummer a quiet, "Thanks for your help," a sentiment Silas couldn't quite comprehend, given that all of this seemed to be the fault of the trespassers of his town. But by the time that had crossed his mind his friend was at his side once again, and they stumbled across the battlefield that the marketplace had descended into, carrying his beloved niece home one last time.

A mindless zombie patrolling across the stone Cresvy paths, by the time he stumbled through the still broken doorway of his home, he had barely realised he'd walked more than a handful of paces and suddenly he was home.

Now came what he dreaded more than he could fully reason.

"Cat?" Flick's voice made him jump at his side, as though he had forgotten she was close to him, he was delirious but wasn't quite sure it was just from blood loss.

Appearing from the kitchen, a smile so contrastingly bright that it blinded the wolf for a heartbeat. She approached with a chuckle, "Was work so hard she fell asleep?" She tutted, but the words were playful and laced with affection as she approached the pair.

Only when she was a few feet away, did his mother seem to notice that something was terribly wrong.

His mother's scream could have terrified the Gods. A sound that would be buried into his soul until the day he died, and it took every inch of effort on his part not to collapse under the weight of the noise alone. His lower lip wobbled but he stood upright, "I'm sorry," was the best he could manage as his mother fell to her knees in front of him. He lowered his niece to the ground in front of her.

Part of him begged anything that would listen that this might turn out to have been some dreadful dream. That at the touch of her grandmother Rosie would leap to life once more, laughter echoing across the halls once more and he could take a great breath of relief.

But it didn't and she wouldn't, and his mother was left simply to wail hopelessly.

To see the person he considered the strongest in Cresvy broken by grief, Silas could barely breathe as he fought to keep his breaths even, sobs shaking his frame irregularly as he fought to find control over it. But it all seemed hopeless.

From the shadows of the corridor behind, Flick was simply left to watch, her own whimpers adding to the broken-hearted symphony.

After a few moments, Catrina spoke finally. Her voice suddenly stiff, replacing the sobbing with her usual firm kindness, "Sy, what's happened?" Only the eyes gave her away, tears welling in the dark browns as she struggled to keep them from falling any further.

Finding the strength to speak properly for the first time, his voice mirrored none of his mother's incredible composition as he replied weakly. Explaining the events of the afternoon, and the tragic outcome despite his best efforts.

He watched his mother's expressions shift and waiver, desperately trying to maintain the strength she was known for. Until in the end she whispered, "You did your best," despite it all his mother knew what the wolf needed to hear, but he found little comfort in her determined efforts.

When her arms wrapped around him in an all-encompassing hug, Silas couldn't help it as he descended into sobs once again. Collapsing against her warm arms, he felt like a four-year-old child again, but he needed it more than words could have ever described.

Catrina gestured, and without needing much further in the way of persuasion Flick joined them on the ground. Rosie's broken form hugged between them, the most they could offer in the way of a farewell to their loved one.

"How are we going to get word to Alice and Theo," Flick's words were gentle, trying to find some sort of logic in the midst of the pain. The sound of his sister's name and her husband were agonising to Silas.

His mother shook her head, "I'll send a bird in the morning," the local posts would have been closed for market day otherwise she'd have stood and done it immediately, Silas was certain of that much. "We'll need to figure something out for a funeral." The monotone to her words were almost cruel sounding, but Silas knew the alternative would have been broken hearted sobbing, and this was the better of the two choices his mother had elected to follow.

As his mother moved to stand up, only then did Silas recognise just how ancient she looked. The jovial youth that had always defied her age, disappeared in the wake of grief, the wrinkles amplified by the frown etched into her expression, and the dark brown eyes dulled seemed to make her look exhausted.

It like an electric shock to the wolf to see, something he'd never considered and had hoped would never have to see.

"We need to lay her to rest for now," Catrina managed, unaware of the thoughts spurring through Silas head, she ran her hand through his hair.

She treated him like a child, but the wolf welcomed it in that moment, needing every comfort he could gain, he closed his eyes.

Inhaling sharply again, hating that every breath he took was laced with the stench of death that now laced his niece's form, he found himself barely daring to breathe except until his heart all but exploded from the effort of holding it.

"Sy, I'm sorry but can you-" his mother needn't have finished as he moved to stand. Taking Rosie once more in his arms as he did so, awaiting further direction wordlessly.

He felt useless enough and would have done anything no matter how slight that might have helped.

Shaking hands moved to clutch his niece's form, he forced trembling fingers to still for fear of dropping the fragile girl. As though death had rendered her bones glass and her skin fine china. Lifting upright again, he realised halfway through straightening his knees. "Where?" The exhaustion of the day stole anything in the way of coherent sentencing from him.

A quick sniff of the air told him Alex had departed the kitchen, or at the very least found a different residence to sleep off the traumas of the morning. But Silas could hardly imagine laying the body of his niece to rest on the kitchen table, as much of a decoration as a pot of flowers or a piece of pottery. His sister and her husband would take a few days to get here, on top of the day or so it would take the bird to take the macabre message to them, but Silas knew Catrina wouldn't conduct anything in the way of a funeral before then.

But where to keep the body until then was a question he could barely begin to consider.

"Her bedroom?" Flick seemed to cringe the moment the suggestion was offered, she added. "Her desk, it might do for the time being?" It was logical enough, out of the way of the grieving, methods could be utilised to maintain the bodies state for the time being until things could be arranged, Catrina was fluent in that sort of routine. But holding funeral traditions were something quite different when it came to one's own loved ones, Silas stifled a meek gulp.

"Her bedroom," Catrina confirmed firmly, casting Flick a grateful glance.

Wordlessly Silas complied with the orders provided, but as he ascended the stairs it felt like great weights tied him down at the ankles.

Pulling each foot up took the same effort as lifting a house from its foundations, but he proceeded despite it.

Knocking his shoulder against the bedroom door, he entered as the door gave way against his efforts. Rosie's still fresh scent flooded his being, to the point where it almost dragged a further whimper from his lips, to the point where he was grateful his mother lacked his stronger senses.

His niece's room was her embodied. The little room was dimly lit by a small square window looking out into the alleyway outside the house, and it was littered with little sketches of flowers, buildings, animals or anything that had recently caught her fancy. Handfuls of discarded papers from schoolwork that would never be completed littered the floor, beside unwashed clothes that would never be worn again. Her bed was unmade, something she would no doubt have returned to a scolding for, had she been able to return in the first place.

The tiny body barely took up two thirds of the desk, a fair amount of room left at either side of the head and feet. Silas hesitated, then moved to grab the small vase from the windowsill at the right-hand side of the room and lay the stems at her head. Something to make the scene less ghoulish but almost immediately regretting the decision. The beautiful colours seemed out of place – painfully so, against the pale and unmoving frame of his loved one. But he had barely come within an inch of the flowers when his mother interrupted.

"Don't," with a suddenness that caused Silas to jump out of his skin. "Please, don't." She didn't offer anything in the way of explanation, but Silas complied stepping away without touching a further thing.

He backed away until his back was against the wall, he stood at attention. Solemn and quiet, he waited for his mother's direction but when she remained quiet, he queried softly. "Mum, what can I do for you?" He was a child desperately seeking confirmation and comfort, and he hated that fact, but he could hardly take back his words.

"My bag is still in the kitchen," Catrina flinched with frustration. "Retrieve it for me?"

He promptly turned; anything that could have gotten him out of the room full of reminders and made his way back downstairs for the kitchen. Torn between wanting to drag his feet to prevent him from returning and hurrying for the sake of his mother. He found a middle ground of a usual walking pace, trying to unclench the stiff muscles that made up his entire frame.

The kitchen had maintained much of the chaos from the morning, an event that now felt as though it had taken place an eternity ago. But a quick look into the living room found his answer to where his colleague had departed to, for Alex was sprawled across the small, tattered couch that stood as a centrepiece to the room. In the depths of an induced unconsciousness, unaware to the grief that tore the world apart just outside his little bubble.

Flick; who had descended down the stairs behind him in a similar attempt to be free of the painful room. Took it upon herself to check on the morning's patient, anything to keep her hands busy and mind preoccupied.

He sifted through the kitchen, much of his mother's haphazard materials scattered in various parts of the tiled room. He made brief efforts to organise the madness, but elected speed was more of a priority over cleanliness, thus snatched together what he deemed would be essential to his mother. Various herbs usually utilised for healing poultices that could be repurposed to create a good smell; something the mask the encroaching scents of death.

Deciding he had done what he could, he shoved them into the leather bag characterised as his mother's medical supplies vessel and returned up the stairs. Though now all he carried was a relatively light bag, the weight felt just as bad as it had moments prior.

He moved to push through the bedroom door again but paused at the entrance.

The sound of gentle sobbing had once more taken over the sounds within the bedroom, and it left Silas with a lump in his throat. He hesitated, wishing to allow his mother with her dignity – not that he'd have ever held it against her given he had already spent much of his time wailing. Silas waited, stiff as a board by the door, breath held for fear his mother might notice him.

After a few moments, he returned to the stop of the stairs. Shifting his weight more now, so the sound of his footsteps could be audible even to all too human hearing. He called out for his mother's benefit, "I've got what you needed mum," hoping that would give her something in the way of time to prepare herself.

When he returned to the bedroom, he found his mother dabbing her eyes casually. Smiling weakly at her son as he entered, "Thank you Sy," her words were more formal than they would have been usually. A jarring sound that came with her attempts at composing herself.

"You don't need to be here," her voice was gentle and reassuring. "This won't be easy for either of us, but I can manage it alone." She assured.

A selfish piece of the wolf wanted to snatch the opportunity to depart. Get out of here and pretend for even a heartbeat longer that none of this had occurred, and that there might be the slightest chance life might have returned to normal.

Despite all of that, he shook his head.

"I want to help," he said with a hoarse, unfamiliar tone. When his mother looked uncertain, he added, a little sharper this time. "Please, mum."

"Thank you, Sy," she repeated, and in truth it was as much for his mother as it was for him that he remained. Despite every wailing instinct that begged him to get out of there and never return.

With a deep sigh, she turned again. Resting her bag against the desk chair for the sake of ease and began setting to work.

"I don't know what to use here, and what to save in case it's needed later down the line." Catrina admitted after a few moments, using her son as someone to bounce ideas off of, even though Silas medical abilities were about as even with the average toddler.

Proper medical supplies were an expense they could barely dream of, thus when there was an herbal alternative that could manage even at a lower degree of efficiency, it was utilised. The only true supplies a hospital might consider not ratchet were in the way of a handful of vials of painkiller, and various antibiotics. But for the most part they were only utilised when absolutely necessary.

But even those herbs were not always easy to come by at the markets, especially during the sodden moons that had plagued the recent months. Silas knew for a fact they were running low, despite his best efforts to search for his mother.

"Mum, I can find things for you in the woods if needed," he reasoned. Not wanting his sister to go without if it meant saving something for someone else, they had spent their lives being selfless. "I'll go further than I normally would, it doesn't matter," he promised. There were no lengths he wouldn't have gone to in that moment.

His mother merely nodded and continued wordlessly.

Whereas her movements that morning with Alex had been effortless and calm, accompanied by a jovial ease that encompassed a woman who loved her work. Now the ease seemed to encumber her, as though steady hesitance was more proper for the situation. He watched as she applied strong smelling poultices to his niece's skin.

A strange part of him disliked the flowery scents that now protruded from his niece even more than he did the now faded smells of death. It was even more unlike Rosie to smell so sweet; it was almost sickly; he resisted the urge to vomit.

His niece's scent was usually wild and muddied, the smells of the bitter ocean wind and pine forests that surrounded the little town. Those weren't exactly something that could be applied to the stiffening body, so this was the best alternative that wouldn't turn the stomach.

The process continued at speed, but they were interrupted by a rapping at the door.

Silas hesitated, taken off guard by the sound he straightened, defensive. After they day they'd been plagued with, most could forgive him for being protective of the loved ones he had left. He sent a questioning gaze to his mother.

"Word spreads fast," she said with a grimace, rubbing her hands together. "Please send them away."

Nodding, he descended back down the stairs, but Flick had beaten him too it. He moved to intervene, knowing her parting words likely wouldn't have been as kind as the ones he'd aim to utilise despite the circumstances.

But what he saw behind the opened door frame stole the wind from his lungs as he skidded to a stop at the bottom of the stairs.

The bored Prince and the King, with the King's Guard ensemble in his wake.

Chapter Eight.

In the brief moment Silas had taken to consider whether he was so exhausted he had begun hallucinating; the group had bombarded into the house. Given the broken nature of the door, the wolf was mildly surprised they had taken the time to bother knocking in the first place.

"We came to offer our condolences regarding the child lost today," the Bored Prince was the only one to speak.

The look Silas regarded the prince with was nothing short of incredulous. *We've a post box and accept carrier pigeons, in fact smoke signals would have been preferred.* Were among the hundreds of thoughts that sprang through his head. *You of all people are not welcome here.* Were among the first thoughts that lit his brain, but he kept them to himself once more for the sake of not being shot on sight.

Despite his common sense and in disrespect of any concept of politeness, the wolf dared to quietly query. "How did you find us?"

Not one of the more obvious questions that came to mind, but his brain was already so frazzled the usual filter was almost non-existence.

"We asked for the town Lycanthrope and were told to follow the smell," a guard muttered, looking around Silas' home as though the very air was infested with rats. "Now I can see why," the particular guard lifted a gloved hand as though to prevent vomiting. The guard's cruel words and mocking gestures sent tension shooting through his veins, his fingers closed to fists but that was all he permitted.

His words drew a handful of chuckles from amid the gathered crowd, even the King's lips seemed to quirk upwards though ever so slightly.

"We assumed there wouldn't be more than one," the prince's tone was a softer, calmer one. An inkling of kindness in the hostile environment his tone had descended into. "We asked around and were told this address…" he looked around and seemed to think his choice of wording. "The directions to get here," was the best he came up with after a heartbeat of uncertainty.

Silas seethed silently but kept his temper for the sake; though it felt as though he might just explode from the effort. "Well you were correct, and I thank you for your condolences, I shall ensure they are duly passed on," the formal tone utilised was unfamiliar to even him. Even the way he inhaled was structured and careful, on edge that anything might provoke or aggravate or even mildly annoy the ensemble. "Now at your leisure, make your way out of my house."

When no one moved to leave, Silas stepped forward a little. His bulk at the centre of the hallway as a means of blocking further entrance; he didn't use it to intimidate or provoke. But at the very least assert something in the way of dominance, in a move more feral than he generally preferred. However, outside of a couple of hands grasping a little tighter at holstered guns, they seemed neither effected nor amused by this decision.

Electricity coursed through the air, with a tension that could have been cut with a rusty spoon. Admittedly Silas had been all bark no bite – unused to having his rare challenges accepted, he feared he would be called on his bluff, and then he would genuinely have no idea what to do next.

Fortunately, it seemed that wouldn't be necessary.

"Sadly, the offering our condolences weren't the only thing we came here for."

The caveat, of course. Silas didn't bother prying further, he merely watched them with arched eyebrows, waiting with mild impatience.

But he wasn't the only impatient one, for the first time the King spoke up. "Enough of this nonsense, we need to speak with you, and we need to do it somewhere in private." Now he could see the King properly, the hood downed from his features the young wolf could see – smell, the blood that laced the older gentleman's very skin like tattoos.

None of it seemed to be his own, but the sight was a terrifying one.

"Okay." The word was unfamiliar and plagued by exhaustion. All Silas could think to do was guide them left, to the sitting room where Alex as far as he was aware still remained dead to the world asleep. Stunned silence accompanying his movements as he pushed open the heavy doors.

"Do you want me to get my mother?" He asked as easily as he could manage.

"No," the answer was immediate and spouted from a handful of mouths across the gathered crowd, and Silas considered them with a nervous glance.

But before much else could proceed, movement from the couch caught Silas' attention. Alex not yet roused from the depths of his slumber, and no doubt would immediately suffer a heart attack from the scene gathered before him. Considering the accumulated ailments of the day, Silas moved to try and negate the situation.

"One of my mother's patients," was the best he could offer in terms of an explanation, or at least all that he could be bothered to come up with.

"We don't need him listening in on this."

Ignoring that he moved to check the still weary and not quite conscious patient's pulse carefully, paying little attention to what went on in his wake. "It will just take me a moment to move him," he muttered after a minute. Rumours spread like wildfire in the little slum borough,

The reaction was far from what Silas expected. "He already knows too much," an unfamiliar voice reasoned, but Silas barely had noticed the threatening tone underlying the words until he heard a single, dark word. "Move."

He turned around to find a gun pointing at him but intended for the man laying oblivious on his back, dozing the world away. Silas looked stunned, uncertain as to whether all of this had been some insane dream.

"Now," a swift movement and a flash of pain caught the wolf off guard. As the gun was used as a weapon to hit him across the cheek, leaving the area warm and his senses buzzing.

Returning to a straightened position with a growl like thunder that he wasn't entirely sure he knew the origin was. "Not a chance if it means you're going to use that thing," he returned without moving an inch either way.

The gun in turn didn't as much as shake from its line of fire. "Move or you will be moved," the guard reasoned with something akin to a smirk on his expression. "I might not have silver bullets, but I don't need to kill you to get you to move, and perhaps a little pain might teach you to obey orders, little mutt."

Silas didn't waver, but spent a heartbeat scrambling for an answer. His outside the swan atop the water, but his brain was the legs frantically paddling beneath until he came out with. "You might not kill me, but you clearly need me for something or other, unless this is a façade you pull in every village you visit," he was amazed the words came out in a somewhat coherent order. "But use that gun in the proximity of my house and I won't help you for love or money."

For a moment the aiming guard seemed to consider, and begrudgingly the gun was returned to its holster.

Now Alex has sat upright, rubbing exhausted eyes all Silas heard of the mumbling voice was, "What in the name of," but he didn't get the chance to finish.

This would be the second time that day Silas had saved the ungrateful Alex's life, and he might have been keeping count if he doubted it would have helped in the slightest after the fact.

"Move him," it was the monarch this time, speaking as though none of the former had happened.

Silas considered for a moment, before calling out. "Flick."

From the kitchen, poised between sheepish and threatening, the red head emerged. Clutched in her grip was a frying pan, and Silas might have chuckled were it not for the fact he knew full well she'd have quite willingly used it had the need arose.

"Help Alex upstairs, explain to mum that we have visitors please?" He asked in a slow steady voice, he'd heard her creeping footsteps midway through the conversation, and knew she'd be as up to date as he was at that point. He trusted her.

Grip released on the frying pan, it clattered dramatically to the ground with a metallic thud as she moved her way through the guards. Paying them as much attention as she might have the average sewer rat, she harboured as much love for Alex as Silas did, but did as she was told without complaint.

Her departure and ascent were slow, hoping to catch what she could of the conversation.

Unfortunately for Flick she had the subtlety of a bull in a china shop, and the ensemble seemed to know what she was doing and thus waited patiently until her shadow had disappeared from the narrow stairs. It was then that pairs of eyes turned to Silas, fixing him with a heated gaze he was quite sure could have burned through the skin.

Only once they were quite sure that no one remained to eavesdrop, did proceedings begin.

"We were ambushed at the Marketplace." The King explained the obvious.

Never! Silas remained quiet; arms folded he leant against the wall in a desperate attempt to seem remotely less panicked than he felt. *I thought that's how all your public outings go*, rather he simply nodded in acknowledgement he'd heard what had been said.

"Seven of my men were killed, and a few dozen bodies were found in the surrounding fields, naturally it is impossible to figure out who were amid the audience and those who were there under more malicious circumstances." the way the monarch referred to the murdered innocents sounded like they were little more than rats becoming casualties to the cat and little more.

"What happened out there?" Silas allowed himself to query at last, against his better judgement but the need to ask built up inside him like a raging fire, and if he kept it inside much longer he feared he might well have exploded from the pressure. "And I don't just mean the ambush, why, how and who is what I'm asking – not the what." He clarified before he could be annoyed any further.

"Someone knew we were coming, and they wanted to stop it," one of the guards reasoned lowly, the anger left Silas' hair standing on end, a brewing storm coming closer. "But outside of the King's Guard and a handful back home, no one knew we were coming today before this morning. Let alone a few days ago which would be the kind of time needed to plan something like this."

The chaos he'd witnessed that morning wasn't exactly what he'd considered a plan, but Silas merely nodded along in silence. "You have a mole," it was his own turn to state the obvious. That seemed to be the only reasonable conclusion.

"We have a mole," the guard confirmed, hatred laced his tone like a venom.

The stench of betrayal seemed to stick to the very skin of the men around him, the fiery blaze of anger in their gazes would have scared anyone. But the wolf remained steadfast in their wake, finding more confidence the further this continued.

It seemed they needed him for something, the what would hopefully soon be revealed.

"How could this have happened? I'm no expert but I imagine you don't just let any man with a gun into your forces," Silas asked a little softer this time. They had been hurt by this experience, their friends had been slaughtered just like his townsfolk and niece, part of him hated himself for being so willing to listen. But he could beat himself up for that at a later date.

Now the bored Prince spoke up, though every inch of boredom that had earlier given him the endearment had disappeared from his expression, replaced by a careful focus Silas wasn't sure a bomb could have shifted.

"The men in the King's Guard are the loyalist around," he answered. Dark green eyes staring into Silas', not with the degree of challenge the wolf was used to – those challenging him for the fun, or the dare were something quite difference.

When he looked at that bored prince, he saw a wolf staring back, even without the lycanthrope blood running through the bored prince's veins.

"Clearly not," it wasn't intended as an insult, but Silas would have been kidding himself by pretending he hadn't noticed the stiffness that had ricocheted about the room at his question. "Again, not an expert, but as far as I'm aware guns don't pick themselves up and decide to start shooting for the fun of it."

"They don't," a guard conceded after a moment of quiet. "But for the time being they might as well do, because we have no idea who did this."

The honesty was refreshing, Silas could give them that much at least.

The next question might have been the easiest in the world or the cruellest depending on who looked at it and how. Silas lowered his eyes to the ground for the first time, something in the way of guilt sparking through his veins though he wasn't sure as to why, as he asked quietly.

"Why would someone want to do this?" He pried, a teacher trying to drag an answer from an unwilling or uncertain student. The wolf was no politician, and he knew little about the world of the monarchy, but he was all too aware this wasn't something one did on a whim. This could well have ended in the death of the assailant, and he doubted someone would do it for the sheer fun of the chaos it had wrought, unless they were truly insane.

And this didn't look like the work of a madman, and Silas had known many in his time.

"Our time in Braxas wasn't necessarily the simple one we advertised," the monarch's words jarred Silas. "It was a peacekeeping mission."

For a moment, Silas allowed himself to take in this information. Blinking slowly, he could all but hear the gears grinding in his head as he worked through the known facts. "Peacekeeping – are we at war?" His heart thundered in his chest as he asked, and the words parted his lips in a shaky, half coherent manner but he didn't care about his eloquence in that terrifying moment.

"No."

Silas should have been delighted by the answer, but something about the tone terrified him. He couldn't quite shake the feeling that he was the mouse and they were the cats. They were here for a reason, but he wanted all the answers before he would offer anything of his own. Whatever they wanted that they might be looking for, at least.

"And the best we can think of is that this response has disappointed someone, that the outcome of peace wasn't what somebody somewhere was hoping for." The Prince answered for the Monarch, with an ease Silas found discomforting.

The wolf recoiled admittedly, Nekeldez had known war. Not his generation but his mother's younger days had been plagued with it, he had heard the stories and known those left broken by it. He couldn't begin to imagine what kind of monster would want to return their world to it.

"Why," his words were a stuttered syllable, scared not for his own sake. Silas was barely allowed a job as simply as what he did at the docks, he wouldn't be allowed within a hundred feet of a proper frontline. Something far crueller than what took place that day at the marketplace, but he was amid the fortunate who would be safe from the battlegrounds.

Not many were going to be as lucky, if war would go ahead.

"It seems someone is wanting to spark a rebellion," the answer came from a guard after a brief heartbeat of contemplation.

The answer wasn't something all that surprising. Rebellions had been present since the very word royalty had been created. Barely a year went by without the word floating about the newspapers, it never seemed very real and rarely did anything come of it.

"Brilliant," a hand run through his thick hair as a sigh tugged from his lips. The answer was lacking but from what he saw it was the best they had to offer. The next question wasn't quite as easy to ask. "Please tell me you have a plan to stop this place from descending into war?" The question was posed at no one in particular and might as well have been asked to the Gods, if they were even listening.

"Mind your tone," a guard lost his patience and offered a warning sound from deep in the back of his throat, Silas regarded him with surprise, but didn't relent in his question. "Regardless of what you've seen today, he is your King and you will treat him as such."

Before today that man didn't know my home existed, Silas had to bite his tongue to keep the words from slipping free. "The question still stands," he offered with a quieter tone, "I think I at least deserve something of an answer. If it weren't for you being here, a lot of people would still be alive."

Mere metres above his head, his niece lay dead on her desk, rather than playing in the streets with her friends. He wouldn't let himself forget that, no matter how amicable these strangers seemed, nor the danger they posed to his little home.

"Get home as quick as possible and tell those who need to know that war has been averted, and to stop the plans that had been prepared if the answer had been something else." The Guard returned easily, narrowed eyes watching the wolf incessantly. Judging the reaction.

Silas had to restrain himself from scoffing, "Sounds easy enough," he was grateful they caught his sarcasm. "What's the catch?" He doubted anyone would seem this panicked if it was as simple as it sounded, they wouldn't seem as trigger happy and nervous as the men before him were.

These were warmongerers, pity was something he struggled to find for them now.

"We don't have one place to travel to," that answer of all that had been offered seemed to be the one they struggled to offer the most. "And we have limited time to do it in."

"And why are you taking the time to tell me of all people, I can't imagine you're going through the entire town telling everyone individually, and if so you probably picked the worst person to start with." If anything, he'd usually have been at the bottom of a quite long list, past the newborns, stray dogs and rats.

A distinct feeling of discomfort ran through the room, so thick Silas could almost see it on the air. They seemed uncertain, as though most of them disagreed with whatever reason had been used to seek the wolf out.

"We don't know who we can trust," It took a lot for them to answer truthfully, but it didn't bring anything in the way of pity to Silas who could hear it. "Outside of the cowards who ran from the battlefields, you were the only one being shot at that we know the placement of, and unless you're stupid enough to allow someone to shoot at you, we think you're someone we can trust."

Silas didn't take much appreciation from those words.

Tension worked through Silas frame, but he waited with thin patience; something that was quickly becoming quite the rare commodity for the struggling wolf.

"Simple math, there are 6 places that need to be made aware," the King took on his son's moniker of boredom, as though it were the simplest thing in the world. Though to the warmonger King it probably was – his life would never truly be on the line in all of this. "And only 11 of us."

A quick glance about the room told Silas such was the truth, himself making up the twelfth number, and that realisation told him exactly what they wanted of him.

"No," the answer came from him with ease and suddenness. "Now if that's all you wanted of me you are quite welcome to make your way out of here, immediately." The words shook as he spoke, an anger he couldn't quite hold back, leaving him almost certain he might well have burst free of his silver bindings just from the anger it brought into his chest.

"Unfortunately, that answer isn't going to be good enough for us," a guard answered, though the discerning tone used told Silas that even he wasn't happy with the answer they'd come up with. "We can barely manage the journey with two per party as it is, and we aren't about to let somebody go it alone."

"I think you'll find none of this is my problem," his tone shook again but this time with the effort of keeping it from creeping above a shout. "None of this would have happened if you hadn't come to my town, and now people I love are dead,"

To the credit of the strangers, they maintained eye contact no matter how he glowered.

"And now you have the balls to come and ask for my help?" He glowered.

"Yes," the easiest and quickest answer the wolf had gotten all night.

"Cresvy might be a terrible place, but we have pigeons use one of them. Hell, a message tied to a horse and sent galloping would probably be a better option," he wasn't sure any of them needed convincing that using his services was a bad idea.

"War is on the horizon and people are wanting to make sure it gets here as soon as possible," scowled a guard again. "If you think every pigeon between here and every major city isn't going to be shot on sight you do not understand the gravity of the situation."

Silas understood the gravity of the situation more than he understood anything else that had taken place that day. And he hated it all the same.

"What's happened today has stolen a lot of good people from this town, and has stolen a granddaughter from her grandmother, if you think I'm going to leave my mother after all of this, you are mistaken." It was a last resort and perhaps offered something in the way of a low blow, but Silas found himself entirely unable to care at that point.

But a voice from the doorway behind them sounded, making even the wolf jump. In the heat of the conversation they had failed to notice someone had been eavesdropping, perhaps saying something about the quality of the King's guard but that wasn't a point Silas was willing to bring up in the moment.

"You are going, Sy," a kind voice in the midst of hate. "And I'm not sure you have a choice."

The wolf turned around, surprise marking his movements and only doubled when he spotted who had thrown her pennies into the conversation. His mother stood teary eyed but fierce in the shadows of the doorway.

"Mum." The word quivered with a mixture of concern and sadness. "You don't need to agree with them just for my sake," he promised – fearful that she might have been saying yes for the sake of keeping the wolf breathing and upright. "They're not going to do anything," it might have sounded like arrogant cockiness on the lips of another man, perhaps, but on the young man's it sounded matter of fact.

"I'm not agreeing with them for any reason outside of the fact that I agree with them, Sy."

Silas recoiled with surprise at this response, his nostrils flared, ears strained. Trying to pick up on the indicators that she might have been lying for his sake, but he found none. Catrina portrayed only her usual fierce calmness, despite the puffy red eyes.

"I can't leave you," his voice was underlined with more quivering than he cared to admit, but now wasn't the time to be self-conscious.

"You can and you will," Catrina entered the room now, approaching Silas until she was close enough that he could see how fiercely she fought to keep her tears from falling. She was being strong for his sake, but there was nothing new in that.

"It means I'm going to miss Ro's funeral," it was nothing short of a choking sound that came from his lips as the realisation struck him. The idea of missing his niece's farewell was something that sent spikes surging through his heart.

"She would forgive you given the circumstances, Sy," Catrina's response was something between heartbroken and firm.

About them the King's Guard, Monarch and the Bored Prince seemed torn between looking away and keeping focused. It might have been amusing to see the kingdom's strongest men rendered uncomfortable by a hurting mother, but Silas had little attention to pay them. His every sense focused on his mother, trying desperately to find a means of convincing her otherwise.

"If you think that after everything they've done today I could even begin to leave with them, if you th-" Silas began but a simple look was enough to steal the words from his lips before he could begin to form them.

"Silas," the word was caught somewhere between anger and fear. "This is so beyond what you want and need," she warned – truly a mother's scolding tone. "Sweet child you only know the stories, and for that I will be ever grateful that you didn't need to see what some of us had to," her voice shook, her gaze glistened out of control, with stars that swam in watering eyes. He could almost see ghosts in his mother's midnight gaze.

For a heartbeat she paused, trying to compose herself. Silas was caught between reaching for her, hating watching his mother in pain but it was as though he were frozen in place. His legs rooted to the ground and the ability to move stolen from him.

"If there is a chance, no matter how slight that you can stop that from happening again," she shook her head, trying to chase memories and ghosts away with the movement. "Then you have to leap at it, Sy," his mother finished, managing to maintain her composure enough to lift her gaze and stare the wolf down directly.

Silas watched her for a moment, before ducking his head to the side with a sigh. It seemed his decision had been made for him, there was nothing unusual there. But if his mother was so insistent, he knew there was never going to have been a choice in the first place.

Gods couldn't have stopped him from complying with his mother's will, especially given how desperate she seemed now. It was something Silas had never witnessed before, and the persistence to her voice could have moved mountains – the wolf in all his strength stood little to no chance.

He swallowed hard, his gaze lingering on the floor for a moment, until at last he finally voiced aloud. "It would seem that I'm in," was all he managed to offer.

Chapter Nine.

The ensemble set into movement as soon as confirmation had been sent their way. The suddenness suggested that they had expected much more of a fight to gain their final ally, but for the most part they appeared grateful it hadn't come to that.

For all their facades, even with numbers on their side a fight with a lycan was something anyone would aim to avoid. Even a chained one, in the confines of his own home the wolf was unpredictable to the strangers, and he could hardly blame them for their cautions.

But now there was a calm to their movements, a certainty and surety that this was their territory now, and they began acting just like it. Silas was left simply to watch as things were stripped from the dining table, a great piece of paper unfolded onto its surface now; a map. Silas studied it, a splash of black by the coast demonstrated their position. He was mildly intrigued, it had been a long time since he'd been in the same room as a map, let alone had the chance to study one close and in detail.

"Don't tear that," a guard's voice jarred Silas from his concentration, feeling quite like a scolded toddler. As though the lightest touch might have left it crumbled, with a sigh and not in the mood to argue. The wolf did as he was told, withdrawing his hand from its surface, reduced to admiring it from a distance. He left his ears half trained on the conversation, but his gaze wandering and curious.

After a few moments of conversation Silas didn't entirely understand or regarded as not entirely relevant to himself. Silas head jerked up when he realised eyes were trained on his form once more, he arched his eyebrows questioningly. Hiding any inch of sheepishness that he had been caught not listening as carefully as he should have been by casual ease.

Clearly repeating himself, "In an effort to make sure that if one team is taken down, the whereabouts and position of the others aren't leaked. We'll pair off, but the King and I shall give you your coordinates," the Guard – whom Silas had taken to be the head of the King's ensemble explained with a bored tone. "And I don't care if the Gods themselves descend from the skies and ask you to tell them, no one can know."

He only offered a simple nod of his head, compliant and obedient through common sense alone.

"Good," the guard breathed, a sigh tugging free of his lips. He looked at a piece of paper scribbled over in writing and began listing names. To Silas he might as well have been speaking in a different language and thus didn't pay too much attention, until. "Mason, and the Lycan."

It was then he realised the fact he knew none of these men's names was somewhat of a flaw. He glanced about the room, uncertain.

"Me," A voice sounded, causing Silas' gaze to dart left. Surprised to find that the bored Prince had spoken, finally he had a name to replace the moniker.

"I'm sure you will keep the boy safe?" The King's booming voice ricocheted across the room, setting Silas with a glare that left his skin burning.

"I'll do my best," he had a sinking feeling that none of them were going to get out of this that easy, and he might need to further enquire as to the King's definition of safe at a later date. But then if he was willingly allowing the prince to descend into something just short of a warzone, Silas began to wonder if it was a reasonable requirement to ask of the wolf.

The King merely nodded, as though the question by itself had been something of an afterthought.

For a while questions were battered back and forth. Silas felt like a sore thumb amid this little army, sticking out and uncertain of his own place.

"We will set off at night fall," a glance out the window told Silas that wasn't quite the period of time he'd have hoped. A couple of hours at most, though the heavy clouds overhead made locating the sun difficult. "Sleep as best as you can until then, we will come knocking at your door when you are needed."

"It will be crowded but you can manage here for the night," his mother offered. The tears still gathered in her eyes but gone was the shake to her voice. As though, and much to Silas's sadness, she had gotten over what was to come and the facts at hand. "There's a study upstairs that you can use to have dealings in… private."

Their orders – however lacking, had been provided. And with little else to be done, the King's guard dispersed amongst themselves. Some taking to the floor to follow the orders to find rest, a couple of others managing to take seat on the small sofas of the living room.

Stunned and wordless, Silas watched this go down. Uncertain of what to do, but after a moment he came to a decision. He had goodbyes to say. Though part of him wanted to put that off till the last possible moment, he knew if he didn't face the music now, he'd have regretted that decision for the rest of his life.

He turned and moved for the doorway to the stairs. But a voice called out.

"If you think you're about to run for it - " a voice warned but he didn't have chance to finish before Silas offered with an all-out growl of frustration.

"You're stealing me from my home with no promise that I'm going to get out of this alive," it took effort to keep still in his place. "I don't think it's too much to ask that I be allowed to say my farewells."

The guard seemed to genuinely consider doing just that, but a muttering from the bored Pr- Mason, prevented his lips from parting. The guard merely nodded, "Fine, but keep what we've told you to yourself," he warned.

Silas merely nodded, before turning and springing up the stairs in a couple of bounds. Following his nose until he came across the only person left alive for him to say goodbye to, Flick.

The redhead all but charged for the door the moment she heard footsteps. Silas didn't dare ask exactly what she'd have done had it been a guard or his mother, for her reaction wasn't entirely suitable for either as she tackled him into an all-consuming hug.

"Sy, I'm so sorry I tried to go down with your mum, but she refused, she made me stay here." She stumbled on her words; Silas hugged her back with a restrained strength. Having to stop himself from shaking with the effort of remaining upright after all that had happened that day.

"It's ok," was all he could think of in the way of comfort. "There wasn't much you could have done."

She looked thoroughly offended at this assumption, her eyes narrowed. "I think you'll fin-"

"Don't, Flick," he asked, the energy seeped from his bones he had nothing left to offer. He slumped to the ground with a thump, he held his head in his hands as he tried to wrap his head around the day's events. Left dizzy and sick to the stomach as he processed it all.

His best friend knelt beside him, thudding to the ground with a gentle, more elegant sound. "Sy, what's happening?" She asked with a gentleness uncharacteristic to his best friend.

With dull, exhausted eyes the wolf regarded his friend. "War is coming," was the best he could come up with in that moment. Despite what the guard had warned, he knew that word of that would spread soon enough and keeping it secret would do nothing but lose him a friendship.

"After what we saw today, it looks like war is already here," Silas wasn't quite sure if it was an attempt at humour or something more macabre.

"That was nothing, apparently," his lips felt dry from just saying it. "That was only the start," he closed his eyes. Trying to decide whether or not to admit the next part, he eventually decided he would, but only in part. For the sake of his best friend's safety above anything else. "I'm to travel with the King's Guard, that bored Prince," he added trying to clarify through a wave of uncertainty. "And try to stop war before it comes."

Even saying it aloud, Silas hated himself all the more for agreeing to partake in it, though under some degree of coercion and not entirely of his own will. Silas struggled beneath the great weight, ,his heart ached from the day's events.

For a moment Flick simply watched him, it was a lot for her to take in. Until she offered with a meek smile, "Of course it would be you, after all that, who would get to travel with a prince," Flick sighed over exaggeratedly, trying to make her best friend smile in spite of it all. "Be honest with us Sy, was this your plan all along."

Silas looked at her, incredulous.

"Of course not," she said with a sigh, rubbing his arm in an attempt at comfort. "What else?"

But Silas shook his head firmly, "No, Flick, I've told you enough," he wasn't entirely sure there was any weight behind what had been said as it was. "This is serious, and they've warned against telling anyone," he considered for a moment, gaze fixed to anywhere but his best friend. "And I think they meant every word of it."

Flick watched him sadly, understanding what had been said and hating herself for it. "Okay, Sy," she avoided argument for the sake of her exhausted best friend. It was unusual but appreciated by the wolf, he barely had the energy left to blink or draw in breath. "What now?" She queried gently, resting her head against the wall they propped up against.

But Silas didn't answer, grateful as in the safety of his best friends' presence, he managed to be consumed by the darkness of sleep. And the last he heard before he was overwhelmed was his best friends' gentle chuckles and the words, "Sleep well, you lazy git."

A not too gentle knocking on the wooden door drew Silas from the depths of his sleep, he jarred upright with an instinctive growl. It took him a moment to remember the events of the day, and he was hit with the brick wall of grief as it all sunk in on him again. The scars were still very new, and the wolf knew all too well this would be a familiar trend for the time being at least.

Though his legs still ached, sleep had done something to heal the majority of the pains he had accumulated the day before. The heavy bruising from hours before had now been rendered much lighter if not disappeared from his frame now, but still his feet dragged.

Pulling the door open, he found the now somewhat familiar features of the bored Prince behind it. "We've been called downstairs," Mason explained, wiping sleep from his own eyes in a very unprincely gesture that once upon a time might have drawn a smile to his features.

He simply nodded, moving with the prince not downstairs once again, but his mother's study – one of few spare rooms in the house now it was overcrowded with strangers. Flick seemed to consider following suit, but she offered a quiet "I'll see you downstairs, Sy," before descending in that direction at a bounding pace.

Silas looked back, nodding to thin air as he was too dazed to act anywhere near normally right now. The early start and unusual circumstances making logical trains of thought a difficult feat, for now he was happy to be led.

The study was bathed in silver moonlight, it almost made Silas jump. It had been the first time in a long time since he had seen the greys and blacks of a moonlit sky, for he hadn't seen the night sky in many years. Being returned to his cell as the sunset and being released just as the sun began to rise once again.

Silas stiffened, uncertain of whether he should have expected his skin to burn at the very touch of moonlight to his skin, or be forced into a form he hadn't taken in many years on the spot. When neither occurred, he wasn't sure if the appropriate response would have been disappointment or gratitude.

He briefly wondered if Mead and Whiskey might be missing him but was drawn from his weary thought process by a voice.

"We have a couple of envelopes for you," the head of the King's guard explained lowly. "You are to open them for nobody, and if on the other end the recipients find that they have been tampered with in any way you will be executed on the spot," but that much was a given by now. "Hand them only to the people we tell you to and take the hand from anyone who tries to take it from you."

He only nodded quietly.

"You two are to head west," it didn't narrow the field much, but those words alone were enough to catch his full attention. "Travel as far as the forests just before Godsgather and when you reach the river crossing, follow the paths north again and beyond there will be a great hill range. Just beyond that is where you'll find the city known as Brynde, Mason there you will find Gregory – you'll remember him from the summer festival and let him know to call off the plans," what plans were the gentleman elected not to convey.

"From there head north, and you will find the city of Rehenney not long after, there you will seek out the town's mayor – it's hard to miss him there are smaller mountains, he is known by the name of Joseph."

Silas didn't dare ask any of the thousands of questions that raced through his head. *What if someone arrived late? What if one of the teams didn't make it?... What if none of the teams made it?* But he didn't dare, there were many flaws but there was neither the time now the ability to find a different plan. It was this or nothing, success or war.

A metallic thud sounded as a small bag collided with the table, the sound associated with a small number of coins. Pretending that he wasn't in the presence of enough coinage to by the entirety of the slum they inhabited, or the nicer parts of Cresvy as a whole, as few and far between as those were.

"Take that with you, don't draw attention to yourselves and only buy what you need to. Find what you can otherwise," though Silas hadn't been outside of Cresvy by more than a couple of miles at most, he couldn't imagine they could have spent that kind of money in a year's worth of travelling, let alone however long it would take them to get to Rehenney.

Speaking of.

"What kind of time frame do we have for all this?" His voice was hoarse and unfamiliar, but his narrowed gaze determined. Upon a glare from the guard he added with a hasty tone, "Your Majesty," in an attempt not to get cuffed.

"Word will have already spread that the King is alive, though not for lack of effort," the head guard explained as though Silas hadn't spoken at all. "It won't be long before remnants of this group come to Cresvy hoping to get the job finished, we'll be long gone of course. But keep an eye out for anyone who might be tracking you and keep out of the cities and populated areas as best as you can, except for Brynde and Rehenney, naturally."

For the most part it seemed largely like common sense, Silas nodded. "And how long do we have?" He asked patiently, having the growing belief that he was seen as little more than a protective decoration in this new employer/employee relationship.

The head guard and his king seemed to consider it for a moment. "On horseback it would take maybe three days," the guard decided aloud after a period of time pondering it. "I recommend you avoid horseback, it will only bring attention to you, on foot it should take you a week, maybe ten days as the terrain can be rough this time of year."

Silas found some comfort in the fact that the guard seemed to know what he was doing, that this wasn't just a guessing game to toy with their lives.

"I can manage that," Silas replied as it was the best he could think of. His stamina was decent given the lycanthrope blood, but he glanced to the prince. "If you can keep up?" He added, not wanting it to sound like a challenge, but genuinely curious.

The prince scoffed, yet the sound was more playful than Silas could have expected. "I think you'll find yourself struggling to keep up with me if anything," he retorted lowly. But the façade of confidence covered the nervousness that Silas could smell on the young man, the wolf all but drowned in the stenches of fear. "Though if we're not allowed horses, perhaps I can ride into battle upon a wolf, I imagine that would be much quicker."

Silas recoiled at that more than he cared to admit, the idea terrified him and not for the ridiculous image that brought to mind of him being utilised as some great warhorse. The best he could offer as response was a quiet, "If horses would draw attention, I can't imagine a lycanthrope running through the woods would do anything better," he replied. Praying to anything that might listen that they wouldn't take that as a good idea.

"Definitely not," the wolf all but deflated at the response from the King, relief sinking through his bones.

The Prince merely chuckled, but neither party had anything else to say.

"Hopefully the dark will provide you enough cover to get out of town unnoticed," the guard explained, "Two parties have already gone, and we've heard no word of trouble nor anything that might indicate they were spotted on the way out."

At this time of the night, Silas wouldn't be surprised if all that lingered in the streets were vagrants and drunkards, neither of which would likely be in much of a position to tattle on them when morning broke. But he understood the need to be careful all the same, he nodded in understanding.

"We'll be careful," Mason's tone was solemn now he regarded Ezekiel, the tone deep and meaningful, Silas glanced at him adding a nod of his own, but not really knowing what to add that could have been helpful.

"Then you may go," the voice was dismissive, and he didn't as much as look up from his papers. A gentleman telling his son goodbye for the workday, not a period of a week in which they might not have seen each other again.

For a moment Silas thought the King was going to move, and even the monarch seemed to consider it. To say goodbye to the Prince with something more passionate than one might considered a brief acquaintance, but as soon as Silas was certain he was about to move the idea seemed to have fled from the King's mind.

Mason, who had either not noticed or was unsurprised – Silas wasn't sure which was worse; had already turned and was making his way from the room once again.

Wordlessly, Silas followed. The pair descended to the kitchen where the welcome was warm and surprising, jarring Silas from his sleepy state into something far more alert.

Flick tackled him so hard he was certain he would have collided with the kitchen floor had it not been for the island blocking his descent. Chuckling, Silas wrapped his arms around her gratefully. "I'm going to miss you, too, Flick," he responded before she had the chance to say anything.

"And I'm going to miss your idiocy," she responded, though despite her laughing words the tears in her gaze were noticeable. "Come back alive, or at least intact, or I'm going to kill you," she warned strongly, Silas was left with no doubt that she meant every word of it.

But as soon as Flick had released him from her grip, his mother lunged at him too, wrapping him in a hug once more which he willingly and gratefully reciprocated. In her hands was a pair of heavy backpacks, that left her arm straining with the effort of holding them both up in one hand whilst hugging her son with the other.

"I packed these for you," she explained hurriedly, knowing time was short.

Silas released her from his grip and looked at her uncertain. He took what was offered and looked through it briefly, before returning his line of sight to hers. "Mum, there was no need we can manage, you'll need this stuff more than we could." Supplies in the form of a small loaf of bread, a few apples, a few sets of clothes and other bits and bobs he couldn't quite see through the chaos.

"Don't be ridiculous," Catrina scolded and offered a similar backpack to Silas' travelling companion, who took it with a notable look of confusion lighting his features. Though despite it he had the common sense to say thank you for it. "I'm sorry, I only saw you briefly I wasn't sure what would fit you, I did my best." She explained in her distinct motherly way that made Silas hate himself all the more for leaving.

"Tell me you didn't do this for everyone," Silas half asked half pleaded.

Her expression was a genuinely mournful one, "I would have done if I thought we had enough," she explained.

"Make sure the portmaster gets my wages to you on Friday, just because I'm not there doesn't mean he gets to keep it," he warned. It wouldn't be much, but it would at least help keep food on the table whilst he wasn't there.

"If you think I'd let him get away without paying what's owed you clearly don't know me well enough," she paused cracking her knuckles, pondering thoughtfully. "You're not the only one in this family able to put up a fight if the need arises."

Despite himself, his mother's attempts at humour left Silas smiled meekly. "I love you, mum," he inserted, surprising himself with the words, but the instinct to say it as though it might well have been the last time he had the chance was strong.

"I love you too, kiddo," she returned with a stronger smile of her own. "Now get going, before you get skinned for taking too much time." She whispered.

Straightening, she moved the strands of hair knocked loose from her ponytail out of her face. Her features turned stony as she forced the emotion from her features. Catrina moved to the door and pulled it open for Silas and his new companion. "Don't get yourself killed, kid," she finished said softly. "And maybe just save the world while you're out there, yeah?"

Silas smiled weakly, "We'll do our best," he promised, moving to salute as he shouldered his backpack and lead the way from his damp little kitchen. As he was out in the bitter morning air of Cresvy, he turned briefly, waving to his family with what he could manage in the way of a smile. Despite the tears pooling in his eyes.

He found his own efforts reflected in the half smiling faces that looked back at him, and Silas forced himself to turn back before he began crying outright once more. "Let's go," Silas whispered weakly, and his companion was kind enough to comply without arguing. Though what reason he might have for such Silas couldn't begin to imagine.

"Lead the way," Mason requested with quiet tone.

Nodding, he cast his gaze across the streets, hesitant. Finding them largely empty but in their little town even the shadows could tattle, and he was aware of every window peering down onto the narrow streets outside his home. Once certain there was no one about to spot them, Silas gestured, whispering quietly. "This way."

Silas moved quietly, habit left him keeping to the shadows as he would in daylight and crowded streets to avoid confrontation. There was no one about, and the streets were covered in shadows, but after an unfamiliar and uncertain day he sought out the known as much as he could. Especially in the knowledge that the next few weeks would have very little of that.

The border of Cresvy was much like the rest of it, ugly and entirely fit for purpose and nothing else. Here the houses thinned, and the treeline began, the only indicator that anything was changing was the change of distinct scent from the industrial stenches of the little town, to the kinder scents of the woodland and open air.

Inhaling sharply, Silas lead the way across the boundary. As he moved desperately trying to shake the notion from his head that these might well be the last steps he'd take in Cresvy.

Chapter Ten.

The pair withdrew from Cresvy at a steady pace, Silas took conscious effort to keep pace with his companion rather than taking the lead. His stamina would outlast his more human companions by a good few hours even with his silver bindings, and he didn't want them both overly exhausted by the end of the first jaunt through being overly competitive. Though in an effort not to offend the Prince's ego he pretended even this fairly mundane pace was a difficulty to the wolf.

Preferring the façade of being the weaker one. It left the climate feeling easier and less hostile.

And he would rather the Prince not rethink his idea of utilising the wolf as a steed.

But for the most part the first couple of miles were undertaken in a comfortable silence, the only noises the soft shifting of night-time wildlife. Silas was more on edge than he cared to admit, the world outside of Cresvy turned out to be unfamiliar and strange. The very shadows seemed to lurk with dangers, and Silas took physical effort to not jump or spook at the slightest unexpected movement. He hoped this would be something he soon got used to, for he feared he would die of a heart attack before the journeys end if he continued jumping out of his skin with every owl hoot.

His companion, comparatively, was almost entirely at ease. As though this was a walk in the park to him, as opposed to a walk… in the woods. The usual roles reversed, Silas felt more human than he cared to admit, but he hoped it was a sensation he wasn't going to need to get used to.

But soon enough the gentle melody of the surrounding woodland became enough that he thought it might make his head explode. He glanced over at his companion, Mason seemed content as a child in a sweet shop, unbothered by anything going on around him.

Occasionally the prince would pause, Silas stopping a few feet away in an effort not to be split up, Mason would study the map wordlessly. Occasionally make slight adaptations to the course and then continue on.

The night was moonless, any light it had to offer stolen by the thick clouds overhead, covered in turn by heavy foliage. When morning came they'd at least have some idea of their direction, but until then it felt quite largely like they were stumbling blindly. And only by virtue of a small lantern and some matches to ensure it remain lit were they fortunate enough to not be entirely blinded.

"What's the plan?" Silas' voice was quiet, uncertain as to whether conversation would be welcome or if the entirety of the next few weeks was to be spent in silence. Something that might well have driven the young man mad, also not a great idea for a journey through the woods. Somewhere between a heart attack and lunacy, the next few weeks would be spent with one foot in the grave and the other on an icy patch.

Fortunately, that didn't seem to be necessary.

"Plan?" The sudden aggression in Mason's tone brought Silas to instant regret, but before he could part his lips and ask for forgiveness, the Prince had continued abruptly. "I was just following you, there was meant to be a plan?"

Gratitude sank through him at this, that the kind and playful façade he'd seen in the midst of the royal guard was not reserved for those of a similar rank. The wolf didn't quite relax, but there was something similar to ease working through his veins, replacing the icy nerves of moments prior.

"I barely know my left foot from my right out here," he explained quietly. "I'd have us going in circles for the rest of time, until we ultimately fell off a cliff I was certain was a lake," his attempt at humour was nervous and staggered, but a sign he was attempting to relax. If only his actions could convince his instincts that things were going to be fine.

But part of him hated himself for his attempts at joking, what was on a normal day his go too defence mechanism to the extent that humour was practically a second language. But after the day of death that had preceded them, and the fact that his niece had met her end because of him, even smiling seemed like some sort of cruel betrayal to his loved ones. The numbness of grief still something that sent ice through his every crevice, refusing to let it flee from his train of thought for even the briefest of moments.

However, he was all too aware that the past couldn't be changed. Instead he'd have to continue in the knowledge he had to make sure his niece's death was not in vain and make her proud of the uncle she had left behind. Not saddened by the state her departure had left him in.

Now wasn't the time for grieving himself into a crippled state, but rather looking to the ones left alive that he could keep that way, rather than those hopefully at peace that no amount of begging or crying could change.

Remember but not focus, until a time he could truly grieve. But as much as he hated it, now was not that time, and he knew maintaining a silent solemnity was going to do little for Rosie's memory, nor the task at hand. Slowly but surely he was getting somewhat of a grip on her death, and whilst still agonising he could find comfort in the fact that he had something else to focus on.

"That's a talent," Mason offered, jarring Silas from his line of thought. "Fortunately, I think we have something of an idea based on what we've been told," he explained. "And with the money we were at least given a map, though nowhere near as detailed as what we saw in the study, it's better than nothing, that and the journey should be fairly simply once we find Godsgather." His companion explained, gone the joking tone to be replaced by a calm focus, a certainty in which Silas was able to find some comfort.

Silas' gaze concentrated on the ground, contemplative but sheepish for a moment. Trying to decide whether or not the next question would have him considered an idiot for the rest of the trip or not, until at last he asked. "What actually is Godsgather?"

From the use of Gods as a prefix he knew it should have had some importance, as those outside of his poorly educated self didn't tend to use that term for fun. But the wolf struggled to apply any meaning to the name, and even any distant memory he did have was evasive in the early hours of the morning.

Mason's smile wasn't a cruel one, "Sorry, I forget not everyone has the kingdom's geographical features driven into them like their life depends on it," the apology was genuine. "It's a congregation point, for the very religious around here. It's the flattest point in the Kingdom, people think it used to be the meeting point of the Ancient Gods. A neutral ground for Sydenra, Kadovy, and Cres."

The Earth, the Sky and the Sea. Even Silas knew those names, though he paid about as much attention to their beliefs as he did the rats running in the sewers.

"It's meant to be the perfect medium," Mason chuckled, seemingly having about as much reverence for the concept as Silas did. "Equally far from the sky and the sea," Silas looked at his companion with an arched eyebrow. "Hey, I didn't say it made any sense, I'm just telling you what I've been told," he defended himself.

"But it's still at ground level?" Silas queried further, part out of the want to fill the silent gaps and partly out of a genuine curiosity. His schooling was minimal, constrained by his mother's knowledge which in turn was minimal due to her school years having been taken up by war.

Not many teachers paid him much attention, so learning was something he appreciated.

Mason shrugged, "Its further from the sky and sea than a mountain, I suppose that's their justification at least." He reasoned, more out of difficulty in finding better explanation than out of genuine knowledge.

He was beginning to see why not many people followed religion anymore, even this basic information Silas struggled to get his head around, but Silas didn't want the conversation ended there. "Why Godsgather?" He pried quietly, not wanting to be deemed an annoying, talkative schoolchild but still curious.

Mason was kind enough to humour him. "Other than it being the most obvious landmark from which to continue?" He shrugged his shoulders. "I think the reasoning is because it's such a sacred route that those travelling it in such inconspicuous pairs won't draw much attention, or those that spot them won't want to bother reverent people." Mason reasoned, "I don't know how much wait weight would hold though, especially if we're working against people bent on starting war."

"Thanks," Silas admitted after a moment of consuming what he'd been told. Unsure of how else to fill the silence but there was a sincere tone to his voice all the same. "I must come across as an utter idiot, I promise I'll keep questions to a minimum."

His companion merely shrugged his shoulders, "My scholars will be pleased I've put something they taught me to good use," his retorted with a chuckle of his own. "It's really no problem, but you're probably giving too much weight to my answers. Most of that was dredged up from lessons spent half asleep, I wouldn't count too much on them being spot on."

Silas smile was watery once more, "You shouldn't have told me that," he scolded a little more boldly than before, his companion set him with a confused glance. "You could have had me revering you as a genius, hanging on to your every word. You've really missed the trick," he said with a sigh, shaking his head. "I'm glad to at least learn something, outside of Cresvy I've never really learnt about the rest of the Kingdom."

It was always such a distant concept, something that had seemed so unreachable to try seemed like giving him false hope. Fantasies of a world he'd never get to see, now he was thrown into the deep end, entirely unsure of where every path lead. He had to trust his companion more than he cared to admit, but at least Mason was proving himself to be an amicable travelling partner. Silas cringed at what it might have been like had he been paired with one of the guards.

The soft patter of raindrops from the foliage overhead caught Silas' attention, the tell-tale sign that the rain that had plagued the last few months was a country wide phenomenon. It was nice to see that would be a common theme even outside of home, that Cresvy wasn't just some dump that the rain liked to make constant fun of.

Mason's steps had brought him closer to his travelling companion. Until they were walking at armlength rather than the handful of metres they had moved with before. Partly because now the terrain grew more difficult, the ground underfoot now resembled something similar to a swamp, so if one of them found trouble the other would be close by to offer help. But Silas hoped it was partly because they were growing more trustworthy of the person prior to yesterday he hadn't known existed.

"Odd that," the prince explained dabbing a water droplet from his face. "Because I thought I knew a lot about this Kingdom, but before the news of where we were docking came through yesterday, I'd never even heard of Cresvy." He considered.

Silas was unsurprised. "I think everyone but those who live there don't know about Cresvy," he returned, stepping carefully. "It was wiped off the maps the moment it was created, and anyone involved who left decided it was a better idea to just leave its memory in the dust." Silas smirked gently, his little fantasy bringing him good fun.

For a moment, Mason hesitated. Lips parted as he sought words to respond, but eventually gave in. "I can see that, your home wasn't the most pleasant place," it wasn't necessarily an insult, if anything it brought a further grin to Silas' expression.

The Prince hadn't spent more than a few days in Cresvy but had already decided it wasn't for him, of course he didn't blame the royal man – Silas doubted that Cresvy was for anyone but rats and roaches. The rest of them weren't exactly there from choice. "There's no need to be so kind," he reasoned quietly. "Cresvy is about eighty miles south of pleasant, even the rats and stray dogs are disgusted that they have to live there," Silas reasoned lowly.

It was only now that Silas had dared to glance in the direction of his travelling companion, did he notice just how severely his companion was shivering. It was surprising how will the Prince had managed to keep the shake from his tone of voice, for even through the rain Silas was able to see the shake of his frame.

"Do you want to stop for a minute, get something drier on?" Silas asked after a moment, seeing that the companion was intent on persisting despite the fact his knees were nearly buckling under the pressure of shivering. "Mum said she'd packed something drier; it might be worth stopping given we didn't exactly have the chance to layer up when we left."

The prince paused, looking back to him with something akin to worry in his green gaze. "It's probably not a good idea to stop until we want to rest," he reasoned lowly. "We're under time restraints as it is, and they wouldn't be too happy if we were stopping every time an inconvenience came up," he insisted, chin high.

Under the strict belief this façade was perhaps as intrinsic as the Prince's very veins, and in an effort not to offend him. The wolf replied, "It's all very well and good keeping pace, but we're not going to be of much help if we drop dead from exposure to the elements before we even reach Godsgather." He aimed to find a balance between patronising and friendly, a right mix of the two might get him what he wanted – a companion who would make it until sunrise.

"That, and we're not exactly under surveillance out here," he reasoned. If he missed the distinct scent of something human out here, even under the scents of the wild Silas would have been very worried about the function of his nose. "And you have my word that I won't tattle," he finished quietly. Not about to force it but hoping his companion would see reason.

Mason cast his glance around, and sighed. "I guess you're right," he reasoned, coming to a stop in the shadow of a particularly large tree. Its foliage so thick that the ground underneath remained reasonably dry and mud free compared to the rest of the paths. "I'm just not very used to not being under observation," he reasoned.

Silas nodded, understanding though he doubted to the same extent. One of them spent their days in the watch of a king's guard willing to do whatever they could to protect him, the other under the surveillance of a town terrified of him. Though, if it meant Mason was so worried as to be concerned about taking too much time in adding extra layers, Silas wasn't sure which he'd prefer.

One form was done through fear of what he could do, the other out of fear of what could be done. Neither pleasant, but Silas doubted Mason had seen a prison cell from a distance, let alone spend every night of the past 17 years in one.

"It's alright, I think we've both got a lot of things to get used to out here," he reassured. Standing at guard beside his companion, keeping an eye on anything that might try to approach in their moment of statutory ease.

Mason spent a moment shuffling through his pack, pausing as he asked. "Are you not cold?"

Even the wolf could admit the cold was getting to him, "Chilly," he responded with a shrug of his shoulders. Still keeping alert to his surroundings, "But I can manage for now." The rain left him restless and his skin itching, almost missing the comparative cosiness of his nightly cell.

A thick jacket and long-sleeved shirt were all that protected him from the elements at the moment, and that still rendered him cold even though he had a fair tolerance to the bitter wind. One of few traits not gifted to him by lycanthropy but rather a lifetime by the sea, the cold ocean air was a regular element he was used to and could be far crueller compared to this. But if he got his coat wet now he wouldn't be able to rely on it later, so for now he managed with feeling a little chilly.

The Prince withdrew a familiar looking coat, and as he donned it Silas' heart panged lightly. He smiled a melancholy expression; it had been a long time since he had seen it. "I didn't even know we still had that coat," his laugh was a little too high pitched, too forced. "Careful, by now it's probably moth-bitten to Kingdom come."

With a flourish, the coat was donned. It was too long on him – finishing just below the knees where on a taller man it would have halted at thigh length, but otherwise Silas could admit that it looked nice. Even if the memories attached to the garment weren't necessarily kind ones. A little creased but not worse for wear from being shoved in a cupboard for years.

"Your fathers?"

"My brother's," Silas corrected, moving forward to pull a cobweb free of the crook of his arm, he added with a chuckle.

"Why's it not with your brother, even somewhat large and rather moth bitten it's a good coat," Mason commented thoughtlessly, chuckling softly as he took efforts to hitch up the sleeves so he could maintain the use of his appendages. Pulling his hood up and smiling, "Warm too, thank the Gods." He added, pausing for a moment, wanting to remain in the dry for a little while longer.

As an afterthought Mason looked up, with mild panic. "Unless... I'm sorry if it's a touchy subject."

It took Silas a moment to catch on to what was meant, and he couldn't help but chuckle at the prince's worry he had caused offence. "Oh, no don't worry, last I heard Luke's quite alive." He assured, stepping out of the trees shelter and turning back. "He married some wealthy girl in a city a few miles east of Cresvy," he explained though probably without need. It was something he hadn't thought about in a long time, "He couldn't wait to get out, forgot most of his things in his rush." Silas took off at a steady walk once his companion had joined his side once again. "I haven't seen him since." The wolf stuffed his hands in his pockets with a sigh.

Mason's uncomfortable silence spoke a thousand words, and Silas briefly wondered if he had spoken too much, he glanced at his thudding feet with mild embarrassment. *He won't even know about Rosie*, he realised after a beat. He wondered if an invitation would be extended to his brother as well, and even if he did find out whether Luke would have bothered coming anyway.

"Your brother has little sense in fashion, it's a good coat," Mason said out of the blue taking Silas by surprise, having assumed that in his idiocy he had cut off any chances at continuing conversation.

Silas smiled at his attempt at conversation, "You should have finished it at little sense," he said with a shake of his head. "Though I think that's just a genetic trait, something about the family, we've always had the common sense of toddlers." He explained with a quiet sigh, a sound that the hefty winds stole to his gratitude.

"Don't make me regret being put with you," Mason warned lowly, striding more confidently now the feeling had been returned to his fingertips. "We've got a kingdom to save, I can't go around making sure you don't fall into rivers and get into arguments with rock trolls."

"I've the common sense of a toddler, not the brain of one. Rock trolls don't exist," Silas warned. Given he was quiet the expert in supernatural oddities, Silas felt he could at least say that one with some form of certainty.

"That's a bit more reassuring," Mason's tone of relief was hopefully playful given how genuine it sounded. "But then..." He didn't finish, hoping he'd gotten away with beginning and not being noticed, however, the hesitation made Silas looked back up at him, eyebrow arched. When the prince saw he had backed himself into a corner, he continued with a more sheepish sound lacing his words. "But then given... your propensity to the wild,"

Silas had to stop himself from bursting into laughter at that one.

"I'm going to ask that be carved onto my gravestone," he managed, rendered breathless with his attempts to stifle laughter. "That is the best description of it I've ever heard," but his laughter was good natured, and his liking of this Prince was growing more and more. He looked at the ground and sighed, "You can call it what it is, I promise I've likely been called far worse than anything you can come up with," Mason struck him as someone too kind to say anything much worse. "Lycanthropy, or my more lupine attributes if you'd prefer something a little posher, whichever you'd prefer." *Mutt is catchier*, he reasoned chuckling to himself.

"I'll bare that in mind," Mason replied after a moment. Trying to compose something of his dignity, embarrassment apparent

Before they could continue something caught his attention and Silas paused. Lifting a hand to block rain droplets from obscuring his vision even more, he spotted the line of the woods, where the trees faltered into the meadows that told them they were almost out of the woods. He grumbled quietly, out there they would have even less protection from the elements. And he might need to rethink not putting on his coat.

Silas was about to continue, to break through the woods border and into the cold open meadow, when a voice from beside him left him mid step.

For all his will to get this done, Silas seemed to have been a bad influence on his travelling companion, who now in spite of his newly donned coat seemed uncertain with proceeding.

"We've made good distance," Mason seemed genuinely pleased after he took a moment to regard his map. Seeming to have regained a bit of his dignity, but he remained quiet for a moment. Seeming to consider something. "Do you want to pitch up camp here for the night?" He asked, and Silas wasn't about to argue. "Given we aren't under surveillance, and you've given your absolute word that you're not a tattle."

Silas had already been sold at the chance of staying dry a little longer, having some fleeting hope that the mornings weather would be a little kinder on aching bones. But they'd journeyed long enough that sunrise didn't feel far away, and the heavy clouds over head remained grey and intimidating, masking both any sight of the moon and the sun.

"I'm ok with that," Silas replied gratefully. "It will do no good getting lost in the night and rain anyway, we'll move faster in the morning able to see where we're going than we will now anyway," his brain tried to convince his heart that this was the right thing to do.

They had a little over a week to complete their task in, and it was true that they were likelier to get themselves lost more than anything else in the darkness of the night unsure of where their steps took them.

He followed as the Prince traced his steps deeper into the woods once more, Silas following hurried suit. Until they were able to find the driest spot they were able to lay their sleeping mats and sleep the rest of the night's hours away.

Hurriedly they cleaned the area as best as weary minds would allow them, ridding it of any obvious rocks and branches and excrement that they could find. Though compared to the cell Silas doubted this would bother him too much, he imagined compared to a royal bed this would be like sleeping on nails, so he made an effort to help his companion out with tidying the area in preparation.

Given a fire was neither possible due to the heavy rainfall, nor a good idea in case they drew attention. The lantern had been one thing, but a blazing fire would be like a sore thumb against the otherwise empty woodlands, and they would rather not take any chances.

Even the wolf was capable of being crept up on in the depths of sleep, and his silver bindings were going to make that an even easier task. The shadows seemed to encroach his very common sense, making him certain everything was a threat, but in an effort to keep himself sane he elected to ignore his instincts to the best extent he could.

Soon the pair had made what they could in the way of a bed, his mother having been kind enough to pack them blankets. Threadbare and worn but comforting enough.

"Good night," Mason's words pulled him from the beginnings of sleep.

That word brought a warmth and a smile to his tired features, compared to his nights in the cell this was almost pleasant. Fleetingly, Silas regarded the prince as a friend, something that took Silas off guard. It had been a long time since he considered anyone new to his life as a friend, for usually it was quite the opposite, and the suggestion otherwise would be considered an insult. But even this early on, it seemed a good descriptor for the man a few feet away.

He didn't bother blinking his eyes open, too much energy had seeped from his bones to even be bothered with that much. Rather he offered with a yawn, "Good night.

Chapter Eleven.

The wolf woke with a start, panic lacing his veins.

His initial reason was the fact he didn't know where he was. The unfamiliar surroundings accompanied by a sudden consciousness sent ice shooting through his veins. But after a moment the memory flooded back through his system, recalling the proceeding day's occurrences and that he hadn't in fact been kidnapped and dumped in the middle of the woods.

A fraction of relaxation worked through him, his erratic heart returning to a more comfortable pace.

A distant drumming; but too irregular for that unless it was made by an especially poor band. Silas sat up, pausing as he shoved off his blankets. He stalked onwards, leaving the Prince in his wake for the time being. Wanting to investigate before he took the time to bother his companion's beauty sleep.

What he found left him uncertain of whether or not he should be worried.

In the fields the pair had come to and immediately retreated from the night before, a road of sorts was now visible through the long grasses. Not cobbled nor tarmacked as what he'd seen at home, rather trodden into dust and dirt from regular usage, and Silas couldn't quite see the end of it.

But it wasn't the path that surprised him, rather what took residence on it. For it hadn't been drumbeats he had heard, but footsteps.

A parade; far less regal and extravagant as what he'd seen of the King's parade. Not the same show of wealth the monarch had boasted, but it was still rather beautiful. Great wagons of dark woods, pulled by shining horses and laced in colour, not one or two of the usual uniform of an army, but every colour Silas could have begun to imagine. It left him caught between awe and fear.

Silas watched them, jaw amid the dirt and eyes narrowed with uncertainty. He spent a heartbeat, trying to spot a banner or colour scheme amid these strangers that might have demonstrated who they aligned themselves with. He found nothing uniform enough to begin to give him any ideas.

It was a tide surging west.

"I thought you'd already bailed," a voice from behind caught Silas off guard, he turned to spot his companion approaching, wiping the sleep from his eyes as he yawned. "I thought it was early, do I really snore that bad?"

Mason threw the backpack at Silas, he caught it without blinking and shouldered it with ease. The weight told him the prince had been kind enough to pack up camp in his absence, and thus retracing their steps wouldn't be necessary. But given the herd ahead, he wasn't entirely sure how they were going to continue with their journey.

But Silas shook his head, gesturing for Mason to come closer. As he complied Silas lifted a pointing finger and gestured, wordless and worried.

Uncertain of what was going on, the Prince came to Silas' side and looked out across the field. He frowned deeply, the sleepiness vanished from his expression to be replaced by some strange blend between worry and surprise. "What's going on?"

All the wolf could do was respond with a shake of his head; he didn't have the words to explain what he saw before him. He had heard stories about the travelling wagons before, small processions similar to the King's the day before passing through. "The Angofwen," he replied quietly, though uncertainty bound his words; nomadic families who never set roots down in one place for too long before moving on to something else.

But this was something different, even to the uncultured young man. He'd heard stories of groups of maybe three or four, a dozen when it came to the larger clans. But this was something entirely different, borderline awe inspiring had it not been for the instinctual worry that it set deep in his chest. From a distance he couldn't be sure, but there must have been a hundred of them, if not more. The last time he'd seen this and the massacre that ended in left Silas tense and worried.

Like he could see every possibility of this ending in death all at once, the images racing through his mind and panic setting deeper into his bones.

"Maybe," the Prince replied, and then out of the corner of his eye, "Let's go find out," he decided quite abruptly, and started through the treeline.

"For the love of the Gods no," Silas answered before he could think properly.

Mason set him with a surprised glance, "Where's your sense of adventure?" Mason asked with an excitable laugh.

It died with a lot of people yesterday.

"The King explicitly told us to avoid groups of people, I think this is going against that order about as badly as you can outside of going to one of the capitals" Silas hissed under his breath. Even he would have struggled to hear a whisper at this distance, but he wasn't taking any chances.

"You said it yourself no one's here to keep an eye on us, and you're not a tattle," Mason reminded.

I'm a terrible influence.

Silas growled lowly, not a sound meant to be intimidating nor the usual tone of playfulness he would have usually deployed. Now it was more of a sound of frustration, to his credit Mason didn't jump at the sound as most would have. "I meant in terms of a sleep in or an extra pair of slippers, not something this stupid," he retorted lowly.

"I don't think we should," Silas started when Mason turned on him, confusion bordering on annoyance brimming in his green gaze.

"What do you mean?" Mason sounded frustrated but not unkind.

Silas started falsely, uncertain of how to begin. He knew it sounded stupid, an assumption based on a feral instinct and nothing more, but the need to follow his gut here was intrinsic. "We're in enough of a rush as it is, and the King said rebels are about. Do you think they'll react kindly to finding us, on a mission to stop them?"

That and from memory the Angofwen harboured no love for the monarchy, and Silas would rather not test that theory.

The prince shrugged his shoulders. "We're not going to be carrying a banner advertising our allegiances, Sy," he returned easily. "And you never know, finding out what's happening here might just help us down the line. Two travellers are hardly going to bring much attention, we're going to be fine."

But Silas wasn't going to accept that answer lying down, "Please. I've got a bad gut feeling about this," he said quietly, cheeks flushing an unflattering red as he spoke with an increasing desperation.

Mason regarded him softly, a mother comforting a child woken suddenly by a terrifying dream. "Its fine, I'll go by myself and meet you back in the woods if I can find anything of interest," he decided and moved again. Pausing when he realised Silas' steel fist remained still clutched his coat's hood with fierce strength. "Err, will you let me go, please?"

He found himself torn between wanting to remain at distance from the great crowd and wanting to protect his companion. The responsibility weighed on his shoulders more than his fear, and again he found himself fiercely despising his moral compass which forced him to help and risk things for a person he hardly knew.

"Fine," he said quietly, releasing his grip so suddenly Mason nearly tumbled. "I'll come with you, but if anything happens I'm picking you up by the scruff and running for it."

The image seemed to bring a smile to his companion's face. "I don't doubt it," the prince replied chuckling, nowhere near as panicked or as worried as his companion. "Now come on," and he set off at a brisk walk towards the parade. Silas left watching for a heartbeat, before moving with a start and quickly catching up.

Recent rains had allowed the fields to flourish, the long grasses almost as high as their shoulders meaning they needed to employ little effort in order to hide. A mere running crouch was enough to disguise their efforts from sight, and the numbers were so large it wouldn't be overly difficult to blend in with the masses.

Among the wagons, people; mostly children ran alongside playing. Their laughter so prominent it was like a constant birdsong, oblivious to the world around them. Dotted about were other families, men and women walking beside the great wagons, less jovial than their children but the atmosphere generally seemed light and calm.

Now they were closer Silas was able to take in the beauty of the wagon train about him. Bathed in colours, the very paint shone despite the poor weather and the mud caked to the wheels, everything about the wagons shone, and the smell of oak wood was a pleasant one. The nomadic people surrounding the train were dressed regally, the colour replicated there as well, no uniform shade but everything under the sun. Wrapped in long, light fabrics that whipped in the wind.

He could have stayed and admired for the rest of time, had it not been for the fear melded with the time restraints on their shoulders.

"It's beautiful," Silas breathed, forced to laugh by the ludicrous idiocy of his own statement.

"Incredible," Mason's response was short but carried something sincere, but the prince was clearly distracted to a degree. He cast his gaze about, how he wasn't rendered bewildered by the masses of movement and colour Silas wasn't aware. "Unfortunately, we don't have time to smell the... look at the roses," he corrected with a brief frown. "Come on! We're here for intelligence," he wove through the crowd, Silas moved to keep up.

Mason spotted a particular group, and decided that would be the best chance of sneaking in. The youngsters so involved with their chase that they would barely notice the new faces of those around them. With any luck they'd be mistaken as a worrisome parent come to check in, and not strangers trying to sneak into the midst of them.

For a while they kept their distance, maintaining pace enough metres away that they could still see the wagons but not close enough that they could be spotted without being overly observant. They remained alert for any warning cry that might go up amid the travelling group, upon which they would have turned tail and run for their lives. But after a few minutes it became apparent that there would be none.

With little other choice or at least on Silas' part, it was time to make their move.

Easing closer step by step, Mason said quietly. "On my count," his words were soft enough that only a wolf could have heard them easily, Silas was left merely to nod. The prince lifted a hand, held out three fingers and began to allow them to fold against his palm. As the thumb descended, the pair launched forward as one.

They folded into the mass so quickly Silas almost lost sight of his friend, by virtue of the now familiar thick coat he was able to catch up and keep sight of him. Almost astonished it had worked, though his heart thundered so loudly now that he was sure it would give them away. He barely dared to breathe, for fear the scent of terror on his lips might have alerted someone to an intruder. But after a few beats, it became apparent they had gone unnoticed.

Silas forced the tension from his shoulders, it remained in his blood and heart, but at least now he walked less stiffly. Against the calm composure of their surroundings, that was as likely to bring attention to them as anything else.

He looked to his companion, hissing quietly. "And what's the plan now?" He cast a glance about, certain the very wood of the wagons was spying on them, prepared for the slightest trip up they might have made.

"Make friends," Mason replied, a swagger to his step Silas wanted to kick out of him. Though he cast a glance about him, where the children oblivious and happy continued to run and play. He kicked a ball for them, spending a moment to partake in their play with a genuine happiness before adding to his companion once more. "As cute as they are I don't think this lot will be of much help, come on, this way!" He decided at seemingly a heartbeat notice and folded into the midst of people to his right. Leaving an uncomfortable Silas to follow in his wake, hurrying at a gentle pace.

After a little ways journey through the proceeding crowds, Mason stepped into pace with a handful of women. Silas moved to walk beside him, content to let his genius of a companion to do all the talking for him.

"Do remind me where we're headed, fine ladies?" Mason's attempt at charm left Silas rolling his eyes.

The trio were dressed in such bright shades of oranges and lilacs that it made Silas' eyes ache to look at, their outfits dotted with bells and beads which left the conversation backing tracked by a pleasant melody.

One woman regarded the prince with an incredulous look, she sniffed at him. Considered for a moment, only to reply with a question of her own. "How drunk are you? Do you not think it's rather early?" She queried.

Silas nearly bent double at that, stifling his laughter with great effort.

Injured but fortunately only in terms of his ego, Mason shook his head. "Not nearly drunk enough unfortunately," he recovered quickly. "I'd prefer to be inebriated; my legs are already killing me I can barely think. Could you at least tell me how much further there is to go?" Persistent, Silas accepted, he could only hope his companion's efforts wouldn't reward him with a slap across the face.

Princely as he might well have been, out here that meant nothing. These people didn't know the Prince from a peasant on the streets and considering they had spent their night with a tree as their only shelter, they probably looked similar to one at that point.

For a moment Silas thought the trio were simply going to ignore them, and Silas and his companion would have to move on in search of more help. He had moved to grab Mason's arm, to pull him out of the fray and insist they move along with pleas for forgiveness left in his wake. When one of the women let out a sigh and answered.

"Well unfortunately you might need to find yourself a wagon to rest in, good sir," her words overly formal. Moulding her voice to be admittedly a quiet good mimicry of Mason's formal tone. "For you've a good half a days' worth of travelling yet before we get there." It didn't narrow their destination down too much, but before Silas could part his lips to offer a question of his own, she added with a sigh. "Malowa, that is. We're headed to Malowa."

"Though how by any stretch of the imagination you could forget that without being drunk to the eyeballs I'm not entirely sure," another of their number offered. Bringing a chuckle from her friends, and a smirk to Silas' expression.

"He's thick as a bag of bricks, and I've the memory of a small child," Silas explained lowly, a little more at ease now he'd learned not everyone had fangs like his. "Thanks for your time, we'll leave you be while we try to fix our sober state."

He said his farewells before Mason had the chance to interrupt, grabbing him by the sleeve and tugging him into the crowd once more.

Once they had descended into the crowds enough that even if the women they had left behind wanted to find them again it would be a tricky task, Silas turned to Mason once more. "Malowa? What's important about Malowa?" He queried breathless. Hopeful that such might be enough information to set them off running once more, out of here and onto their quest once more.

Mason seemed annoyed; his features twisted with uncertainty. "I remember hearing about it, I know it's important to the travelling folk, but for the life of me I can't think as to why."

We'll find a library in the nearest city and do some reading, just let us get out of here! Silas thought but had enough sense to keep to himself.

"And what do you suggest now," was the least snarky response Silas could force from his lips. His gaze constantly travelling as the pair continued forward, moving now not through the tide but with it, their steps in comfortable pace with the strangers about them.

But before Mason could respond, Silas felt a tap on his shoulder that made him jump out of his skin. A voice from behind them sounded, "Well it's nice to see some youngsters so interested in learning more about our people," a gravelly but not necessarily threatening tone sounded at Silas' shoulder. "Odd given our children usually have such stories taught to them from birth pretty much, those words sent a tension ricocheting through Silas. "But then, I'm beginning to think you two aren't children of our people at all, now are you?"

Silas moved to grab his friend but was second to the prize as the newcomer grabbed the prince by the collar and pulled him to a stop. "I think it'll be a good idea if you come with me," the crowd parted around them to prevent knocking into those who had stopped, but otherwise it was apparent no help was coming.

On instinct alone, Silas lunged forward, moving to grab his friend back with a movement so quick it was a blur to look at. But he learned the hard way this newcomer wasn't alone, as someone else stopped him in his tracks. The wolf having to make effort not to tumble forward. His own assailant moved to grab his collar, but a gasp sounded before he had the chance.

"A Lycan!" The shout of genuine astonishment went up, leaving Silas frozen in place. Here he was surrounded and truly vulnerable, and he wasn't sure he could protect his friend.

The man who'd grabbed Mason released the prince and moved forward, grabbing Silas by the chin which he jerked upright, so they were face to face. Silas stared into the dark brown eyes of the man, seeing his terrified form reflected back at him.

It would have been his moon kissed eyes that gave him away, he should have thought that through more, and he would have gouged his eyes out on the spot if he thought that might have gotten them out of the situation.

"Come with me," after a moment the man seemed unperturbed, and when it appeared, initially Silas contemplated just about anything else.

When it seemed they had little other choice, the pair exchanged a glance, and proceeded to do what they were told. Following the stranger as he moved at a steady pace with the flow of the caravan's traffic.

They wove through the crowd, and it seemed they had gone on for miles after a short time as their assailants showed no sign of stopping. Only when they had reached the head of the wagon parade, to a quite beautiful vessel did they come to a pause. "Wait here, and don't do anything stupid."

Their morning had been made up of nothing but stupid decisions, but Silas only nodded in response.

"I'm sorry," Silas whispered to the Prince, all too aware that for all of his caution it had been himself who had given their position away.

"Don't be just yet," the Prince replied with an effort to create an easy façade. But Silas could see his own fear reflected in the green gaze of his companion, they were left to ponder their fates for a moment, as the man disappeared into the wooden wagon for a moment. Silas wondered if someone would appear to execute them.

In the wake of the head wagon a handful of people followed in close quarters, atop beautiful horses of shining blacks and greys. Far different creatures to the scraggly half-starved beats he had known at home, and free of the immense tack the King's guard had utilised. But Silas admired them less than he admired the men and women atop them, only here did the colours embodying the rest of the wagon train dilute to a more sombre pattern. The swords lacing their bodies, no doubt a number more hidden about their bodies told Silas exactly who they were. Guards.

Guarding what?

Silas and his companion kept careful pace, though the travelling guards paid little attention to either of them he was struck with the sensation of being carefully watched.

He wasn't left in discomfort for too long however, as his gaze lifted up at the sound of creaking wood emanating from the caravan, the rich reds and golden laced fabric that offered a cover to the caravan's entrance parted, and out if it stepped a worn man. He lifted a massive hand, gesturing for Silas and his companion to step forward and join him. With seemingly little other option, the pair did as they were told, scrabbling to find purchase on the steps of the still moving caravan, they entered with little in the way of elegance.

The small compartment they found themselves in was small but elegant, plush pillows and rugs littering the ground. Various golden decanters littered the ground, but looked surprisingly organised given the context the little room was in. The scent was intensely herbal, reminding him of the scent circling his mother after a long day's work, it was a familiar and pleasant smell.

But there sat on a central cushion, was a gentleman that would have made most of the horses outside appear dwarfed and pathetic. Against the tight nature of the caravan's room he was almost comical, if his very presence didn't draw awe and astonishment.

The walls around them were laced with banners, the first Silas had seen since coming across the caravan trail. Compared to the uniform banners of the King he had seen, these were wild comparatively, handmade and extravagant, dappled with paint but somehow more beautiful than the ones Silas was used to. Each differed in their patterns, but the one common theme central to each of them was the proud falcon symbol at the centre of it.

His bulk meant eyes were drawn immediately too him, covered in clothes of dark blues and pale, ruddy red shades. His hair was up in a bandana, but strands fell free to reveal thick black strands that framed his dark face. His eyes were a strange contrast, something between ancient and eccentric that Silas couldn't quite put his finger on, but there was a kindness to the man that emanated even from a distance that the wolf trusted.

Not enough to put his guard down, but the tension that had worked through his system seemed to dissipate some here. But this man was incredible.

Man was an unkind word for the person that appeared in front of the pair. For as little in the way of education Silas had gained, the stories that circled the man were known even by youngsters and the ancient. More myth than man, suddenly a lot of things made a lot more sense about everything they had seen that day. But he hadn't begun to believe this as an option, namely because he had been long convinced this was a man who existed in legend and tales alone.

The Angofwen King.

Chapter Twelve.

"Sit," less an order more an offer, Silas' reaction was immediate and compliant, falling to his knees onto a cushion without a word. The prince a beat behind him. Whereas the wolf's reaction had been out of intrinsic respect, the man beside him clearly had less of an idea who this was.

For a moment the monarch permitted the newcomers to make themselves comfortable. More at ease – though perhaps forcefully so, Mason slouched back into the thick cushions. Despite his comfortable position, even from the corner of his eye Silas could see the stiffness to his posture and the tension working through his body.

The traveller lifted a golden decanter from its spot on the floor, "Something to drink?" he queried, lifting it in Silas' direction.

The wolf quickly nodded, all too aware all of a sudden just how thirsty he was. "Please."

Beside him the prince nodded with equal eagerness, "I'd appreciate something," the prince showed some restraint in his town of voice, whereas the desperation seeped through the wolf's guttural tone more fiercely.

The gentleman who had brought the pair here revealed a pair of small cups, offering them to both parties. Into which the gentleman poured the liquid, the scent was a similar herbal scent to the rest of the wagon. And the soft whoosh of steam that battered his chin when the wolf lifted it up to sniff told him it was tea.

Aiming to be subtle, as not to offend their host but still worried about the prospect of a poisoning. The wolf sniffed carefully, by virtue of his mother's skills he had some knowledge of the common poisons, namely nightshade and hemlock.

The prince had lifted his gaze to meet his, questioning with a similar caution. "Chamomile," the Nomad King was kind enough to pretend he believed their caution was to do with the flavour, not the ingredients.

"Chamomile," Silas confirmed taking a hearty sip.

Grateful the prince followed suit, and after a few moments of appreciating their drinks. The Nomad King began speaking again. His booming tone strangely kind and reassuring, "I'm Malachi," the pair had been put so at ease they had almost forgotten they weren't here exactly by invite. The man's gaze was a deep, burning brown – a perfect replica of the dark brown eyes of the symbols dotted about the room, and just as watchful. "And you are?"

"My name is Mason," the Prince's efforts to make his voice rival the King's was notable and amusing. "My companion is Silas," the formal tone returned to his voice, the casualness Silas had become accustomed to all but forgotten.

But Malachi regarded the Prince with as much interest as he might a mediocre child's drawing, his gaze settling on Silas with a warm fierceness. His tone remained kind, but there was something about the way those ancient eyes burned into Silas that made him restless. "You're the lycan?" He queried as the casual tone one might apply when asking about the weather recently, as though he wasn't capable of seeing the glinting silver of Silas' eyes.

Taken aback, he hadn't heard spoken kindly in a long time, most people used it as though it were a venom being spat out. Like the very effort of saying the word would infect them with the curse, Silas nodded. "Yeah," was the best he could think of.

His laugh was a booming sound, delight lacing it and so sudden and boisterous it took Silas effort not to smack his head on the caravan roof when he jumped out of his skin. "I've not been fortunate enough to meet one of your kind in a long time," he said sadly, as though theirs was a dying species in need of protection not extermination. He moved forward, clasping Silas' hands with one all-consuming hand, and clapping his shoulder with the spare. "It is a pleasure to meet you, Silas."

The wolf regarded the Nomadic King as one might have considered someone having recently and randomly sprouted a set of fine antlers. The words were stolen before he could form them on his lips, confusion and nothing short of it.

In all of his efforts to remain calm and polite, even Mason looked confused by this turn of events. Neither of them had met a person so willing to accept a lycan into their midst, outside of his family and Flick it was something to be disgusted of, not revered.

Malachi seemed to have sensed the confused nature of his companions and elicited a sigh as he sat back down onto the cushions. Watching them with a frown, he considered for a moment before he said lowly.

"No doubt this is not a reaction your used to, then?" The tone was something caught between amusement and genuine pity, those watchful eyes never parted from Silas frame, leaving him feeling dwarved by even a fleeting glance.

Silas almost laughed at the suggestion, "Far from it," he admitted quietly.

A bulky hand reached out once more, to touch Silas but this time the digits reached not for his skin but the clothes covering it. Strong fingers brushed the fabric, considering for a moment. Dark eyes glinting with recognition, as though from the very touch and in the darkness of the caravan's compartment he could sense the presence of silver woven into the wolf's clothes "Your skills have been wasted no doubt," he spoke with a shake of his head. "A wolf in chains."

The pity in the man's voice made Silas hate himself all the more, he forced himself not to shrink away from the King's soft touch. His gaze lingering on the ground, "Hardly chains," his tone was forcefully more jovial than what he'd been utilising. "It's meant I've been allowed to walk free all these years; it was that or execution."

What had been intended to make Malachi less pitiful only succeeded in sparking a degree of anger in the old man's eyes. "Well I'm glad you didn't elect execution," Malachi decided, releasing the young wolf from his grasp and resting back against the wooden wall. "For it would mean I wouldn't have the joy of meeting you today."

"If you don't mind my asking," Mason's tone broke the darkness, Malachi humoured him with a dark glower. "Why are you so pleased to meet him?" The Prince struggled to find the words, decide an order that would offer the least in the way of offence possible. "In the kindest way possible," he added quietly in an effort not to offend his friend.

Upon seeing the look the King regarded the youngster with, Silas wasn't sure Mason could have been entirely silent and not raise some anger in the kind older man.

"Of course, someone of royal blood wouldn't understand," the Nomadic King's nose wrinkled as though able to scent the stench of royalty on the Prince's very skin.

"I'm not - " whatever thought he had formed was quickly discarded as he elected a different path. "You're a king yourself, are you not – the Nomad King?" If he hadn't known Malachi from the face or the context, it seemed he had connected enough facts through the name at the very least.

"A moniker, and one Ezekiel would no doubt have me shot for." Malachi returned with ease, undeterred and unworried by the Prince's efforts. Having lost what Silas believed to be infinite patience, the gentleman gestured for his guard. "Deposit him outside, we don't need him for this."

Before the guard could deploy to comply with his orders, Silas moved with an immediacy that surprised even him. "No," he responded quickly, more demanding than he had intended his tone to be, he immediately panicked. "Please, no, he's a friend." *An idiot friend, but a friend all the same.*

For a brief and terrifying moment, Silas was convinced that would be the end of both of them as the Angofwen King set them with a gaze, the intensity such that the wolf was sure it would set his skin ablaze. Until, finally. "Fine, but by virtue of your friendship alone. Know I have no love of the King nor any of his kin."

Beside him, Mason relaxed notably; what he'd have done in the event of conflict Silas didn't know, but he was grateful that for now it wasn't going to come to that.

However, the curiosity Mason had sparked in Silas didn't relent. He lowered his tone, his gaze fixed to the ground as he quietly prodded. "But please, if you could answer his question I would be appreciated," he aimed to mould his tone into something as formal as his companions – it seemed somehow fitting. "I've never met anyone that doesn't regard a lycan with anything but hatred and fear," for the sake of finding answers he ignored his family and Flick. "If for the sake of my ego alone, please do tell me?" He asked, allowing his lips to twitch into a slight, hopeful smile.

Malachi regarded him, the pity returning to his gaze but that was preferred compared to the sudden and combustible anger he had demonstrated moments prior.

"I don't know how much you know about the Angofwen," when shaking heads met his words, he continued. "But our Gods aren't the ancient ones followed by city dwellers," Silas might have found it amusing that Malachi regarded city dwellers with more disgust in his tone than he had a lycan. "Rather, our gods are Malo and Irena," the solemn tone left Silas bowing his head – it only seemed fitting. "The fauna and the flora, the very world around us," he reiterated.

He lifted a hand, pointing a finger at Silas. "Most people will consider you a monster possessed by a stupid beast," Silas might have been offended had it not been something he'd heard a thousand times. "To my people, you are something to be envied." He explained with a sly grin, Silas cringed beneath the gaze once more. "You are a body Malo herself has decided worthy of implanting one of her own creatures, believed you worthy of the gifts of her own creation. I know some people who would sell their right arm and left leg for something like that."

Part of him wanted to believe it, the other wanted to run far from the idea. If some God had decided to do that by allowing him to be attacked and nearly killed at such a young age, all to be rendered an outcast and a monster among everyone he knew. It wasn't a destiny he'd have chosen.

But then the kind tone was perhaps something he could get more used to.

None of these were things he wished to convey to the kind King, a sincere gratitude for answers no matter how unagreeable he found them shot through his veins. The wolf lowered his head, and said a genuine, "Thank you, King Malachi. I do appreciate it."

Malachi shook his head, "I'm sorry you've had to spend your life being told anything different."

"Unfortunately, that wouldn't be the end of our questions," Mason dared to speak up, and Silas wasn't sure if he should have admired his friend for that decision or revered him as the biggest idiot he knew. Something which had a fair amount of competition at this point. "Why are you headed to Malowa?"

After all he had learned in such a short period, Silas had entirely forgotten that had been their original intention in joining the wagon train.

However, Malachi shook his head. "A question in return for a question, I'll give you the first one for free, remember that generosity," the dark tone he regarded the prince with compared to the gentle kindness he did the wolf was jarring to Silas. "Why is a crowned Prince and a lycan travelling alone when this Kingdom is on the brink of war?"

Guilt ripped through him, partly for the fact he had no certain answers and partly because those he did have, he had been forbidden from sharing. The very aura of this gentleman lent itself to those surrounding wanting to share; despite having known the Nomadic King not even an hour Silas was struck with an intrinsic need to trust him.

"Unfortunately, we're not able to say," Mason broke the news before Silas could begin to think of an excuse. It was easy and blunt, polite but unwavering in his tone.

If he was annoyed by the prince's statement, the Angofwen monarch didn't hint such in the slightest. Not a twitch of the eyebrow or a quirk of a frown that might have made his expression readable, and those dark brown eyes were fixed to Silas intently.

Lowering his gaze, he responded the only way he could. "I'm sorry but he's right, we're under orders." It wasn't his fault that it was the truth and he had little choice in the matter, but that made the guilt nonetheless bone deep.

Briefly the King seemed to consider prying further, and when the guard straightened nearby Silas tensed instinctually. But then the King simply shook his head, "Very well if you insist."

Gratitude flooded Silas that this wouldn't end in a fight, or even anything further than a slightly heated discussion or the exchange of fleeting frustrated glances. Silas wasn't someone adversary in nature, but here of all places it seemed outright rude to even try.

The King shifted and stood upright, bones cracked as he moved, gesturing to the fabric entrance to the caravan compartment. "You two are welcome to leave now, and may I thank you for speaking with me, it has genuinely been an honour, Silas." He all but ignored the prince, who had taken little more than a decorative role at that point, something the wolf was very unused to it, but would rather it wouldn't become a theme.

Silas was happy to comply, but his companion didn't move from amid the plush cushions. Arms crossed and gaze dancing across the King's regal features, "You might be willing to go without answers," Silas wasn't sure if that comment was directed at himself or their host. "But our question has still gone unanswered, what's in Malowa?"

Through spite alone Malachi seemed to consider telling them to take a long walk off a short pier, but the response didn't come from him but the guard behind Silas and Mason. "Word will spread quickly enough, why keep it to ourselves?" He offered, Silas glanced backwards, nodding his head appreciatively for the man's efforts.

But when he turned back, he realised that might well not have helped.

"I imagine you know this better than you let on," he explained lowly, his voice something between kind and mildly threatening. "But war is on the horizon, we head to Malowa with some of the other clan heads, to discuss what our next move is."

By strength of will alone Silas kept still and silent.

"The King only returned yesterday," Mason chose his words carefully, but his tone maintained its casual tone. "How have you already got such a large body of people on the move so quickly? That can't be possible in just a day," his disapproving and untrusting tone made Silas worried.

Malachi's chuckle wasn't the same enigmatic tone it had been before, this time it was a sad booming noise, made as though he wasn't sure what would have been a better choice. "My people have felt conflicts in the winds for a long time, kid," he responded, treating the Prince in the most human way he had since the pair had entered. "We gathered two days ago to consider things, and then yesterday the attack happened."

Ezekiel hadn't been joking when he'd explained that news travels like wildfire in their little kingdom, Silas didn't know whether to be impressed or scared.

"The meeting at Malowa will determine where you ally yourselves then?" Mason pried further, and for the first time since their entrance the wolf turned his gaze from the Angofwen monarch and onto the Prince. "Who?"

"Kid if you think I'm sharing that much you clearly are drunk," Silas almost smiled at that.

It was worth a shot, he supposed. "I suppose that's fair enough," from today the newcomers had definitely earned more information than their hosts.

"Are you at least able to tell us where your headed?" Malachi queried, this time out of genuine curiosity rather than the hopes of gaining something that might be used as leverage.

"Godsgather," Silas answered quickly with a half-truth. It might not have been their end destination, but for now it was their focus. That and the destination of the landmark was explanative enough in its own right it might not draw too much attention nor further questions.

"Our path doesn't cross with Godsgather directly," he explained – not what Silas had expected. "But we can drop you off near Clemmensgate and you can make your way from there?"

"We're meant to be avoiding larger cities," Mason spoke sending a meaningful look at the wolf, but before either the King or Silas had the chance to respond he added. "But Clemmensgate is small enough it shouldn't be too much of an issue." He said with a nod of his head, then after a look from Silas, added with a slight almost laugh. "If it is agreeable with my companion, we'd like to take your offer. Our feet will no doubt be grateful for some of the journey being made for us."

Silas nodded more eagerly than he cared to admit.

Malachi smiled a vibrant smile once again, the animosity or frustrations of beats before seemingly forgotten and discarded. His mighty hands clapped together producing a sound that would make thunder spook, "Brilliant," his tone was that of a gentleman who had spent the last hour laughing and joking with friends, and Silas was grateful to hear joy return to the jovial monarch's booming voice, beside him Mason remained stiff and his expression motionless.

The Prince's lips parted as he asked lowly, "How long do you expect it to take for us to reach Clemmensgate?" He asked, unperturbed by his Grace's happy movements.

But Malachi had lifted himself upright, parted the curtains and glanced outside. For a moment Silas thought he had departed, and the pair were to simply enjoy the rest of their journey in comfort, but he returned after a beat. "We should reach the town within two hours," he decided.

How the King knew that given Silas' recent look outside he had seen nothing of interest outside of a woodland, field and grass, the wolf didn't know and wasn't about to question. If they ever met again Silas would be surprised, but for now he was grateful to be able to consider the man a friend, however fleeting.

"For that time feel free to make yourselves at home," the extent to which he extended that to Mason sincerely Silas wasn't entirely sure, but he was happy to disregard that much. "This caravan is yours if you want it, drink, sleep, whatever you please." Malachi didn't return to his seat. "If you don't mind, I've been crowded in here long enough, I'm going to be outside for a short while," the King explained.

Silas could hardly blame him; the wolf was a dwarf in comparison and he still felt cramped in the small compartment – half a life in a cell had made him used to it but that didn't mean he found it a familiar nor comforting setting.

"Thank you, sir," Silas replied with a nod of his head.

Malachi nodded, offered a farewell and was gone from the caravan, his guard seemed to consider something for a moment, and then followed suit. Leaving the wolf and his companion in the warmth of their plush pillows and the comfort of their own company.

The silence between them was strained but Silas wasn't sure how to fill it, Mason mused in quiet. Taking a further drink of his tea, his gaze watching the curtain. He was waiting, careful and observant but attempting to façade at casual and ease. Both of them were out of their element here, but the Prince was faring worse it would appear.

The Angofwen King's departure left the room suddenly feeling far emptier, as though the joy had left with him. The pleasant and familiar smells remained, but seemed more diluted now, though that wasn't something Silas thought too much into.

"What do you think?" Silas chose to break the silence after a few moments, sure that if they were being listened to the wolf would have either heard them eavesdropping, or their resulting conversation would be nothing too noteworthy. Even in the depths of his most trusting state Silas wouldn't have been so stupid as to discuss what they'd promised not to share in the middle of an unknown camp.

"I don't know," he answered after a beat. "And what I do know I'm not going to speak about here, we'll talk better when we get out at Clemmensgate," he added as an afterthought, a little kinder than his initial statement.

The wolf sat back amidst the plush comforts, the herbal scent that reminded him so of home was like a lullaby. "You think it was a good idea to agree then?" He queried lowly. "Even if it's a small city, the King warned us to avoid crowds."

"We were given money, we might as well find somewhere to spend it," Mason responded, Silas wondered whether it was worth asking to buy something from amid the caravan train but decided against asking. Left with the belief his friend might take some offence in the suggestion. "And Clemmensgate is as much of a city as Cresvy, if memory serves. I don't think it will offer too much of a problem to us," Mason said definitively. "Your mother's provisions were lovely, but it will be worth finding more as we go," Silas licked his lips. Remembering the loaf his mother had left them with what felt like an eternity ago now, and to add emphasis to the idea, his stomach let out an almighty growl.

"Speaking of," now the hostility seemed to have dimmed from his friend's frame, the wolf grabbed his backpack and sifted through it carefully. Finding the loaf his mother had packed them, slightly dinted from the weight of clothes and extra supplies on top of it, but it smelled delicious, though something rotten, ancient and rendered to crumbs would have been appetising to the wolf in that hungered state. "Want to share?"

Mason briefly considered saying no, Silas could see it from the way his thick eyebrows furrowed together however momentarily. But eventually he gave in, "Fine, I think I could eat you right now, I'm starving."

"I don't think I'd be very nutritious," though muscular he was skinnier than the prince, a life of malnutrition versus luxury. "And fortunately, that won't be necessary, unless human pie sounds more enticing?"

Snatching the loaf tearing it carefully in half and returning the other portion to Silas, the prince smiled meekly, using the pastry to gesture emphatically at his companion. "For now, this will do, just don't get on my nerves," he warned, his voice deepening in a sweet attempt to sound threatening.

Tearing off a small portion, he ate it – savouring the taste. His mother's recipe was mundane, her talents had never really wandered into the realm of cooking, but right now it tasted like home, and even though they were still only a few hours from home, the sensation of home sickness was beginning to set in.

It would be a long time before he would be back, and the reminders – however tiny, would have to be enough for now.

Now his hunger was satiated, far from full but enough that he didn't fantasise about ripping his friend's shoulder from his body and chowing down like it were a fine steak. Silas settled back into the warmth of the cushions, careful to spend a moment battering the crumbs out of the fine fabrics and out of his clothes where they might have caused an infuriating itch at a later time.

"What do we do now?" Silas asked once his friend had finished too.

Tilting his head to one side, he deliberated quietly. "Not a clue," he answered, torn between curiosity and common sense. Casting a glance to the fabric exit, the sounds and smells of the outside world were tantalising enough to waver Silas' most steely common sense.

"Stay in here?" Silas queried, it seemed that with every encroaching moment the walls folded in closer to the pair. "Or do you want to go flirt some more?" He allowed a little laughter at that, remembering his unfortunate attempts at befriending the trio of women outside.

Mason scoffed, "That wasn't flirting, that was a tactical attempt at finding out key information."

"Whatever you want to call it, it was pathetic," Silas returned easily.

The Prince simply shook his head, defeat mixed with amusement, the man seemed at a loss for witty response so left that train of thought where it had finished. "As exciting as it would be, I think it's probably a good idea to stay where we are for now, if Malachi's response was anything to go by – it might be a good idea to not let an entire wagon train know there's a lycan in their midst."

Silas paused, before offering lowly. "Just because it's not a good idea for me to show myself," or his eyes would have been a more accurate descriptor, "Doesn't mean you need to be bunged up in here with me," they were to spend the next couple of weeks in tight quarters. He wouldn't have blamed the Prince for wanting to take the chance to have time by himself.

It was true that the Prince needed to be careful, but in his current untidy and misshapen state someone who guessed his status would have to be psychic or would quickly be deemed a lunatic for having come up with such an idea.

Whilst perhaps a sore thumb compared to the beauty and colour of the rest of this place, he would have been a pitied creature to look at not something that drew attention. Thus, Silas wouldn't have minded too much had he wished to separate, even for a short period.

Even if they had become friends in a short space of time; Silas would have to live with the knowledge that they had lived very different existences. And there were some paths he was never going to be able to follow the Prince down.

Mason hunched forward, torn between choices. Silas could smell it on the Prince's skin that he hated this place, if Silas felt cramped the other man felt outright claustrophobic. Though perhaps for reasons he wasn't entirely aware.

The shake of his head demonstrated an initial intent to refuse, but the glint in the Prince's green eyes made Silas doubt he would be truthful with him. He had gone to say something further, but a question cut him off before he had the chance.

"Do you mind?"

His words were that of someone searching for the slightest reason to stay, for fear guilt would replace the longing to see the outside world again. But Silas wasn't about to give it to him, he knew the Prince would only be miserable staying in their cramped little compartment for too much longer. And Silas had no want to see that.

He shook his head, his response genuine. "Not at all," he sunk back into the plush cushions – largely for dramatic effect and to convince his friend. "Enjoy yourself, all I'm going to do is catch up on sleep," he rubbed his weary eyes. With a full stomach, aching feet and a quenched thirst – accompanied by the scents that reminded him of home, the need to sleep pushed at him like a gentle wind.

"On second thought," Mason moved and faceplanted into the plush cushions, laughing as he thudded into the softness. "I might join you; I'm shattered."

But Silas was aware the Prince's insistence was largely for his benefit. "Not a chance," he growled lowly from the little den he had created about him. He made effort to mould his tone into something sterner, more defensive but the playful glint of his silver gaze gave him away as having little true malicious content. . "I've got dibs, you go make friends."

Upright again, Mason looked at him with grateful eyes. "If you're certain?"

"Stay safe and wake me up at your own risk."

"I'll bare that in mind," Mason responded with a chuckle, moving towards the curtains, but cast a gaze back before departing through them, adding as an afterthought. "Sleep well."

"Stay alive," the wolf retorted lowly, but the Prince had disappeared before the final syllable could part his lips. He watched the curtains swing close, little choice but to hope Mason would return soon enough and in one piece.

Chapter Thirteen.

Something jarred Silas from the depths of his sleep.

He had no idea what it was, nor for how long he had been contently dozing. But one moment he had been in a world chasing bunnies and stargazing, the next the sensation of being carefully watched ricocheted through his very system. As he lurched upright, attentive and careful all at once, on edge by something that might well have been a gust of wind.

Fortunately; unless the wind had recently taken a human form and was terrible at sneaking around – it wasn't the wind that had awoken him.

A woman, long silk fabrics of deep reds and golds similar to the garbs he had seen the Angofwen monarch marked with, she stood bent at the waist and paying very little attention to the previously dozing wolf. Silas' elder by quite an age, but beauty still marked her features and elegance laced her posture. Her hands holding a pair of decanters, making a clear effort not to rouse Silas from his sleep.

"I'm sorry, I was trying not to wake you," the stranger conceded gently.

His second reaction was to look to the corner of the room, where he and Mason had discarded their rucksacks for the time being, the newcomer might not be an assassin but that didn't mean she wasn't necessarily here to steal. The Angofwen King's caravan was laced with beautiful things, and whether a thief would even bother with the muddied rucksacks was doubtful, but still Silas didn't find it worth the risk of not checking.

Fortunately, the bags remained where they had been unceremoniously dumped.

Now he turned his attention to the newcomer, it took him a minute to compose and realise what she had said, and despite himself he smiled weakly.

It was a general rule of thumb – don't try to sneak up on a wolf, but Silas wasn't going to hold that against her. "It's okay, sorry," he mumbled moving to wipe the sleep from his silver eyes. Now he had realised there was no threat, or he had come face to face with the worlds least threatening assassin, the adrenaline had drained from his body. Leaving him in the all too human state of grogginess as he tried to rouse himself from this sleepy phase. "Who are you?" He realised, this woman might not have been a threat to him, but that didn't mean she should have been allowed in the monarch's compartment, and he would rather not be deemed overly welcome to find out they'd been robbed due to his ineptitude. His gaze flickered to the golden decanters she held in each hand.

Unwavering and unperturbed by Silas' careful observation. "Lenore," she responded, grabbing the second decanter by the handle and offering her spare hand to the wolf, looking at him expectantly as she waited for him to shake it.

Mildly surprised by the offer, he doubted a hundred years could have passed in this place and he would still be unused to the kindness they should him. He shook it gently, "I'm Silas."

"I know," she responded, withdrawing her hand and using it briefly to push back her long locks from where they had flittered about her features. "Kai told me," it took the wolf a moment to realise she referred to the Angofwen monarch. "You're the lycan?" A question Silas had the feeling she knew the answer too.

Silas was taken aback even more than that, he had assumed after their conversation the King would make efforts to not spread the news. That or his guard had tattled, but neither seemed overly likely options to this seemingly strange woman.

Apparently gifted in reading minds, Lenore shook her head with a chuckle. "Kai has never been a good liar, but don't worry he won't have told anyone else," she promised with a solemn tone Silas believed went rarely used but didn't render him any the less uncertain. "I'm his wife – I believe that leaves me privy to at least something he wouldn't share with the rest of the clan," she explained easily. If she was concerned about sharing close quarters with a wolf – even a chained one, she did little to exemplify such in her features. "Plus, I'd have to be quite the idiot to miss those silver eyes from this distance."

An instinctive hand lifted to rub self-consciously at his face, embarrassed and caught off guard. But Silas knew it wasn't as though he could particularly lie, pretend that his eyes were a fashion statement and nothing further, he merely nodded in acceptance.

"It's nice to meet you?" He was uncertain as to whether it was worth even trying to play at politeness, but if this was the wife of Malachi; a queen in her own right, it meant he should at least make efforts to be friendly. Especially if he were wanting to keep Malachi as a friend, he came across as the type of gentleman who would take offence to his wife on a personal effort.

"Quite the pleasure," her expression was the same degree of unreadable as the King had expertly demonstrated, she didn't carry quite the same enigmatic charisma as her husband had. But the kindness in her dark brown eyes shone through despite the refined posture, and if this was someone Malachi liked, Silas doubted she could be a nasty person.

"Do you know how long I've been asleep?" Earlier pauses of silence had been more comfortable compared to this, but now he sought to find ways to breach it, feeling that with every second that passed in emptiness, the woman grew more watchful and intent.

Discarding the decanters to the side, she sat not on her husband's chair but a cushion beside it. Likely out of respect rather than a preference in seating, not that the wolf would have told on her for taking residence on the makeshift throne the King had utilised.

"Kai left about an hour ago," she countered, "But we've not made great progress, one of the wagons at the rear of the train broke a wheel, we had to take the time to get that fixed," she added before Silas could query as to the whereabouts of Clemmensgate from their position. "But we should reach Clemmensgate in maybe another hour or so." Lenore clarified further.

"Have you seen the gentleman I came in with?" he asked her further, and when she allowed him to say that uninterrupted or without presumption, Silas forced himself to take some comfort in that. "He went to explore, and I'm not entirely sure I trust him not to get himself killed out there."

It wasn't meant in offence to the Angofwen people, but rather the degree of doubt he harboured for the Prince, especially given how willing he had been to throw himself into the midst of the wagon trains. Common sense hadn't thus far been demonstrated to be a thriving trait, and whilst Silas didn't exactly have a leg to stand on to that extent, especially as he had been proven to be vastly wrong.

It was worth ensuring his companion hadn't been left dead in a ditch somewhere.

Without the monarchical moniker he usually toted, Silas wasn't sure the Prince would be as careful as he should have been. But then, toting that title among these people Silas wasn't entirely sure that would be of help either.

"He's... making friends?" Lenore decided after a moment of deliberation as to how she was going to choose her wording. "He's interesting one," she added grinning. "He's far more tolerable than most members of the royal family I've had the... joys of meeting," careful emphasis indicated it had been anything but.

Lenore spoke about Mason with far more kindness than her husband had at least. Her laughter wasn't as booming as Malachi's had been but seemed almost more genuine and sweeter. Someone used to the shadow of her husband and didn't bother to match him, happy in her own way.

The wolf cast a worrisome glance at his companion, uncertain of how to ask the following, before he said quite gently. "What do you have against the royal family?" He tensed in worry that the question might repulse the chances of friendship. "Malachi was the same... I don't understand," he admitted, his knowledge of the world was admittedly poor, but all those he had known in his limited experience had displayed only affection for the royalty, bordering on reverence for those on the throne.

The look the Queen regarded him was one of uncertainty, tension in her own frame as though fearful that she might get into trouble for answering. But she relented, seeming to trust the newcomer, or at least of the opinion anything he wasn't too dangerous.

"The Nekeldez royal family have never had much love for anyone outside of a very strict set of people," she responded with a shrug of her shoulders. "Ezekiel might be kinder than some of the past kings, but his reign is still new compared to some, and time will still tell just how far he might be willing to follow in his mother's footsteps."

Silas considered this, uncertain and wordless for a moment.

They might have known each other for very short period of time, but Silas admired her already, and her honesty was something that he appreciated.

"Anyway, enough of that, your friend appears to at least be breaking the usual mould," she flourished a slender hand dismissively. "Do tell me, how did you meet such interesting young... gentleman?"

Unthinking Silas parted his lips, and almost began quite enthusiastically but stopped himself barely. He straightened, trying to sense out a trap where he might find one, but he had the increasing belief his companion was far more gifted to that extent.

Lenore watched him, batting long dark lashes in a half playful attempt to seem innocent, but both parties were aware that the woman had been caught red handed.

"Not an overly interesting story," Silas lied with what he prayed would come across as ease and casualness. Uncertain as to how much further prying he would be able to stand up to before crumbling like a poorly built house in an earthquake. "And I think you know better than you let on that I'm not in a position to tell much anyway," Silas arched an eyebrow.

Lenore's smile was a black hole, drawing in the unexpected until they didn't realise before it was too late. "Can you blame me for trying?" Her ember eyes were lit with a burning youth that contrasted with the wrinkles of her dark skin and otherwise ancient demeanour of the women. All at once she seemed far younger and far older than something her features seemed to betray, playful but wise, naïve yet omniscient. "We don't often get visitors, especially not of the interesting variety. Unless you count monarchs attempting idiotic treaties." She added with a rumbling chuckle, setting back against the plush cushions. Entirely at home, whereas Silas couldn't help but feel like he stuck out like a sore thumb.

But he felt safe, and his curiosity and overly trusting characteristics ended up getting the better of him. "Do nobles often try to make peace?" He pried, genuinely interested. Of the stories he'd heard Rehenney nobleman and the Angofwen avoided one another like the plague, both entirely happy to live lives as though the other didn't exist. This was the first he'd heard that they had ever tried to make friends, and what he'd known of both parties made that concept seem impossible.

"Now child this isn't a one-way street," all at once the youthful features seemed to drain away and she became a mothering creature, condescending but gently so, Silas was a child being taught a lesson it seemed. "If you're not going to give me any answers, I most certainly am not going to be overly forthcoming with my own."

"Can you blame me for trying?" His cheekiness got the better of him.

"The wrong traveller joined camp it would seem," Lenore commented, the laugh stifled but her gaze glittered with unsounded amusement. "You're far more fun, your friend seems entirely full of hot air and not much else, you're quite good fun."

This had been a day of firsts; he had never been the interesting one. The terrifying one, yes, the useless one, regularly. Interesting was at the bottom of a quite long list of descriptors he'd heard in his lifetime, and the way Lenore spoke made him think she meant it.

"I won't let him know that, I fear it will burst what seems to be quite a fragile ego," she commented further when Silas failed to. "Someone far used to being at the centre of attention," she said with a sigh, but her words weren't hurled like an insult, rather offered as a conversation topic. Prying, but not too deep nor too cruelly.

What he did know was based on very little information. But thus far he had found his companion a kind one, and not what he had expected of someone of royal blood. He shook his head, "I wouldn't say so," he replied. "He's a good man, and kinder than a lot of the people I've known," he added with a meek chuckle. Kicking out his muscled legs, feeling the cramped nature of the compartment beginning to get to him.

"Uncomfortable?" Her change of topic was abrupt.

"Fidgety," he corrected. He had spent half a life in cells, but this was self-imposed, and freedom was inches away but forbidden. That and even in the context of his night-time home, he disliked remaining in one spot. "I've never been a fan of sitting still," he admitted aloud, the first

She chuckled, "I might not be a lycan, but I can appreciate that much at least," she returned, a form of give and take that settled the conversation into a comfortable flow. She paused, considered something but then decided against it, instead adding. "But then the Angofwen have never been a people that enjoy sitting in one spot all too very long," she added, running slender fingers through her thick hair in a brief attempt to tame its wildness. "It's like asking the wind to stay put, impossible."

"Or lightning to act politely," it was something his mother had constantly thrown his way as a child, the memory sparking a smile across his lips.

"Indeed," but her voice was distracted – she leaned closer; gaze not fixed to Silas' eyes but rather his shirt. Long, dark fingers entwined with the fabric, much as her husband had done as she studied it. Spotting the silvers lacing his clothes without needing to be told about it. He resisted the urge to flinch away, not wanting further pity from someone he was beginning to consider a friend.

"You've spent much of your life in places like this, I imagine little wolf," that wasn't another demonstration of her mind reading capacities, Silas knew that on an intrinsic level. The way her fiery gaze glowed showed empathy, a knowing Silas wasn't sure the source of.

He simply nodded.

Silas worried that might have been the end of their conversation, as she didn't speak again for several moments. Silas parted his lips, trying to find a means of filling the silence but finding his imagination lacking, thus he quickly shut them again, feeling quite useless.

After several, strained minutes. She spoke again.

"The people who would usually keep you in chains are long gone now, kid," she decided eventually. "And from the looks of your friend he wouldn't mind too much." She brushed the hair out her face, using the opportunity to release his sleeve from her strong fingers. "One of these days, maybe let yourself out of those chains, see what happens."

It hadn't been something he'd contemplated – for so long it was something he'd considered impossible. He shook his head, "I'd kill people," he knew from experience that was all that could come from a wolf left free to roam. Releasing a breath of air he hadn't realised he'd been holding as he said quickly, "I've killed people," he further clarified, the sound catching in the back of his throat.

"You're a full-grown man, not the scared child you once were," he didn't pry as to how she knew those further details, scared of the answer more than he cared to admit. He was unsure whether to be grateful or worried about how she avoided his murderous history. "You can control yourself better than you think," her words were calm and kind. "I've known others who wouldn't be controlled by silver, no matter how much they were laced with, if you were as out of control as you insisted, these silver bindings would do little more than slow you."

Silas looked at her with a start, unsure of where to begin. "You've known other Lycans?"

Her smile was a pitiful one, but Silas was left with the impression it was self-applied. "Wolves aren't the only creatures bound by silver," she explained with a shrug of her shoulders. "But all stories for another time."

The wolf moved, wanting to speak more, learn more, ask more. But the way the Queen shrugged her shoulders was final, and Silas knew he wouldn't get any more information from the beautiful elder even if he tried for years.

As pleasant as their short conversation had been, Silas was all too aware of the likelihood of ulterior motives. He watched her for a moment, moon kissed gaze staring into flame burnt eyes. "I've enjoyed this," he admitted genuinely, and hoped such would be clear from his voice for fear what would come next might ruin what little friendship the pair had built up in their brief conversation. "But why are you here?" He elected was the easiest way to word it in order to offer the least offence.

Her smile was wildfire, unpredictable but beautiful. "Curiosity," her response was quick and not something that she needed to think about for more than a heartbeat. "After all, how often is it that you get to meet a lycan?" She asked, tilting her head.

Silas had never met a single one, except the fateful day he had become one himself. It was a fair point.

"And now you've been kind enough to humour my curiosities, I had best make movements," Lenore explained, lifting herself upright. Snatching the decanters up and moving for the door with little further ceremony.

Silas watched her leave, offering a farewell of his own in turn. Wondering if she left in more disappointment than she gave away with words or expressions, saddened that she hadn't gained further information for her husband, but Silas wasn't sure.

However, she didn't have the chance to get through the door, before another person parted the curtains. Mason re-entering the carriage, cheerful and perhaps mildly tipsy – he had only been gone an hour, but it seemed he'd had a great deal of fun in the short time he had been gone.

"I'm glad to see you made it back alive," Silas greeted his friend, withholding the laugh which threatened to break his lips as his friend slumped into nearby cushions.

Lenore didn't give his friend the chance to reply, as she interrupted with a heart guffaw. "We are a noble people, we wouldn't let your friend get himself killed," she promised, chuckling. "What other… problems might arise," *namely inebriation*, "Well I've got to be honest that's not exactly our fault."

Silas nodded, falsifying solemnity in his expressions. "That's fair," his gaze fixed to his friend's form, content and merry in the early stages of inebriation. It was good to see that he took this mission seriously. "I'd hoped he'd have a stronger constitution than this, surely all those courtly wines would stiffen him up for a day like this?" He commented, genuinely surprised the strong-willed man had been quickly rendered even tipsy in such a short period of time.

"No idea," Lenore responded, but she moved to leave once more. "I'll leave you two to recover a little before we arrive," she decided, nodding her head in a signal of farewell. But once more she was halted before she could part through the curtains.

A sudden stop in momentum lurched Silas forward in his seat a few inches, pulling upright it took him a moment to realise what had happened. Their wagon had come to a stop, quite a sudden one. He looked to the Angofwen monarch; confusion bright in his silver gaze. "Are we here already?"

But from the dark expression marring her features, Silas could guess something wasn't right.

"This can't be right, we can't have reached Clemmensgate already," The words didn't seem pointed at anyone in particular. Lenore stood, moving to part the curtains, she disappeared without allowing her companions a word in.

Silas in turn lifted himself to his feet, ignoring his oblivious companion and moved to follow her. But was forced to retreat as the doorway was filled by the form of Malachi, Lenore following suit quickly. Both of them looked panicked, the expression seemed out of place and bizarre on the previously so strong monarch.

"You need to get out of here," he said lowly, the tremble in his voice so slight it made Silas share their panic. "We're being stopped, the wagons searched. It won't take long before they find you, and I don't think they will appreciate finding a Prince and a Lycan in our wagons." His explanation was hurried, but despite all of it the kindness to his voice rang through all the same.

Confusion ripped through the wolf; a sudden eviction hadn't been what he expected.

"Please," Lenore reiterated, her elegance and composure of before struggling to maintain the forefront as fear began working to replace it. "Not only for your own sake, our people will suffer if they are found to be harbouring you."

"What?" Silas struggled to get his head around everything that had been thrown at him all at once, he was caught between needing a better explanation and complying and getting the hell out of here. "Who?" He panted, breathless as he watched the monarchs grab the Prince from his spot amid the cushions.

Malachi shook his mighty head, "No one is carrying your King's banners, so we can only assume that-" the King was interrupted by the uproar of shouting from outside, but he hadn't needed to finish all the same. He could guess the answer anyway, rebels.

On his legs one second and nearly tumbling the next as they were thrust unceremoniously from the wagon.

Now outside, the sun finally parting through the clouds, he could see the wagon train beginning to unfold into chaos. The children that had bounded without worry alongside the carriages were now being hurried away by worried parents, shouts ricocheted across the open fields. Weaving throughout were a group of people dressed in such dark colours they might well have been painting a target to their backs, they looked so strange against the shining rainbow that made up the Angofwen train.

Some feral part of him was driven by the need to take off running and find safety, abandon all forms of ties he'd made in his brief time here and fend only for himself. Another part was too terrified that it rendered him fixed in spot, like roots had taken place around his feet and refused to let him leave. Something smaller still was more loyal than all those parts combined, and even if he'd been able to – he was going nowhere in that moment until he had certainty of exactly what was happening.

All the same he was terrified, as Silas was left only to stare, wordless as he watched the peace of moments prior descend into fear, and chaos, and pain.

Surrounding the carriage were the men and women in dark blues and greys who had surrounded the carriage when the companions had originally come to the carriage. They were at attention, prepared to protect their king at all costs, but Malachi was having none of it.

The King's voice sounded easily above everything, despite all the shouting. "Spread out," he warned, gesturing emphatically. "Make sure as few people as possible are hurt, I can look after myself." Though Silas had no doubt that the Angofwen king was more than capable of keeping himself safe, he was surprised that the guard was dismissed all the same.

For a moment the guards hesitated, exchanging glances briefly and then complied with their orders.

Malachi's gaze followed the guards briefly, before he turned to the pair. "If you head north from here, you'll hit the woods again. It won't be as quick as it would be if you followed the road but-" he trailed off; Silas followed his line of sight to see that the road ahead of them was blocked off by a large group. For whatever reason they had decided to block entrance into Clemmensgate, but it didn't seem like they'd have much chance to ask as to why.

"But it'll get you there all the same, if you follow the river's flow it will get you to the hills just outside of Godsgather, and it's pretty obvious from there." He was condensing as much information as he could into the shortest amount of space possible, Silas listened intently. Trying to burn the very words he spoke into the back of his eyelid, knowing full well the slightest detail forgotten could be time wasted. And right now it was becoming more and more apparent that was time they couldn't lose.

The Queen removed the fabrics that laced her shoulders, the red and gold shimmering in the pale light, she passed it to the wolf. "Take this, use it to shield your head it might well save your life," she explained.

Uncertain but compliant, he pulled the silk over his head into something resembling a headscarf, a not uncommon accessory among these people so it wouldn't draw too much attention. And would shield his eyes enough that someone wouldn't be able to spot it from a distance.

"Thank you," he breathed meekly, trying to compose himself before they were thrust from the safety of the wagon's shadow, sent on their way and left to hope they made it to the treeline alive.

But before Lenore had the chance to respond, Malachi interrupted.

"Lenny go with them, escort them as far as the eastern treeline, and meet me in Clemmensgate by dawn."

His tone was commanding, and from the surprise in his Queen's gaze Silas could assume that wasn't a regular theme in their conversations.

For a moment the older woman was visibly torn between agreeing and otherwise, "And if you don't make it to Clemmensgate?" She asked lowly, not exactly the first question that would have come to Silas' head, but he wasn't one to judge.

"Then thank the Gods that you're finally free of me, and enjoy some alone time," Malachi's response contrasted severely with the dark fear in his gaze.

Silas interrupted from where he was propping Mason up, the Prince delirious but quickly catching up on the fact that something was very run. "There is no need, we can take care of ourselves," he promised – not wanting a family torn up for his own sake.

Malachi turned his attention fully to Silas for the first time, his gaze burning through the wolf's form. "You might not have been willing to share what you're here doing," he explained lowly, all too aware that if they waited too long all of this might well have been useless. "But it has to be better than what's happening right here, whatever your King is intending, I hope there is some form of logic to it. This…" he trailed off, his gaze cast across the rest of the wagon train, chaos reaping wherever the eye could see. "If this is what war will be looking like, I want it ended before it can even begin." He finished lowly; Silas had to stop himself from trembling beneath his intense gaze. "I need to stay here, make sure my people get out of this intact," a King truly loyal to his clan, "But you need to get out of here safe, and make sure whatever you are here to do – make sure you succeed."

Lenore's gaze fixed to him, contemplative for a beat despite the madness of the world about them. "Okay," she agreed.

Understanding that anything he could have further interrupted with would be useless and pointless, the wolf was left to step back. His heart thundering at that point so fiercely he was sure it would draw a rebel too them, give away their position and render all of this effort to nothing.

"Stay safe," she warned him, her voice shaking but her eyes and posture fierce and insistent. "I will see you soon, so for the love of the Gods don't do anything too stupid whilst I'm gone."

Malachi's smile was genuine, despite the flood of emotions that backed up his dark eyes. He pulled her close, embraced her hard. "You have my - " he didn't finish in time for his wife to close the distance between their lips. Silas looked away, self-conscious and awkward.

"You have my word," he finished when the two parted, Malachi released the woman from his bear grip and turned his attention to the two younger men. "Stay safe," he added to them as an afterthought, but his tone was honest. "And I can only hope one day we meet again."

He took Silas' unoffered hand and shook it firmly; with his inebriated companion the monarch didn't bother but Mason probably wasn't in much of a position to notice that much. "Now go."

Chapter Fourteen.

Malachi pulled away from the trio, lifting his voice above the crowd he began hollering. Drawing attention to himself and hopefully away from those he left in the wagon's shadow.

For a heartbeat Lenore watched him go, then gestured at the pair. "Let's go," she hissed.

"Not just yet," Silas froze at a sound, but turned to gratefully see a friendly face; though not something he had a high bar for at the moment. Leaping from the wagon's entryway, a pair of bows and arrows gripped carefully in his grip. "Take these, they'll prove of use."

The Queen reached and grabbed the bow and arrow quiver, treating it with a familiarity that Silas envied. He blinked in surprise when the second one was thrust into his own hands. "I have no idea how to use this thing!" He stammered.

"You'll be of more use than your friend," Lenore replied easily, the guard having departed in pursuit of his King. "Keep it as a back-up, you never know," she warned, and Silas could only nod.

By then Mason had become somewhat more aware, better able to remain upright of his own accord. Now the dreariness in his dark eyes was replaced with a fear that was bone deep. He was attent, any lingering cheeriness all but drowned from his system as adrenaline took its place. Silas would have to explain later, but for now they needed to make sure they survived until later.

Instinctually, the Queen took the charge, and with few other options Silas and his companion followed suit.

About them chaos raged, but the trio went largely unnoticed as much of the guard had surged further than through the wagon train, and those who had paused to check the first wagon had gone in pursuit of the rampaging King.

But their luck didn't remain for long, as a shout echoed from behind them.

"Run," Lenore warned, "I'll keep them busy and catch up in a minute."

He moved to stop her, the bow felt heavy and useless in his grip, more a hindrance than it would have been a help, but unless he elected to have a drastic change in life choices it would likely be his only form of protection. He stammered, but only nodded. Watching her for a heartbeat as she drew back her bow and began taking shots of her own.

Turning, grabbing Mason by the hand, he continued his charge. Only the beginning of the treeline in sight by then, but if the Queen could succeed in preventing their pursuers from making any further ground, they might just have made it out of here alive.

War was on the horizon, and there were a lot of people desperate to make sure it came. And they were willing to do anything in their power to ensure that it did. They had known to expect rebels plaguing their path, but something of this size terrified Silas to an extent he hadn't expected.

Silas knew that this problem wouldn't have been confined only to the borders of Clemmensgate, barely a drop in the pond compared to some of Rehenney's larger cities. If this degree of protection had been instilled to check people going into the city were savoury, Silas worried what kind of trouble the other teams might face.

He bore none of the King's sigils – which might just let him get out of this alive. The other parties were dressed to the teeth as members of the King's Guard, even without his wolf genes he could have scented that much from a mile away.

If nothing else, it made it all the more apparent as to just how essential their success was. If they wanted the war over before it could even begin, they would need to get this done and done right, for fear the rest of the King's missionaries wouldn't be as fortunate.

But then an arrow shot by him, missing his right arm by the breadth of the hair. Proving that in spite of the Queen's best efforts, they had continued to be pursued, all Silas could hope was that these were new, not the same pair as those who had originally been following them.

Instinctually, Silas hurled himself at the ground, pulling his companion with him. In an effort to hide themselves from anyone attempting to stop them in their tracks.

Scrambling to find grip on his bow, he sat up. Fingers struggling to find purchase as he drew back the drawstring, nocked an arrow into place and let go. It went an entirety of five feet, compared to the thirty it would need to have gone in order to come within spitting distance of those making their pursuit of the pair.

He swore loudly, knocked again and attempted a second time. This time finding something in the way of more luck, at least it went a distance down the hill though no doubt aided somewhat by wind or the pity of the gods. But still came nowhere close to those following.

To his credit, they too hit the floor, expecting a more talented bowman to be taking shots.

No doubt it would take them less than a minute to realise the dastardly absence of one, so they had to take their opportunity whilst they had it. Grabbing Mason by the arm, he yanked him upright too and took off again.

Naturally the sound of footsteps followed them only a couple of beats later, but once in the heavy treeline they might have more of a chance of losing the followers. At least Silas and Mason had speed on their side, though Silas might have been naturally the quicker one, Mason to his credit kept up fairly well despite stumbling feet.

Those following were armoured to the bone that weight might well have saved the running duo.

They had no idea Silas was a lycan, nor that Mason was a Prince. It should have been impossible at this distance. So, either they were very neat and careful about the death records they kept, or they had no intentions of letting anyone get out of this alive.

The rebels were out for blood on anyone who they thought might be allied with the King.

Beyond them, the wagon train continued in chaos, Silas feared for them. But for now he was too busy fearing for his own life.

What felt like an eternity later, the treeline was within spitting distance. They thundered on, the shadows of the heavy foliage quickly covered them, but the ground underfoot became unpredictable. Tree roots everywhere, they lunged a few feet attempt not to collide through them, only to tumble metres later, the ground snatched from under their feet as they were sent plummeting into the dirt.

It seemed that their luck was out of order at last.

Scrambling upright again, but the moment of being downed had allowed the pursuers to catch up. Silas looked up to find bows pointed at them both, Silas panted. Lifting his hands in a show of surrender, praying that by some miracle that might just have worked.

Mason on the other hand, either due to a newfound sobriety or because of the opposite grabbed at the bow Silas had dropped. Not bothering to reach for the arrows, he lunged to his feet and swung as hard as he could. To his credit he managed to collide with the head of the man closest to him, he crumbled beneath the blow a cry tugging free of his lips. But another merely lunged for Mason, taking them both to the ground where they wrestled briefly.

The wolf moved to help his friend, only for a further assailant to descend upon him. A punch to the face jarred his head back. A growled rippled from his lips before he could catch it, the hood falling from his head now revealing the full extent of his features, though if his opponent noted the silver of his eyes, they made no acknowledgement of such, moving to hit him again. They sparred, Silas all too aware of just how useless he was.

Lashing out, his fist collided hard with the face of the man, a crack sounded but otherwise there was seemingly no effect to his blow. The stranger parried, taking note of Mason's efforts as he swung with his bow too, attempting to find advantage wherever he could against the lycan.

But the battle wouldn't need to continue further than that, as before he could deliver another blow – the man fell face forward into the dirt.

At first, he froze in place, confused and panicked. Then he noted the arrow protruding from between his shoulder blades, and when he looked up he spotted Lenore weaving through the trees towards them, their saviour and of that he had no doubt. A further arrow quickly nocked and aimed for the gentleman currently attempting to pound Mason into the dirt.

Relief flooded through every inch of his system, a shot to the heart that left it pounding through his bloodstream. He was shaking where he stood, not from a blow he received nor from adrenaline, but in truth genuine fear and surprise from everything that had gone on.

The remaining assailant was quickly felled in a similar means, having seemingly not noticed the newcomer in their attempt to render the Prince's face into pulp for daring to fight back. "Thank you," was the only thing Silas could manage to say, knowing full well that the Angofwen Queen had just saved their lives, and in fact his offer of gratitude was likely ridiculously petty.

"We're not done yet, little wolf," the queen returned panting from her sprint, and blood tainted her features, but from the lack of visible wounds Silas assumed it was not her own. That or she was incredibly good at hiding the extent of her injuries, "Come on we have to keep moving."

Silas nodded firmly, trying not to concentrate his gaze on the bloodied bodies they would be leaving in their wake. He forced any notion of pity from his frame, it was either him or them and even he had to admit he would prefer them dead on the ground then himself and his companion. He looked behind them, for now at least, they weren't being followed.

And if they wanted to keep that a common theme they had best get moving, and quick.

Mason – bruised and a little worse for wear, any inkling of drunkenness now thoroughly shrugged off; stood up. Grimacing as he moved already stiffening muscles, Silas regarded him with a pitying look, he moved to grab something, found it absent and looked to Silas with worry bright in his gaze.

"We left the rucksacks in the caravans," Mason stammered, genuine terror laced his tone.

Dread worked through Silas all at once. He could all but picture them discarded in their little corner of the caravan, he turned immediately. "We need to go back," there was no doubt in his mind, and had already moved to take off running in the direction they had come from. Death might have faced at every shadow back there, but he knew death would only be more widespread if they failed in their mission. And without those rucksacks they might as well have been dead men walking.

A hand grasped his arm, and without thinking he yanked it away, eliciting an angered growl that someone had attempted to stop him, but stifled it quickly when he found Lenore still clutching his sleeve. Anger reflected in her own gaze, "Don't be idiotic, you'll get yourselves killed, and I did not just go through all that – kill other men and women to make sure you got out of there alive, just for you to hurl yourself back in the fray." She demanded; her anger was a fire in her gaze.

"If we don't get those rucksacks back, a lot more are going to die," his voice trembled.

Mason spoke up, his own voice equal in emotion but far firmer than what Silas had managed to say. "In those rucksacks are the ability to end this war before it starts," he explained, his own gaze lit with desperation as he tried to persuade their companion that there was no choice but to go back.

The older woman straightened, her gaze darkening with thoughtfulness for a moment but she still didn't release her grip. "Come with me," her tone of voice was entirely different, gone was the desperation to be replaced with something more akin to determination.

"We ca-" he didn't get the chance to finish.

"Come with me," she repeated lowly, pulling Silas sleeve. "Trust me, I might have an idea."

The use of might worried him, but with little other choice they complied.

Together they trudged through the trees, and in spite of further attempts at prying the Queen refused to offer anything further in the way of answers. Her eyes focused on the paths ahead, concentration emanated from the elder, and Silas wasn't sure that a nearby explosion could have jarred her.

Just as Silas moved to stop her, thinking all of this had been a ploy to get them further away from the chaos and that there had been no plan all along. The Queen stopped of her own accord, cast her gaze around and sat down with a thump.

"Don't speak," her eyes were closed but it seemed she had sensed that Mason's lips had parted. Her hand gestured upwards, "Don't move, I'll be back soon," just as Silas moved to interrupt unthinkingly, "I said don't speak," she reminded him with the tone of a teacher scolding a school child. "And if I'm not back soon…" she trailed off, before shaking her head firmly – like a dog trying to shake a flea, "Carry on without me."

Confusion laced the looks that Silas and Mason exchanged with each other, but seemingly few other choices, they sat before her and waited.

It happened slowly at first, and Silas had barely noticed anything had changed until all at once it was rather obvious. The woman was fading, her face furrowing with concentration slowly dimming until the trees behind her were growing more visible, and then all at once, she was gone.

Silas could do little more than stare, whereas Mason lurched forward and grasped at the air where Lenore had formally been sitting. Only to fall through the space, he landed on his hands, looking back at Silas, sheer confusion in his green blinking eyes. "What in the name of the gods?" He asked after a minute aloud.

"I have no idea," was all that Silas could manage to stammer out in response to a question he wasn't even entirely sure had been directed at him.

Now all they could do was wait.

In hindsight they should have asked a better definition of what 'soon' was to the Angofwen Queen, as minutes soon stretched into eternity.

Mason had moved to ask the very thing that had been propped on Silas lips, when the need was discarded. As suddenly and all at once, Lenore reappeared before them. As though she had never been gone, and the two men had simply entirely lost their minds.

But this time clutched in her hands, was the two rucksacks so carelessly forgotten in the chaos.

All Silas could think to do was stare, but the first thing that came from Mason lips was unfiltered, a little stupid and perhaps mildly offensive. "You're a witch," he stammered.

"You're observant," her retort was easy and unthinking. "Why little prince, do you no longer want my help?" She asked, eyebrows arched and stance challenging, as though she feared an outright attack from the people she had risked her life to save. She hurled the two rucksacks to either party.

Wordless, Silas grabbed the backpack easily and sifted through it, until tucked into the little pocket he found the note. King's seal intact and seemingly untouched from the madness that had gone on, it seemed impossible, and the wolf found himself shaking with gratitude.

"You're welcome by the way," Lenore added, clearly trying to compose herself. She shivered like a dead leaf barely clinging to a tree in the midst of a bitter wind. Her gaze stern, contrasting with the shudder of her entire frame.

If the queen noticed the astonishment the pair were staring at her with, she didn't acknowledge it. "Come on, we need to get going," she said and turned away. Making her way through the woodland, simply assuming the two men would follow her without thinking into it too much.

And like oblivious lambs being willingly led to the slaughter, Mason and Silas followed suit.

The two boys trailed behind their leader, silent and uncertain. Silas could have quite easily taken the lead, to some extent because the woman was the one who knew the way for the most part, but out of a newfound respect. And given he had been all but flooded with respect for the monarch the moment he had discovered who she was, now he all but revered her.

For a few miles they walked just like that, the hours passing by in a nervous quiet as they wandered through the massive woodland. For the first little while, Silas couldn't help but constantly cast his gaze backwards, ever terrified that the very shadows would contain enemies set on ripping them limb by limb.

But as they travelled, that terror lessened. Mostly because he might well have suffered a heart attack from the uncertainty.

Soon even Silas' legs began to ache lightly with all of the effort of this walking, and how his companions were managing, Silas wasn't sure. Though from looks of Lenore, she continued only as a means of ignoring the pair following her, desperate to keep the topic of conversation just about anywhere other than what had just occurred.

Now a little more at ease, though still incredibly curious to the point where Silas was certain he might explode, and from the energy protruding from Mason at his side – his companion was in a similar boat. He at last asked one of the simpler questions that came to mind, something that might not anger their companion, and might have the most chances of getting a reasonable response.

"Are all the Angofwen witches?" He felt like a small recently scolded child daring to ask something of his mother after a recent smacking.

Her response wasn't one that he expected, a short sharp laugh. But it was less out of amusement, but not out of annoyance. The sound burst forth due to something angry inside the queen, and the sound was one that might have left a God scared.

"Gods no," she whispered, her tone harsh. Though the shaking had long disappeared from her frame, the Queen looked exhausted and her feet dragged. In spite of that, the same determination that seemed intrinsic to her very character remained all the same. "Some of us have magic, that's true enough, but if the witches knew that much, I don't think the Angofwen people would last longer than a week," she admitted running a finger through her sweaty, dark hair.

"But I thought you said you were Angofwen," he asked at last, keeping his gaze fixed to the ground underfoot. "That they were your people." But the way the Queen turned that flame gaze upon the wolf made him instantly regret the choice to say anything further at all, but just as he was stumbling over his words to find a means of apologising, the Queen had already begun to reply.

"They are," her voice was more defensive than any of them had predicted it would seem. "I am Angofwen, far more than I am a witch anymore," she added with a voice so close to a growl it would have made Silas nervous.

A sigh pulled from her lips, as she continued unprompted. The emotion to her voice something between sadness and anger as she continued. "I haven't considered myself a witch in a long time, little wolf," she explained quietly. Her amber eyes ablaze now, "I fell in love with Malachi when we were both little more than children," memories danced in her watering eyes. "But the witches are people of the skies, and the Angofwen are people of the earth," she shook her head. "And my people hated me for it, I left them long ago, haven't seen a single one of them since," she stopped, stifling something akin to a whimper but forced back into something angrier. "Today was the first time I've attempted magic since I left," she finished at last.

Well that explained why she shook like a precarious leaf afterwards; all Silas could do was nod.

But from Mason's lips came something more surprising, "Thank you," he said in a low tone, as though every other word of his vocabulary had been ripped from his head and that was the best he could think to offer.

Even the Angofwen queen seemed to light up with genuine surprise at the child's offer of gratitude. She smiled for what seemed like the first time in eternity, "You are welcome, Mason," her voice returned to something Silas considered more familiar to her frame. "Now come, my little Wolf and little Prince, let's make sure all of that wasn't in vain."

Chapter Fifteen.

For the better part of half a day the trio continued, the river Silas and Mason had been warned to keep an eye out for was nowhere to be seen, but both parties trusted their leader in spite of it. And after a while, the thundering sound of crashing water sounded.

Swelled by recent rains and spanning a couple of hundred metres wide, the part they were headed for had built in steppingstones. But by now the waters all but flooded over them, hiding most of the steps from sight and the remaining few had only the very tips visible over the dark waters.

He looked to Lenore, uncertain. "I'm not sure it's a good idea to try crossing here?" He half stated half queried.

She only shook her head, "We don't need to here, it's disappointing as it would have made life easier, but if we head downstream a couple of miles there's a proper bridge we can use." She explained, though took a moment to study the water further, and added. "It doesn't look like the water is high enough to have flooded that too," but her uncertainty was far from settling.

Thus, the trio turned and headed east, following the meandering path set by the thick river. Now the crashing made it difficult for his human and magical companion to hear one another, meaning elevated voices was a necessity. Here the heavy foliage that had protected much of the rest of the area grew thinner, but fortunately the rain had begun to let up somewhat. The scents of wildflowers, ancient trees and fresh water flooded the wolf's nostrils, generally a pleasant scent.

A general curiosity crossed the wolf's mind, and with his caution lessened by her already having proven that she was willing to share to some extent. He asked with as loud a tone as he dared to use, "If you don't mind my asking, what other powers can witches use?" He asked.

Lenore cast her gaze back, scoffing lightly. "If you're going to keep asking questions," she began with a shrug of her shoulders, "You might as well be decent enough to call us by the actual name, using 'witch' makes you sound like a small child," she scolded, adding a tutting sound for special effect.

Colour flooded his cheeks as he was forced to ask, "And what would that be?"

"Never mind that, you make yourself look like a child anyway," she corrected herself, her chuckling audible even above the rush of water. "The proper word is the Volendra," she finished with a sigh.

Silas kept his gaze fixed to the ground, while witch was infinitely catchier, Silas respected her wishes more than the sake of his own ease. "Okay, so what other powers can the Volendra use?"

The shake of her head was visible even from the few metres in her wake the two men were, her thick hair flying about her shoulders by the gesture that demonstrated vast disappointment with her companions. "Honest to the Gods," she muttered in a tone only loud enough that Silas could catch.

"We are creatures of the skies," she entertained their curiosities kindly enough in spite of being of the clear and increasing belief she was surrounded by idiots. "Thus, we have some degree of control over the wind." Silas saw her flex her fingers, and his eyes widened with anticipation, but nothing happened, and her hand was snatched in front of her and out of sight. Her next words were littered with embarrassment, but she didn't mention it.

"Which is how we can Windwalk," she continued quickly. "That's what you saw me do, we become one with the air and it allows us to travel to spaces we've already been without need for… more mundane means of travel," she clarified to Silas' gratitude. "It's how we can fly too, though that was never something I was very good at," she added, managing to laugh lightly at her own expense.

Silas was genuinely impressed, he had heard of wit- Volendra, in stories his mother had told him, but even her knowledge – something he had always considered to be infinite, now seemed lacking.

"Interesting, isn't it, Mason?" The royals might have harboured little love for the magical, but he hoped his companion would come to see the woman a friend as he slowly was.

"Hmm, little Prince, do tell us what you think." Lenore's voice sounded again, challenging but not in the playful way Silas had seen her before. This was a predator threatening someone else they considered a threat, and Silas felt a lot like someone trying to play the peacemaker. Even if Lenore was their elder by a good few decades, it seemed that history raised the animosity between them more than simple mediation would heal.

Mason didn't answer immediately, his gaze lowered in a way that Silas assumed was meant to portray annoyance, but the deep inhalation the young man made caused the wolf think otherwise.

"I've been meaning to tell you, but the chance really never came up," Mason's response wasn't what either of them had been expecting it would seem. "Things just got mad, and well we've barely had much of a chance to breathe since we set off without things happening every step of the way." Silas watched his companion intently, and while Lenore didn't turn around to look, Silas could tell from her posture – slightly tilted towards them, that she was listening carefully all the same.

"I'm not a prince," he explained at last, sending Silas recoiling with surprise. "At least not by blood I'm not."

Silas' nostrils flared, and he regarded the prince desperately trying to catch his sent, catch hold of anything that might indicate he wasn't telling the truth. For the sake of not starting an argument he might be trying to falsify the facts, but he found none. His companion's heartrate remained steady, and the scent of sweat didn't change enough to indicate a lie.

Lenore, oblivious to any of those factors that allowed Silas to come to the immediate decision. She turned around for the first time, not coming closer but her hands settled firmly on her hips. She watched him carefully, "You're kidding," she said lowly.

"He's not lying," Silas interrupted before Mason could stick up for himself. "What do you mean you're not a prince?" He asked further, his tone firm and free of the shake that his emotion tried to add.

Shy all of a sudden – something he would never have connoted with the young man, his gaze lowered and blinking sharply. "I was taken in as a kid, Ezekiel isn't my father, as far as I'm aware I don't have as much as an ounce of their blood in my system, and if I do its no doubt from some very distant relative, I've never heard of."

Both the wolf and the Angofwen Queen regarded the young man, rendered a boy by embarrassment, discomfort and sadness brought on by the admission. Silas wanted to move to comfort his friend, but somehow the very idea felt out of place.

Unprompted yet fuelled by the need of someone shrugging off a heavy weight, Mason continued quietly. "I grew up in the capital, my mum and dad worked as a maid and a butler for the previous Queen," he explained, now the shudder to his voice became more apparent, but he continued all the same, looking all the stronger for it even if his tone was shaking. "There was an assassination attempt, one of about ten I've since found out about, and my parents were among the ones caught in the crossfire," he moved to wipe hair from his face, but Silas spotted how he desperately dabbed at the tears. "The Queen took me in, out of duty more than anything else, and I've been there ever since."

To say Silas was shell shocked would have been putting it lightly.

He looked at his feet, muddied and worn from the days efforts but there was nowhere else he could feel like he could look.

"I'm sorry to hear it," the Queen's tone was sincere though her eyes remained narrowed. "But from what I've seen you don't hold much love for my people either, regardless of the blood in your veins," it wasn't forgiveness but nor was it hostility.

Something akin to a laugh pulled free of Mason's lips. "They might not be my true family, but I have known then more than any other family in my life, I think it's only human to share their beliefs," he admitted though looked more sheepish now. "But now I've met you, I can understand more than I did that you're not the monsters I've always thought."

That much surprised Silas, he was far more a monster than anything the pair of them had met that day, but he had seen none of the animosity Mason had portrayed thus far.

"The King might not be a good man nor was his mother a good person either," he admitted finally, crossing his arms with a tone much firmer now. "But without them I would be dead of starvation a long time ago, and I have to thank them for that much at least."

Pity wasn't quite the word for what lit Silas, something closer to understanding would have been more appropriate but he was all too aware neither feelings would likely have been welcomed by the proud man. He shook his head, chuckling once more again because he had few other ideas of how else to fill the awkward silence between them. "I had no idea," he admitted, of the increasing opinion that he knew nothing of the world.

No response came, until with a rumbling sigh. "I'm so used to having it thrown around like an insult," he explained, running his fingers through his hair thoughtfully. "I've sort of come to assume that everyone knows."

Lenore had listened and considered to what had been said, her blazing eyes fixed on the sheepish Mason, unwavering. Her lips sealed shut, and the tension working through her jaw visible even from a distance, her posture stiff but her facial features demonstrated consideration.

And despite all of that, it didn't seem that she could find a way to respond.

Silas might not have known much, but he knew magical creatures received little love from the former monarch, and the present King though on the throne for several years now, had not made his opinion overly known just yet. All the same, her family and many families had been hurt for a long time, and the admission of one young man that they might have been wrong wasn't going to fix that.

Instead, she simply shrugged her shoulders, and gestured for them to follow. "Come on, if we make good distance we can be at the treeline by sunset."

Rather a boring way to finish, but all the wolf could be grateful for was that it didn't finish in something more hostile. He glanced to the young man, his stance still stiff as though he too had expected something more to come of it, but he relaxed visibly when the Angofwen Queen turned her back on them and continued to lead the way through the woods.

Obedient sheep, the two men followed in silence.

But after they had been walking for an hour or so, Silas paused instinctually. Something catching his attention, though it took him a heartbeat to spot what.

Through the woodland, a small herd of deer chewed hungrily on the damp grass underfoot. Oblivious or unfearing of the humans they had crossed paths with, Silas' senses came to focus. Nostrils widening in some gesture more feral than he might have usually permitted, but then it wasn't every day he came across animals in the wild, and not of the delicious category.

His companions had taken a beat further to realise that one of them had fallen behind and turned to look at him. Lenore approached, coming to stop at his shoulder and quickly spotting where his line of sight had wandered.

A chuckle pulled free of her lips, "Not many wander these woods, at least not long enough to go hunting," she explained lowly. Her burning gaze dancing across the peaceful, pale copper forms of the deer a few feet away. Quiet and admiring, "They know we're here," she reasoned, seeming to understand the wild beasts on a level more intimate than Silas could begin to understand. "But they don't realise there's a reason to be scared."

Silas would have been happy to leave them that way, no matter how his stomach had begun growling at the sight of them he was content to leave peaceful things peaceful. Anything else in these woods seemed out of place and unnecessary.

Lenore, on the other hand, seemed to have different ideas. "Go after them," she prompted out of the blue.

"They might not fear humans at a distance, but if I go stumbling about them I imagine they might have a few qualms," Silas returned, amused, shaking his head.

"I don't mean go in as a bull in a china shop," she queen responded with surprising charm. "Shift."

The idea made the wolf grimace, looking at her ludicrously he backed off a few feet and continued down the path. Gesturing for her to follow, "Don't be ridiculous, come on let's get going," he insisted, not wanting to even humour the idea.

She remained fixed in place, watching him depart without moving to keep up. Now Mason had become rooted to the ground too, seemingly equally curious, though he didn't offer input of his own. Happy to let the two argue it out among themselves, it seemed he'd used up his quota of frustration for the day and was happy to let the others take up the slack.

"You don't need to be so scared," on the lips of someone else it might have sounded condescending or rude, but on the elderly queen's tone it sounded nothing but kind. "Now or never, and you're not going to hurt anyone but me and Mason out here if things go wrong."

Lenore seemed to miss that was the source of his apprehensiveness. "I'm not doing it," he insisted, fiercer now.

The Angofwen Queen regarded the wolf calmly, whereas Mason's expression was something torn between anticipation and mild fear. The former one fortunately seemed to overtake the latter, otherwise the young man might well have been running for the hills too.

But when she spotted the genuine fear lighting Silas' silver gaze, she let out a soft sigh, disappointed more than annoyed. As she'd said, it wasn't every day someone met a lycan, though it left Silas under the impression that he was an experiment to be watched, an entertainment piece. Not the danger he could well have genuinely posed to the man and woman beside him.

Yet something deeper, a curiosity of his own perked through the hesitation.

Taking a deep breath, he stepped forward, he didn't move to strip – as odd as that might have looked in the middle of the woods. He simply watched, trying to find the courage to take the first step into something he hadn't done in the better part of two decades, and had not yet done of his own volition. All he had known from that form was pain, blood and death. Most wouldn't have blamed him for the uncertainty Silas was posed with when thinking of it.

He watched, wordless. Trying to muster something – be it annoyance or out of genuine want to find some form of control in a world that seemed to be ever diminishing. His fingers tightened into fists, drawing blood as his fingernails pierced the skin from lack of concentration. The pain was brief, something he wouldn't have noticed had it not been for the slight patter of a blood drop slapping against the dark of his trouser leg.

Forcing movement into his legs, he walked forward, hoping the momentum might well have pulled the shift out of him. Despite his aching frame and sore feet, it would have been as simple as removing the outer layers of silver, it would have been that simple. But his problem wasn't in the physical, but entirely in the realm of the psychological.

Put simply, the wolf was terrified of himself.

He continued moving, and for a brief moment thought he might well have managed to force matter over mind. But all of a sudden something stopped him, nothing of the world around him but again something mental. His legs stopped moving without having ordered it, and no matter how he tried it felt like someone had locked great chains around his legs, rendering them incapable of movement no matter how hard he tried.

And though he hated to admit it, he had the key to his chains. But today wasn't the day he had it in him to use it.

An angry growl pulled free of his lips, angry at no one other than himself.

Missing his ear by the breadth of a grass blade, an arrow shot past him and landed into the flank of one of the deer. Its herd darted about it, gone before the body had fully hit the grass, now newly stained by its blood.

Silas blinked, uncertain initially as to what on earth had happened, he turned back to spot Lenore shouldering her bow once more. Shaking her head, but otherwise her features were unreadable.

For that Silas was grateful, so disappointed and angry with himself that he wasn't sure quite how he might have managed seeing it reflected on the features of a friend.

"Never mind," Mason broke the silence when the Angofwen Queen failed too, moving forward but not towards the would-be wolf, but rather the newly felled deer. "It doesn't really matter," the other man was clearly trying to be helpful, but no doubt didn't understand just how much his words fuelled Silas' raging self-deprecating fire.

He deigned not to honour that with a response, Silas turning to watch as the Volendrian knelt, grasping the animal by the hooves and hoisting it above her shoulders. It landed with a thump, head lolling to the side in a macabre show, lifeless eyes staring at nothing but piercing through Silas' very core.

For the first time since, the queen looked at him again. Nothing in her ember eyes outside of her usual observant, but neither pity, nor anger nor kindness marred the concentration. "I didn't want the deer to die of old age, thought this would be a kinder fate," she explained with a shrug of her shoulders. "You can either eat it when you find somewhere to stay in Vergily, offer it as a gift, or dump it in the lake. Your choice," on the lips of a stranger or someone less kind it would have all sounded like pointed insults. On the beautiful Queen's, it was simply matter of fact. If unnervingly emotionless.

Mason nodded in response, but Silas offered a response. "I can carry it," if he was to be of no other help this afternoon, he might as well have tried to be helpful in that way.

Lenore watched him momentarily, he could see the cogs of her brain turning as she sought a reason to say no, but eventually shrugged the weight off and passed it over. She hadn't struggled under the weight, it was fairly heavy, but she hadn't wavered in any notable way, but Silas believed some intrinsic part of her understood his need to be helpful after an utter demonstration of futility.

Shouldering it with ease, little more than a juvenile rabbit against his broad shoulders. He inhaled sharply, "Shall we get going?" He half asked half pleaded.

The Angofwen Queen only nodded and began leading the way through the woodland once more, the pair of friends quickly falling into pace in her wake.

Silence took hold of the world around them once more, the birdsong and wind continued backtracking them but now it seemed distant. Silas in his own little world and happy to stay there, he could only hope his choice had been the right one. All he knew was negative outcomes from his more feral side, and miles from help and an enemy at the flanks, now of all times was not the opportunity to be experimenting with whether he had lost his more murderous streaks.

It wasn't long before in the distance the small wooden bridge came into sight, more rickety than he would have originally hoped but better than the steppingstones at the very least. For once Cresvy had a one up on just about anything else in the world, as even its bridges looked like a breath of wind wouldn't send them flying. This looked precarious and worrisome, but from Lenore's statements and insistence, Silas knew there didn't seem to be much other choice.

Maybe five minutes had passed until they reached the little wooden bridge, and unfortunately on close inspection it didn't prove to be anything more hope instating.

"One at a time," Lenore's voice pierced the water's roaring song, ever louder now they grew closer to its meandering paths. "I'll go first, and I'll shout when I'm safely across."

"Scream if you're dangerously across," Silas added, exactly what he'd have done to save her he wasn't sure. But events with Alex had proven he wasn't against getting wet to save a friend, or even an enemy at this point.

The queen merely nodded, and slowly but surely began making her way across the little bridge.

Mason and the wolf were left to only watch, hearts frozen in place until she disappeared over the horizon, the width of the howling waters claiming her frame from sight, and Silas could only wait. Rooted in spot until he heard the "I'm across," yelled.

Relaxation pushed through his frame, but they were far from out of the woods. "Go," he told his companion. Reasoning it would be better for the young man to have a helper on either side of him, as fond of Mason as the wolf had quickly become, he didn't trust his abilities quite as much as he had done the Volendrians. He couldn't imagine many safer places than having a witch on the one side and a wolf on the other, but then even if he lacked the bloodlines – Mason had been raised as a prince.

Offering no protest, Mason too made his way onto the half rotten wooden path. Shifting one foot slowly after the other, until he was swallowed from sight. Once more Silas was left to wait, hopeful and silent until he heard, "I'm here."

Now there was little left to put off, though the idea of running home briefly crossed his mind at that point. He refused to show himself a coward any more than he already had that day, and it was time to face the music.

Silas touched boot to dark wood and began making his way down the bridge.

The process was an agonisingly deliberate one, a cold plunge would hardly have killed him, unless the waters happened to be flooded with silver and wolfsbane. But his earlier experience, as stupid and unnecessary as it had been left him shaken and uncertain of himself. Like the very wolf in him had been stripped without him knowing, and now he felt more vulnerable than he ever had done before.

Mason looked at him triumphant, and the wolf couldn't help but smile in response. Lifting the deer briefly to position it more comfortably now comfort could take precedence over being hurled into cold water. "Glad to be on hard ground?" It was the young man's turn to read minds it would seem.

"Infinitely," he admitted, digging the toe of his boot into the grounds a bit and kicking upwards. Allowing a little dirt to shower his friend in a playful gesture, drawing a sharp laugh from Mason in the effort. Hoping doing so would reiterate that he was absolutely fine, not just to himself but his companion.

The bright smile of the not quite prince told Silas he had been at least somewhat successful, but in terms of himself Silas wasn't quite so certain.

"Not far now," Lenore assured with something hinting at kindness to her tone. "If we can continue it won't even be dark before we reach Vergily."

This knowledge added something more spritely to his walk, and once more the trio set off through the woodland. Despite solid flooring now underfoot, Silas couldn't help but feel like his head was still swimming.

He could note the trees beginning to thin, and the grass grew longer here now that more light was visible through the heavy foliage overhead. But the first sign that the little woodland was coming to a close wasn't the sights nor smells. But rather the sounds.

Rather than the soft, natural sounds of the woodland, a more distinct sound broke through the pleasant peace. Faint and distant, but quite distinguishable from the rest of their little world, the thrum of a city that felt unfamiliar to Silas, as though it had been an eternity since he had last seen one.

Once the trees had thinned off and the treeline became visible, Silas could see the sun setting over Vergily. Here he saw that it was less a city and more a quite humble village, but still he could spot the people moving about the streets even from a distance. Their vantage point up in the woodlands above offering a fine opportunity to just sit and watch for the rest of time.

A darker feeling in Silas couldn't help but realise just how easy an attack could be launched from a point like this.

Either way, here was where they would leave their companion. The woman neither of them would have been alive without. Silas turned, setting his gaze on the Angofwen queen, a voice lit with gratitude broke the silence. "Thank you for everything, Lenore," he offered, bowing his head respectfully. In spite of it all, his thankfulness was truly sincere.

And despite all of the experiences the last day together had brought her, Silas found his sincerity reflected in her blazing eyes. "It has been a pleasure to meet the both of you, though hopefully someday it might be during happier times so we can better get to know one another." She returned, though her gaze didn't flick to Mason, Silas believed to some extent he was included in that offer.

"You too," Mason dipped his head more respectfully than Silas had expected to see of his companion, but then he turned his gaze onto Silas. "Come on, let's get going." It was less a demand more a statement, and something Silas understood the urgency of. If battle had begun so close, it might not have been long before it spread to here as well.

"You might as well take this with you," Silas thought as an afterthought, taking the bow and arrow set from Mason and handing it back to Lenore.

She thought for a moment, "Are you sure? It might prove to be of some use to you," she insisted, moving to hand it back.

Silas only shook his head, though looked to Mason for confirmation and found him doing a similar thing. "We're both useless with it, it will prove to be more a hindrance than it is a help," he replied and was grateful when she accepted this and shouldered it. "That and we're probably in far too much debt to you and your people already, might as well try and pay some of it back whilst we can.

Lenore merely shook her head, "Not a debt, a friendship," the elder woman corrected, and Silas beamed childishly at this. "Now hurry on," she said, Silas understood this was probably someone who didn't enjoy overly long farewells.

Mason departed first, casting a glance and a final wave back at the Queen as he moved through the long grass, and Silas had moved to follow him, when an arm grasped gently to his long sleeve. He looked back to find Lenore watching him carefully one final time.

"Do remember child," she said gently now they were out of hearing distance. "You're free of your chains now," she explained in a dark but meaningful tone that left goose bumps flickering across Silas' muscled arms. "Don't be so scared of yourself, see what you truly are."

Silas grimaced at the further insistence, looking to his feet as he sought the answers that might not have left their friendship in a bitter light. He found something he thought might work, parted his lips and looked up, only to find out he was already too late

For the Angofwen Queen was already gone once again.

Chapter Sixteen.

Alone again, the pair descended upon Vergily in silence.

Behind them the sun began setting, the dim light fading as they crossed through the little towns entrance gates. No one was there to oppose them, aside from a handful of people enjoying the last of the dying light, it didn't seem that anyone was there at all. Had it not been for those few people the wolf wouldn't have been surprised to learn that they had stumbled upon a ghost town.

The village was small, compact like Cresvy but on a lower level. Though the smell here didn't quite resonate as terribly as it had done at home, here it smelled like fresh morning dew and stone. Aside from the general rumble of life that Silas had heard from a distance, this place was peaceful. It seemed like a distant universe from where the Caravan attack had occurred.

Some of the tension released from Silas for the first time in what felt like an eternity, here he felt safe enough to lay down his guards. The biggest threat that could be offered here it would seem was twisting an ankle on the uneven dirt roads. Even if vastly different, this place felt almost like home.

"Let's see if we can find a shop," Mason expressed his plan of action quietly, "If Brynde is going to be anything like Malowa, I don't know how easy it will be to find anything we need without drawing attention," he reasoned quietly. "Might as well try to stock up here, and only find things when absolutely necessary."

Offering a nod of his head, it was all reasonable. He gestured to the doe still settled across his back, "What do you think we should do with this?" He asked, though not overly heavy it was becoming rather annoying to tote it around like some macabre decoration.

Mason considered to point briefly, only to shrug his shoulders. "I guess we could sell it, we don't really need the money given we still have what the King gave us," he touched a hand to the deer's side. Studying it up close for the first time, and to his credit didn't grimace when he came into contact with it as Silas might have expected of a man like the not quite Prince. "I think it'll fetch a reasonable price," he added with the tone of someone who had very little idea of what a reasonable price might be.

The young man had lived a life in which everything he wanted had been paid for him, not something Silas blamed him for but still an amusing point. Rather than voice those opinions aloud, he nodded his head wordlessly, his gaze constantly travelling, less out of concern and more out of curiosity for what this oddity of a village might have to offer.

Allowing their feet and noses to choose the paths, they had no idea of what direction to follow but time was somewhat limited. If the King had been correct it would take a day to get to Brynde from here, and then a further two to get on to Rehenney. With a maximum of ten days to get there they should theoretically have plenty of time, but Silas wasn't going to put the idea that something might go wrong to bed just yet.

Though the brief trip with the Angofwen had saved them at least half a day of time, Silas was ever aware it would only take one trip up for that extra time to be lost, if the past two days had taught him anything it was that time was a commodity when war was on the horizon.

Instinct, hungry bellies and a strong sense of smell drew them through the town. Weaving through small houses for the most part but nothing of interest aside from the occasional inn, not exactly what they hoped to spend their money on.

Until their feet eventually took them to something akin to a town square, where the narrow dirt roads opened into a central area, shops littered the sides and people wandered between them. Peaceful, no one noticed the entrance of the Lycan and the almost Prince.

Much of it was little market stalls similar to his mothers, but to the far corner was a large stone building, about which a variety of people lingered on the steps of. Further scents of food stuffs wandered towards the pair on the breeze, leaving Silas licking at his lips.

Nodding in the direction of the shop, the wolf tugged on his friends sleeve and lead the way through the gathered crowds. Most of whom happily soaking in the suns dying rays before they returned home for the night, few paid either of them little in the way of attention.

The pair pushed through the shops wooden doors to be presented with the pleasant smells of herbs, freshly baked bread, and a handful of meats still roasting above the fire. That same fire cast the room in a dark golden light and left the shop rather warm. Silas took the opportunity to shrug the coat from his back and hang it upon a provided hook by the doorway. He did, however, quickly returned the rucksack for safekeeping, that and the money was tucked carefully into one of its pockets.

He had briefly forgotten that a deer rested upon his broad shoulders and realised it might well have been rude to carry the carcass into a clean shop. But when he was neither stopped nor scolded, he quickly placed that too beside the gathered coats, and followed deeper into the stone shop.

Keeping back, Silas allowed his companion to approach the counter and begin conversing with the gentleman working behind it. He kneaded a large piece of dough carefully on the counter and greeted the pair with a cheerful tone of voice.

"Good evening," Mason greeted, appropriating a less formal tone of voice than Silas had thus far become accustomed to. "We're going on a journey for a few days, and wondered what you might suggest we take with us in way of provisions?" He asked, allowing the vendor to lead them down the path of what they'd need, as in truth neither of them had too much of an idea. Especially if they didn't want to survive the next few days off a loaf of bread and deer alone.

Happy to leave his companion to negotiate, Silas allowed his gaze to wander. The scent of fresh bread emanating from the counter was tantalising, and left him licking at his lips, salivating slightly at the combined sight and sound.

The pastries were ornate, from those woven into braids, to the ones decorated with little dried fruit pieces in little patterns. He doubted they would have the money to branch into the more elaborate items, it seemed a waste of somebody else's money, but that didn't mean he couldn't appreciate the hard work of another.

"Good, aren't they?" the baker asked when he spotted the wolf ogling the bread pieces, a kind if slightly amused grin lighting his expression.

"Incredible," Silas breathed in turn. "I've never seen anything like it!" He exclaimed, allowing a soft laugh of his own at how childish he sounded. Though after the couple of days he had, he could hardly be blamed for enjoying himself just a little, especially following all the stress and fear. A little joy couldn't be scoffed at, no matter where it could be found.

The baker only grinned with a nod, and continued his negotiation and conversing with Mason, happy to leave the wolf in his own little world of exploration.

Forcing himself away from the pastries, namely for fear he might well have begun drooling over the fresh baked goods and have to pay for them anyway. His gaze wandered briefly over the meat section but found it largely unexciting. Thus, straightening, he moved to stand beside his companion once more. To see the baker quietly bagging up some loaves of bread, and some wrapped variants of meat he couldn't tell the source of through the brown papers.

Seeing that, he asked in a polite tone, gesturing back to the deer at the doorway. "Do you have any use for that?" He queried, reckoning this would likely be the best place to ask.

Looking up from where he was finishing up, the baker looked to the felled animal briefly, only to shake his head. "Sorry, we have an arrangement with the Brynde mayor and a few of the farmers that I'll get the meat from there, it'll turn heads and I'll get into trouble if I'm seen selling that." Despite his negative answer, his tone seemed genuinely apologetic.

It was hardly heart-breaking news; the wolf only shrugged his shoulders. "Not a problem, thanks anyway," if worse came to worst they would just leave it to the first finder somewhere out in the square. There was little use in keeping it, neither Mason nor Silas knew how to skin a deer from scratch, and the effort of portioning it into meat and cooking it, as well as having to further carry it for who knew how many lives, it was too much effort for their short but exhausting journey.

"But," the baker added after thinking for a moment, handing the bag over to Mason which he quickly placed inside his large rucksack. "If you turn left outside the shop and travel down the street a short way, you'll come across an Alchemists, they might have some use for it, I know the owner – Elizabeth, she'll give you a fair price for it if she can find use to it."

For a moment Silas contemplated saying no, they were in enough of a rush without having to go on some wild goose chase for what might not work in the end, but before he could Mason nodded his head. "Thank you, we'll give that a shot," he replied with a smile. Looking to Silas while he asked, "How much did you say that was?"

The vendor gave a price, and Silas withdrew the little leather bag their savings were kept within and passed it to Mason, allowing him to do the counting given it had never been his personal strong point, "Is that good?" The other man asked somewhat awkwardly, glancing back at the wolf.

He shrugged his shoulders, he considered it a fair price. The sellers in Cresvy would have sold a rat for the price of a house if they thought they could get away with it, so the honesty was refreshing and something he appreciated. "It's good," he nodded, smiling to the baker hoping he wouldn't take too much offence in how outright Mason had asked the question.

If the baker was offended, he was more concerned on getting a sale than giving the youngsters in his store a lesson on manors. He gratefully accepted the money and watched as the pair turned for the door once more, "Goodbye, and good luck!" He called as they departed.

Silas smiled back at him, "Thank you," he said once more, before following Mason through the shops exit, in the marketplace once more, the rucksack and felled deer returned to his shoulders.

In the brief period of time they had been within the shop, the sun had already set below the horizon. The square now darkened and gloomy, but a handful of people still remained in the town square. Setting about gathering their things in order to return home.

Mason had turned left, but Silas called to him before he could set off down the little street they had been directed down. "Is it worth going to that much effort, or should we just find somewhere to leave this and continue on to Brynde?"

"I thought about it," Mason admitted lowly. "But he said it was an alchemist, we might be able to find a few things that we can use for our journey, healing herbs and the like which might come in handy if things go... well wrong," he added, running his fingers through his hair, the wind battering at it making it look rather unruly. "Your mum taught you something about herbs, yeah?" He asked hoping for affirmation that his idea was a decent one.

Silas agreed somewhat, he would hardly be able to save someone's life if something went severely wrong, but it might be useful to have a few things that could help if something mild went wrong. An herb that might help aching feet would be particularly helpful if they were able to come across something that specific.

"I'm hardly a doctor," he replied sheepishly, "But I see what you mean. I think it's worth the time," he confirmed, and with that the pair departed down the street to the left of the little store.

The street narrowed once more now, the stones underfoot turning unstable into narrow cobblestone paths. It was darkened, no lights offering an explanation of when and where the unfamiliar paths would weave left and right, so Silas took the lead. His sharper eyes better adapted at seeing through the dark, though Mason kept pace just behind him fairly easily.

It only took a short while before they found themselves in the wake of the small stone shop, its outside was no different to any of the other shops they had been graced with in their time in the little village. But etched into the wooden signs on its storefront demonstrated this place was a different one, the sun and crow that demonstrated an alchemist's abode.

Exchanging a look with his companion, the pair entered.

Almost immediately Silas was flooded with the heavy scents of herbs, contrasting with the familiarity of his mother's home, here it made him almost nauseous. Bombarding his nostrils until he had to make an effort in order not to grimace visibly under the harsh scents.

He looked around, but it seemed only the pair of them were here.

"Is anyone here?" Silas called into the darkness, but no response came, and he looked to his companion, confused. "What should we do?"

"Maybe she's gone home for the evening?" Mason responded, uncertain. It was late, and Silas could have understood and willingly taken that as an explanation. But something in him told him that it was something quite different. "Come on, let's go."

But Silas didn't respond, instead prying further into the shop, ignoring the young mans called warnings. Something didn't feel right, and he wouldn't have liked leaving without finding out what was wrong.

He wove through the high bookshelves, stacked to breaking point with books, jars and flowers until Silas was impressed the wood holding them up was yet to collapse. He found his way to something that looked like a counter and peered around it nervously.

What he saw their tore a shout from his lips without him having ordered his body to yell. "Mason, I've found her!" He yelled.

There against the wood, a woman lay motionless, dead to an unobservant eye, but a careful study made Silas spot the rise and fall of her chest. He lunged forward, in the back of his conscious mind he remembered hearing his friend respond but couldn't have pinpointed exactly what for all the money in the world.

Gentle fingers found the spot beneath her chin, there he felt a wavering pulse. So weak he thought at first he had imagined seeing the rise and fall of her chest, but eventually found the rhythmic sensation and sat up.

Strong hands finding their points on her chest, he began pumping up and down hard. Desperately trying to force her heart into beating once more, the unconscious woman writhed beneath his touch but was otherwise unresponsive.

By then Mason had come to join them, and a surprised shout ripped from his own lips. "Good Gods," he panted, kneeling beside the woman's head, parting her lips and attempting to force air into her lips. Lifting upright again only after every few beats before beginning again.

Just as Silas was beginning to give up hope and leave her be, the woman lurched upright with surprise.

Stumbling backwards, his hands held up in surrender in case they were about to receive a scolding for their intrusion. Even if they had no doubt saved her life, Silas knew not to assume that kind of thing. The stranger – assumedly Elizabeth unless she had been a burglar went terribly wrong.

Elizabeth gasped harshly for a few moments, before dragging herself upright relying on the counter for aid. "Thank you," she said as an afterthought, as she might have done to someone delivering her the newspaper not the two men who had saved her life. "And how can I help you today?" She asked, forcefully casual she leaned against the counter. Either in an attempt to look at ease, or because her shaking legs struggled to keep her upright currently.

Silas had to restrain himself from laughing out of the ludicrousness of the situation, he regarded the woman as one might have someone who had recently sprouted antlers out of the blue. She looked him in turn through narrowed eyes, tense and uncomfortable.

"You're a lycan," it wasn't worry in her tone necessarily, but she had the good sense to be weary when she spotted it.

The wolf cringed under the observation, shifting on the spot and half expecting that to be enough grounds for this alchemist to have them kicked out of the little shop.

"And you're the alchemist, and I'm Mason – that's Silas if you care about that at all" it was Mason who replied, seemingly already growing bored of this common conversation he'd heard already. "We've helped you now would you be so kind as to help us?" He wiped his sleeve across his lips, Silas looked to the garment to see it was now stained in dark colours. "And you can do that by explaining first what the hell just happened?"

Elizabeth merely shrugged her shoulders. Pushing long golden locks behind her ears, "I'm an alchemist, you said it yourself, I was experimenting." She lifted a small goblet with a flourish from under the dark wooden counter, inside was a midnight blue, steaming liquid that turned Silas' stomach just to look at it, "I was trying to find out a means of reversing the rotting process in meats," she explained, looking disappointed more than she did perturbed by everything that had happened.

"It seemed it didn't work too well." She spoke as though this was a regular occurrence, something Silas wasn't sure if he should admire her for or worry about her sanity because of.

You can say that again, Silas silently hoped she would put the liquid away again. Just looking at it made him uncomfortable, everything from its scent to its colour looked entirely unnatural, he felt like just looking at it would make his skin corrode.

"I'm sorry for your loss," Mason's tone was mildly sarcastic, watching the cup of liquid as though it were prone to sudden hurling. "We wondered if you could help us," he explained further, stepping aside so that if this alchemist did decide to start throwing it would at least give him a minute to spot her intentions. "Me and my companion are journeying and were hoping you might provide some herbs for our journey, just in case we come across any maladies during our trip." Mason explained easily.

"Where are you headed?" Elizabeth asked, not moving for her shelves but rather withdrawing a great book from beneath the counter and pulling it open. A brief look inside made Silas notice it was a stock book of exactly what the shop held. He found this idea insane, given the size of the store and how randomly things seemed to be scattered about it, he could imagine any sort of book being accurate enough to keep stock of everything, even if updated regularly and carefully.

This was the sort of place that left the wolf with the sensation that things just randomly appeared in the shop and would stay there for the rest of their lives.

"A village east of Rehenney," Mason replied easily, Silas wasn't sure as to why he had elected to use a slight truth but said nothing for the sake of the lie. "Our sister has had a child, and we are going to give our congratulations."

Silas assumed it was better to give a reasonable lie than outright explain they weren't in a position to give away those details. He merely nodded, cementing those details into his mind in case they were asked again at a later time, so that they'd be able to keep a stable lie up, rather than end up convoluting the tale in a means that might get them into trouble at a later date.

But the alchemist watched them carefully, "That's a pretty short journey, surely you don't need herbs, can't take you more than a day to get there." She returned, as though she was able to smell the lie on the air as easily as Silas could.

"We're hypochondriacs," Silas returned, deadpanning in an attempt to appear believable.

For a moment it appeared the vendor would kick them from the shop without another word, "You're a lycan, last time I heard you don't hurt easy, at least nothing that won't heal," Silas forced his expression not to waver or change under her slight interrogations. "But then, I've never been someone to turn away a buyer," she said at last, something that let the tension release from Silas' shoulders. "Do either of you know much about herbal medicine?"

"My mother taught me some things, she's a doctor back home," Silas explained lowly, not wanting to come across as a complete newbie nor someone who could be taken advantage of and loaded with useless herbs they wouldn't need in a million years. "So I know some of the more basic herbs and what they can be used for, how to make poultices, that kind of thing." Silas explained, Mason stepped back letting him take the lead, as this was more the wolf's forte.

Thus, they continued, Silas explaining his brief understanding of herbs and their application. And in the end they came to an agreement on what would be a necessity for them to take with them on their journey. Willow bark, to ease pain in the case of injury, chamomile leaves for general maladies, ginger root to ease nausea and various other herbs that might help along the way. They were quickly portioned and bagged, before being offered to the pair.

"Thank you," Silas dipped his head, but then remembered the original reason for their entrance here. He pointed to the carcass he had deposited at the door, "The baker in the square mentioned you might have use for it?" He added.

Elizabeth leapt over the counter easily, her near death experience long forgotten it seemed as she had regained her strength. She considered the doe momentarily, "I think I can find some uses for it," she decided, moving to lift it from its position on the wood floor, but Mason stopped her.

"How do you hope to recompense us for it?" He asked, they were yet to exchange monies for the herbs, but didn't want it to be excluded from the equation if it might have saved them a few pennies here or there.

She chuckled, "Do you two have a shop of your own? You'd be good at it," she returned, straightening and thinking for a minute. "Consider it an exchange for the herbs," she decided with a shrug of her shoulders, "Would you find that an amicable trade?" She added, turning her gaze onto the pair, questioningly.

Mason grinned meekly in turn, "And the whole saving your life from your own idiocy aspect?"

Elizabeth considered briefly, eyes narrowing as though with true annoyance but there was something to the glitter behind her blue gaze that demonstrated a lack of true malice. "Consider it a debt to be paid off at a later date, now get out of here. I have a potion to perfect."

Silas turned to do just that but cast a glance back carefully. "If you're sure, we won't be back to make sure you're not dead any time soon?" His tone was playful, but carefully so. Not wishing to overstep any bounds, especially given that she had already proven to be cautious having noticed his true nature.

The alchemist bared her teeth at him in a grin that didn't spread to her eyes, but still she laughed. "I'll be fine, now get lost before I change my mind." She returned easily, and wordlessly the pair did just that.

Chapter Seventeen.

Stocks newly refilled, the pair headed north once more. It didn't take too long until Vergily was a distant memory, gone even from the horizon as the climbing hills hid the place from sight.

Darkness consumed everything, and Mason had tied a length of rope from his rucksack Silas' to ensure they wouldn't lose each other. Silas heard the gentle thud of his companion's feet, but even he couldn't see the human from this distance.

Even the lightest breeze sent it whipping about and might well soon be leaving them black and blue. But instinct left him fairly certain he wasn't about to drop face first off a cliff edge, but his companion wasn't so fortunate.

In order to keep his friend safe, the rope remained in spite of how annoying it was.

The woodland that had provided their cover for the past few miles grew sparse now, leaving Silas feeling as though they were vulnerable to the very rabbits

Mason's pace was admittedly frustrating, his human feet beginning to drag as the ascent grew all the more harsh. That and the terrain was far from ideal, mud disguised rocks which meant the pair were prone to stumbling every other minute, whilst Silas didn't want to hold his companions more human aspects against him, he found it increasingly difficult as he wished to speed ahead, whilst Mason seemed to linger in his wake.

"If we make it to the peak of this hill range," Mason said between poorly stifled gasps for air, Silas aiming to remain patient as he moved alongside the young man. "We should be able to see the Godsgather plains, and Brynde will be just before it." Despite his clear exhaustion, Silas could hear the hope in his tone, and smiled lightly.

"It won't be that far I'm sure," he added with the hopes of reassuring.

Not stopping as he manoeuvred to take the map from his rucksack, he acted as though he had something to prove. A losing game when playing against a wolf, but Silas had already slowed his pace so much that he felt like he was actively having to stumble over his own feet in order to keep shoulder to shoulder with his friend.

Lifting the lantern to the parchment, he studied the little map with great care. Considering in silence for a moment, Silas kept his distance, waiting for news with the best façade at patience he was able to muster.

"The little creek you heard a few hundred metres back is there," he jabbed at a point on the map Silas couldn't decipher. "So, unless there's another nearby, the peak should be visible within an hour or so," he decided through narrowed eyes. "And then we should have climbed over it within at least three," he finished with a half-smile as transparent as the waters they had crossed not long ago.

More for the sake of Mason not exerting more energy than he needed to rather than the necessity of it, silence dwelled over the pair like a heavy shadow once more. Occasionally his companion would gasp harshly, as though having forgotten to breathe in the first place though in truth it was from his desperate attempts to keep his panting under lock and key.

By then he had only just begun to break a sweat, when he offered quietly to Mason. "If you want to take a break, grab something to drink, I won't hold it against you," Silas said. Pulling his collar up against the blustering wind, all the more prominent the further they climbed against the steep hills.

Something like hope sparked once more in his gaze but dimmed again quickly. "Not for my sake," he insisted with a grimace. Quickening his pace as though to prove he was entirely fine, "If we do well we can find somewhere to sleep in Brynde, maybe even with this famous Gregory and get some decent sleep," he reasoned, the word sleep made Silas' heart quicken in turn. It was something he pined for, the last couple of days already left him drained and exhausted.

But he wanted his friend's health to come before anything else. "It's already dark," he insisted. Running his fingers through his hair, he hated himself for the words that next came from his lips. "I don't mind sleeping at the peak, but it might be worth taking a break just to drink and gather our thoughts for a moment."

If Silas was certain he was going to lose his mind from the monsters he swore he could see dancing about the midnight plains, he had no idea how his friend was managing to remain sane. "That and it will give us a chance to catch our breaths and rub sore feet," even the wolf's boots were beginning to wear sores into the soles of his feet. He would appreciate the chance to relieve a little of that pain, and even if Mason refused to admit it he was more than certain the young man was in a similar boat.

Yet still Mason seemed uncertain, Silas could almost hear the shake of his head even if he couldn't see it through the darkness. But when the silence went prolonged for a few moments, he had reason enough to find hope sparking again in his chest.

"Fine," he grumbled lowly, clearly unhappy about being the slow one in the relationship, despising having to burden the little party with lingering. "But we're only resting, we can set up camp on the peaks. It'll be safer there anyway," he reasoned, clearly trying to convince himself over the already long persuaded Silas.

"Whatever you say," he said and before the latter word had pulled free of his lips, he had thumped bottom to ground and intended to stay there as long as he could steal. For his companion's sake he wanted to let them catch their breaths and consider their next steps, that and he too was desperate to let his aching legs rest for a moment. "Do you want an apple to eat while we wait briefly?" He asked, allowing a grin to tug the corner of his lips upright a touch.

"If I must," he grumbled though with no true annoyance to any part of his words and caught the apple Silas through to him and began chewing gratefully. The would-be Prince considered briefly, so much so that Silas could hear the cogs whirring in his brain, before asking. "If you were wanting to build a fire, a brief one, I would not be opposed," the shiver to his voice was more apparent now he was able to catch his breath some.

The more human aspects of his companion were becoming clearer, and Silas had to remember that if he didn't want his friend to freeze to death. He was of the increasing opinion that the young man would rather freeze to death or die of exhaustion than he would have admitted that he wasn't as strong as he liked to believe and was in need of a little help.

Not about to scold him for such, Silas set to work building what he could of a fire. That and even the wolf could feel the cold beginning to seep through his silver jacket.

Fortunately, the grass here was reasonably dry, and the tinder they'd bought from the baker's shop was dry enough for the sparks to catch. It was small, a pitiful sight to an outsider but they were more than happy despite its pathetic size. Grateful for the heat it emitted, both of them huddled close to the bristling flames.

Soon the roaring crackle of burning wood and dried leaves broke the night-time, offering light through which Silas could better see the exhausted expression darkening his friend's expression.

Letting the flames dry him, he was content now to be in silence. Soaking in as much warmth as he could before Mason decided it was time to get moving once more, but it seemed that silence wasn't on the agenda of his travelling companion, as a gentle voice broke the quiet.

"Sy?" a voice began tentatively. The tone of someone not entirely sure he wanted to ask what he was about to ask, instinct telling him not to whereas curiosity was tugging him closer in spite of that.

Uncertain, he looked up mid chew. "Yeah?"

For a moment Mason didn't answer, and the wolf would have been happy to pretend he'd never heard the starter in the first place. Until a somewhat sheepish tone was heard once more. "Why don't you shift?"

Admittedly that brought a frown to his face, a couple of days of friendship was great but he never usually revealed these things unless necessary. And there was a genuine part of him that feared he might lose a good friend if he did dare to explain in further detail more than what he had already departed with in that short time.

"You don't have to tell me," he added quickly, shifting in his spot as though desperate to occupy his hands, like momentary lapse in movement might have made him explode from the embarrassment. Those green eyes pierced Silas' skin once more as he added, "I was just curious. I mean if it were me, I'd be desperate for a skin outside of this one, I'm useless next to you. If you stripped of the silver, I don't think I'd dare be on the same hilltop." He attempted a laugh, but it sounded dull and fell flat.

That's the very reason I don't want to shift, he responded in his head, *enough people are scared of me, I'd rather not add to the list*.

Using his apple as an excuse, he continued chewing it long after it had been swallowed in order to steal a little more time to think over the question. Think of a way to respond that wouldn't hurt his friend's feelings.

What he eventually came out with was the truth, but a small part of it. Happy to keep some secrets to himself for the time being, his voice was quiet, only just audible to the human senses over the soft crackling flame. "I killed people before I was put in these chains," he explained lowly. "And I have no solid proof that such isn't exactly what I would do when I take them off, and only when I do," *if I ever do*, "Am I willing to even try it."

"You said you were a kid when it last happened," Mason insisted with a little more confidence now, but his words remained kind. "You'll be under more control now surely?"

He simply shook his head, "That might be true," he was man enough to admit that much. "But what if age does nothing accept strengthen my body and weaken my mind?" He challenged in turn, though his tone remained gentle. "When I was young, I was easier caged, easier stopped. But now I'm full grown, and for all I know I will be all the more unstoppable," with frustration he hurled his finished apple core into the darkness. Hearing it thud to the ground somewhere in the distance, his silver gaze fixed to the dancing flames in front of them.

"For all I know is the minute I take this silver off is the minute I lose…" he trailed off, a lump forming in the back of his throat that he couldn't quite swallow, nearly choking on it. "The minute I get rid of the silver I might just get rid of myself, and that's not something I'm willing to test." He finished, sitting back and avoiding eye contact at all costs.

The truth of the matter was that there weren't enough lycans in the world for a particular study to be conducted to find out the answers he had been asking since the day this happened. And the one he had ever met, had been killed almost as soon as their encounter, though the scars it had left him with still lingered more than the curse it had implanted.

Seeming to accept this answer, the young man remained quiet a few beats longer before adding. "I'm sorry I asked," in someone else's tone it might have sounded insulting or rude. But Mason made it sound sincere, and Silas took some comfort in his assurance.

He shook his head mournfully; pity was the one thing he never wanted. "Don't be, I'm happy enough like this," he lied. But a chained life was better than no life, and that's all he would be left with if he tested these things and they went poorly.

The pair proceeded their brief moment to rest in silence, Silas liked to hope his companion remained quiet due to trying to regain as much energy as he could. But a darker part of him was all too aware that the reason came from a sadder reason than that. Silas concentrated on the crackling fire, content in its warmth and trying to focus his thoughts just about anywhere else.

After a short while, Mason lurched onto his feet. "Come on," he decided seemingly out of nowhere. "Let's get going, we can have a proper sleep when we're at the peak," Mason stated, and Silas was neither willing nor in the mood to argue.

"Give me a minute," Silas answered, "You get packed up I'll find some water to dowse the fire with," he didn't see the point in using what could be difficult to come by drinking water, if they were able to find a local water source to use it. Pulling the spare canteen from his pack, he stood upright and continued down the hillside a short way. Tracing his own scent in order to return to the little creek they had come across a short while ago.

It wasn't difficult to find, the sound of rushing water lead, the way alongside his own scent. It took him only a few minutes to find it, and he knelt down to gather some of its liquid.

But as he looked down, a soft sigh pulled free from him.

Now the moon had arched further into the sky, it shone down quite beautifully onto the clear surface of the little creek. And as the wolf knelt before it, he spotted his own reflection for the first time in a few days.

In honesty the person he saw staring back was unfamiliar. On a day to day basis the wolf had been someone who despised looking at his own reflection, though not out of ego. Now he could see the scars lacing his skin – he wasn't sure if it was just because he hadn't seen himself in a few days and had thus forgotten their severity, but the man looking back at him was a stranger. His thick hair a mess and his moon kissed gaze glinting in the faint light.

Silas grumbled to himself, smacking out at the water and sending droplets flying in smooth blow. It blurred the reflection and he pushed away from the riverbed, shaking his head with frustration.

He felt like a child for his immature show of frustration, and quickly moved to dry his hand upon his dark shirt. "For the love of the Gods," he muttered to himself, shaking his head as he filled the little canteen up. It wasn't natures fault that he couldn't stand the sight of his own reflection tonight of all nights.

Returning to his feet, the young man turned and began retracing his steps. Thanking the Gods that no one had been around to spot his moment of childishness, he would have been happy to forget the little incident for the rest of his life.

Their little makeshift camp had been tidied to the extent that outside of the fire and Mason standing beside it soaking in the last amount of warmth he could, Silas would have struggled to pinpoint the fact that there had been a camp there in the first place. The place still stank heavily like the pair of them, lacing the very area despite how short they had been there for, but no one else would be able to pick up on that. Anyone who might be following wouldn't be able to pinpoint their tracks from this place alone.

Dumping the canteens contents across the fire, it sizzled and roared with frustration at the attempt on its life, but the efforts were short lived. Silas swiftly went about kicking dirt over the ashy pit, and soon the pair were ready to leave. Any suggestion they had ever been there in the first place all but wiped from the area.

"Everything good?" Mason asked, too knowingly for Silas' tastes.

He can't know. "Fine," his response was quick and too defensive, it wasn't as though he had committed some atrocious crime. If self-hatred was a crime he would have been put away a long time ago, and unless his crime for being a lycan had been acquitted without him being told, Silas assumed he could get off scot free to that extent. Of all the worries he put into the world, that was at the very bottom of a rather long list.

Shouldering his backpack once more – only an additional weight to those that already burdened his broad shoulders. The pair set off once more into the midnight black, following the ascent of the hills in silence.

Their energy, or at least Mason's, now renewed tenfold. Their journey took a quicker and easier pace, especially as the steep ascent of the landscape began to lessen underfoot. Their path became winding and relatively easy to the difficult initial few miles they travelled, and Silas could actually feel his aching feet at that point which offered great relief. Though the sores would remain for a few further hours, they weren't as bad as they had been.

As they ascended, the winds grew ever the more bitter and Silas pulled up his collar against the howling winds. Mason took a moment to remove a spare coat from his backpack and pull it on, preferring that against the chances of freezing to death on this lonely hilltop.

When it felt like an eternity had passed, though up here they had little concept of time given the difficult to spot moon. The peak finally came into view, the midnight sky seemed to part to reveal the edge of the hills, beyond which they could finally begin their descent into Brynde.

The pair instinctually sped up, excited for the journey to be over as well as hoping to catch sight of the city they had sought for so long. It took only ten minutes for them to be at the very top, and now the sight of the valley bellow took the breath from their lungs.

Both had known Brynde as the walled city, the capital of the surrounding areas it took great pride in who it let in and out. But this close it was a sight neither of them could have imagined, as it took even Mason's breath away at the sight of it.

It was massive, the magnitude of the city unlike anything Silas had ever been before. Set in the great valleys just a few miles from Godsgather, its glowing lights shone even from the distance the pair found themselves at.

"It's beautiful," Silas said for the first time, genuinely in awe.

Mason merely nodded, though not out of spite did he continue his silence, rather genuine surprise at the sight it would seem. After a few heartbeats of silence, he said lowly. "Do you still want to sleep here and descend in the morning?" He asked.

Urgency was part of what he said next, but also a want – a need, to get closer and find out more. The city seemed to draw him in, it had a gravity that was difficult to resist. "No," he admittedly sheepishly, wanting to take off at a run if anything.

Though he would have happily done so if his companion had expressed a wish to stay, from the expression on the young man's features, Silas knew they were in agreement.

"Me neither," Mason responded with a meek laugh. "Come on, let's go."

Chapter Eighteen.

The descent into the Brynde valley wasn't the problem, compared to the harsh steep hills of the journey prior it might as well have been a walk in the park comparatively.

Once they were in the foothills, however, it became apparent just how difficult this portion of the journey was going to prove to be. The walls towered into the skyline, at least a dozen metres tall and a good few feet thick. Those stone walls circled the half of the city facing the hills, and the back half was flanked by a great lake, with the flat valleys of Godsgather visible in the distance. Entrance without invitation seemingly impossible.

Silas could only hope toting the King's seal and ward would be enough to grant them access.

The pair made their way towards the great city, but closer inspection demonstrated that the walls wasn't the only obstacles. For windows marked the walls every handful of metres, and at each one a guard stood, armed and waiting with the first guns Silas had seen since he had departed from Cresvy.

It seemed that Brynde hadn't heard word that war was cancelled.

Forcing himself not to cower in the shadow of these walls, Mason lead the way as they skirted the walls at a distance, until they found their way to a great pair of metal gates. Etched high into the wall face, shining in the pale moonlight.

Despite it being in the midst of the night, it seemed they weren't the only ones trying to gain access.

A line of people laced a good few metres of the wall, men and women, young and old, able bodies and crippled. People of all sorts had flocked to the city; they too had heard of war on the horizon, Silas assumed. Thus, here they waited, desperate and uncertain of what their world was coming too.

The pair folded into the line silently, muddied and exhausted – they became invisible against a mass of strangers. They remained shoulder to shoulder, amid the pushing and tussling it would have been all too easy to lose one another.

Even if they were here to help, Silas could barely shake the feeling that they were in enemy territory. A bizarre concept given that this of all places should have been the safest spot they had been in the last couple of days, yet Silas struggled to keep his calm all the same.

Brynde, unless something drastic had happened in the last couple of days, was one of the major cities in the area, and a stronghold for the King's barracks, that was clear enough from the number of people that laced the tall walls. An attack here would only be done by an insane man, but that didn't render attack an impossible concept. The guards atop the walls weren't pointing their guns at the grass and stone underfoot, and the slightest toe out of line would no doubt bring a rain of bullets down upon them.

However, no one about them seemed in much of a position to even try. Exhausted and decrepit, Silas couldn't help the surge of pity which ricocheted through his system. They sought the safety of the city for it didn't appear they had many other places to go. These were farming communities and distant villagers that didn't harbour in the comfort of Brynde but the outskirts, without the good fortune of walls to protect them from the oncoming storm.

Silas wanted to lift his head back and shout, that war wasn't coming, that it had been prevented and that there was no need to hide or seek solace or abandon their homes. But he knew he had no other choice but to keep quiet and blend in.

Progression was slow, at good few dozen people in front of them at that point. Silas wasn't sure if he should have been grateful that he had declined a sleep at the hilltops for it would only have added to the line they had to stand in, or disappointed at the time he could have used for sleeping was instead wasted on standing about, bored out of their minds. However, there was some gratitude to be found in the fact that at least they could stand still, after a couple of days of heavy travelling, it was some relief to know they'd be here for at least a little while.

Or at least if they were allowed entrance.

Just in their short period here, Silas had seen families be turned away for no rhyme or reason outside of the whims of the guards. Silas prayed they would believe that they needed to converse with the city mayor, if they couldn't, the wolf couldn't begin to imagine what they were going to do.

But now wasn't the time for worrying, as the truth of the matter was there was little they could do to change the minds of the guards, all they could do for now was sit and wait. Silas forced those exact thoughts through his head as best as he could, refusing to allow himself too much time fretting over things that he couldn't presently change.

By the time they had managed to progress towards the front of the line, the moon had set, and the sun was now beginning its steady ascent into the sky. Now flames about the kingdom were put out, and Silas could get a better look of what they were faced with.

Oddly enough the great stone walls were no less intimidating this close, but he saw the faded oranges and browns of their heights. He familiarised himself a little better with the landscape outside of the city walls, long rolling open fields with a single proper path leading up to the gates. Though they remained at the back of the line, no new joiners yet to occupy the space behind them. Silas could see the spots on the horizon that demonstrated he and Mason would be far from among the last.

The great gates that parted the walls weren't the only obstacle in that regard. Rather, there were a second pair of smaller gates in between. Where searches and questioning occurred, a single group permitted in at a time, which would usually take a handful of minutes before being turned away or permitted in. More often than not the former option seemed to be the one chosen, but every time the metallic screeching of the second pair of gates sounded, Silas found a little comfort in the fact that at least there was a chance this might just work.

Finally, Silas and Mason were the people at the front of the line.

Stiff and uncertain but trying to façade at ease and surety, they didn't want to come across as having anything to hide nor as offering a reason to not be permitted entrance.

The initial set of gates were parted, the previous pair of occupants expelled and teary eyed. Silas tried not to pay too much attention to them, as he and Mason stepped through the mighty gates. Trying not to shudder as he crossed enemy lines.

"How many in your party?" A gruff voice sounded, and Silas looked to the source, a massive man armed to the bone, sitting behind a small desk that was so dwarfed by him it might well have been considered comical. He didn't look up from the sheet of paper in front of him, the quill clutched to tightly in his dark hand, Silas was impressed it didn't snap beneath the steel grip.

"Two, sir," Mason was the one to answer, quick but formal.

The scratching of quill on paper sounded, Silas resisted the urge to glance curiously at the paper. "Hmm," was the only response the blunt man offered in response to this. "You will be searched, no choice in the matter unless you want to be turned around off the bat," he explained as an afterthought. Bored by the process, but his tone gave little doubt as to whether there was the chance to argue.

Nodding, a pair of further guards stepped forward from behind the desk. They too were armed to the bone, but they offered something of a sympathetic look which Silas appreciated at the very least. He submitted himself to their prying hands, allowing them to search wherever they felt necessary, thanking the gods he had never been the ticklish sort.

His guard was a man of similar height and stature, commendable given the lack of lycan genes. But strong hands probed his frame, carefully checking every inch for any sign of a hidden weapon. Part of Silas panicked briefly, as though by some miracle an arrow or dagger might have appeared on his frame to offer reason for either guard to protest their entrance.

Had either guard thought to study him more, it would become apparent that Silas was someone who needed no concealed weapons, but his secret remained just that.

Silas stiffened with surprise when the man said, "This one's clean," before stepping back behind the desk once more. Mason's guard taking a moment further to do his checks, before proclaiming something of a similar sort.

Hopefully the light in the room was so poor that it was difficult to see the silver of his eyes, that or this trio didn't know the signs of a lycan. Either way the wolf thanked every deity he knew the name of that he wasn't simply shot and chained on the spot.

Moving shoulder to shoulder again, Silas had quickly learned that was where he felt the safest. They turned their gazes onto the guards once more, the wolf could only assume that the number of occupants in their party wasn't the only question, unless those who had been refused before were atrocious counters. He waited, silent, all too aware of every passing heartbeat.

"And why do you come to Brynde this fine day; a lovely holiday planned do you?" The sarcasm all but glowed from the head guard as he lifted his gaze for the first time from his paper and onto the companions. Behind them, Silas heard the quiet chuckling of the other guards, he inhaled slowly in an attempt to take control over something right now.

The quick exchange of glances offered the power of the conversation to Mason, who composed himself far easier than Silas as he replied with, "We are here to speak with the mayor, Gregory." He replied easily, as though it were the easiest think in the world.

Sat behind his desk, the man smirked like a cruel cat. "Ah of course, what times are best for you and I'll see if I can get that scheduled in for you!"

Neither the would-be Prince nor the wolf found this amusing, but the guards behind them clearly had never heard anything funnier in their lives. As optimistic as he tended to be, even Silas knew it wouldn't be that easy to gain entrance, and from the mocking tone of his guard he was all too aware he shouldn't get his hopes up.

"We're messengers from the King," was the killing blow offered so easily by Mason. Unblinking and unperturbed by the laughter of the guards, he was a man with a mission and wasn't about to have those efforts extinguished by the mockery of some idiots.

Silas might have been impressed were he not too busy being terrified.

To Mason's credit, that statement alone was enough to stop the guards' laughter in its tracks. As he turned his dark gaze onto the young man, as though trying to break him into admitting the lie just by a single look, and in fairness Silas wouldn't have been surprised to learn that tactic was something he'd found success in before. Those eyes could well have sparked fire just by glancing briefly over kindling, Silas could feel his skin boiling just by being under them for so long.

For the first time the guard lifted himself to his feet and moved around the desk, he came no closer than a metre, and leant comfortably against the desk. Arms crossed, and gaze observant as he considered this information briefly.

"And what proof do you have of that?" He pried, though his tone was kinder this time, but that wasn't much of a comfort when surrounded by three massive men armed to the teeth. At either side of them the two other guards had perked up, curiosity simmering from them as they moved closer. Not close enough to be in arm's length, but close enough that Silas' hair stood on end at their proximity, a warning of oncoming lightning.

Mason looked to Silas for the first time, and Silas needed no verbal order as he quickly pulled off his rucksack and began sifting through it. Finding the two envelopes, kept carefully pristine in their little pocket, the King's seal shining proudly on the fold. He pulled them out and passed them over, Mason took them gratefully.

The guard moved to take them, but Mason snatched them back before he had the chance. "We've been told only to permit Gregory to look at these letters," he explained not unkindly before allowing the Guard to take them. "Please, look but don't open. Our heads will be taken if they are found to have been tampered with."

If the guard had heard those orders, he made no acknowledgement of it as he took them.

Carefully rotating the letter, he held it carefully beside the flame to check the validity of the seal. Silas watched, barely daring to breathe as he studied the letters one by one. Saying nothing as he did so, though the guards in their wake continued gossiping quietly to themselves, the audience seemingly intrigued by the ongoing. Though he couldn't imagine life as a guard during times like this was an overly exciting role, but the way they were being watched made Silas' skin writhe with discomfort.

After an agonising and infinite wait, the guard spoke aloud again. "I'm going to need to open this," he said simply, and moved to do just that.

Silas didn't remember giving his legs the order to move, but suddenly he was close enough to hear the flutter of eyelashes every time the guard blink, which he suddenly did rapidly in surprise at just how quickly the wolf had moved. "I'm sorry but we can't let you do that," he explained simply, moving to take the letters back.

The guard blinked at him ludicrously, and from the audible pound of the older man's heart Silas knew he had taken him by surprise. "If that's the case, unfortunately I cannot grant you entrance." For now, the guards didn't move to kick them out, but Silas heard them tense in place with preparation.

All at once his mind began racing with ideas of what they might have to do if this altercation was enough to get them thrown from the kingdom. The idea of trying to either climb over or dig beneath the walls flew through his mind briefly, but those were both impossible and idiotic ideas. Brynde was impenetrable, and the walls would have been felled long ago had it been so easy to get into the walled city. This was their only chance, but what they would do if this failed, he had no idea.

"Joshua, Reese, take them out of here," he commanded lowly with a wave of his hand. The two guards moved to comply when Mason spoke again, more desperately this time, but the shake of his voice was audible only to Silas fortunately.

He shook his head, moving closer but not as aggressively nor as suddenly as Silas had done. "If you do this our King will not be happy," he insisted with a terrified tone, but it was falsified to an extent. Hoping his own worries might be passed onto the guard, plant a seed of uncertainty which would sprout into a massive tree, using which they might just breach those walls. It was hardly a lie, but the danger it would put the guards in would no doubt massively outweigh that either of the companions would be, but that wasn't information this trio needed to know.

"Imagine his response to learning his own messengers weren't even permitted through the gates, let alone aloud to have the mayor find out about what he has to say," Mason shook his head exaggeratively. His façade at worry enough to persuade even Silas.

The head guard's eyes narrowed to slivers, "If it were so important the King would surely understand my need to check your documentation," he countered as though it were the easiest thing in the world, depleting Silas' hope notably. "At times like this anyone could claim that, it's not all that difficult to create a false seal if you know the right steps and have seen one before," convoluted but Silas listened without stating such. "For all I know you are simply assassins sent to murder the mayor, and it would be on our heads for letting you in were you to succeed."

Beside him, Mason stiffened with discomfort at this. Knowing all of them were fair points even if they weren't applicable to either of them, or his lips parted to respond but for a heartbeat he failed to find anything convincing to fill the silence.

Again, the head guard moved to order his guards to get rid of them, but Silas interrupted before he had the chance.

"Surely the incredible guards of Brynde can manage with two people," he staggered over his own words, but hoped they sounded convincing enough to not be beheaded on the spot. "Anyone knows the stories of how incredible the guards of this city are," he hoped a little ego stroking would go in his favour. "Especially those surrounding the mayor, there can't be too much harm in letting us simply discuss with the mayor, and if our intentions really are malicious. Surely we won't be permitted within a hundred metres of him?" He reasoned, feeling like an idiot but a hopeful one.

The guard regarded them in silence again, and when his eyes narrowed a shade once more Silas was convinced that would be the end of their tenure within Brynde. But he wasn't about to give in that easily. Once more his head began racing to find something else to say to them, but fortunately it turned out to be unnecessary.

"Joshua," one of the guards stepped forward obediently. "Take these two to the mayor's quarters," he said with a defeated sigh, his gaze not once leaving either of their forms. "On your way stop by the barracks and gain some support," Silas could see the nod of the guard's head from the corner of his gaze. "And if they as much as put a toe out of line, have them chained and tell me," he finished. Crossing his arms and looking Silas directly in the eye, "I'll find great joy in placing their heads atop spikes."

The wolf had no doubt that the guard exaggerated even slightly.

"Yes sir," the guard nodded in agreement, turning to look at the pair once more. "Come with me." the pair happily followed the gentleman without complaint as the gates parted before them, revealing the true glory of Brynde through its entrance.

From a distance the city had been beautiful, up close it was nothing short of magnificent. Even the nicer parts of Cresvy would have been staggered in comparison, and the slums of his hometown would have wept at the sight of its extravagance.

It was uniform but beautiful, each house built from a similar red brick to the great wall surrounding and protecting them. Gardens marked the borders of each little home, in an identical means that should have been impossible but instead was awe inspiring.

The buildings which weren't homes were churches, cathedrals, shops and things of the like. Touching the skyline, with banners marked in colours of all kinds were strewn across them, even the little lampposts lining the streets had received a similar treatment. Each towering post marked with flowers tied to the foot of them.

But they weren't here to admire the scenery, and instead the guard turned left and continued down a particular street, and what they were faced with was what Silas could only assume was the ugliest part of the city.

Brynde's barracks was a fat, squat building. Lacking the colour that made the rest of the city beautiful, it was simplistic, matter of fact and fit for purpose, absolutely nothing else.

Joshua lead them through the great doors, boring dark wood that moved stiffly, resistant to let anyone into suffer the ugliness of its building up close. Succeeding in breaking through, the guard straightened, and bellowed orders into the darkness.

"Persons without orders, line up." The sound echoed through the small hall.

It took only minutes for people to respond, and soon no less than a dozen people were crowded into the little entryway. To the city's credit, it didn't seem much of the ego stroking had been exaggerated, they were quick to respond to orders, and ready to do what was necessary for their city.

"We are to accompany these two to the Mayors quarters," he explained the same bellowing voice, his gaze fixed only to a wall as he delivered his orders. "If they put as much as a foot out of line, they are to be escorted to only our finest cells, where they shall await execution."

Hearing that very word sent a shudder down Silas' spine, but he stood unmoving beside Mason.

Orders delivered and men gathered, their little regiment moved out.

The little group headed upwards, the city angled at a natural incline as they moved wordlessly towards the tallest building in the city, something Silas could only assume was their destination. No building so regal could have any other purpose that he could think of.

Every guard was armed to the teeth, and though Silas doubted they would carry silver on their person, he knew his friend wouldn't have the same protection.

That among other more obvious reasons, Silas didn't revolt. He moved obediently and silently up the paths towards the mayor's towers, doing his best not to as much as glance at either those surrounding them, nor his friend.

In comparison to the quarters, the rest of the city might well have been considered a dump. It was massive, enough to house a town in its very confines, with towers pointing skywards. Palace would have been a far more fitting word.

Joshua broke from the crowd as they made their way up the paths, a shout going up before he reached the great metal gates. Only smaller than those used to enter the city itself by a barely noticeable fraction. Adhering to his shouted orders, the great gates parted effortlessly.

Inside was even more beautiful, something Silas hadn't been capable of beginning to imagine. The floors a shining marble, and chandeliers lit the halls with candleflame. A spiralling staircase lead the way up to another floor, and paintings of every colour littered the walls. Those of past monarchs, landscapes, animals, everything. Silas could have spent a million years here, and he was certain every time he re-entered the room he would be able to find something new to admire.

"Wait here," Silas wasn't sure if the order was directed at him or the little army had accumulated, but the wolf did just that as the guard disappeared up the great staircase. They waited in silence for a while, only then did Silas and his friend dare to exchange a brief glance.

After a few minutes had past, Silas began to grow worrisome. Panicked that in spite of their efforts they would still be declined at this stage and hurled from the city, he couldn't imagine any other reason. Except perhaps that the palace was so large that Joshua struggled to pinpoint the whereabouts of the mayor, but that idea made him no less concerned.

Until finally the silence was broken by the sound of boots slamming against marble once more, accompanied by the lighter thud of less carefully guarded feet.

The man who accompanied Joshua wasn't as old as Silas had expected, but he was dressed in all the magnificence that the wolf had come to expect of a man of such stature. He came to the front of the guards, who parted obediently though by no more than a couple of inches in order to permit the mayors eyes to study the pair of them.

For a moment the mayor seemed to consider them, rubbing his chin with a long, pale finger. "Bring them to my drawing room," he decided after a beat, and without hesitation the guards began doing just that. Changing direction so jarringly Silas nearly stumbled over his own feet, as they were directed through the halls, past many rooms until they were stopped before a particular one.

"You may leave us alone in here, wait at the door." The mayor decided.

This decision surprised even Silas, the idea he would be so willing to be alone with the strangers and without help was a bizarre one. "I can take care of myself with just two people, and I will let you know if I need any help," he insisted, and the guards, whilst uncertain relented.

The mayor pushed the doors to his drawing room open and entered. The two friends shoved in as well behind him, the door slammed shut before they had the chance to take in their surroundings.

Whilst smaller, the room was beautiful too. Sofas lined one wall, and bookcases the other. Leather-bound books left the room smelling pleasant but ancient, and a mighty oak desk stood as a centrepiece to the room, behind which the mayor contently settled himself.

"I'm Isaac, how can I help you today?" As though he were doing them some great service.

Silas blinked at him slowly, confusion lighting his very bones. But as he was struggling to compile a sentence, Mason interrupted. "Isaac? We're here to see a Gregory?" The would-be Prince interrupted.

"Unfortunately, Gregory is unavailable at this time, do please tell me what your problem is, and I can see what I can do to help." If the man, Isaac, had been annoyed by Mason's insistence, he showed none of this on his stone features.

It was Silas' turn, shaking his head firmly. "I'm sorry, sir, but we're under orders. We can't do what we're here to do until we are in the presence of Gregory, we're not intending to be rude. But there is a lot standing on this," he explained quietly.

The man let out a sigh, shaking his head as he said lowly. "That's quite unfortunate, you see," he began lowly. "As unfortunately, Gregory was killed in his sleep two nights ago."

Chapter Nineteen.

The ricocheting shock might well have been attributed to grief under other circumstances, but it wasn't for the man who had been lost, as prior to a couple of days ago Silas had never met let alone heard of the man. Rather it was a pain that he connoted with a loss of a different kind, rather the fact they had come all this way, and now it might well turn out their efforts were fruitless.

Maybe in spite of all of this, war would come all the same.

Silas exchanged a fleeting glance with the man beside him, a surprise equating to terror reflected in the green gaze of his friend of the past three days. Neither of them could begin to comprehend this revelation, something between exhaustion and terror made them numb to the world.

"An assassin was able to get into his sleeping quarters and stab him, by the time morning came he was cold and none of us had any idea." Isaac explained with the casual tone of someone informing the pair about recent weather patterns, "Gregory was my father, and for the time being I am taking his role until word comes back from the King as to who he would prefer in his place, though we believe that will still be me." He added, a smile lighting his expression.

He wouldn't have minded smacking the smile off the man's face, but he remained statutory.

Beside him Mason began speaking again, recovering from the surprise quicker than his companion. "Unfortunately, I don't think you're going to be hearing back from the King any time soon," he explained in a quiet tone, "I am a ward of Ezekiel, and we returned from our journeys in Braxas three days ago," he revealed a lot all at once but none of it brought much of a reaction from Isaac outside of the occasional glint of surprise, but despite that Mason continued seamlessly.

"Our efforts there were successful, we were able to avert war and we are here to prevent plans from attacking Braxas going ahead," the words spilled from Mason like water from the skies. "But we were met with an ambush and a lot of us killed, the King survived but we have reason to believe those responsible were wanting to ensure those attacks did go ahead, and plunge Nekeldez into war."

As he finished, the young man removed one of the letters from his rucksack once more and presented it to the stand-in mayor wordlessly. The King's seal still shone atop its pale white paper, untampered with though not for want of trying from outside parties.

The makeshift mayor's expression remained steadfast as he listened to this, and if he were surprised by any of the information that Mason provided, he made no indication of such as he listened.

Isaac took the envelope, studied it briefly before slicing through the paper and reading through its contents. He looked up after a beat, gestured to the sofas settled in their wake and said a quiet, "Do sit," though it was an afterthought, his concentration clearly concentrated elsewhere.

Silas and Mason retreated a few metres to the back of the room and sat down on the sofas as ordered. Silas slumped forward, his elbows on his knees and his head on his hands. His brain rushing as he considered everything that had happened.

Mason looked more exhausted than he had done in all the time Silas had known him, which wasn't saying a great deal, but it was a pitiful sight. The burden of the last few days built up and weighing down on him now, the bags beneath his green eyes were plentiful.

Once more the door opened, revealing a worried looking Joshua behind it, he stormed in. When finding all occupants peaceful and waiting, he frowned in an expression Silas couldn't decide whether it was disappointment or gratitude. "I just wished to make sure everything was okay," he explained, sheepish and wanting to retreat quickly. Seemingly having convinced himself that they had managed to pull of the quietest murder the Kingdom had ever known.

Isaac's gaze lifted from where he had been intently reading, narrowing on the newcomer. "Things are fine," he seemed annoyed but little else by the intrusion. "Do you doubt your searching abilities, surely you wouldn't have permitted them entrance without making sure neither of them carried a weapon?"

For a moment Joshua seemed to consider searching the pair once more, but instead simply nodded his head. "Of course not sir, I will leave you now," he retreated from the room quickly and without a word, Silas watching the door slam in his wake.

But the makeshift mayor didn't return to his concentrated study of the presented letter, instead his gaze returned to the pair of men in front of him and gestured for them to return to their previous spot. Which they did without question nor complaint.

Up close Silas could truly study Isaac, and he discovered the stranger to not be all the much older than either Silas or Mason. How he was maintaining such composure given the events of the last few days, Silas could admit he admired him to that extent. Knowing he would have been falling apart at the seams had his mother died, and he knew from experience of how he had reacted on the news his father had died, though that felt like a lifetime ago now.

Isaac didn't say anything at first, lifting the paper closer to his eyes and reading through it briefly once more, before sighing. "I'll admit, this does make things make a lot more sense." He said, but before either of them had the chance to respond, the mayor had already continued. "My father's death was an inside job, it's the only way. Though security has been upped since, it would have been near impossible for someone to have breached those walls without being able to be inside the city already," he explained, and Silas was left to simply nod and listen along. "I assume these efforts were coupled with what happened to the King," he explained, a fair stream of logic but Silas knew his opinion would be unwelcomed.

He was little more than dirt among the diamonds in this room, and every word his companion or the stranger made simply drove that fact home all the more.

Mason spoke up once more, "You have rebels in your city?"

A lump rose to the back of Silas' throat at the cheek of Mason, how willingly he had asked such a sensitive question was either a very confident move or an incredibly stupid one. Silas stiffened, watching the makeshift mayor expectantly.

Isaac's gaze waivered for the first time, something akin to annoyance blazed in his gaze so briefly but was gone almost as quickly. "It would appear that is the only reasonable answer."

As reasonable as it might have sounded, that didn't offer much in the way of answering the other ten thousand questions burning through his head. For the first proper time, Silas dared to speak up in a quiet tone of voice. "Have you found anyone you believe to be the culprit?" He aimed to mould his tone into something similar to Mason's, to make himself feel a little more at home here, but a rat, or rather a wolf, was never going to feel overly at home in a palace. It was like finding a burning fire in a riverbed, the two things simply didn't mix.

"As I said," to his credit the stand in mayor didn't sound annoyed by Silas' interruptions, but he had made it apparent he was quite the expert in remaining polite above all else. "It was hours before we discovered the body, ample time for any person to have gone missing in." He explained, considering the pair for a moment. "Before you ask," he added a little more harshly at this point. "But we have checked, none of our staff are presently missing without justified cause."

Mason and Silas sighed in unity, no matter how much more they were told, it seemed only more questions were piled onto their heads.

"Well I am sorry about your loss," Mason's tone was genuine. He at least had known Gregory, however briefly, and Silas could only nod in agreement. "But the questions still stands, will you stand by the King's orders, stand your men down and cancel what plans your father had for an attack on Braxas?" He pried lowly.

The mayor looked at them for a moment which quickly spanned into an eternity. Briefly Silas wondered if he'd heard them in the first place, but just as Mason moved to pry further as to the answer, the mayor moved again.

Isaac stood finally, Silas watchful as he moved around the desk, pausing before he reached the door. At this point Silas began to feel somewhat like a decoration, but he considered Mason as an afterthought too. "I'm going to consider what you've told me today, what are you to do once you're finished here?" He asked.

"We're to head to Rehenney," Mason explained, "To give similar news to the mayor there."

He took this in as he seemed to with every other piece of information thrown his way, calmly and thoughtfully. "It's a fairly short journey there, but I understand you are likely on a timeframe," he said with something nearly sincere in his voice. "Do you have the time to stay here for a little longer, until I can properly consider what I've been told today and come to an answer."

Part of that unnerved Silas, he'd hoped the answer would be a simple yes. In what world would he want to proceed with attacks on Braxas, when the very King of this place didn't want to proceed with it. What sane man would want to proceed with war, if there was a chance that numerous lives could be saved, and it could be averted.

As far as he could tell, this mayor was no idiot nor insane.

He exchanged an uncertain look with Mason, who contemplated this briefly. "We're exhausted," he admittedly lowly, in a tone that might have brought a laugh from Silas had he not been so shocked by everything else. "I think the pair of us would appreciate a good break, if that's okay with you?" He added, not wishing to impose.

The mayor only grinned slightly, "I imagine we can figure something out, Joshua," he called as he pulled open the drawing room door and entered the corridor outside once more. Silas and Mason following suit at speed. "Find these two a spare room and let them rest until I call for them – undisturbed," he added knowingly.

Joshua nodded obediently, lifting a gloved hand at which the guards moved to accompany them, but Isaac spoke up once more impeding their eager momentum. "They are friends, Joshua, there is no need to treat them like wild animals."

Either disappointed or uncertain, the guards except for the one deemed as Joshua dissipated from their close proximity to the pair, and Joshua was simply left to lead the way.

Fortunately for their aching legs, the journey wasn't too long. Though compared to three days-worth of travel anything over a hundred metres could well be considered too far. As they were led up a set of stairs – nowhere near as extravagant as the great one found in the entrance hall but neither of them had the energy to complain too much about them.

Silas realised they were likely in the staff quarters, as here it was simpler and a little more boring. Gone were the fine paintings and the marble floors, it was bitterly cold and barren. The doors crowded together; the ample space provided for the ludicrously large entrance hall clearly stole from the space provided to the people who kept this place running.

Comparatively, the barracks could almost be said to have been beautiful.

Seemingly at random, the guard stopped, turned left and opened a door. Revealing a room empty except for three beds, freshly made but otherwise not much inside aside from a chest of draws, a fairly barren bookcase and a small square window peering onto the gardens below. "You can sleep here," he explained with a steel tone. "I will come get you when Isaac wishes you to return."

He barely took the time to note Silas and Mason's nodding heads, before he turned and shut the door behind him. Silas didn't fail to hear the sound of a key in the lock being turned, locking them in with no exit except for a drop from the window that might leave even Silas hurt.

Mason moved wordlessly towards one of the beds, slumped down on it into a position that might well be mistaken for death. Silas assumed he'd been dragged into sleep the moment his head neared the pillow, but as he moved to claim a bed of his own, a voice muffled by pillows sounded.

"What do you think?"

Sitting down on the bed slightly more elegantly than his accomplice, the wolf shook his head. "Stiff, could do with a new mattress but it will do." He decided, trying to smile but the gesture felt fake and pointless.

The man elicited an annoyed grumble, lifting his head from the pillows and manoeuvring so he lay flat on the length of the bed rather than half hanging off it. "That's not what I meant, and you know it," the would-be Prince scolded.

His gaze fixed to the little window, Silas had known exactly what his friend was meaning, but answering that question would mean he'd have to admit that he had no idea what to think of any of this. "I don't know," he admitted, still sitting cross-legged atop the bed. "I guess we shouldn't be surprised that the attack at Cresvy wasn't a singular, focused attack," he considered, trying to compile his thoughts into a logical or at least coherent sentence. "But if that's the case…" he trailed off.

"If that's the case, how are we to know any noble is left alive in the rest of the Kingdom?" Mason finished more bluntly than Silas would have, but got out much of Silas' line of thinking quicker and better than he'd have been able to.

Silas cringed at hearing his worst fears aloud, "Exactly."

Again, silence fell between them, though the wolf could all but hear the cogs whirring in their brain as they tried to process everything they had learned in the short space of time. By the end of it his head was rendered aching, and still no answers were produced despite his best efforts.

"But if they're wanting this war to go ahead," Mason continued after a minute, his head turned now so Silas could at least see his face through the thin pillow. "Why would they kill the men willing to launch the attacks, prepared to launch the attacks!" He exclaimed; his tone laced with poorly restrained anger. "I just don't understand." He admitted at last.

None of this made sense, though Silas was of the increasing belief they only had half the facts.

In an effort to prevent his friend suffering more than necessary he spoke up quietly. "I think the best thing we can do is wait until Isaac calls us back to his quarters, and see what he thinks of all this, and what his next move is intended to be." The wolf spoke gently, running his fingers through his hair and pulling it out of his face, the need to keep his hands occupied frustrating. "I don't know how long that will take, but in the mean-time we might as well try and get some rest."

He felt utterly useless, but that had become a common trend.

His companions features moulded into pure frustration, at the lack of understanding as well as the lack of choices. Mason sighed and nodded his head, "I don't think we have much choice, unless you fancy trying to dig through the floors."

A downwards glance told him the likelihood of that was about as equal to all of this turning out to be some cruel prank. The floor was cold concrete, the pair of them could have lived three lifetimes consecutively and not made progress of more than a few inches through it.

"Probably not," Silas admitted. "Sleep it is?"

"Sleep it is." Mason confirmed and piercing green eyes closed shut without another word.

The little room soon filled with the light snores of the would-be Prince, exhaustion had quickly provided for a swift sleep, but Silas wasn't so lucky. He pulled the covers over him and up to his chin, desperately trying to find some form of comfort and warmth in the threadbare duvet and paper-thin mattress and naturally found none. By now it was a familiar sound, a couple of nights together had left it an expected backing track.

Yet still sleep didn't overwhelm his senses.

No matter how sleep deprived the last couple of days had left him, the thunder of thoughts bounding through his head made the idea of sleep difficult. He closed his eyes so tight and held his breath so forcefully he hoped unconsciousness might take him, but still he didn't succumb to sleep.

The wolf was in enemy territory – an idea he still couldn't shake no matter his best efforts, and he wasn't about to fall asleep in the viper's pit.

A growl of annoyance inadvertently pulled free of his lips, he shifted the covers off him and left the bed. Glancing over to Mason, if he'd heard the short outburst he made no acknowledgement of it, his breathing rhythmic and his snores regular.

Silas smiled at the sight, though he felt it looked more like a grimace.

For a few moments he paced like that, increasingly certain that if he continued like this it wouldn't be necessary to dig through the floor, for he would wear away at it slowly but surely. But after a moment he bored of that, reasoning it would be of little use to waste his energy and increase the ache of his legs if they were to continue their journey shortly. But given sleep wasn't much of an option, he needed something to occupy his mind.

His gaze fixed to the little bookcase.

It was poorly stocked, either the items left behind by previous occupants or perhaps just one leisure the palace offered its staff. Approaching the small wooden fixture, he knelt before it. Considering it briefly, dust and cobwebs clung to the shelf, and the occupants smelled old and slightly damp.

Running a finger across the leather casings of the books, a large portion of them were history books. About the palace, the monarchy, the area, and admittedly that did spark his interest. The last three days had proven just how little he knew about his own Kingdom, and he reasoned this could be a good chance to find out more.

He pulled free a copy, the movement was stiff and difficult as though the book had been sitting there for many years. He sat at the foot of his bed; the stone floor nearly as comfortable as the actual bed, and began flipping carefully through the pages.

The book was named 'A History of Nekeldez,' not an overly exciting title but something broad enough that he thought he might find something interesting in its pages. He began reading, the process was slow – his minimal schooling meant that he could at the very least read, but the longer and unfamiliar words made it painfully slow compared to others.

Still he persisted silently, its ink was faded, and the information was outdated; the latest monarch it named wasn't one he recognised, so he knew it was at least two monarchs late.

He read about the felling of previous noblemen, through rebellion, their own squabbles or quite rarely simply by means of old age or illness. Few of these people seemed to live peaceful lives, Silas noted with narrowing eyes. He might have smiled to learn that history always seemed to repeat itself, but given it was his own people at risk now, not strange names on paper he found it strictly humourless.

His efforts had brought him maybe twenty pages deep after an hour or so, when the sound of footsteps from outside the corridor made him sit upright. His gaze narrowing as he stood up, prepared for whatever the door would open to reveal.

The viper's pit was full of surprises, and he intended to be careful at every chance.

Silas snatched his rucksack up from the corner of the room and pocketed the book for later reading. He reasoned no one would notice a single book had gone missing from any of the rooms and doubted anyone would mourn its loss all too much.

He stood, waiting for whatever fate would greet them on the other side of the door.

It swung open to reveal a frustrated looking Isaac, eyes darkened with annoyance as he regarded the two, bored. "Come with me," he explained and left the room without waiting for either of the boys to respond. "Isaac is ready to see you now."

Chapter Twenty.

Their return to the drawing room was tracked by silence, a more comfortable one now that they weren't surrounded on every edge by guards, but still the pair remained stiff and weary.

The trio pulled to a halt in front of the drawing room door, but before it could be pushed open someone on the other side already had done the honours, revealing a stranger behind it who shoved past them without a word and hurried through the corridor. Joshua stiffened noticeably at the sight of that stranger but ushered the friends in all the same.

"I hope you slept well," Isaac said without looking up from where he was positioned at the desk. Seemingly having not moved an inch since they had last seen him a couple of hours ago.

Silas and Mason merely nodded in response; it didn't matter as Isaac didn't look up.

"You may leave, Joshua, I wish to continue this alone," he ordered, still scratching quill to parchment as he hurriedly wrote something. Eyebrow furrowed in concentration and arm arched carefully around his work in case prying eyes dared look too closely.

Considering refusing for a brief second, the guard parted his lips to argue back, decided against it and turned once more from the room. A loyal dog, even if he wanted to disagree it seemed the guard would never go against the word of his superior.

Isaac paused, no rhyme or reason aside from ensuring the guard was gone from the doorway. When it seemed no one was about to eavesdrop, he began with a firm tone. "Do take a seat," he offered, gesturing to the pair.

Rather than the sofas at the very back of the room that they'd utilised before, a pair of wooden chairs had been provided in their absence, not quite as comfortable as the plush couches. But both the wolf and the would-be Prince took their seat without argument. Though it left them feeling quite like school children preparing to be scolded by their teacher.

"I've considered what you have told me and discussed the next course of action with some of the city advisors who left a few moments ago," the mayor explained. Sitting back against his seat, a façade at casualness that Silas was barely able to see through, but when he did he could sense the fear coming from the strange young man. "And I have a proposition for the pair of you." Isaac finished.

Admittedly that hadn't been what Silas expected, watching him carefully, curiosity melded with worry as to what would come next.

Mason, something impatient but not quite rude to his tone of voice didn't let the mayor finish. "I know you understand that we are under a deadline," he explained, restless. "Before we can consider that, can you please let us know whether you intend to stand your father's troops in Braxas down." The tremble to Mason's tone didn't portray fear but poorly contained frustration.

The gentleman shifted in his seat; slight annoyance sparked in his gaze, but it never once shifted from the pair as he spoke. "While I might be new to this, I think it's generally good manners to be politer to your superiors than that." Isaac warned, Silas nudged his friend with his elbow in an effort to bring him back to the ground, but his efforts failed.

"I am a ward of the King," he wielded the phrase like a weapon.

He sniffed at this, amused by the assertion. "No bloodline then," Isaac's calm tone entirely contrasted with the cruelty of his words. "Here your word is about as good as that of a sewer rat, so I remind you again. Mind your tone."

Mason moved to speak again, "Mason," he warned before he had the chance.

He didn't look happy about it, but he shut his lips and sat back. The wolf left hoping his apologetic tone would save their heads from being placed atop spikes.

The makeshift mayor seemed to have a very strange definition of friends.

"Forgive him," Silas asked lowly, continuing before Mason could interrupt. "It's been a difficult few days, and we have both seen and lost a lot," his tone remained infinitely calmer than he felt. "You'll understand if we're a little touchy right now."

For a moment Silas was certain this would be the end of their time in Brynde, that a moment of heated frustration had ruined everything and that they might well be killed on the spot. Then the makeshift mayor relaxed a fraction.

"I understand," he said, his tone steel but calm once more. "This is no doubt a difficult time for all of us, and that's not going to stop any time soon." He shook his head, distracted for a moment his gaze wandered for the first time. Watching the large window that sat to the corner of the room, leaving the room lit in a warm afternoon glow.

Somewhat calmer, seeming to have seen reason, Mason remained steadfast as he repeated again, politer this time. "Will you stand down your father's men?" He repeated.

"That's what I'm here to talk with you about," the gentleman avoided the question as though it might spread the plague. "But first I have more questions to ask," he added.

Neither of the young men liked it but it didn't seem that they had a great deal more choice other than to sit and offer what answers they could. Left only to pray by the end of it their mission would find some success,

Under their expectant gaze, the mayor continued swiftly. "Where did you say you're headed?"

"We're going to Rehenney," the wolf reminded kindly.

Recognition flickered in the dark brown gaze of the mayor, he considered this for little more than a heartbeat then nodded. "And you are to deliver a similar message there to the one we received."

Given neither of them had opened the second letter, they didn't know the contents of it, but could only assume. "Exactly," Mason spoke before Silas could, though he would have offered a similar reply, it was better to pretend they had all the information rather than none of it.

Pulling the second envelope from its place, he lifted the sealed envelope to demonstrate his point. The King's rose littered seal still flawless on the envelope's close. "We're to deliver it to a nobleman who resides there, Joseph."

Isaac gestured, expecting the young man to hand the letter over to him, however, Mason didn't hand it to him and instead tucked it once more into the pocket. Looking up, "Unfortunately we're under orders to give that one to Joseph and nobody else, I'm sure you understand." His grin darkened a shade, daring the mayor to challenge that decision.

The nobleman didn't. Nodding his head understandingly, though not appreciatively.

"I see," his voice was stable and his gaze scathing the pair of them carefully. "Unfortunately I don't think I'm going to be able to let you get away with that."

The threat to that statement made alarm bells ring in Silas' head, he stiffened but didn't move from his position. A patient wolf prepared to pounce but not willing to just yet. He cast a questioning gaze over the stand-in mayor.

A brick wall beside him in the effort to not shake as he spoke, "I'm sorry to hear that," he said, crossing his arms but that was the only movement Mason permitted himself to make. "Can you explain to us why?"

The politeness of it all was bizarre to Silas, having grown up in a far less civilised place arguments like this would be put to bed through bloodshed and fists.

"Simply put, me and my advisors, as well as some close friends don't consider stopping war beneficial to my city," he explained, the smile of a cruel cat etching its way across his expression. "We have been given many reasons to wish war upon this country, and the felling of that coward King from his ill-gained throne is merely atop the mid three."

Mason looked like he had been punched, Silas felt like he'd been dropped from the highest tower.

Now he accompanied his words with a shake of his head, "So no, I shall not be calling off Brynde's forces from their efforts in Braxas," he finished proudly. "War has been long coming to Nekeldez, and this is something a lot of us have been waiting a long time for.

The would-be Prince shifted beside him, and Silas tensed in case the need arose to catch any punches he might have been considering hurling, but Mason didn't He merely hunched forward to look the man closer in the eye.

On his part, Isaac looked like he might well have been expecting a hurled punch, merely regarded the King's ward with a bored look.

"Why are you telling us any of this?" Mason asked, not among the first questions Silas had expected, but he wasn't about to interrupt. "Surely its counter-intuitive to tell the missionaries of the King your plans to foil their mission?"

A guttural chuckle sounded. "Do tell me, where exactly is the King right now?" It wasn't a means of finding out genuine information, no tactical question but rather a mocking statement. He knew the state of the world at present.

Mason's confidence faltered, he didn't. No one except the head guard did.

For all either of them knew the King was dead, but one they weren't about to share willingly with a man who seemed to be contemplating that man's demise.

Isaac's smile brimmed only larger, until Silas was certain it could only be painful to maintain that expression. "That's where you too come in," he continued with a shake of his head. "Can you genuinely say that you're loyal to that coward of a King?"

The pair stared at their companion, incredulous.

Outside of three days ago the wolf had never had much of an opinion on the King, he was a distant fairy-tale to be regarded only in stories of his incredible feats. Though those feats were largely handed to him by virtue of a bloodline, having a discerning opinion of a monarch wasn't a leisure afforded to someone from Cresvy.

In short, no, Silas didn't have an opinion on the King, nor any particular loyalty to him. But that was something from the lack of necessity, rather than a dislike of the King.

None of this was something the mayor would care about, however, as in truth the question hadn't been pointed at him but rather the young man beside him.

The ward of the King and given that much Silas was surprised the question needed asking at all. For the answer was obvious.

"Of course I am!" Mason's stuttering was defensive, angry that the question had even dared to be asked in the first place. "You could be executed for this nonsense, are you incredibly drunk or simply insane." Brave would have been the first descriptor that came to Silas' head, but then right now there didn't seem to be much of a difference between the two.

Something similar to disappointment darkened the mayors face. "And outside of a familial tie, why would that be?" He was persistent, Silas could give him that much.

If it weren't for the fact that they were deep behind enemy lines, Silas and Mason would have taken off running at this point. But given the fact that the likelihood of getting out of here alive seemed to be lessening with every word, they were trapped mice thrown into the lion's lair.

"He saved my life," Mason's response was immediate and unthinking.

And a lie. From what he had told Silas the young man had become the King's ward by virtue of his accidental murder of Mason's parents. It was out of no duty or love that Ezekiel kept Mason in his household, but something more akin to embarrassment about a mishap.

Silas kept that to himself, knowing Mason would likely be more willing to punch him then he would be this makeshift mayor.

Isaac laughed again; the guttural sound regurgitated from some hateful place deep in his chest. "One noble gesture, after a lifetime of cowardice and idiocy."

For his friend's sake the wolf stepped in, asking lowly. "You keep saying that, and yet you have no proof?" He asked, prying for more answers that they might build an idea off of.

"You should know from your journeys in Braxas, how desperate he was to get out of this potential war, no?" He asked setting his gaze on Mason, acting as though Silas hadn't spoken in the first place, little more than a ghost to these people. "The idea of war terrifies the King, he is not worthy of that throne, there are many people who would do far better in his place."

"Yourself included?" Silas asked darkly.

Isaac's smile was stiff as he regarded the wolf properly for the first time, "I'm barely used to mayor, friend. I would not doubt be just as useless," he replied with a shake of his head. "I know quite a few candidates who would be far better, however, and the Kingdom would thrive under a new bloodline."

Silas didn't know how to comprehend any of that, particularly under the increasing belief they were here only to be slaughtered now their allegiances had been demonstrated. Mason moved to say something further but wasn't given half the chance.

"What I do know, however, is that this city and everyone like it across Nekeldez has been burdened with paying off the infinite taxes of the King's, to give him a lavish lifestyle and keep enemy kingdoms he has succumbed to from taking what's his." Isaac stood, earlier Silas had assumed their age to be similar, but suddenly all at once the young man was morphed into something far older.

"I can see that you really suffer." Silas returned before he could stifle his first retort.

"Brynde used to be something far more beautiful," he looked down upon his newly earned city, distracted. "Much of this palace is in an ill state of repair, and we've had to lay off more than half our staff just to keep up with tax payments."

Sell the chandelier. Silas managed to keep that to himself. He had no pity for this man.

"And you would thrust this kingdom into war because you don't like paying your King's debts?" Mason's tone was riddled with confusion. "That is your duty as a nobleman, it's the way it always has been."

Isaac shook his head, "If it continues as your father insists, there won't be much of a Kingdom left standing in a few years." He responded, turning from the window once more but he didn't retake his seat. Instead using the vantage point of his height to stare down upon the young men. "It's not just big cities like this that struggle, the smaller villages are left on the brink of starvation, your king's debts are killing your kingdom."

"And you think war would fix that?" Mason asked, scoffing.

Shifting from one foot to the other, "I do," the certainty to the newly dubbed nobleman's voice was infuriating.

"Because war is a cheap feat." Mason all but growled.

"A one of cost in return for our Kingdom's autonomy back, and our people pulled from poverty and starvation."

Silas had been silent; he had known starvation as well as seen it. It was common as the rats in Cresvy, and he had long lived in the knowledge that they weren't the only ones. It had never crossed his mind that it might have been the fault of the King, but now it seemed to make a lot more sense, and it sickened him to his stomach.

Beside him a vein in Mason's neck was prominent and a vivid blue colour as he struggled to keep his temper. But the truth of the matter was that he struggled to find a means of responding, the stand-in mayor's points were fair, and at this point neither of them could have really said anything that might have convinced this man otherwise.

"You would ally yourself with the very sort who had your father killed," Mason scoffed, his tone genuinely one of disgust. It was a low blow, and one even Silas found to be distasteful.

The reaction it took from the mayor; however, was something neither of them had expected.

Isaac moved with sudden speed, making to punch the daylights out of the would-be prince in sudden anger that surprised the both of them.

Silas reacted unthinkingly, putting himself between the more breakable prince and the angered mayor before an eye could blink. He shoved the mayor away.

He expected his reaction to bring further angered blows, he began stuttering with surprise at his own sudden defensive movement. But what Isaac replied with wasn't what he had expected, something akin to surprise mixed with curiosity in his gaze.

Before the mayor could respond, however, the guards burst in. Apparently having heard the crash and clutter of the mayor's inelegant stumble and thinking an attempt on the mayor's life had been made. "Isaac are you okay?" It was Joshua once more, gun unholstered and prepared to unload bullets into anything he found in that little drawing room.

Yet the mayor didn't look to the newcomers, his gaze fixed upon the young wolf's. "A lycan!" He stated in genuine surprise, Silas' silver eyes finally having been noticed. The dim light, a careful distance and the general lack of care had kept it secret thus far, but he knew he would have been incredibly lucky to get out of this without them noticing. Thus naturally, to a person who had almost no luck in his entire life, he had been found out at the worst time possible.

Running a finger down his chin; contemplative. "I'll admit this changes a few things," he decides. Then turned his gaze to the guards and gestured for them to come closer, "Joshua, be so kind as to escort these two to the dungeons."

Ice ricocheted through Silas' veins, and he leapt forward and away from his guards, defensively. He might have been about as adept as the average toddler in combat, he assumed his strength and speed would offer something in this situation and given they hadn't known until then that he was a lycan he doubted they would have silver on hand.

Lunging at the first person who was dumb enough to come into range, he threw a punch which shattered the man's nose. Something which would usually render Silas feeling guilty exhilarated him now, the scent of blood driving his actions as he moved again. To his opponent's credit, the pair parried for a moment, Silas having the upper hand for the few beats their little fight lasted.

Yet in a show of genuine intelligence, the guards didn't go for him but rather his much more human friend beside him. A yell of pain and surprise ripping from the King's ward as a harsh blow was delivered to the side of his head, sending him collapsing to his knees with a painful sounding crack to the marble floors.

Joshua held a gun to Mason's head, and looked to Silas, "Stand down, or we'll kill him."

Silas' eyes widened, and he didn't have much other choice as he lowered his hands and loosened his fists into stretched fingers without hesitation.

"Only the finest cell for our good friends of course," he added smirking, as Silas and Mason were dragged away.

Escort was a kind word for the shoving, kicking and threatening which proceeded the order.

Silas and Mason stumbled along as they were unceremoniously dragged from the drawing room, Isaac not giving them as much as parting look as they were pulled away.

In the chaos Silas had no idea where the left and right turns took them, retracing their steps would be impossible. But then Silas had a sinking feeling the need would never arise, and that this would likely be the last journey he was able to take.

A yowl dragged from his own throat as a punch ricocheted across his cheek bone, he didn't stagger beneath the blow, but it was painful, leaving the space throbbing and warm. Something feral in his chest knew that would likely be among the gentler strikes he would receive today.

The pair were dragged through the corridors, neither had much chance to take one step before they were being shoved again. They weren't going especially slow, but anything a beat under the speed of light was too slow for the guards – enjoying themselves a little too much.

Fortunately, or incredibly unfortunately depending on how they looked at it, the journey to the cells was a short one. A long, stone staircase took them from the main entrance and down, down, down until the daylight didn't breach and the only form of lighting was provided by the sporadic lamps lighting the pathway.

The clang of metal sounded, and the pair were thrown through the opening, before Silas could as much as blink the barred door had been slammed shut once more. He whirled on the spot, still on his knees in an inelegant crouch, the growl that pulled from him was entirely feral, a dangerous but unfamiliar noise that seemed to echo across the stone walls.

Most of the guards scurried back a few inches, Joshua remained statutory, watching and grinning.

"Please," he grumbled, bored more than anything else. "If you could shift you would have done it on the way down," he said unbothered. He regarded Silas, something akin to curiosity in his gaze as he considered the crouching, pathetic man. "Why can't you?" It was a rhetorical question, and even if it hadn't been the Gods wouldn't have been able to drag an answer from his bloodied lips. "Silver on your person?" He wondered aloud, leaning against the bars. "You don't seem to have much other use, why oh why would you want to get rid of your own purpose?" He snorted; the mockery seemed more natural in his voice than any attempts at politeness he'd made earlier. "Rendered into weak, cowardly, nothing. No wonder you get on with the King."

In a show of confidence he wasn't sure the source of, Silas growled. "Come closer and I'll show you just how useless I am."

The young guard simply laughed again, shaking his head he retreated from the bars but not in a show of fear but more of convenience.

"I doubt you could throw much of a punch in there against me," he decided aloud, but his words were more matter of fact than they were defensive. "Fortunately, I have nothing to prove to you especially not in the state you're in," he took hold of the door and shook it for good measure, ensuring it was locked before moving to turn away.

"You, however, might just have something to prove in the next few days," he called over his shoulder as he began to depart. "Who knows, play your cards right and you might be allowed out of this dingy little cell within the year."

Chapter Twenty-One.

Exactly how long passed, neither of the companions could begin to imagine. It could well have been minutes, hours, days, or only heartbeats, in that dungeon, time was a distant concept. Whatever measurement most applicable to the period he had spent there, every unit of it had been spent in pain for the young wolf.

Initially the bruises, shock and grief of everything that had gone on ripped through to his very core. The crushing understanding that they would likely never see the light of day again, and that all the efforts and losses of the last few days had been for nothing, that no matter what they were always going to trip at this obstacle was like swallowing a poker.

But before long the mental pain would become the last of their worries.

Their original cell had only been a halfway house. In the meantime the rattle of metal and banging of hammers sounded, whether that was just for special effect to make them more worried about what was to come or not, they had no idea. At least not for the time being.

A short while – or maybe a long while, after they had originally been dumped there, the young man was dragged out of the blue from his uncomfortable spot beside the would-be Prince and deposited quite unceremoniously into the one beside it.

Nothing seemed different apart from the absence of Mason, it took him a little while longer to realise the true maliciousness of the new context. A pair of handcuffs now kept his movement to a minimum, and a collar encircled his neck, just short of being tight enough to make breathing impossible.

The wolf had already spent the better part of his lifetime in a cell, three stone walls and a barred one was far from an unfamiliar setting for the lycan. But this was something quite different.

It began with a fierce headache, and before long even thinking was inordinately painful.

Only when Silas was able to drag himself close enough to the bars of his cage did, he realise the extent of what had happened.

The very bars were laced with silver now, that accompanied by the circles encompassing his wrists as well as that in his clothes rendered his every breath agony.

During that time, nothing of Silas was Silas'. The silver stole everything from him and encompassed anything that remained, from his sweat to his bones to his very thoughts, whether that was a blessing or a curse the wolf couldn't have said for all the money in the world.

In the little cell beside him, Mason was able to do nothing but listen and pray to the Gods he wouldn't go mad as all he could hear was his friend's choking and desperate screaming only metres from where he sat, but unable to do a damned thing.

Apparently, the King's ward wasn't worth much outside of the potential for a ransom; he was permitted to sit and look pretty as time passed, as any injuries delivered would surely only lessen the price offered.

But the wolf was worth something outside of a ransom, and they worked to weaken him to breaking point, and use him for their own.

His attempts at offering comfort either went ignored or unheard, the would-be prince was left only to pace and circle in his little cell, trying not to bring up what little food he'd had in the last few days. He knew these guards weren't going to clean up after him, nor offer him the materials with which to do so, and Mason wasn't going to be left to rot in his own waste.

Fortunately, his cell offered no view of the ongoing in his companion's cell, but the sounds carried like a dry leaf on a harsh wind. Mason's features contorted and struggled, he would return to pleading, begging, shouting for the guards. Desperate to stop his friend from going through a single further minute of this.

But the guards were as capable of hearing as Silas was.

It hadn't felt like it had even been a couple of hours in that solitude of stone and silver and pain, that the guards returned.

Paying about as much attention to the would-be prince as one would the average rat in the street, they approached Silas' cell, and looked down at him contemplatively. No sympathy, or anything even akin to human emotion in their gaze sparked as they watched him.

As far as any of them were concerned – the lycan was something to be moulded and ordered, nothing human left within him after the bite that had cursed him.

Joshua watched through the bars, peaceful and smiling for a few moments. Before he asked in a low voice, seemingly unperturbed by the torment of his victim. "Now you've had some time to think about the situation," he said, bored if nothing else.

The wolf didn't answer – he wasn't in the position too.

Demonstrating something a little more humane in the frustration that followed, the guard tutted softly. "I'll take that as a yes," he gestured emphatically to the men watching from a few feet behind them, and the silver bars were opened. The wolf dragged from where he had been curled on the floor, pulled through the opening and dumped on the ground again. Uncollared, it was thrown to the side, but they at least had the common sense to leave the cuffs encircling his wrists.

Now that breathing didn't feel like he was drinking acid, the wolf lifted his head up and stared blankly for a few moments. A baby uncertain of anything in the world for a few moments, his eyes blinked trying focus, and when he the memories flooded back, he started in surprise. Silver had altered his thinking patterns, and it took him a minute to remember who he was, where he was – what he was.

Squatting down beside him, Joshua demonstrated something in the way of patience as he permitted the wolf to catch his breath. Pulling something from between his teeth and flicking it away as he waited, making a façade of just how at ease he was in the presence of something that could have killed him in the space of a heartbeat.

But in that state, the wolf was about as threatening as a newborn pup.

And Mason despised having to see his companion in this state. Tears flooding his eyes as he fought to keep them from falling with everything he had.

"Now you've had the chance to see what you'll be faced with for the rest of your life," the guard took great pleasure in what he said. The wolf's pain was a source of entertainment and nothing further to the fowl man. "I have an offer for you."

Looking up, he struggled to sit straighter from where he had been left belly down in the dirt. He shook harshly as he straightened onto his knees, but now he could look the stranger in the eyes and listen, trying to hold onto what left of his dignity he could manage.

That cat like smile spread again, he looked at the wolf as though he genuinely offered something out of the kindness of his heart. That the two had been friends for many, many years, and not a man and his captive as he continued darkly.

"What the Mayor has so kindly decided to offer you," he explained running his fingers through his hair and pulling it out of his face. This casualness was no façade now, something entirely different. "Is a place outside of this cell, among his own guard where you can live life free of your chains and your silver… and your fear," he added with a smirk. "And all you have to do is swear your allegiance to Brynde and its mayor."

The wolf didn't respond, his gaze not shifting from his assailants for a few moments. But otherwise he said nothing, then something stiffened within the weakened wolf. And he did the only thing he physically could in that moment outside of raising a weak arm to fall flat again.

He spat on Joshua's cheek.

Considering this for a moment, he then straightened once more wordless for a moment, gesturing for his guards again. "Very well," he replied unperturbed, rubbing the saliva away from his chin with the sleeve of his jacket. "I'll give you a little while longer, let you think things over a bit better, maybe?" He decided, lifting a gloved hand to gesture once more.

At his movement, the guards had the wolf on his feet and backtracking before the wolf was able to as much as reply, and all of them were gone from the room in the space of a heartbeat. The wolf's moans and cries returning to the air once more, ricocheting about and embedding themselves into the very stones of the walls about them.

That interaction apparently left the guards not thinking that they shouldn't poke a hibernating bear, but rather trying to rile a cornered snake was a brilliant and quite fun idea. For what continued was not as kind as gentle interrogations or questionings.

Rather the wolf was forced from his cell, freed from his collar, and had the very love of the Gods beaten out of the young man. Silver rings laced fingers that would be driven into his chest, head, any part they believed that particular day was in need of a thorough pulverising. He would be drowned, have every inch covered in silver and allowed to just wither and scream where they left him.

All of them seemed to find great joy in their little game, to them they weren't hurting a human being but simply they were the cats playing with a mouse. But unlike in that scenario, they had no intention of ever putting the wolf out of his misery not until they got from him exactly what they were wanting.

Neither of them slept for the duration they were there, whether that was a horrendous period of many months, or only a few hours. But the idea for the agonised wolf was impossible, and whether out of sympathy pains or through simple impossibility of the concept.

But after a few events just like that, Mason had no idea how much longer his friend was going to last. Lycan or not, the would-be Prince couldn't understand how the wolf hadn't given in and begged to still be permitted to be free of that cell.

Mason wasn't sure if he should be impressed by his friend, or terrified for him. For every time they failed, the guards seemed to only come back with something worse. Mason wasn't quite sure how much further they could go without outright killing the wolf.

Or maybe that's their intention, Mason thought, trying to distract himself by putting any inkling of logic onto the circumstances they found themselves in. *Maybe they've found some witch to revive him, so they can have as much fun with him as they want without consequence.*

The would-be Prince had no idea, as far as he could tell there was no logic to any of this. Let alone humanity.

The little cell had been flooded with darkness, the few lamps available had been dimmed and now Mason was left to only take in the consuming midnight black of the dungeons. Every shadow seemed to writhe with monsters' mere metres from his place, and in truth the would-be Prince had no idea in those moments how he maintained his sanity.

And whether by the time this was over, whether or not his travelling companion would have any of his left.

But something painful struck the young man when he considered that part, the fact that this was never going to be over for his companion.

His voice gently broke the quiet are between them, his voice genuinely terrified but something sincere laced it all the same.

"Sy," his voice was hoarse from the lack of use and his own gentle cries. "I won't blame you if you give in to what they want," he explained. His father might just pay the ransom and let him out of his isolated hell, but that opportunity wouldn't be present for his wolf friend. "Do what they want, join them. I won't think any less of you for it."

The wolf only responded with further cries and screams; Mason wasn't sure if the man had even heard what he had said in the first place. He slumped back, closing his eyes and desperately trying to keep himself from crying any further.

The first reasonable period of time past undisturbed, the only sound was the intermittent whimpers from the wolf, but eventually his exhaustion made it impossible for him to make much further sounds. His harsh, struggling breaths soon replaced the pained cries, but Mason wasn't sure which of the two options he would have preferred in honesty.

But naturally it would never have lasted long, as the thunder of footsteps down a staircase sounded once more and Joshua's face, alongside a handful of others as they returned to the cell.

"I hope the pair of you slept well," though the head guard paid almost no attention to Mason where he sat watching them from his cell, his attention as ever fixed onto the wolf's form. The would-be Prince for the first time in his life had been rendered little more than a decoration in this context, a starter compared to the main course that was breaking the exhausted wolf.

"You know the drill," he spoke to his guards, who complied quickly and wordlessly. Unlocking the barred gates and pulling the wolf from his spot and into the open once more.

By now that little hallway was already littered largely by the blood he had spilled in those few days, and his features were swollen and almost unrecognisable. The exhaustion was apparent just from a single look at the wolf, but still he didn't relent or even retort outside of his one act of defiance however many hours beforehand.

Joshua swung – but relented at the last beat, his swing falling short as he let out an exasperated sigh. "You know what? No." His voice boomed across the room, though the wolf didn't lift his gaze from where it had become affixed to the floor. "This is clearly not working," he said with a sigh and began circling the wolf, coming within punching distance without too much concern.

"Bring me the King's brat."

That order took the guards by surprise, but it lasted no more than a beat as they quickly lunged to comply with his orders. Mason too was soon dragged from his spot and hurled onto the floor beside the unmoving wolf. Mason free of his little prison for the first time in however long, felt no safer here. He looked down at his hands, to find them stained red from where he placed them on the floor.

Still the wolf didn't move as much as an inch.

"It'll be a shame to dull this silver on your revolting skin," the guard considered as he turned his attention to Mason for the first time. Circling around the pair of them for the first time, his movements elegant and refined. "But then they've made contact with a lycan, so I suppose that boat has long sailed by now."

His burst of laughter was quickly replicated by those around them.

Still the wolf didn't budge.

"And if his own pain won't change his mind, maybe, just maybe he might for yours."

Joshua lunged; Mason flinched; and finally the wolf budged.

"Fine, fine!" The wolf's words were stammered and desperate, the genuine panic laced his tone as he spoke for the first time, the sound was hoarse, pained and raspy. Tears began to pour from his face, "Please, I'll do what you want, just don't hurt him!"

Joshua straightened, Mason relaxed, and the wolf simply watched. Red eyed and desperate, the would-be Prince didn't know whether to be grateful, heart broken or disappointed that his friend had given in. In the end, it was a mixture of the three, all marred by something bittersweet and grateful that his friend might make it out of this alive.

"Everyone has their price," Joshua said mostly to himself, shaking his head he removed the silver rings from his thick fingers. "And I'll admit, for a mutt you've got a pretty good moral compass."

His attempts at mockery made Mason grimace and flinch on the behalf of the wolf, but behind those bars he was useless and could only watch as the young man sat and listened to the hatred and vile words poured upon his head.

But the wolf seemed only numb to the world around him at that point. Wordless and broken.

The guards grabbed Mason by the armpits and dragged him backwards a few feet, depositing him on the ground once more and leaving him there. Returning and slamming the door shut, but they didn't move to do the same for the wolf, for the first time leaving him there, allowing Joshua to consider things for a few moments. From his point all he could do was look away and try to ignore it, but the sounds of the proceedings just outside of his cell continued, turning his gut as he tried to ignore it.

"I'm glad you've come to consider things how we do, mutt," he spoke as he continued to circle, a proud man revelling in his success over the broken and weak. "I truly think we can learn to work together, and truly make the most out of this relationship."

Joshua struck him again, a movement that made Mason jump in surprise but barely made the wolf move an inch. He seemed to have expected the gesture, but despite that had made no attempt to dodge it in the slightest.

Again, the head guard grinned that cat's grin, "I thought so. Come on, let's give Isaac the good news, bring him down here, and we can show him just the kind of power we have delivered into the armies of Brynde." He finished, regarding the wolf like something he had earned through hours of sweat and tears, something to be proud of, not disgusted by. Though the reasons for Joshua's disgust were something entirely different to what would have brought it on for most people, anyone with even an inkling of humanity in their veins.

He nodded to the guards, who were more hesitant at first, but moved to do as they were told all the same. The trio of strangers thundering up the stairs, leaving the wolf, Joshua and one of his guards waiting in the dungeons bloodied hall.

Joshua watched as his men departed and came to squat before the exhausted wolf once more. Grinning at the broken man who didn't as much as lift his gaze to meet the assailants. "We'll give you a few days, heal up a little huh?" He decided, brushing a piece of hair out of the wolf's face, who for the first time lifted his gaze to look at him. "And then we can see what you can really d-" but he wasn't given the chance to finish his tirade as a scream ripped from his throat.

Mason lunged to his feet again, tearing for the bars to try and see what had happened, and what he saw took his breath away.

Joshua's body falling with a thud to the ground, a shadowed creature leapt over the newly felled body. And where the young man had once stood, a wolf rose in his place.

Chapter Twenty-Two.

The would-be Prince watched in shock as the wolf paused in place. Massive with muscles prominent beneath a thick, sandy brown coat. Its eyes danced about the chamber, the only bit of the man before which was familiar to Mason shining despite the dark, that moon kissed gaze.

How much of that man remained? Fear shot through the would-be Prince as he pondered whether Silas' worst fears might well come true.

Fortunately, the gaze didn't remain fixed to Mason for more than a beat, as its lupine features turned away and sprang across the newly felled body. Making for the staircase up and out of the dungeon, following only the scent of fresh air and some distant memory of where freedom might lie.

Panic rather than blood shot through Mason's veins as he saw his companion turn away.

"Sy, Sy please!" He yelled after him but had no idea whether the man he called for remained anymore, and for a heartbeat it seemed it might have been true.

Then once more through the darkness, closer this time so close to the steel bars of his cell all of a sudden that the would-be Prince stumbled backward in surprise. Expecting his arm to be bitten clean off as much as he expected help.

Approaching the bars once more, though with enough common sense to keep some sort of distance, he said quietly. "Are you still there, Sy?"

No response, and Mason felt much the idiot for even trying it. No idea of what further to say, he shook the door with all of his might, but found it unyielding and steadfast. The young man swore to himself; he didn't know how much longer they'd have until the remaining guards returned with the makeshift mayor, and if they descended to find this. Silas was as good as dead.

Joshua lay just a metre or so from the front of the cell, blood pooling about him. Mason stifled the gagging that instinctually came to mind, but on his hip he could just about see the ringlet of keys. Sitting, a steak tantalising the starving, a distant lake mocking the dehydrated.

If he could just get close enough, he might well get out of there alive.

Trusting the wolf more than any sane man probably should, he came closer and knelt down. Heart racing as he took his eyes of the lupine creature and shoved his arm through the bars. It only just fit, the metal scraping his limb as he forced it through as far as he could manage. Grasping at the space where the dead man lay, but to no avail.

It seemed even if he chopped the arm off and used that to reach further, it was pointless. The body was just too far away.

But just as he had begun wallowing in fear, a heavy thud and metallic screeching sounded. The bars shaking, and he leapt back in an effort to save it. He looked up, to find the wolf body slamming the bars with all his might.

Without thinking he staggered back as many feet as the small cell would permit, watching the wolf work with bated breath. One eye on it and one on the staircase, they were still alone but for how much longer he didn't know.

This continued for what felt like an eternity further, and the panic returned to Mason's very heart.

"You need to get out of here Sy," he said desperately between the horrendous metallic banging, worried that anyone close enough to the staircase leading down might soon hear what was going on and come down in order to investigate. "I might get out of here alive, you won't."

If the wolf either heard or understood what had been said, he made no indication of it, as he sauntered back once more and lunged again. The bars indeed had become misshapen and crooked, but not yet enough to permit the young man to depart through them.

Desperate and pleading now, "Silas ple-" he didn't have the chance to finish, as finally with a groan and cracking sound, one of the bars cracked beneath the relentless efforts of the wolf. Mason's heart soared, hope returning no matter how slight.

"Move," he hissed, and whether by luck or understanding – the wolf did as he was told.

On either side of the broken bars, those still standing were bent. Taking a deep breath and picturing every thin object he could think of, the would-be Prince desperately began pushing himself through them. It pinched, scraped and hurt quite a bit, but if it saved him he would have willingly left a leg or arm behind him in an effort to a scape.

After some desperate squeezing, Mason was free once more.

"Come on," he demanded, and the man and his wolf ascended the stairs as fast as their legs would permit them.

Soon the wolf took the front position, taking the long winding staircase five at a time, leaving Mason in his wake as he fought to keep up with everything he had in him. Only spotting fleeting glances of his friend's plumed tail as he bounded ahead.

If the wolf could get out of here alive, the would-be Prince would find some comfort in that.

Every heartbeat he spent on that staircase made Mason all the more certain that they would come across an obstacle. After all of this to be killed on the stone steps, if not dragged back to the cells for the rest of their lives, no matter how his legs ached, heart raced and lungs burned, that idea was enough to keep him running through adrenaline and will to survive alone.

Then all at once the bright lights of the main entrance were upon him, and Mason stumbled out into the extravagant marble of the palace hall. He breathed, the idea that they might just be free of this alive suddenly all too real.

He spotted the door and took off running for it. Silas following suit with a scatter of claws upon marble, now in the light Mason could spot the red running down his muzzle and staining the sandy colours of his chest fur. The King's ward tried not to concentrate on that too much, not blaming his companion by any extent of the imagination but knowing after all this was over – if it ever was, the young man would hate himself for that.

If the young man were ever to come back to the world.

Suddenly the distance contained in the palace's main entrance seemed infinite, every step seemed to only take them an inch whilst the exit stretched a hundred miles away. But their progress was progress, and the handful of people in the hall were only left to watch and stair. Either unaware that their home had been home to a lycan and a king's ward in the first place, or not stupid enough to be willing to interfere with their desperate attempt at freedom.

Naturally, however, it was never going to last.

"After them," an almost familiar sound boomed. Mason was able to take a fleeting glance back to spot Isaac descending that elegant marble staircase, his guards beside him, bewildered for a beat at first, then all at once they were moving. And the chase was on.

Now their movements were backed by the clatter of boots and shouting voices, bullets flew about the main entrance, and by virtue of luck alone Mason didn't feel the piercing heat of one.

"The doors get the doors," a shout followed, and Mason panicked as he saw civilians move to follow orders meant for guards. Genuinely unsure whether Silas would know the difference between an enemy and an unfortunate but innocent spectator.

Luck was on their side, but still Mason forced his feet faster, knowing that at any moment it could well run out.

The wolf reached the door a good few beats before Mason was able to and lunged through its gap. And half a beat later, the would-be prince was through the massive doors and into the open light of Brynde. The breeze and sunlight that he thought he would never feel again were sudden yet welcomed friends, and his nearly cheered with gratitude.

But they were far from out of the woods, and a further glance over his shoulder told him that freedom from the palace was far different from freedom from persecution.

If the distance of the main entrance had been infinite, the distance between the palace and the walls of Brynde seemed like it would take a hundred lifetimes to cross. As he took off pounding down the hill. His aching feet thudding rhythmically down the stones as the wolf charged on ahead.

Behind him the fervent shouting of the pursuing guards soon began echoing down the hill in their wake, the sounds of gunfire continued but less regularly now. Rather than the chaos that had ensued moments before, they had composed and were taking true efforts at aiming now.

Gulping hard, it mightn't have looked elegant, but the would-be Prince began zig zagging his path like an erratic and panicked sewer rat. Desperately bounding on, praying that now of all times he wouldn't trip and stumble. A single misstep here would be the death of him in the wrong scenario, and a lifetime in those cells might well be worse than death anyway.

Fortunately, the panic that had made the walls seem an infinite distance away didn't delve into the realm of reality, and the stone houses, shops and churches of the main city of Brynde were upon them nearly immediately. Here they found something more sheltered, places to hide almost everywhere.

"Silas," Mason shouted, but the wolf had bounded on ahead. The young man took the moment to shelter in a small nearby alley, hoping letting the guards lose sight of him might give him better chances, especially in their seemingly fruitless pursuit of the wolf.

At least if the wolf was able to be free before the guards caught up, the would-be Prince might be able to hide and follow at a slower pace, not drawing as much attention in this city full of people as a wolf did. The sandy creature was a bull in a china shop and might as well have carried a sign alerting everyone around him of his presence.

Their pursuers were weighed down by their armour, weaponry, which matched with the few beats of a head start allowed the wolf and his companion to make fair way down the hill in advance of their assailants. Still the adrenaline and the fear of everything that had gone on left his heart racing until he was certain it would explode from his chest.

But the sound of his own thundering heart and thudding footsteps was soon drowned out. The King's ward heard the regular chime of a bell, and he looked to find the source. Spotting the palace at the top of the hill, and knowing it was some sort of alarm.

Alerting the city to the presence of an enemy in their walls, a call to arms that could have been heard from the hills beyond the city walls. Mason was quite certain even the gods could be roused by the amount of rockets the palace now emitted.

Mason grimaced and took off running once more.

The city which had once caught their breath in its beauty, now seemed to writhe with enemies and potential monsters. He wove through, keeping his head down and trying to steady his breath, hoping to blend into the masses and be lost in plain sight.

But a glance in the reflection of a nearby window told him just how bad of an idea that was.

The man who stared back at him was grimy and dirty, exhaustion left his eyes baggy. He didn't know how long he had been there, but that period was enough to steal his familiar features and make him look hideous. Mason grimaced, took a moment to attempt to wipe some of the grime free of his face, and instead took off running again.

Little idea further than try to stay in a straight line, he could see the towering walls of the border, but the placement of the gates remained less certain. With little more direction than a headless chicken running about the farmyard, he could only do his best.

Most of the inhabitants of Brynde had flooded to the streets, the sound of the chiming bell rousing them from whatever they had been doing. Confusion seemed to light the atmosphere ablaze, though eyes weren't particularly fixed to him, only those who noticed his desperate run tended to turn and look at him. And even they didn't have the chance to react before he was gone again, skimming through alleys and dark corners.

Shouting sounded from nearby, and Mason tensed in place. Panicked that his companion had been caught, but soon he recognised the sounds of orders being howled above the incessant chiming. Explaining what was going on, and who they were on the lookout for.

Fortunately the damned bell had some advantage to the trespasser, for it muddled the orders and made it difficult to pinpoint different noises. If they could make the most of that confusion, it might be one of few helping hands the pair would receive for the foreseeable future.

Taking shelter in the shadows of an alleyway, he heard thundering boots and shouted voices, but they didn't stay in place. Running past where he hid and paying little consideration to the would-be Prince, either they had spotted the wolf further ahead – naturally the source of their main attention, or Mason had been successful in losing them.

Inhaling weakly, he hurled into the main streets again and continued in his desperate run. Close enough to the pursuers that he could see the advancing guard, but not so much that they could see him watching their direction and electing a different path.

The King's ward kept up his charge, his breath coming in harsh uneven pants as he struggled amid the unfamiliar stone city. But his progression was continuous, and he went without drawing much attention fairly well.

Until in his wake a voice shouted, "Stand down."

Slowly he turned, hands up in surrender for fear he might be shot on the spot. When he had rotated he spotted a single guard, split off from the rest of the group, holding a gun pointed directly at his head. Finger grasping the trigger, regardless of how much luck he'd been graced with, it would take a miracle for the stranger to miss at this distance.

The guard approached a few feet, observant and worried. Clearly expecting the wolf to appear out of the blue and rip his throat from his body, leaving him bleeding out in the alleyway. When this didn't happen, his pace sped up – confidence emanating from his frame, a grin laced his lips, but the anger in his gaze was prominent and terrifying.

"I don't think they'd mind too much if I brought you back dead," the stranger growled in a tone that Silas would have been impressed with, the shining muzzle of his gun not leaving the young man's gaze once. "You killed my friend," he continued, something tearful lighting in his gaze but that burning and insistent determination couldn't be extinguished.

Mason tensed, eyes closed and expecting nothing but the darkness of death to overpower him. But for the second time that day, and for the hundredth time it seemed since they had first met, the wolf saved his life.

From a nearby alley the wolf had lunged forward, colliding with the gun wielding stranger with the impact of a sudden brick wall. The pair thudded to the ground, from the scream that tore from the guard's throat, cut short out of the blue, Mason knew it was over for the other man before it had ever truly started.

He hated the relief that flooded through him, but right now it was him or them.

The would-be Prince would never know whether that had been coincidence or genuine effort on the part of the wolf, but whichever it was he would be forever grateful.

But right now was far from the time to offer thanks, and struggling to force the shiver from his frame, Mason gestured for his companion. "Come on," Mason breathed not quite able to get his head around the fact that he was still alive, "We don't know if anyone will have heard that scream." He explained, and the two took off again.

Now with the wolf thundering at his side, it wasn't quite as easy to slip through the streets as unspotted as he had done before. Silas might as well have been his own, moving siren, alerting to the world around him that they were not welcome here.

However, the danger of a lycan in the streets wasn't enough to make even the most loyal civilian to start chasing. Only the guards continued their pursuit, though for the time being out of sight, but the screams of surprised that launched from the civilians they passed was going to draw attention at some point, and the pair could only hope that they would be long gone before the guards were able to pinpoint particular screams.

For now it added only a melody to the thunder of their footsteps, the pounding of his heart and the heaving of his breaths. As well as the scatter of claws against the stone floor from Silas, the world seemed to roar by as the surged on at speed.

Whether out of sheer desperation, luck, or the virtue of the very gods themselves. The great gates which marked the exit to Brynde came into sight, Mason's heart soared. He found some unknown source of energy renewed as he surged forward, feet pounding against the hardstone floors of Brynde as he wove through the crowds, quickly parting for the wolf and the King's ward.

They might just get out of this alive after all.

A few feet before him Silas continued to run at full speed, it didn't appear that he was yet to break a sweat, though through the fur it was difficult to tell. The wolf didn't stumble, didn't pause, didn't hesitate. Mason knew he wouldn't have thought twice about tearing through the crowd and through anything that might block the way.

"Get out of the way," now the young man cared not for whether the guards would spot them, in the midst of their all-out sprint that was only one of their millions of worries, none of which they could pay much attention to, instead their focus fixed to the way out and the tantalisingly close freedom.

Rather, now Mason yelled for the sake of his friend, ever unsure whether Silas had any control in the matter, but for the sake of later guilt he did what he could to keep the death toll to a minimum, the wolf was doing all of this to save their lives.

But the by behind the wolf wasn't going to see it that way when all of this was done.

"Close the gates," the shout went up from various places, the realisation hitting the guards that either the wolf would get out or both of them, and the repercussions of that would be on their heads. Despite it, the pair ran on.

Only by the grace of the gods did they see that the exit gates were parted, in hindsight Mason realised it was likely that they were only purposed with use as an entrance, and that an exit set would likely be somewhere or other. However, they were hardly here to comply with the rules, and they certainly weren't about to break their run to find out directions for the proper exit.

Before them Silas burst through the gates just before they closed, and Mason followed a few beats before. But the entrance guards had been gifted with the aforethought to slam the first set of gates closed first. Mason moved to snap the second set shut with an almighty, metallic grown.

At least that way they would only have to deal with one set of guards at a time.

He turned, panting breathlessly to find Silas tensing to lunge for the guard marking the entrance. Who looked fit to need a new pair of trousers by the time all of this was done, whether to keep his dignity or the pair he was to wear to his funeral was yet to be seen.

"Silas don't!" Mason yelled, but now not out of the worry for his friend's guilt. They needed something of the guard. "The keys!" Mason yelled, desperate and all too aware that the remaining guards were only a few hundred metres away at most.

The guard didn't move, "Keys!" He repeated desperately.

Now the wolf was nose to nose with the stranger, the growl emanating from him scared even Mason who considered himself an ally at that point. "It is not worth losing your life to that wolf because of your job, please, the keys!" He all but begged, voice shaking until he wasn't sure it was comprehensible.

Shaking like a dead leaf, the guard relented. His trembling fingers left the little corridor between the gates lit with the metallic tingling of keys smacking together, and he hadn't it over to the would-be prince, who lunged for the first gate and set to work desperately trying to open them.

The wolf didn't move from his spot, keeping the stranger pinned to the wall on the off chance he decided last minute heroics would be a good idea.

Doing his best not to think about what followed, and how easy it would be to poke a gun through the holes in that gate and end them there and then, Mason forced the key into the padlock, unlocked it and jarred the great gates open. "Silas come on!" He yelled, and the two tore through the gate before the stranger they left behind could even think about reaching for his gun.

His feet were free of the gatehouse less than a heartbeat before shouting went up behind them again. Thinking not about keys, gunshots sounded but not directed at either of them, rather the lock Mason had taken the time to bolt before turning to the second one. It gave way under fire, and the guards were on the chase once more.

Mason cursed himself for being so stupid as to hope they might have been entirely free once outside of those walls. It would take a lot more effort to be free of their desperate pursuit, and now before them was the great hilly plain, familiar from a distant lifetime.

But they would be cornered mice if they attempted to find a hiding place on those barren fields, they needed to think of something else.

The next question, however simple, flawed the young man. Left or right.

His decision was split and made on fly, there was no chance to think about it. The last time he had been outside of those walls felt like it had been a lifetime ago, and he was too exhausted to picture it well enough outside of a blurred image.

Left only to pray that he made the correct choice, the young man started right. Taking off at a hasty run, gesturing as he did for Silas to follow him.

"This way," Mason panted, still unaware of if Silas was listening or understanding a word he offered but he found some comfort in at least trying to. He could remember seeing a woodland close to the walled city from when they were on the hilltops, if they could find it, they might just be able to lose their pursuers there.

Beside him the wolf set off running again, paws colliding now with mud and grass. A more natural setting for the creature to find himself in, his speed increased evermore, despite Mason being certain that was an impossibility.

Free of the silver chains the wolf had known all of his life, he was even stronger than he had already demonstrated himself to be.

Together – though at an ever-increasing distance, they skirted the towering walls of Brynde, breathless and hurried. He kept to the shadows, but soon in their wake the sound of metallic crashing of boots as they were pursued at speed. Now their head start was less, but despite his exhaustion he wasn't going to let it decrease any further.

Their luck not yet out of order, Mason was able to spot the woodlands in the distance.

Somewhere close by he could hear the now nearly familiar thud of paws.

The distance between themselves and the woodland began to close, though the sound of footsteps was distant it was an ever-present warning that one misstep would be the death of him. He charged on, long grass whipping at his face as he charged, drawing blood from the various wounds it inflicted at speed, but that was nothing compared to the wounds that might be wreaked if he paused even a beat too long.

Mason continued until the darkness of the woods were upon them, shielding the light from sight and offering them shelter. He took a moment to turn back, trying to see the guards and he spotted the grass still moving behind them. They weren't gone yet, but here was the best opportunity for them to lose them once and for all.

A small part of the would-be Prince was petrified that they might never give up, but he couldn't concentrate on that too hard.

Despite how desperately his legs wanted him to give in and collapse to the forest floor, he continued his desperate run. Lunging over sporadic tree roots, sliding through the thick muddy patches and struggling through thickets and nettles. Fortunately the wolf led the way, offering something in the way of safe paths and managing to keep his legs moving one in front of the other without breaking a leg.

Somehow over the past few days, this had become something in the way of a routine.

Until finally, the sound of following footsteps faded into nothing. Though they ran on a while, just in case it was some ploy to get them to relax only to be caught on the spot. Eventually, it seemed that there was no one left following them.

Resisting the urge to collapse to the floor, Mason came to a stop. Shivering from head to toe, his breaths panting as he fought to catch his breath. Silas too came to a hasty halt, the wolf didn't pant or seem remotely unperturbed by the all-out run the two had been subjected too, but then Mason wasn't paying too much attention.

His vision was blurred, and his lungs were burning, but still through it all the sensation of relief took precedence over all of it. Through desperate and harsh panting sounds, the young couldn't help but laugh out of sheer gratitude that they had managed to survive. Elation surged through his body, all the pain and fear of the last few days slowly dissipating.

Then he heard a sudden and nasty thudding sound.

Mason looked up, uncertain as to the source. Until he spotted the wolf downed, on the ground, and a pool of blood slowly spilling onto the ground around him.

Chapter Twenty-Three.

When Silas awoke again, he had the distinct feeling of someone who had been recently dropped off a fifty-foot wall.

A groan tugged from his lips as he sat up, memories faded and distant, for the only thing that mattered in that moment was the agony ricocheting through every inch of his muscled frame. That muscled frame currently portrayed a hundred shades between black and blue and that was only based on the upper half of his body. For the lower half of him was hidden beneath a thick blanket, and he found himself resting on… *a bed*?

Dropped off a fifty-foot wall, onto concrete, he corrected with a grimace.

Further inspection revealed a thick layer of bandages around his chest, skilfully wrapped to the point where moving was difficult. Something of a gift given that even breathing currently made the pain nearly unbearable.

Dropped off a fifty-foot wall, onto concrete, and then run over by a herd of wild horses. He corrected even further. He moved his hand to investigate the bandages further but found the act impossible. Looking down at either hand, he found silver bands lacing his wrists, and tied to the sturdy arms of his bed.

It wasn't just any bed; it was a hospital bed.

He had no memories of the nights before, but voices lit his memories. Unknown sounds that had come to him in the dark. He shook himself, shaking at the hideous memory and desperate to find someone to explain any of this for him.

The young wolf tested his voice, "Hello?" The sound was unfamiliar, jarring from lack of use for Gods only knew how long. He had no idea how long he had been asleep, but he knew it had been no brief nap.

His last memories were of the dungeons in Brynde, and when that came back to him after a few moments he cringed with a mixture of panic and fear. *Where's Mason*? How he'd managed to get here was something he could figure out later, but whether his friend was alive or at least intact took a prominent place in his brain.

Grunting with the effort, he tested the fortitude of the metal arm, the pain was fierce, and the fixture was steadfast. His frustration flickered through his gaze, but he allowed the limb to lay flat again. Right now the slightest movement was like setting his skin ablaze right now. His healing abilities had been restrained by the silver and the general exhaustion which captivated him.

He could well have been asleep for a month and closed his eyes in order to sleep a further year, and he doubted this exhaustion would have departed. It was an all-consuming sensation, that accompanied by the pain made him wish for the sweet relief of death in that moment.

The click of a door handle tugged the wolf from the depths of his melancholy and macabre line of thought. He stiffened, all too aware that he might as well have been a mouse cornered by a lion but still, he tensed. Prepared to do whatever was necessary to defend himself and get out of there.

His memories of whatever came prior to this were fleeting, but the need to be protective were intrinsic and bone deep.

Yet the expression that greeted him was kind enough, not the hatred brief nightmares had led him to expect. Her voice was kind as she said with seemingly sincere excitement, "You're awake, thank the Gods!" But didn't give Silas the chance to return before retreating from the doorway, shutting the door and leaving Silas alone once more.

He was left simply to stare at the door, blank of expression and confused of mindset.

Fortunately, he didn't have to wait too much longer before the door snapped open once more, no revealing a much more familiar face in its doorway.

Mason took one look at him; elation quickly lit his features and he was at the bedside with a speed even Silas found impressive. "Thank the Gods," he stated, hugging Silas as best as he could give the other man was tied firmly to the bed.

Relief worked through him at the revelation his friend was alive, he accepted the hug with gratitude for the friendly embrace. Particularly when every part of him screamed that the last few days had been filled with nothing but cruel encounters. But as the would-be prince released him from his steel grip, Silas realised just how badly the efforts had hurt him. He said nothing, but apparently the grimace which crossed his expression revealed the truth.

Mason cursed with embarrassment, "I'm sorry I wasn't thinking," he pleaded with genuine panic.

Silas' laugh was weak and shook his entire frame with the effort. "It's alright," and the young man meant it. But his gaze narrowed, and his tone turned to something more solemn and worried, "Mason, what happened?" He asked.

The young man's features moulded into pain; a brief study informed the wolf that his companion wasn't injured outside of a couple of light bruises. Those scars were something more mental, and something not as easy to shake. "What do you remember?" His voice quiet and quivering.

Nothing, and that's what frustrated the wolf to his core. "The last thing I remember is being in those rotten cells," he said.

But what scared him the most was the blackness that followed those memories.

Mason hesitated, prompting Silas to ask again. "Please, Mason," he said with as much firmness to his tone as he could force despite the shaking. "I need to know."

"Another time, Sy," the King's ward insisted with dark eyes, tears welling in his own green gaze, but he forced them down, rubbing at the area with the sleeve of his shirt. "Right now you need to concentrate on healing, and telling you is going to do nothing to help that."

Frustrated and uncertain, he clutched at his friend's sleeve with what little leeway the handcuffs provided him. "Mason I need to know," he insisted but his tone wasn't cruel or mean, rather genuinely insistent and pleading. "With this silver on my wrists it'll take me as much time as it would a normal human to heal, I can't wait that long."

Catching the change of subject like a well thrown ball, Mason managed a weak laugh. "Yeah I'm sorry about that, I tried to promise them that you weren't going to hurt anyone, but they weren't having any of it," he explained with a sigh. Investigating the cuff with curiosity, seeing the burned and raw skin beneath, but Silas knew that wasn't from the recent use. "But it took us so long to make you…" He trailed off, and Silas stared at him, lips parted and heart hammering.

"Did I shift?" The words tumbled from his lips before he could stop them.

But he knew the answer before he heard it, brief flashes of fangs and blood and fur blinking through his memory all at once. But still those very images had plagued his nightmares for a long time, and until he had absolute affirmation, he might just keep hold of his sanity and be free of his worst fears.

Mason grimaced visibly tensing, mentally kicking himself for the slip up. As quickly as he caught himself, the wolf wasn't slow enough to have missed the sudden stop. He stammered on his words, searching for a lie, searching for anything that might save him. And coming up entirely and frustratingly empty in spite of his best efforts.

"Yes," he admitted eventually, wringing his fingers with an expression of clear guilt. "Yes you did."

Terror and guilted bolted through Silas' own veins, the next question left him stuttering and struggling to form words. Finally, he spat out, like it was a foul tasting and burning drink on his tongue as he managed it at last. "Did I kill someone?"

Again, the young man's silence told all. He too began stuttering and struggling, his gaze lowered and desperate to find an excuse to lie. But Silas could already sense the intention to lie before Mason could even begin to say it, the thunder of Mason's heart audible despite the pounding panic of his own.

Eventually the young man seemed to see sense, that lying was going to help neither of them nor eventually he answered meekly. "I'm really sorry, Sy," he began but that was enough of a confirmation for the wolf to want to scream.

The guilt was all consuming, and the tears were all but overflowing. His scream of anguish was a stifled one that echoed across the little room. His control was gone, the pain, the exhaustion and the confusion of the last few days came hammering down on his head all at once. Until he felt fit to explode from the agony of it all.

Mason panicked visible, "Sy, please," he said hoarsely trying to get a grip on the conversation once again. "Silas, you did it to save the both of us," he promised insistently. But backed away from his companion, watching helplessly as the wolf struggled to get a grip of his control. After a few moments, the King's ward added bleakly, "If it weren't for you doing that, I have no doubt that the both of us would still be stuck in that little cell."

Memories of his companion's screams danced through his watering eyes.

The King's ward wasn't entirely sure he could survive a second round, let alone his companion.

But despite his best efforts the young man was inconsolable, however, his next renewal of efforts was cut off. As once more the little door opened, revealing not the friendly woman from before, but a solemn if somewhat bored older man. Dressed entirely in white, he approached the bed with a nod of his head to Mason.

"I'm glad to hear that you're awake," if he spotted the great amounts of distress his patient was in, he made no efforts to either ease them or ask as to what had happened. "How are you doing?"

For the first time Silas seemed to come around a little, he inhaled sharply and tried to concentrate on the matter at hand. Part of him realised how ridiculous he appeared in front of strangers, and as with most things the young man wanted to be private during his more devastating moments.

"I hurt." His voice hurt too much for him to put together much more of a comprehensive response.

The gentleman hadn't offered his name, and simply approached the wolf without too much worry about it. He peeled back the blankets to reveal Silas' bandaged chest, undressed them a shade to check the bandages underneath.

"It won't heal properly until he's free of the handcuffs," Mason explained with the tone of somebody who'd had to explain this a number of times already. Speaking for his companion while the wolf struggled to form words.

A new gratitude sparked through the hurting young man.

Shaking his head with annoyance, the doctor regarded the King's ward with a bored expression "And as I've told you before, I'm not about to permit a lycan to go running around my hospital, it might be slow but it'll no doubt be good for him to feel a little human."

Right now, the last thing Silas wanted to feel was his humanity, it felt like slowly but surely it was being drained from his body. He felt all too human, entirely aware of every crevice and cranny of his body, and the fact that not a single part of it was without pain.

"I won't shift," Silas promised, the voice croaking but insistent. If he had it his way, he would never do it again. His constant fears had been proven correct, that his wolf side would bring nothing but pain and grief and death. He had to choke back the follow up statement that nearly ripped free of his lips unbidden, *I can't shift ever again*, it was a mantra he intended to live the rest of his life by.

Frustrated for the sake of his companion, "There is no point in leaving him to suffer like this, can we at least unhook him from the bed?"

Hesitation and annoyance melded through the gaze of the doctor, but at last something in him softened and he relented. Either from looking at the pitiful form of the wolf and realising even if he wanted to, Silas wouldn't have been able to kill anyone right now. Or he was sick and tired of having to argue with the persistent would-be Prince.

A small key was produced at speed from his coat pocket, forced into the lock of the small handcuffs and quickly released the left arm. Silas pulled the limb away, rubbing the rawness around his wrist with a grimace, but muttering a thankful sound to the doctor.

"If you have my clothes from before," he said, all at once away again of his naked form beneath the duvets. The thin layer of material all which masked his dignity for the time being, and desperate to be clothed again. "That will do well enough to keep me tame," he said as his right arm too was released. Now a free, he carefully remained still. Every movement conducted with great thought in an effort not to worry the doctor.

Mason looked sheepish, his gaze drifting to the floor as he found himself short for words once more. For the usually charismatic and quick-witted King's ward, it was something quite new to find him struggling to speak.

The doctor, however, was having none of it as he said impatiently. "You're welcome to wear the ashes of what we burned," he grumbled, wrinkling his nose with disgust at the thought. "By the time you... became human, it was so bloodied and muddy that it was washing it would have been nothing more than a waste of water."

Deflating at this, he understood but that was one of few things that he could find comfort in. His portable chains that kept him human and safe, the one reminder of home. But he had plenty of clothes of a similar sort.

"I understand," he said managing to keep his tone even, "I have some more in the..." he was cut short, realisation sparking in his gaze. "The rucksacks." He could still picture them where they had been deposited by Isaac's desk, before all of this had turned to madness and fear. All their food, their herbs, their clothes... the King's remaining letter, gone.

Panic surged through him, but Mason portrayed only grief in his gaze. Fully aware of all of this, clearly having had to go through the same worry Silas was now burdened with, and again that spark of guilt surged in his chest.

Mason merely nodded meekly, "I know."

Certain that the wolf provided no threat, the doctor collected the handcuffs and pocketed them. "I will see if we can find a better means of restraining you for the rest of your stay, see if we can provide you a little more freedom."

"Thank you."

The doctor merely nodded, "You're quite welcome," he said with a shrug of his shoulders, though with a tone of someone who believed something quite different. And was gone from the room without another word, leaving Silas and his friend alone once more.

Now alone, the wolf turned his gaze back to the would-be Prince, curiosity melded with a genuine fear as to what the answer might be as he asked. "Mason, how long have I been gone?" His heart thundered so hard he was certain it might be audible.

Frowning but honest, "You've been unconscious for about two and a half days."

Cringing at this, his eyes hovered over Mason's as he asked again, "And how long were we... there?" He asked finally, his voice finally working into something more familiar now he had the chance to put it through its drills.

"I'm not sure," Mason admitted with a sad tone. "When we left it was the twelfth," he responded, but this was information Silas already knew, he kept hold of his patience by the tips of the pinkie fingers. "And well today it's the twenty first."

This information was delivered like an electric shock to the system, and Silas' eyes widened until they might have envied the breadth of the full moon. He calculated quietly, running the numbers through his head again and again desperate to figure out an answer that was kinder, more reasonable.

Their time in the dungeons had spanned three days.

To Silas it might well have been either an eternity or a few seconds, neither made much difference as it wasn't the amount of time but rather what had happened during it. And more importantly how long remained that they might be able to finish this in.

Ezekiel had given them a conservative estimate of at least ten days, hoping it would take at most a week, but that limit had been and gone. If they wanted this war to be averted, they truly needed to get going and now.

Only his physical difficulties stopped him from lurching out of bed and setting off now, his will, intention and everything else would have willingly gotten moving then. Mason stepped back with surprise at the sudden surge of energy that emanated from his companion.

"Come on, if we get moving now we might just make it."

Inhaling quietly, the King's ward seemed to consider this for a moment, and the silence between them was tense and anticipatory.

"No, Sy." Was all he said at first, but quickly continued without allowing Silas the chance to interrupt or argue. "Now I know you're awake and healing, I'm going on ahead to Rehenney, but if you think I'm going to let you come, you're a mad man."

Silas had made no pretences that he was anything but a madman but persisted.

"And you are a madman if you think I'm going to let you travel their alone."

Shaking his head so violently it was like he was trying to rid his hair from fleas, something between a laugh and a choking sound pulled free of his lips. "Look at you Sy," the young man gestured emphatically to the wolf, still flat in the bed. Silas wasn't sure if Mason sounded angry or saddened or somewhere in between, but all he did know was that he saw the guilt reflected from his own soul into Mason's dark green eyes. "I thought you were dead, I thought you were going to die." He struggled over his words. "I'm not going to let that happen again."

The young man had never felt more mothered, even Monarch might have found this somewhat dramatic. But beneath the frustration he found some gratitude in that his friend cared for him, but that didn't mean he wasn't going to argue over it.

"And you think you're going to fare any better without me?" He scoffed.

He might have expected Mason to look hurt at this, but he remained resolute and unwavering. "No, but I'm willing to take my chances, Sy." That was enough to shatter his heart, knowing that his companion would rather die alone than risk his friend any further.

But the wolf too shook his head, "But I'm not," he returned. Sitting up as best as he could, mostly in an attempt to prove his wasn't entirely useless, but the limbs were weak and shaky from the lack of proper use. His head felt dizzied from the effort, and he bit back the urge to throw up from the exertion, feeling more human than he had done in a long time. Despite all of those things, he managed to look his companion directly in the eye.

After all they had been through, Silas wasn't willing to let his companion take this suicide mission, not alone at least.

"Mason, after all we've been through if you think I'm going to drop this at the last obstacle you don't know me at all." He insisted, looking his companion directly in the eye, commanding his attention now even if the King's ward wanted to look away. "People have died, we have suffered and been through so much. And all of it will have been in vain if I give up now."

Everything might have ached, but he knew that pain would be nothing like what he would feel if he agreed to relent, and later found out that his companion had been killed.

They had started this together, and Silas would be damned if they were to finish it apart.

"Mason, I don't care if I have to take those handcuffs and tie us together," Silas finished with determination, not exaggerating even in the slightest at that point. "I'm finishing this with you, whether you agree to it or not."

The would-be Prince's lips parted, more than ready and willing to argue back, eyes narrowed and desperate. But again, he found himself speechless, understanding that this was a losing battle and there was no version of reality in which the wolf was going to take no as an answer. He might not have liked it, but it seemed he was accepting of it.

"I hate you sometimes."

Silas didn't blame him and managed a weak smile as he replied. "Don't worry, if we do this right, we won't need to see each other again after this."

Chapter Twenty-Four.

A journey of a thousand miles might well begin with a single step, but it was that very first step that proved to be an unforeseen problem.

Now the ache and pains of everything they had endured over the last few days felt all the more crippling, and that accompanied by the fact he hadn't moved from the bed made his legs about as stable as a newborn calf taking its first wobbling steps.

The doctor had sent a nurse to their room once more, and the friendly woman from before explained that she was here trying to get him accustomed to the waking world once more. But first the need to get out of bed was a prominent issue.

Inhaling sharply, the wolf utilised the arms of the bed to garner some leverage as he surged his bottom half off the bed. All too aware of his naked nature, he accepted the towel provided for his dignity with great gratitude. Wrapping it around his lower half, leaving the upper part of his body free but that was hardly his primary concern.

Fortunately, the surge of insecurity about the revelation of his heavily scarred upper body was lessened somewhat. Knowing that Mason had already seen this and was unlikely to comment, and that the nurse who had treated him would already be privy to this part of him. That and the fact the nurse was an older woman, such that she would have seen the war that plagued the country in her younger years – Silas was probably not the worst thing she had seen.

Though the fact that his wounds weren't comparable to those inflicted in war was hardly a selling point to most people. The kind nurse kept her smile and gentle tone throughout their conversation, as they discussed briefly what the best course of action would be to get Silas up and moving.

To his credit, and despite the far from elegant nature of the next few efforts, Mason remained steadfast. Willing to do whatever was necessary for his friend, after all they had been through the would-be prince assumed it was the absolute least he could do.

His habitat at current was a quite large room, one that left him with the feeling that normally it would be packed quite a bit more. But then he assumed it was likely that the doctors had evacuated the area to make room for the wolf, aware of the danger he might pose and not letting any of the more vulnerable patients near him.

Brief guilt caught through him at this idea, not wanting anyone else to be inconvenienced for his own sake, but all too aware that there wasn't much he could do about that now. He was brought back to reality by the nurse's gentle voice. He looked to her, on edge.

"Ready?" The nurse queried, stepping a pace back or two to provide him the space to stand – and if necessary, catch him were he to fall.

As I'll ever be, but he remained silent, they were helping him, there was no need to be disheartening.

Again the sensation of being heavily parented struck him, like a child stumbling into his first steps. The thought made the weakened wolf grin a little at the idea, and it was that happy thought that he used to fuel his first attempt.

Shakily he stood up, grabbing onto the nurse's offered hands as he worked to find his balance. For now he found a little victory in the fact that he'd managed to straighten without falling face first into the floor. His smile was triumphant, childishly so, but he saw that very ecstasy reflected in the green and blue eyes of Mason and the nurse before him.

Carefully withdrawing her arms, Silas was unwilling at first but permitted her to retreat a beat. He teetered a little, finding his balance a little trickier without something to lean on, but he quickly accustomed himself to it again.

I've been doing these for years, why is this so difficult. He was annoyed with himself; precious time being wasted.

"You're doing great," her compliment was sincere. "Now see if you can't try out a couple of steps towards me."

Steeling himself, the wolf took one step forward before his knees buckled beneath the weight and he was sent stumbling to the floor with an inelegant thud.

"Oh how the mighty fall," Mason offered in an attempt to inject humour into the tense atmosphere, he knelt beside his companion and offered him a helping hand to get up with, the nurse doing something similar at the other side. "The dangerous wolf, face first in the dirt."

Silas sent him a silencing glare, but his grin was present despite it. "Less a dangerous wolf and more a newborn pup right now," he corrected.

Utilising the help offered, he returned to his feet once more. Free of the silver he could feel the aches beginning to lessen, it would be a few days before they were gone completely – the aftermath of the wounds' severity as well as the prolonged amount of silver he had been subjected to both during and after the ordeal.

Again he was forced upright, largely through the help of his companions did he remain on his feet. And he admittedly dreaded the moment they would let go but knew if he wanted to be out of here soon, they would need to hurry up.

They released him once more, taking one step, another and then another. Until he had reached the edge of the room, swivelled slowly around and looked at them with mild triumph. His dignity somewhat ruined by the face first plant into the dirt, but it wasn't enough to burst his happy bubble too much, maybe deflate it a shade.

"I'm impressed," the older nurse said with a bright smile.

He was too, but he didn't admit. "Thank you," Silas said genuinely, knowing he would still be tied unmoving to the bed had it not been for Mason and this kind nurse.

"You're welcome," the nurse responded but her gaze narrowed. "But you'll need to forgive me, I have other patients to see to right now, and do need to get on with my morning rounds."

"I think we can manage from here." Silas replied nodding.

Smiling gratefully, "You'll be able to find some spare clothes in storage if you leave here and take a right, it'll be the third door on the right," she explained hurriedly, adding a gesture in order to reiterate her point, but Silas only nodded.

The wolf nodded, grateful for the fact the remaining part of their journey wouldn't be conducted half nude. The nurse departed with a farewell, and Mason looked at Silas with a shake of his head. "You're going to be the death of me or yourself, I'm just not sure which one will come first."

Shrugging nonchalantly, "Again, after a couple of days it's not going to matter too much," he breathed, thankful to have the freedom of movement back.

"We need to find the doctor before we get out of here," he added. The memory surging back to him like a cold shock, so unused to the lack of silver on his frame. He highly doubted the clothes the hospital had to offer would have any silver laced in them and could only hope the doctor had found something that might suffice. Mildly concerned he might need to tote around those silver handcuffs as an accessory, an earring perhaps. "Hopefully he'll have found something."

Mason regarded him sadly. "Sy, I understand if you insist. But do you really think it's necessary?"

"Yes," his voice was steel, ice and terror melded together into some strange combination.

For a moment it looked like the king's ward was going to disagree, and his lips parted with preparation to defend himself. But instead the other young man shook his head, defeated and mildly frustrated but nothing else. It seemed that neither of them was in the mood to even attempt to argue with one another at this point.

"Okay, you go find clothes, I'll find the doctor and get back to you."

Glad that they had come to a consensus, they made for the door. Mason departed left, more used to the hallways after a few days of living here. But to Silas it was unfamiliar and mildly uncomfortable. White walls and tiled floors, it was all simplistic, hygienically so. With very little life to any of this place, he inhaled, trying to familiarise himself with this place briefly. Before he spanned right and delved down the corridors.

Bare feet padded carefully down the tiled floor, thankful for the short distance from here to where he could see the third door. A nurse and his friend were one thing but being subjected to strangers seeing his scarred abdomen was something he could have happily lived without.

The storage cupboard was sparse, a clothes rack at the rear with a handful of garments; the leftovers from patients of past. Silas could only hope they had been forgotten and not… stripped off those who would no longer need them. He trudged to the back of the room and began searching through the offerings.

The only options that would feasibly fit him, as it was mostly children's and women's clothes, were fairly basic something he was grateful for. A black pair of trousers that were baggy and loose, but that could be fixed with a simple belt he found slung across the racks top.

He donned them, pairing the simplicity with a further shirt. It wasn't a flattering look, but he was grateful for the disguise it offered his marred frame, he looked around briefly for a jacket and found the best option was an oversized jumper of sorts. He decided he could go without, hoping he could find a better option down the line.

Exiting, he came to a halt when he spotted Mason and the doctor returning down the corridor and called a gentle greeting. All too aware that there might well be other patients still sleeping in the surrounding rooms.

"I found something that I believe might work," the doctor explained, and revealed the item that had been folded across his forearm. Revealing it to be a simple jacket, it would perhaps be a little tight, but it might offer something in the way of warmth. But that wasn't the problem that came to mind.

"Thank you, but it's not what I was meaning-" he was interrupted before being able to finish.

"You misunderstand me," he returned, eyebrows furrowed with annoyance that Silas dared to doubt his intelligence. "Much like your normal clothes, these linings are laced with silver," he explained, parting the jacket to demonstrate the insides. "And before you ask no I don't mean the colour," that felt more biting, but Silas didn't apologise for the time being. "It has been sewn with silver thread, truly silver thread," he added.

Doubtful and uncertain, "Why on earth do you have something like this?" He asked, taking the garment with gentle hands and studying it briefly. To humour the doctor he donned it and moved briskly, testing it out.

Annoyed by the endless questioning and doubting of his abilities, the doctor crossed his arms and watched the wolf with a grumbling sound from deep in his chest. "One of the nurses is of dwarven descent," he explained easily. "They believe silver to have healing abilities, and often their garments are laced with it, just as yours would be."

This fact brought a weak, watery smile to his expression. Mildly amused by the fact that what prevented his true healing abilities was what spurned it on for another species, interesting. The wolf considered but was grateful.

"Thank you so much," he said after a moment. Feeling truly safe after a moment or too.

"You're welcome," the doctor replied, somewhat more kindly this time. Though that wasn't a particularly difficult bar for the elder gentleman to pass. "It won't be as effective as it might be when all your garments are sewn with it, but I should imagine it'll provide what you are searching for."

Looking to his companion again, "We should get going," he offered. Desperate to be free from this place and in the wilds again, the ever-present deadline was descending over their heads like a storm.

However, Mason couldn't respond before the doctor interrupted. "I forgot to tell you," he explained with the tone of someone distinctly annoyed by being the hospital carrier pigeon. "Levi was wanting to see you before you set off."

Mason grimaced, and Silas could only look on in bemusement.

Annoyed but it was mixed with amusement rather than anger, Mason sighed. "I told him no."

"You've met Levi, yes? Do you really think he was going to take that as an answer at face value?" The doctor returned; arms still crossed. "Go find him, or I'm never going to hear the end of it," and he was gone again before Mason could respond.

"For the love of the gods," the King's ward muttered.

"Levi?" Silas pried, looking down at his companion once more with confusion.

The young man simply sighed, gesturing for him to follow. "Come on, I think I know where he's going to be, and it'll be easier for him to explain it to you."

With few other options than to listen, the young wolf followed his companion as he led the way down the winding corridors. Deeper and deeper until they parted through a great set of doors, and into something akin to a canteen.

No one as much as looked up when Silas and his companion limped into the eating area, unaware of a lycan in their midst or content to at least finish breakfast before they succumbed to death inflicted by one.

Here the tile floor opened into hard wood, and little benches littered the area. To one side a great cauldron was settled, and the smell emanating from which was sweet and quite delicious. Porridge, and the very sight made his stomach rumble.

But rather than towards the food, Mason wove through the tables. They were littered with small groups of people, mostly bandaged, with crutches or other signs of injury and or illness, and the room was littered with the sounds of laughter and conversation.

His experiences of hospitals were far more drab than this, depressing places of death and sadness, not jovial laughter as though this was a school rather than a hospital. But then he doubted those things would be allowed to take place in the context of the dining room, and today of all days Silas was happy to hear the sounds of laughter and chatter. Far better than the screams and cries that had plagued the days before, and then nothing but prolonged darkness.

Mason lead the way through the tables, until they reached one fairly central to the line-up. There a gentleman sat, someone who could have made most mountains look dwarfed in comparison, he sat playing absent mindedly with a bowl of porridge. But when he spotted the pair approaching, that solemn expression slipped into one of genuine happiness.

"I'm glad to see you've joined the world of the living," the man greeted, older than Silas and Mason though not by many years. He stood up promptly, garnering attention from those around him as he rose but was quickly ignored, and he offered a large, dark skinned hand to the mildly bewildered Silas. "I'm Levi ."

Mason hummed in affirmation, "He already knows and has been fairly warned," the King's ward replied leaving Silas mildly worried about who on earth this gentleman is. "Sy, you hungry?" He asked casting his gaze back at the young man.

Entirely unsure of what was going on, Silas nodded. "Starved."

"Well I've already heard his sales pitch," Mason said, shrugging off his coat and placing it on the bench, gesturing for his companion to take a seat. "I'll go get in the queue and bring you back some too," he decided. "Try not to kill him, bit arrogant but he's not too bad." He grinned and departed, leaving the wolf alone with the stranger.

It wasn't common that Silas felt like a small man, even without lycan genes his family were of large and muscular builds. But compared to this dark-haired gentleman, he might as well have felt like a mouse.

Arching a questioning eyebrow, that was apparently enough to spur the gentleman on.

"Listen, your companion has been regaling me with your recent adventures," the young man explained, and when Silas' gaze lit with surprise quickened his tone. "Don't panic, he only gave away the key details under a bit of pressure, it's not every day you come across someone who looks like they've recently been struck by lightning and then throttled by a giant," he explained, despite the humour to his tone, those wise eyes were lit by something pitying.

"I understand," he responded with a shrug of his shoulders, attempting a façade of ease, if Mason decided to reveal some details Silas assumed there was a reason to it.

Nodding thankfully, the gentleman continued. "Anyway, I am an ex king's guard, or retired rather," Levi 's words were unhurried and casual, odd given that such a statement was usually toted around like a weapon in its own right. "And I genuinely think I can help you on your journey."

A thousand questions came to mind, but before he could begin to compile them into a logical order, Mason had returned carrying a pair of bowls. Handing one to the wolf and beginning devouring the other hungrily, "Has the enigmatic idiot convinced you yet? Cos he's been trying for the better part of two days with me and is yet to get the hint it's a no."

"Yeah well given that the only reason you've given me for refusal is because you're worried I'll get myself killed, I'm inclined to persist," Levi returned, turning his dark gaze onto the other man with an arched eyebrow. "Enigmatic idiots like me are generally quite difficult to say no to I'll have you know."

"I'm beginning to see that," Mason muttered between spoonfuls, now his attention turned to Silas. "What do you think?"

"Why would you want to come?" It seemed like they were being sold something, but the price was yet to become apparent.

Levi shrugged his muscled shoulders, "Boredom, the need for adventure, lack of the will to live, take your pick." He returned, none of them were overly enticing options, and Silas was in half a mind to take Mason's side and refuse his wishes to join their little team. "Okay fine," he said when he could sense that neither party were picking up what he was putting down. "I can see when some kids need my help, and I'm not going to be able to live with myself if I hear you died before you got there down the line."

"He's a lycan and I'm as tricky to kill as the average cockroach," Mason returned easily, licking his lips as he finished and pushing the bowl aside, whereas Silas had barely dipped his spoon in. Silas smirked weakly at this, though recently it had proven to be an apt description.

Unperturbed by this statement, he shook his head. "Yeah and your lycan has been beaten and a solid enough boot can kill even the most fortified cockroach," he returned with equal wit and ease, "A little extra help isn't something to scoff at."

Eliciting an exasperated response but turning to Silas now for the Levi al decision. "What do you think?"

Silas wasn't certain that even if they said no this gentleman wouldn't follow them all the same. He regarded the man, flaring his nostrils and thinking carefully. From lack of use his senses felt overly human, but they were soon kicking into gear and he found no signs that the gentleman was lying or had anything malicious to his intentions.

Offering a sigh of his own, though less annoyed given he'd only had a few moments of this and not the days Mason had been subjected too, he shrugged his shoulders. If this man had truly been a pester or annoyance, the King's ward wouldn't have even entertained the prospect of coming to say goodbye, so the wolf assumed that to Mason, Levi was little more than a pester not a true threat.

"Even if we say no I don't think he's going to take that as an answer," smug but playful the massive man leant back on his bench, arms crossed with pre-emptive triumph. "But then I'm a pretty fast runner and we can meet up later on if you can ditch him quick enough."

Levi's facial features dropped, and Silas grinned at his own minor victory that he had managed to trick the older warrior. "I'm kidding," he muttered with a shake of his head, and the gentleman lit up with a grin once more. "I really don't see why not," he finished to Mason.

The King's ward simply sighed, though accepted Silas' answer as final and turned his gaze to the newcomer. "We're under quite the time limit, collect your things and meet us here in ten minutes." He informed, though a slight commanding tone laced his words.

With a smile that Silas wasn't sure death would be able to wipe, he stood up and moved to leave. But turned back when he thought of something and asked, "Will you still be here when I get back, or am I going to need to do some tracking to prove my worth?" He asked, a wicked but playful tone lacing his melodic voice.

"Be quick and find out," Silas returned with equal ease, and the gentleman was gone.

The ten minutes they had offered him wasn't even half-way over by the time the ex-guard returned to the group, a back now placed upon shoulders and that grin still replicated on his features. "I'm ready when you are," he informed, with an ecstasy Silas wished he could replicate.

If the option had been there, he would have slept for the rest of time. But right now it didn't seem like they were going to have even time for a ten-minute nap in between journeys.

Now with a third party, the wolf and the King's ward departed from the little hospital. Godsgather just visible in the distance, but few other things were visible from here.

Initially he thought nothing of it, but after a few moments' worth of travelling, Silas couldn't quite shake the feeling that something wasn't quite right.

"How do we get to Rehenney from here?" He queried, and Mason pulled out the map that the hospital had offered him. Larger than the one the king had provided them, and more detailed towards the place it was made, fortunately this particular valley.

"Well we're about here," he jabbed a Levi ger at the parchment. "We follow the hills this way and travel north from where we would have been at Brynde, but for obvious reasons we'll give it a wider berth than we otherwise would have." He explained easily.

But Silas' frown didn't disappear. His worries confirmed, from here Brynde should have been visible, at least somewhat. He paused, using his hand to shelter the sun from his line of sight, he looked down upon the valley.

"That's all well and good, but where's Brynde?" He interrupted.

Mason parted his lips ready to respond, and Levi did the same. But they both paused when they spotted the same problem Silas had.

All they could see amid the great valley was Godsgather far in the distance, and the mass fields of farmers in between them. As well as a few lakes sporadically placed about the landscape.

No Brynde.

"I… I don't know."

Silas looked genuinely confused, struggling to see a version of events or angles from which Brynde wouldn't be visible from their vantage point. Where Brynde had been, now only sat flat open fields, largely unused and ready for the coming spring, tilled and further blackened by the recent rains.

But then it dawned on the wolf, as he used the map to pinpoint exactly where the city should have been visible based on where they stood. He gestured with a hand until he found what he believed to be the point, and the realisation stole the wind from his lungs.

Where his finger lay was the great expanse he had previously assumed to be farmer's fields. But it wasn't the black of a dead field being prepared for a spring of use, it was the smouldering remains of a city. Brynde.

Chapter Twenty-Five.

The wolf gasped audibly, and the would-be Prince stumbled to his knees.

He held no love for Brynde, so it wasn't grief that sent him stumbling. Part of his nobler characteristics like to imagine his knees had buckled out of unexpected exhaustion – that the lack of use had made him weary all of a sudden.

But the truth of it was the sheer shock that rocketed through his system.

The city they had been so in awe of not a week ago, the city they had been chained and tortured and broken in, rendered to ash and ruin.

"What – what happened?" Silas breathed, but neither of his companions had answers for him.

Levi removed a pair of binoculars from his and held them up. "It looks like an attack," Silas growled with frustration at the lack of information outside of the entirely obvious, but he wasn't finished. "I can see banners," he added further, the signature of a conquest, but this wasn't conquest they saw. It was a slaughter.

Mason spoke with a choking sound, "What colours."

All at once the answers pre-emptively flooded his system. Still he waited.

"I can't be sure, the smoke it makes things hard to see," Fin might have known them only a short period of time, but it seemed he knew enough about them to know how much the answer could well mean to the King's ward.

"Tell me what colours or give me those binoculars," his voice shook, and the anger was quite unprecedented in Mason.

With certainty that left Silas wondering if he'd struggled in the first place. "Grey and purple."

For a moment they didn't entirely have, they stood there in silence. Watching the smoke pillars arising from the city in great puffing clouds, turning the grey sky even darker. From here Silas could pick up on the faint smells of smoke, but something instinctual told him it wouldn't take them getting that much closer for another smell entirely to take hold.

If these were the actions of a coward, Silas daren't consider the actions of the brave.

Mason looked as though a bomb had been dropped on him, the in between of the action and the necessary reaction in which Silas could hear the whirring of the gears in his head. The frown on his features broke Silas' heart.

"Maybe he didn't know you were there," Silas reasoned, desperate to ease his friend's grief. "Maybe this was separate, there was word in the rebellion this might just be a reaction to this. We were meant to be long gone from the area; he will have thought you were safe."

All his reasonings seemed entirely logical to the wolf, but the young man didn't make any acknowledgement of even having heard what had been said. Finally Mason shook his head, compared to his shaking body it was a difficult motion to catch.

"No," all he could manage to respond with. "Isaac sent ransom notes, thought he might at least be able to get a few pretty dimes for me," Mason's eyes teared up as he spoke. "Those were sent days ago, the King would know very well where I was, or should have been at least."

Had their escape occurred even a day later, Silas and his companion might well be amid the bodies, burning and abandoned in the midst of the valley below.

"This might well have been a rescue mission," the ex-King's Guard offered, and Silas lit up with the idea, after all it would be Levi over any of them that would have known any of this. "He might have taken the city in order to find you, and when he discovered you were gone taken… that as a form of revenge."

But Mason was having none of it. "We've been living at that hospital for the last few days," he insisted bleakly. "We're the only one in the area, the only big one at least. If anyone survived… that don't you think we'd have been the first to hear?" Mason growled with something that Silas might well have made himself.

"This was no rescue mission," he finished lowly. "No one can have escaped that, we'd have seen something, heard something." Again the young man looked like he was considering punching something, be it a tree, the ground or one of the two men beside him. "This was a massacre and nothing sort of it."

Ezekiel had destroyed an enemy and had done so believing that he would be killing his own ward as he did it.

Both Levi and Silas sought words of comfort, words of reassurance, any kind of words that might have made this situation better. But they both came up short and felt useless because of it, and Mason simply stood and watched, broken but refusing to show in on any of his features.

The wolf simply sighed, moved forward and pulled his friend into a hug. It was the best he could manage, and he felt quite like a parent comforting a child after a nightmare but given the last few days Silas felt it was the absolute least he could do.

Mason sank into the hug body and soul, shaking as he did so but the gratitude seemed to sing from his very bones. Until he moved and Silas willingly released him, feeling entirely useless that such a meagre gesture was the best he could manage in the moment.

Allowing his companion a moment to compose himself, he asked gently. "What do you want to do now, Mason?" Silas worded it carefully, aiming to make it apparent that all the choice was with the King's ward – though that could no longer be applied as an accurate descriptor, he supposed.

Steeled again and gaze turned to stone, "We get to Rehenney." He decided.

Silas wasn't sure whether he should feel admiration the despite all of that the young man wanted to fulfil his orders, sadness that he felt the need to hide the emotions that were no doubt bolting through him, or gratitude that his companion was made of far tougher stuff than he could ever dream of being.

"We don't have the King's letter, we're going to need a plan to get anywhere near Joseph," was all he responded with.

"I'll figure something out," he returned weakly.

And Silas had no doubt that he wouldn't.

Regardless of what had happened here, their mission was something further than familial bonds. They had a war to stop, vengeance could be sought at a different time.

But the remnants of Brynde looked far too much like war than anything Silas could imagine occurring in Braxas. *How can he hope to keep his throne if war in foreign lands is unthinkable, but he will do this to his very home?* But it wasn't a question he allowed himself to ponder on for too much time longer than that.

Levi had stood aside, silent and watchful, but overall kindness seemed to flood his aura. "I'm sorry," his words were sincere but laced with the tone of somebody who had absolutely no idea of what else to offer in turn.

"Thanks," Mason's chuckle was humourless and stiff. "Now come on, let's get going."

For the first time in known memory, Silas felt like a burden to the group in terms of his speed. He was exhausted, something he wasn't going to be able to shake probably until this was all over. He felt frustratingly slow, though he remained in pace with his companions he couldn't help the insecurity that they were steadying their own paces to permit him to keep up with him.

He would heal, he had to remind himself of that somewhat forcefully. Even with the newly donned silver jacket that would slow the process some, he would heal. And for now he would have to push through the pain and not be too much of a burden to those around him.

No one wanted to come within a mile of the smouldering corpse which had been such a beautiful, and heavily populated city. It didn't take too long for them to be in the foothills of the hill range, the descent accompanied by daylight made it an even quicker journey than their original descent had been.

But there was a reason that they had all been dreading the descent, and even a thousand miles their proximity to its ashes would be considered as being too close to the sad sight. The scent was already rotten and horrific, the smell of smoke seemed to cling to his very lungs and make breathing impossible.

Silas should have felt some sort of delight at the sight, knowing those who had half driven him mad through torture had died with the horrific city. But the wolf knew that the city wasn't resident to only the cruel and vile sorts of this world, there would be innocents within those walls.

Such thoughts brought further questions to his head, what felt like the thousands upon thousands, increasing his belief ever further that he understood frustratingly little in this world. With a quiet voice the young wolf asked.

"If the King was so intent on keeping quiet, making sure no one knew of his return so he could get messages out without people trying to interfere," Silas reasoned quietly.

Mason seemed to pause, trying to compile an answer but he shook his head. "It seems the King was more mysterious than I was led to believe," he replied quietly. "He never said where his team was going, maybe it was one of the cities with one of the larger barracks, Exul or Kretya?" He offered; eyebrows furrowed as he sought answers but came up empty. The frown returned to his features again, "But those are all southern cities, it would take far too long for them to get here, surely?" He asked, a man in the midst of many doubts.

"I don't know," Silas admitted with a shrug of his shoulders, uncertain as to whether these were questions he would ever find an answer too.

Before them, however, Levi was shaking his head with a frown etched into his own features. His laugh was pitying and somewhat doubtful. "There are rumours about the big cities, places like Exul, Kretya and even Brynde." He admitted rubbing a stray hair out of his face, he took the lead of the party but only by a few steps. And he quickly caught the attention of both of his companions, who sped up a few beats in order to walk in line with the larger gentleman.

When he realised he wasn't going to get away with leaving the pair on a cliff-hanger, the young man shook his head with a bleak chuckle.

"In the days of the former queen, I was in her service but after these rumours," he explained as a long way of saying he had taken no part in the former war. A necessity given some of the things it was rumoured members of the Queens guard had been forced to do for the sake of their monarch during those days. "That to ensure key cities remained loyal, or to have a get out clause if it was thought they were going to fall under enemy hands." He explained.

"She would have a special material revered by the dwarven people, alleged to be able to take down mountains though that's never been proven, but more than enough to take down a reasonable sized city." He explained lowly, the grimace lighting his expression just at the thought of it. "There are dwarven names I wont even begin to try to pronounce for fear of being struck by lightning, but most of us just call it Single Spark, cause, well that's all it takes, and everything's gone."

The idea was horrifying, enough to bring a nauseous wave across the young man. "What kind of person would plant that?"

The guilt that had shot through him at the very sight of the city had almost crippled him, the fact they had been unable to help accompanied by the sheer number of innocents that resided within those walls was agonising. The fact that a human could inflict that kind of pain was difficult to fathom. *Is it the same type of King who spends so much money going on journeys abroad while his own Kingdom starves*? His stomach rolled.

He was never going to agree with the mayor much, but here he could see some of the truth in what had been said. Even if he hated to admit it.

Mason scowled cruelly, but the gesture was only to be expected in that moment, he gestured at the city burning in their wake. "What kind of King would set it off?" He challenged in turn, but the question fell on flat air, as neither of his companions could even begin to have any idea with which they might answer his question.

Wordless the little group continued on.

Not long before the sun set, the smouldering pit that Brynde had been reduced to had disappeared from sight. Even Silas couldn't see it amid the fields and small woodlands that dotted the area between them. Gone from sight but never out of memory.

But now Rehenney was on the horizon, or at least would theoretically be within a few hours, and if they persisted at pace enough they might just make it within the time limit that the King had set them. Their progress was fair, Silas feeling energy renewed far quicker than even he had expected of it. And given that Mason had received a good couple of days' worth of rest from journeying, and Levi was new to the journey all together, their speed allowed them to cross the countryside at a good pace.

Just as nightfall descended upon the trio, the burning lights of the city of Rehenney came into sight on the very horizon, and a surge of gratitude shot through Silas.

The dot of the city had begun to widen and come better into sight, when over the next hill the trio came across something unexpected. An encampment, or rather a massive one.

Initially something hopeful sparked in Silas, the beautiful colours were akin to the ones he had seen on the Angofwen caravan train so long ago, and he thought he might just be about to reunite with friends. But a quick whiff of the air told him this group were strangers, friendly or otherwise he didn't know, but now wasn't the time to find out.

"We have enough time," Levi decided, gesturing eastward where they might be able to skirt past the encampment without drawing too much attention to themselves. "If we had that way until we spot the border, give it a little more room and then continue down we can avoid it entirely." He decided, at ease but gentle of tone. All three of them all too aware that such a large encampment so close to a big city likely wasn't a happy sight.

But they weren't here to ask questions and interrogate, they were here to get to Rehenney as quickly and safely as they were able to.

Thus the trio spanned right and began their careful and precarious journey once more. Thankful for the cloak of early evening, the darkness providing a disguise for the three young men. It seemed like they might just have made it without difficulty.

When a voice from a little way down the slope sounded, "You there, stop!"

All at once the trio considered setting off at a run, but the stranger was upon them before they could even begin to think of trying.

The woman who approached had long, silver blonde hair and eyes of burning amber brown as she approached them. Gracing her frame were various pieces of jewellery, all incredibly beautiful shades of blue and grey, glittering in a seemingly impossible manner given the dim nature of the night upon them. Her head was graced with a simple tiara, and Silas struggled not to eye it admiringly, even if not his type – the wolf could admit this was a beautiful woman. Four people followed in her wake, roused from their posts by her shout and surrounding the trio before they could truly think about what was going on.

Slender fingers wrapped around a spear, though an ungainly looking weapon she carried it with a certainty that left Silas with no doubt she could spear the three of them with very little difficulty and not break a sweat whilst she was doing it.

Yet she carried it with a calmness, held loosely at her side and not posed to strike off the bat.

"Only the very brave or the incredibly stupid would dare come close to a camp as large as this," her tone was difficult to read, but they were accompanied by a soft sound as she tutted like a condescending teacher, her arms crossed, and eyes narrowed. "Now pray tell, which one of the two options are you. And why?" She asked.

Silas watched carefully, moon kissed gaze piercing through the dark.

A smile unexpectedly split her expression, "A lycan," she sounded mildly impressed.

The wolf tensed at the sound, for the last time he had heard that phrase it hadn't been long after that chaos descended upon them. The ache all at once returned to his frame, and it took some effort to keep his knees from buckling as fear ricocheted through his muscled frame.

"Unfortunately the question still stands, a lycan would be welcome in my camp." She explained, but turned her gaze to the pair beside him, "A King's guard less so much however," she decided through narrowed eyes.

"Your little friend I'm undecided on," Mason blushed a deep shade of red at the woman's piercing stare.

Levi was the one who responded the quickest, a far more apt liar than either the wolf or the king's ward. "I'm an ex-guard actually," all good lies had some concept of truth to them. "And I'm a mercenary at present, I've been ordered to bring these two to Stedda, they're on their religious migration you see," he said bowing his head with a degree of reverence. "We've just departed from Godsgather and intend to reach the city within the next few days."

It was a fair lie, and the perfect time of year for it to sound reasonable. As the spring months descended, a lot of young people would begin such journeys. They were perhaps a little early, but nothing that would make the lie unbelievable.

Her eyes softened a shade, as she considered the young boys. Mason stepped closer to his companion, laughing in a hopefully persuasive attempt at sheepishness. "Naturally I'm the one in need of protection a little more than Silas here," he explained with a bright grin, hoping to come across younger than he actually was.

"I don't know little one, I imagine you're quite the fighter when you want to be," she reassured with a chuckle. Seemingly deciding the trio of strangers were no threat to her camp, "It is getting late, you three would be quite welcome to join the camp for the night if you'd like?"

"We appreciate the offer," Levi returned with a nod of his head. "However, we were hoping to reach Stedda by late tomorrow, and currently we're a little later than I care to admit." His accompanying laughter was booming and convincing.

"Unfortunately I think it'll be safer if you find someone to camp down with, not necessarily us but certainly there will be in safety in numbers on nights like this."

"Forgive us miss," Mason spoke a little too eagerly, but his attempts at shyness were enough to make the sudden phrase seem more out of nerves than a desperation for answers. "But why would you say something like that?"

Her frown was etched into her features now, she shook her head. "I guess word hasn't spread as far as I thought it had," she explained with a shrug of her dainty shoulders. "War is on the horizon, and rumour indicates that the King intends to send out word tomorrow."

Silas knew this to be a lie. "I can't believe it," he breathed with some truth to the statement.

"Unfortunately it doesn't seem there's much to disbelieve," she continued with a frown. "That is why we are here, a lot of communities are pre-emptively declaring their allegiances, hoping to avoid difficulties later on." She explained with a frown, the distinct impression of someone who would rather do just about anything else.

"If you don't mind my asking," Levi asked politely this time, "Who are you, and who is your…community?"

Her smile was all consuming, "Do forgive me, I just tend to assume most people know. But then I'm not too familiar with these lands," she said with a shake of her head. "I am Niamh, the queen of the Cresine."

Chapter Twenty-Six.

At the revelation, Silas had to restrain his jaw from dropping to the grass underfoot.

While he had never been a worshipper, a lifetime living by the sea meant he was all too aware of the Cresine, and the woman before him might as well have been a God in her own right.

Her chuckle was melodic but kind, those storm cloud grey eyes wise but kind. "You've heard of me then?"

Silas felt certain this was a dream, that he remained in those dungeons in Brynde and that all of this had been some cruel hallucination and he would soon be dragged out of. That seemed the only logical explanation for any of this, young people dreamed of getting to meet a Cresine, let alone be fortunate enough to meet the Queen of them.

"People haven't?" Silas managed, wide eyed and feeling like a small child.

It took a beat longer than it should have for the wolf to realise that the would-be Prince and ex-King's Guard were looking at him with confusion.

"Sy, should we be bowing?" Mason's voice was quiet and slightly nervous.

Colour flooded his cheeks at the realisation, and he was knelt bowing in the grass. Head low and quietly pleading mostly to himself that the woman would forgive them for their idiocy. Beside him, though slightly less eager – Mason and Levi also slumped into a courteous bow.

"No, there is no need to bow," her chuckle was so kind it was all consuming. Leaving Silas with the sensation of having been bathed in the glow of her warmth. She gestured and the trio stood wordlessly.

"I'm sorry, Sy, but please tell me what's going on?" Mason said with mild frustration.

"The Cresine," he was all at once insecure that he realised he would need to explain a people in front of those very people. "They're a sea dwelling people, underlings of Cres himself."

To his infinite gratitude, Niamh seemed to have decided that was a fit enough description. Her head nodded, like every other of her movements this far it was a regal and refined gesture. "I believe the more common tongue word would be mermaid," though at the cringing expressions of the guards that surrounded her, she corrected herself with a further chuckle. "Apologies, merpeople."

Looking a little less offended, the guards who were still yet to say as much as a word relaxed.

"I didn't know merp- Cresinians," the word was unfamiliar on Mason's lips, but he was doing his best all the same. "Ever came to shores."

Niamh shook her head with a sad sigh, the sound was enough to make Silas want to spend the rest of his life ensuring that sadness never crossed her mind another day in her life. "We usually wouldn't but as I said. War is on the horizon, and tradition can be set aside for the time being if it might mean we can save lives."

Respect at that point seemed to all but flood the wolf's system, but now he understood the need to be a little more dignified than that. He nodded, understanding.

"If you don't mind my asking; what are you intending to do for the King?" Levi's words were carefully organised, with the hopes of not offending the woman.

For a brief second the woman looked annoyed, and Silas quickly spoke up. "Forgive him, we have been journeying for a few days now and I'm sure you appreciate that we're exhausted by now," he knew that was understandable enough from the infinite bags pooling beneath his eyes.

She relaxed a little, paused briefly – considering whether to bother or not, and then responded with relative ease. "One of my tribes inhabits in the waters between Braxas and Nekeldez," she explained with a shrug of her shoulders. "I've not had many specifics, but I'm assuming its something along the lines of permitting the safe passage of Nekeldian ships and prevent Braxishian's from getting too close." Her smile was wickedly playful. "As I'm sure you can imagine, we're quite good at the latter, but will be doing our best with the former all the same."

"I hate to break it to you, your highness, but the King doesn't reside in Rehenney," Levi spoke up, his tone not offensive or rude, more matter of fact with a gentle scatter of amusement littered into the tone of voice.

Grateful he wasn't the only one mildly confused by this, though quite embarrassed that it needed stating, he was left only to hope that the queen wouldn't take offence in their statement of the obvious. But her smile didn't fade even for a heartbeat.

Her laugh was gentle, "Oh gosh I wish someone had mentioned, I'd best wake the camp up and change direction," she said with playful worry, "I'm aware. Fortunately, whilst I am not used to these lands, I do know that much at least." She responded, "These are trying times and our original plans fell through, a messenger caught us on the way to Myaelle, and informed us of the change of plan, and that we are to meet the mayor of Rehenney instead and get things sorted."

Part of the wolf longed to tell her none of this was necessary anymore, that she could return home to a peaceful life for the foreseeable future. But even in the depths of his reverie he was all too aware that was a bad idea for all involved. Thus he simply nodded his head with understanding.

Niamh turned, casting her gaze on her camp. Someone who should have been a near literal fish out of water seemed entirely at ease, whereas her guards seemed to jump and stiffen at the sight of every shadow. She frowned briefly again.

"Hari, go find them a spare tent to rest in." She requested, and one of the men immediately set off at a run to fulfil her orders.

Her chuckle sounded again, "I fear we might have been subject to quite the scam, naturally we don't keep this sort of thing on hand, so when we asked the vendor likely told us we were going to need far more than we did," she shook her head, her laughter the melody of a gentle sea breeze. "But never mind, it appears that was fortunate now."

From here he could see the people gathered at various fireplaces, laughing and drinking the night away. Peaceful and happy, there weren't many of them, maybe a few dozen but nothing more. Guards for the most part, ensuring the journey was made safely and without issue, but compared to the guards he had become accustomed to these were a jovial and relaxed people.

Though the concept of war was heavy on their heads as it would anyone's, these people continued with life as normal. But then he supposed from the seas, the war would be of little concern to them, a distant nightmare that wouldn't interrupt in their lives too much.

Silas could understand that and envied them that much.

It didn't take long before the guard, Hari returned up the hill. Nodding his head politely to the queen as he approached, he explained. "We've found something that will work, if you'll follow me?"

Quite willingly, they followed at a steady pace.

They were led down a weaving little makeshift path, until they passed by the warmth of a prickling fire and into a simple tent. It was a dark grass green, small but enough room to fit the three men comfortably enough. The little fire was local enough that its warmth spread to the area, and Silas was grateful for the chance to rest his head.

"Will this do?" Hari asked.

"I'd prefer something with towers, a more regal entrance and guards of our own to secure the exit," Mason responded with folded arms. "Maybe even a moat," the young man deadpanned, but it didn't last too long as a grin broke through the stone features. "It'll do brilliantly, thanks so much for finding it for us."

Nodding his head, he turned and moved to return to his post. The trio of young men left to watch as he retreated through the darkness, and then they too turned. Pushing through the entrance to the little tent and set about making themselves comfortable.

A big blanket had been lain pre-emptively across the ground, with a couple of more folded in the corner for use where needed. The night was bitter, but the warmth of the fire was enough to make the temperature comfortable for the time being, though as the night progressed Silas knew his more human companions would need them.

"Is now a bad time to mention I sleep naked?" Levi asked with an arched eyebrow, considering the blankets with careful hands, pulling them over his lap in an attempt to garner a bit more warmth.

"Is now a bad time to tell you that you're going to be sleeping outside?" Mason returned easily.

But now he was in the confines of the tent, Silas was struck for the first time with the realisation he would rather do just about anything else. He had spent the last few days refined to a bed, conscious or not, and the days before that in a dungeon.

"Are you two going to sleep now?" He asked, distracted and already wanting free of the tent.

Mason looked up from where he too had settled comfortable on the ground, "I think so," he admitted looking tired. Levi had already settled himself down quite comfortably, and looked like sleep was about to take him within a few minutes. "You?"

Hoping not to offend his companions, it wasn't anything against them after all, but he nodded his head all the same. "I think I'm going to explore a bit," he didn't want to admit just how antsy he was feeling and would have accepted staying had Mason indicated that he shouldn't go.

But the king's ward only nodded, "Stay safe," he responded, a yawn parting his lips before he could say anything further.

Silas chuckled, "Sleep well."

Trying not to shake the feeling that that was becoming a bit of a common theme, the wolf turned around again and parted the tent doors. Out in the encampment once more, the bitter night air felt refreshing on his lungs.

Relaxing again, the ache by then had eased enough that movement wasn't quite the pain that it had been previously, though the bruises were still visible in places. In the disguise of darkness he hoped they wouldn't be too noticeable, hoping he might be able to find a friend among these strangers.

He spanned right, following his ears and nose to find a congregation of people in which he might be able to fulfil those wishes.

He journeyed a silent mouse through the camp, until he found a large communal fire. There a good handful of people were scattered about in the long grass, sat cross legged in the warmth of the fires glow. Silas joined them hesitantly at first, prepared to quickly turn back if anyone made it apparent he wasn't welcome. But for the most part he went either unnoticed, and he was left to make himself comfortable.

Closest to him were a pair of young women accompanied by a gentleman, they were relaxed and at ease. But Silas didn't fail to notice the spears scattered around, in place just in case they were needed he reminded himself, but the sight made him stiffen all the same.

He shifted on the spot, watching the crackling fire dance to the whims of the gentle night-time breeze.

The pleasant smell of liquor littered the area, flowery scents that seemed to stick to the very air around them. No one seemed overly inebriated from first glance, but the wolf didn't know how these people reacted to alcohol, or whether they had some stronger stuff that he wouldn't be used to. He wasn't one to judge, but wasn't about to partake with strangers, though no one looked overly prepared to offer him any of it.

Good to know they're very serious about protecting their queen, he thought with amusement, chuckling before he realised he wasn't alone, and was quick to silence the sound. *Getting drunk when they're in enemy land.*

But then from the general relaxation of the camp, they considered this enemy camp as much as someone would consider their neighbours kitchen an enemy trench.

"I can't believe how pretty it is," a voice broke him from his quiet contemplation, and he looked right to see that the gentleman had spoken.

Confused briefly, a grin split his expression when he realised what they were referencing.

Of course, sea dwellers wouldn't be used to fire.

"Are you making fun of us?" One of the women accused, eyes darkening a shade.

Colour flushed to Silas' cheeks; they might have appeared young but as with the queen they might well have been his elder by centuries. "I didn't mean offence," he said quickly, holding his hands up as a means of apology.

"Forgive Helaena," the other woman interrupted with a role of her eyes. "She clearly doesn't know how to treat a guest of the queen," her voice was lit with warning, and Helaena shrunk beneath it, though still looked distinctly annoyed.

"Its not a problem, I was being rude," Silas promised. "Its just not something I've really thought about before," he said running his fingers through his hair, "That Cresinians wouldn't be used to fire," he added clarification, watching the fire still.

"True enough," the gentleman answered with a chuckle. "I'm Jude, that's Aro and you already know Helaena."

"Silas," he returned with a nod of his head, smiling politely at the strangers.

"What on earth are you doing in a Cresinian camp, if you don't mind my asking?"

Remembering the motive that Levi had come up with, he responded easily. "Me and some friends are on a religious journey, we're heading to Stedda tomorrow, and your kind queen has let us use your camp for safety for the evening."

"Of course she did," Helaena's laugh rumbled, shaking her head. "That woman would welcome a giant's child if she thought we might be able to help."

Taken aback with surprise at the woman's statement, Silas blinked at her. He hadn't imagined someone referring to a monarch with such distain. "We were incredibly grateful," that was a lie, but it didn't matter too much at the minute, the insistence had been mildly inconvenient but nothing they would have scoffed at.

"I'm sure you were, and she will have wanted to help sincerely," Aro returned, resting back in the long grass with a yawn. "But I do wonder if she should stop looking to help others as much and turn her attention more inward."

Before Silas had the chance to consider this or even begin to respond, Jude responded by slapping a hand flat across his companion's lips. Silencing her before she could even think of saying anything further, and Silas flinched at the suddenness of the action.

"Sorry about her, we're tired and a little less sober than our queen would prefer us to be."

Understanding on an intrinsic level that they were tired from journeying, more than Silas knew he should admit, but still he recoiled somewhat from the revelation. He sat back, "Its alright, I understand," he responded easily, though on the inside felt quite the opposite.

But now the atmosphere had shifted notably, and the wolf became aware of eyes watching them carefully. Silas straightened, feeling tension ricochet through not only his own frame but rather the entirety of the people around him, unseen eyes piercing through the darkness that seemed to burn holes through his own skin.

He falsified a yawn, drawing a hand up to his face, he stretched and was on his feet before things could turn sour. He didn't believe they would, but this group was tight knit, and if one person got into a fight Silas doubted there wouldn't be a number further ready to pounce and quite prepared to back up one or their own, regardless of whether that person was in the right or not.

"It was quite lovely to meet you," Silas said dipping his head in a façade of politeness, trying to pretend he wasn't half as concerned as he felt. "But I've only just realised how tired I am, and I have lots of journeying to do in the morning, so if I am going to make my way to bed."

"You too," *lie*, Silas could smell it on the air, but he smiled kindly all the same.

He didn't stick around too much longer to find out whether or not anyone else had anything to say in farewell. And began weaving through the maze of tents once more. The sounds of the campfire had quickly silenced in his wake, careful to check he wasn't around to eavesdrop, but the time he had been moving for a few minutes the laughter returned to the air again. And a sensation of relaxation pushed through his veins once more.

With a sigh he realised he would have to retreat to be again, defeated and with no new friends accumulated. But the next question was trying to figure out how to get back.

Normally he would have tried to follow his own scent back, but for the scents of the world around him were too overwhelming. The strange scents of a new people were overwhelming, and beneath it he struggled to catch hold of anything familiar.

Shrugging, he had time to waste he supposed. He would just have to go for a wander and try to figure out his way home. At a gentle stroll, the young man began following the paths that compartmentalised the camp the camp. His trudging steps taking him down the barely worn long grass, happy to wander for the time being, anything to be free of a tent's confines in that moment.

The tents were a mismatch of colour, and he briefly remembered his own being some sort of shade of blue which should hopefully have narrowed things down a little.

However as he crossed through the tents, he heard a voice which made him pause in place. It was inconspicuous enough, but the tone was angry to the extent that it made him stop in fear that he might well have done something to bring it to him.

Nothing. It took him a beat longer to realise it was someone inside one of the nearby tents which was the source. And that there wasn't a single voice, but three.

He ducked down, even if no one was overtly nearby that didn't mean he wasn't going to be caught eavesdropping. And as quietly as he could manage, he began doing just that.

"If we're careful enough no one will even know we left our tent tonight," a deep man's voice sounded through the dark, clearly making efforts to be quiet but unaware of the presence of a lycan in the confines of the camp.

"Its not worth the risk, another time definitely but right now there's just too much going on, there's too much of a chance of getting caught. It might seem ideal, but another opportunity will pop up a different time, this close to one of her allies is not worth the risk."

A booming laugh sounded, but it was a malicious and cruel sound that made Silas uneasy.

"No land dweller will ever be an ally of a Cresine, and she is an idiot if she thinks she can convince them otherwise,"

"That might be, but rather it be her head than ours," a third voice still sounded, a woman's tone logical but condescending. "If things go wrong, all the better."

"But things won't go wrong, and then we'll be stuck in some land lubbers war."

Silas' heart pounded so harshly he was certain it would have been audible to those within the confines of the tent, but no one came out and executed him on the spot much to his gratitude. It was beginning to dwell on him just what was going on here.

The sparks of rebellion didn't seem to just be in the context of the Nekeldian monarchy.

And if this strange man wasn't convinced otherwise, they intended to make movements tonight.

But the wolf didn't set off running, and instead remained still, quiet and listening. His mind raced, trying to collect more answers and not react unnecessarily.

"And the answer is not to fell a queen who has sat on the throne for 800 years," it was the woman who responded, "At least not now and at least not here, another time when we can ensure our people are secure and safe." She insisted equally annoyed by all of this.

"Our people will never be safe when we insist on making deals with land dwellers which will result in death and pain for some war we need take no part in." The males deep voice sounded again, "I don't care what you guys say. But I'm doing it tonight, and you guys are welcome to help me. But get in my way and I will not hesitate in taking you down."

Silas was moving before he could hear anything further. Initially he sought the queen's tent but knew he would be of no help alone. He surged for his own tent, desperately forcing his legs faster and faster.

He had never intended to get involved in the politics of another people, but he wasn't about to allow an assassination to occur under his own nose. He wove through the tents, and all but collapsed with gratitude when he found the one he had come from and tore the door open.

Inside his companions were asleep, but that was quickly rectified. "Mason, Levi get up," he demanded, and he was out of the tent again in an instant and on the move. If he was to squash a small rebellion he would find it difficult to do it alone.

Bewildered and tired, the pair followed his wake. Both fully clothed in spite of the guard's previous promise, they followed him, jogging to keep up. "Sy what in the name of the Gods are you doing? Come back to bed," Mason said but followed anyway, trusting the instincts of his companion despite the bizarre nature of what was going on.

However, he didn't have the time to answer their muttered questions and was grateful when they hurried to catch up with him and not hesitate with the want to find out answers. Silas was thankful for their loyalty, even from Levi who was new to the group hurried to keep up and help out his new friends wherever possible.

Taking the charge, the young wolf moved through the tents as fast as his legs would take him in spite of the uncertain paths. Mason and Levi moving at speed to ensure they were able to keep up with the panicking wolf.

Instinct lead him, that and the fact the particular tent had a flag swinging from one of its legs, indicating its difference to the rest of them. Silas surged forward, left only to hope that he wasn't going to turn out to be too late. He tore through the great doors, to find the queen conversing with one of her own guards, calmly and with nothing to worry about.

Colour flushed to his cheeks, but that didn't stop him. "Forgive me your majesty, but I need to speak with you and it truly can't wait a moment longer," his words were sincere, and he hoped the woman would hear that.

The guard turned, a familiar face from earlier but the name was unknown to the trio. He looked like he was about to execute them on the spot for the intrusion, that or kick them out of the tent and perhaps the encampment from annoyance.

"Stand down," the queen responded quickly and was on her feet. She regarded the pair with confusion, her tone neutral the kindness from before gone, rather replaced with something a little more weary now. "This had better be good, or I might regret not letting Adria kicking you out."

"This is going to sound ridiculous, your highness, but I have reason to believe your life is at risk."

Adria's hand gripped harder onto the spear at his side, offended by the very insinuation that he would allow an attack on his queen to go down without a fight on his own part, but Silas ignored this.

"I was walking through camp and I overheard plans, I'm a lycan – they believed they were being quiet," he was realising all too fast just how ridiculous all of this was sounding but praying they would see the logic behind it. "I'm sorry I saw no faces, but there were at least three of them. Intent on making sure your intentions to create an alliance with the," he had to stop himself from using the word land dweller as he'd heard it so regularly a few moments before. "And they're intending to do whatever is necessary in order to complete it."

The guard looked at the pair incredulously, not permitting his queen the chance to interrupt. "You can't believe this your majesty," he scoffed with narrowed eyes. "We brought only our most loyal guards for this journey, no one would be so stupid as to attempt to take down the Cresinian queen, let alone one of her own circle."

Panic shot through him that he wasn't going to be believed, that he would be turned back and he'd wake in the morning to find that the queen had been killed.

"Did your companions hear any of this?" Her calmness was a comfort.

Beside him Levi and Mason shook their heads in synchronisation. "Are you sure of what you saw Silas, you didn't mishear?"

How he would have misheard a murder plot Silas wasn't sure, but before he could respond the King's ward spoke up instead. "If Silas says its true it must be," Mason spoke with a confidence that sparked gratitude in the wolf's heart. "He wouldn't make this kind of thing up just for the fun of it, nor would he mishear. If he heard this, there is a genuine reason to fear for your life," he said so certain even the Gods might have been swayed by his insistence. "Your majesty," he added as an embarrassed afterthought, not the type who would usually need to think of that sort of thing.

The queen considered this briefly, watching the trio through narrowed and concentrated eyes. She said nothing, and Silas was again worried that they would be kicked out in spite of their best efforts. Silas watched, hopeful and terrified all at once.

"As much as I hate to admit it, I believe there may be some truth in your words and some malintent in my armies," she returned, turning her gentle gaze to the guard who looked back at her with something akin to shock in his gaze. "Adria, go find Hari and Faline, I can trust those too at the very least," her laugh was humourless but still kind.

Straightening, Adria moved to leave the tent. But never had the chance to cross the threshold as he started reversing in retreat hands raised and panic apparent.

And following the thud of his body, six people entered the tent. Each person carried a spear gripped between skilled fingers, and each pointed at the members of the tent. The three spare landing on the queen and watching carefully.

Though the queen had been given the largest of the tents Silas had seen by far, the tent all at once became crowded. Zooming in on the threat and fear immediately rocketing through his frame as he moved to respond but realised there was very little he could do.

"Unfortunately, your majesty, your little friend is correct in what he's said," the face was unfamiliar; but the voice wasn't. It was the gentleman with a deep voice from before, and either his friends had been convinced that this was the right thing to do, or there were more friends willing to turn against the queen than Silas had begun to imagine. "And equally unfortunately, we're not going to let you leave this tent tonight, or ever again for that matter."

Chapter Twenty-Seven.

Silence devoured the tent; it could well have lasted only a second or the rest of eternity as everyone individually processed what had occurred. A paralysis rooted Silas to the spot, and he had no idea what the hell to do – the queen's only true form of protection now lay dead on the tent floor beneath them. Shout and pray someone else would hear and come to protect their queen; but if this many people were willing to help in the assassination how many more were aware of the intent and wouldn't come.

Half a second after the stranger's entrance, the decision was made for Silas as the shout went up from Levi. "Protect your queen," his voice was a lion's roar and he moved with a similarly feline grace, he lunged. Weaponless but brave all the same, Silas and Mason hesitated a beat and launched forward to join him, with no idea of what else to do instead.

The ex-King's guard spoke with the experience of a man who had spent his life protecting monarchy and moved with the loyalty as though Niamh was his own queen. Levi launched downward, grabbing the spear from the fallen Cresinian and wrenching it free, now armed and even more dangerous he launched into the fray.

With speed on his side but very little else aside from confidence provided by the fact he would heal from any non-fatal blow. Silas lunged for the one who dared come nearest to the Queen, dodging the spear by the skin of his teeth, he was able to catch it before it was withdrawn. But the sharp yank backwards unbalanced him, and a kick to the back of his knees sent him tumbling.

He spiralled but caught himself a beat before he smacked into the ground and used it as leverage to launch upright. Kicking the guard in… ungentlemanly places, but the resultant cry of agony and surprise told him his low blow had reached home.

Their shouts and yowls hopefully would be enough to pull anyone close enough to their aid, but a lot of them had been at the communal fire. Silas wasn't sure how far away it would be, but he doubted the sound would travel too well given the bitter wind and inebriated nature of the Queens people.

He could only hope and do their best to keep going until help did come. If it ever did, he didn't allow himself to entertain the idea that they were the only ones willing to protect the strange queen, the idea was a terrifying one, and right now there were more than enough terrifying things in the confines of the tent to keep him quite preoccupied.

In their wake the King's ward held back, keeping in front of the queen and prepared to do just about anything to protect her from assailants. The last line of defence, though unarmed and minimally trained Silas knew the young man would do everything in his power.

His loyalty wasn't easily bought, but Silas knew that if they were going to go down they would go down together, and Mason wasn't going to abandon them in the heat of battle.

Silas yowled as a spear caught his abdomen, though the force wasn't enough to impale him entirely, it left his already bruised abdomen bleeding again. A fleeting hand lunged to cover the area, the blood flow gentle enough, mostly stifled by virtue of the tight clothing wrapping his frame, gratitude flooded through his system.

He would have thanked the Gods, but right now he was already giving thanks to every god he knew the name of that he was alive still. A further few inches up and that could have ended far worse than it had done.

Grimacing, he parried the blow, swerving left and avoiding colliding with Levi by the skin of his teeth.

But the gravity and impossibility of the situation was slowly but forcefully dawning on them. They had survived this long by virtue of the narrow tent entrance alone, offering not enough room for the 'guards' to spread out truly and fight properly. Whereas the wolf and Levi were able to make better use of the space to dodge and withdraw.

However, this would only last so long, and Silas could already see his companion slowly deflating. Strike after blow were parried and sent stumbling back; these people weren't used to fighting on the land. A further advantage the young man assumed, but they had the numbers and the weapons, and Silas was feeling all too human all at once.

And slowly but surely, the two men found themselves being pushed back. With every step forward they managed to gain parrying and fighting back, it seemed that they were only insistently shoved back, it was like trying to change the direction of the tide.

Still no signs of help appeared miraculously through the tent opening.

After all this, it appeared to the wolf that it would be here where he had his last stand. After all the efforts to get to Rehenney they would be felled at an unforeseen obstacle, on the very steps of the city itself. But he would have done it willingly to protect his friends.

He fought furiously, desperately dodging and parrying where he could. He made some leeway, managing to collide fists with flesh and not sustain any further major injuries outside those in the realm of grazes and jabs. But no the tent seemed to become smaller and smaller with every passing beat, and even Silas found himself sweating and out of breath from the efforts.

Finally, the trio and the strange queen were pressed at the tailbone by the tents furthest wall.

"Kneel." The word was thrown like a weapon, and the four had little choice but to obey.

Niamh kneeled but her chin remained high, her gaze bitter and cruel as she stared her assailants – people she had previously believed to be loyal friends. She shook her head, staring each in the eye as she considered with a low tone of voice. "Why?" Was all she asked. Her voice didn't tremble, her eyes didn't water. She was the steadfast mountain, unmoveable despite weapons raised to her throat.

"Why do you think?" The deep voiced man asked, his gaze burning.

"Were you bored and felt like a change of pace?" She returned; her tone humourless.

The gentleman surged forward, his spear kissing her neck, but he pushed it no further. "We did this because you are a coward who would enslave us to the whims of some King who has never held a lick of love for the Cresine." The stranger shook as he spoke, but the determination and anger in his voice and gaze was nothing short of lethal. "That man would rather see us extinct and ruined than he would help us, and yet you leap to his aid the moment he asks."

Niamh moved to respond but she wasn't given the chance. Now his trembling voice was only just short of a shout, and his tone trembled with anger. "None of us ever wanted to do this, but you left us no choice."

Niamh shook her head, pity if nothing else in her gaze. "And why didn't you tell me? This could have ended so many other ways," her head shook with the mourning only possible from someone impossibly ancient, she was as calm as the sea. "There was no need for it to end like this."

The gentleman scoffed, horrified by the idea. "Like you would have listened," he didn't lower his spear for even a beat. His gaze burning holes through the queen's skin, and yet still she didn't waver even a beat.

"Of course I would have," she responded gently. "Broja I can see you want none of this, this would have been over long ago had it been the case." She spoke again, the first inkling of desperation becoming apparent to her melodic tone of voice. "Stop this nonsense, and we can continue like it never happened, I promise. I have known you more centuries than most people can count," she watched him unblinking. "None of you want this, please, we can find a better way."

Beside him the guards relaxed a frame, seeming to think this might be over. And a hope sparked in Silas that this might well have ended in an amicable means.

But, that kind of luck had long been used up for the young wolf.

"Oh I will finish this." The gentleman, Broja didn't waver, and the five people at his side quickly picked up their spears again. "The truth is you are a coward, Niamh," he said with a shake of his head. "Gone is the Queen who felled the city of Atlan, gone is the queen who raged war against the pirate Kings," he considered for a moment. "Gone is the woman I swore my allegiance too, and given it is by blood oath I am bound to you, there is only one means of ending that." He stepped forward again, posed to end this without allowing the queen to respond.

"Yes that woman is gone," Niamh returned with a mourning sound to her voice. "Because that woman was tired of all the killing she had done in her life – she realised there was a better way. And the last fifty years of peace the Cresine have known demonstrates that yes, life is possible to go on without constant battle." She returned, the ease and certainty of her tone seemed impossible in contrast to the sharp spears pointing directly at her throat. "It might not be as glorious, but I have seen my people truly happy for the first time in a long time."

Broja considered this wordlessly, and some idiotic part of Silas thought this might just have ended there, the strange assailant accepting this version of events and giving up there and then.

Of course that was too good to be true, "Not everyone is happy," and he surged forward again, spear poised.

Silas had lunged unthinkingly.

He collided with the spear not with his hands but with his abdomen, screaming with surprise as it pierced through his chest and the young man hit the ground hard. Bleeding heavily.

The pain was sharp and shocking, his gaze turning white with pain as he felt his hands grow wet with blood. But then slowly but surely the white consuming his eyes, faded into a shade of pale, bloodied red.

Now the pain spread across his frame, not located just in his chest but flickering through his veins like the spread of a plague that he could pinpoint beat by beat.

His skin was on fire, tiny needles poking through every inch of his skin. He could feel his bones breaking one by one, slow, meticulous and agonising as they reshaped one by one. His face elongated into a muzzle, and his mouth tasted like blood as flat teeth sharpened and for a brief beat he went deaf as his ears disappeared as the shift took place.

Until he stood not on two legs but four, in wolf form for the second time in the space of days, whereas before this week it had been the many years.

He had no time for questions or puzzlement, he lunged. Colliding with the astonished guard, the fight was on again. This time with energy renewed, and an advantage on their side.

Silas was just about ready to begin his slaughter – the humanity he had begun his shift with all but disappeared now the scent of blood had flooded his tongue and nostrils. Feral instincts very much in charge of his every movement, with nothing but the infliction of death on his mind, if his mind was present in this form at all.

A scream from behind him sounded just as his paws collided with the head colluder, his fangs bared and pressed to the skin of the gentleman's neck. Only a beat before his fangs had collided did the sound pull him back to reality, and then a beat later something as strong as a brick wall collided with him.

He surged aside, landing hard enough that the shift was forced into him. Unconsciousness nearly tugging at his senses, but he quickly roused again, breathing and struggling. He realised he was soaking wet, and when looking around he realised that he was not the only one, and not a small enough amount that someone had thrown a bucket over them.

Their assailants too were on the ground, coughing, choking and spluttering as they struggled to breathe. They too astonished by what had just gone on, and were shaking now either with fear, from the cold or somewhere between the two.

Panting hard and bleeding still, Silas turned back to try and figure out what in the name of the gods had just happened, but what he saw wasn't much of an answer.

At the centre of the tent Niamh had stumbled to her knees. Her hands poised at either side of her, droplets of water still bubbling at her fingertips, a mere sign of the rushing water which had been there moments before.

The grass underfoot crunched, dead and browned and it struck Silas exactly what had just occurred.

"Enough is enough," her voice was shaking for the first time and the beautiful blonde looked exhausted, her features drained of the ample energy, and suddenly she looked so much older. Not in terms of complexion, but rather her posture sagged, and her eyes saddened. .

Then of all times a person appeared at the doorway, "Helaena," her voice was grateful, though the woman screamed at the sight of Adria on the ground, and the bloodied small battlefield. A beat too late to have been of any true use. "Take these men outside, find a few others – that you trust, and I will be out in a minute."

Shell-shocked by the scene she had come across, and with some uncertainty, but Helaena quickly complied with her orders. Gripping a spear skilfully in her hands, she began herding the traitors out of the little tent. Briefly looking down at the body of the felled Cresine, leaning down and pulling him onto her shoulders as though he weighed as much as the clouds, and following the six out. When she parted the tent doors, Silas could hear her begin shouting orders out in the dark.

"You couldn't have done that earlier?" Mason's voice was caught between frustration, relief and ludicrous amusement. As though he expected a moment later to be told this was a dream, a coma induced hallucination, or he was in fact dead.

The Cresine Queen shook her head, struggling to her feet and stumbling as she did. Levi lunged to hold her up, and she gratefully accepted his help. "I didn't know that was possible," she returned her voice little more than a croak compared to its original melodic tone. "I'm miles from the sea, this shouldn't have been possible."

And from how exhausted the action had left her; Silas couldn't help but agree that it probably should have been.

"Whatever that was, I am incredibly grateful for it." Mason's voice was weak.

Silas turned his gaze on him, trembling something caught between anger and confusion ripping through his veins. He stared at the remnants of the jacket, what should have been his safety blanket that prevented any of this from happening, the garment he had been gifted at the hospital.

And it dawned on him what had happened.

"You lied to me." His voice was so deep it could have been mistaken for a growl, and his anger was a burning fire in his moon kissed gaze. It was like nothing he had ever known, the fury something he could barely contain for fear he would shift due to the lack of silver. He restrained himself by the skin of his teeth but shook with the effort. What resulted was anger melded with disappointment, confusion and most importantly the sensation of betrayal.

"I did." Mason's response was calm, but his gaze watery. Either from the confrontation with a wolf he considered a friend, the assault, ensuing battle and near experience with death, or something stemming from the two. He too had received something in the way of a drenching as a result of the queen's sudden lash out, he looked like a drowned rat. But for the first time in a long time, Silas felt no pity for the King's ward.

"Why?"

However, before Mason could respond the queen beside them spoke up. "I'm going to go sort things out," she explained, a thin sheen of sweat still coated her pale skin but her voice didn't shake as much as it had before. Clearly not wanting to be a part of the quite personal conversation which would go on between the wolf and the would-be Prince, she departed. Giving the pair the privacy of the bloodied and drenched royal tent.

Silas watched her go, before turning his attention back to the would-be Prince. "Why?" He demanded again, his voice shaking with poorly restrained anger.

For a moment Silas thought he would be refused even that dignity, as the young man remained silent for a beat, not making eye contact with his companion. Silas moved to ask again; deadlines be damned he was going to get answers if he had to wrench them from his friend's lips.

Betrayal like this was a bitter stab, the blade drenched with poison as he was stabbed from behind.

"Why?" He demanded a third time now, the word tearing from his lips accompanied by a growl which would have made any sane man flinch at the time, but the young man simply turned his gaze up to meet the wolf's.

"I thought I was doing you a favour." Silas almost laughed from the idiocy of it. "We couldn't find anything in silver outside of those damned handcuffs, and having you tied up for the rest of the journey was hardly an option, so we thought it would be kinder to lie than let you think you were going to tear our throats out every beat of the day."

It was a fair reason, but Mason wreaked with the distinct stenches of a lie.

"Tell me the truth or you can get out of this tent," Silas knew he sounded heartless, but in those minutes he didn't care.

Mason's cheeks reddened and warmed. "I did think I was doing you a favour," he corrected lowering his gaze again. "Silas, you've spent your life in chains. You deserve freedom, and you deserve not having to live your life terrified of what might happen if you lose your silver. I thought this was going to be the best opportunity we were going to get!"

Silas was shaking where he stood, "I could have killed you!" *I nearly killed those guards*, but he struggled to find the same amount of guilt in that respect right now. No doubt he would be drowning in it at later gate, but for now all he felt was anger.

The would-be Prince shook his head, remorseless. "I knew you wouldn't, Sy," he responded bravely, a confidence in the wolf that Silas had never been able to match even slightly. "In fairness to me I hardly expected us to be attacked at the last field before Rehenney, I thought this was going to be so much simpler." He too sounded angry in that moment, but not at himself nor the wolf, but rather the circumstances in which he had been caught.

"Exactly what did you expect, Mason?" Silas returned, keeping his distance only by virtue of his self-restraint. "Did you think you would reveal this in a few weeks-time, and we would all laugh about it and I would feel so much better about everything?" He demanded.

Either he didn't know how to respond or didn't want to. Though the wolf hardly gave him the chance to respond. "This was selfishness and nothing short of it, Mason, and you went against my will and could well have gotten yourselves killed."

Levi who had maintained something in the way of an oath of silence for the proceeding minutes, watching the ongoings with awkward nervousness of someone entirely new the dynamic. Finally spoke up then.

"I'm sorry Silas but I think you're being unfair there; he meant no harm. And let's be entirely honest none of us could have imagined that this was going to end the way it did."

Now the fire in his silver gaze was extinguished, now replaced with an icy flint state that only just withheld the tears of pure frustration that threatened to tumble if he didn't hold himself together. "If he didn't foresee harm coming from this he's either an idiot or has absolutely no regard about my wants and wishes, take your pick." He all but snarled.

Neither responded for a solid minute, until.

"I only wanted the best for you Silas."

"And if you wanted the best for me you would have listened to a single word I had to offer on the matter in the past week, but no. You decided you knew me better than I know me, and you put yourselves at risk because of it."

He stopped, trying to catch his breath and keep himself still all at once. All too aware of the fact he looked like a drowned rat in those moments, but appearances made him nonetheless dangerous. He ran his fingers through his dark hair, trying to wrap his head around what he considered to be nothing short of bitter betrayal.

"And what if you had been wrong, what if in the middle of the night something had made me jump, I shifted and killed you both?" He continued, forming a somewhat cohesive argument in spite of the anger which left him shaking. "How do you think that would have gone down when I returned to the King, that I slaughtered his ward like a sheep in the night? Do you think I'd have lasted more than a minute before he had me hung, drawn and quartered?"

Mason stuttered at this. "I... I," the would-be prince struggled, but the words didn't come to him. "I didn't think about that," he admitted after a moment.

"Yeah I can see that, and that's the problem."

Silas surged through the tent but didn't go for either the King's ward or the ex-King's guard, but rather through the parting between them.

"Where are you going?" Levi asked, the calmest of any of them, but genuine pity pricked on his dark gaze.

"Out of here," Silas responded with the obvious.

"Are you not coming with us?" The statement from Mason brought a ludicrous level of anger from the wolf, and he inhaled sharply.

"I'll come with you to Rehenney," he growled lowly. "But after if I never want to see you a day in my life," and he was gone from the tent without a further word on the matter.

Chapter Twenty-Eight.

Silas roused before the rest of camp; the sun was only just cresting on the distant horizon, but the others wouldn't follow suit for a good few hours yet. His body ached, yearning for just a few more moments of sleep but he resisted the urge to snuggle down and return to the dreamy realm.

The queen had been kind enough to provide him another tent, somewhere solitary for him to rest his head without the distraction of all that had gone on the day before. As memories began flooding back to him, mental wounds still fresh enough to be forgotten. Both his body and his heart ached, but he pulled himself upright and set into action.

Parting the flap-doors of the tent, the young wolf descended into camp in silence. It seemed his only companion was the gentle, rhythmic birdsong that danced along the air. A jovial sound that felt like outright disrespect to his pain, but he could hardly take out his frustrations on nature herself.

Camp was slowly bathed in the golden light of early morning, offering warmth to the still mildly sodden wolf. He sighed, grateful for its greeting; seemingly the only constant of recent. As all he thought he knew now seemed to feel like a bitter lie.

If he'd had the opportunity, he would have remained statutory and bathing in the warm sunlight. Content to let the world pass him by without too much thought, but he was all too aware it was time to face the music.

After tonight he wouldn't need to see Mason ever again, and he had to find some comfort in that fact, if nothing else.

The night before, in the peaceful hours prior to the chaos and heartbreak, the trio had agreed to rouse at dawn. So that they might depart before the rest of camp, not wanting their alibi of being on a journey to Stedda to be revealed as a lie.

If they completed tonight successfully, the encampment would arrive to a celebration that war had been averted. With explanations only of a group bringing joyful news, but otherwise no connection needed to be made between Silas and his companions, and the messengers of such brilliant news.

Now more accustomed to camp and its array of senses, that and the dim morning light made the paths easier to follow and familiar spots more apparent, the wolf wove through the camp silently. His tent positioned as far from his previous residence as he could possible have made it, but still the journey was over all too soon.

He moved to part the tent doors and rouse his companions; but was stopped in place when it was rendered unnecessary. As Levi departed from the tents confines and jumped with surprise at the sight of the wolf lurking by the entrance.

Does he think I'm here to finish them off in their sleep? He considered briefly but didn't ask aloud.

"Sleep well?"

Had it not been for his resolute intention to remain silent, the wolf might well have laughed at the statement. Hardly the pleasantries he had expected after the confrontations of the night before, and the casual tone utilised depicted someone calm and at ease.

Despite this the wolf said not a word, narrowing a careful stare at the King's guard, who fortunately was quick to catch on and said nothing else.

Only a couple of minutes had passed before the would-be Prince also retreated from the warmth of the tent. Shivering against the cold at first he didn't notice the wolf standing a few paces away, "I might see if we can borrow some of those blankets," he explained to Levi, hugging himself in an attempt to keep some warmth close to his skin.

Levi said nothing, looking pointedly from between the two. Mason looked up, paled at the sight of Silas and gulped audibly. "Morning."

The wolf didn't answer.

"Are you ready to set off?"

The silence was something even the birds and gentle winds didn't interrupt.

"Is this going to be a common theme?"

His pointed look was the only response he offered, and Mason's sigh sounded. Silas could see the puffiness around his green eyes, but the prick of guilt that might usually have brought forth remained absent. Silas couldn't help but wonder if the efforts of the night before had all but killed any compassion from his system.

No, he still had compassion. But the betrayal revealed the night before was still a bitter and cruel creature, lingering in his shadow and reminding him with every breath.

Mason deflated when the wolf failed to answer but pried no further. Rather, Levi spoke up, breaking the painful silence between once good friends. "Her Majesty has asked us to bid her farewell before we leave," he explained.

Glancing to him in confusion, Silas didn't have the chance to ask – he had no oath of silence towards the King's Guard except for in the context of stupid questions. But the older gentleman continued before he had the chance.

"We don't need to tell her where we are headed, keep the pretences of heading to Stedda." He clarified, and Silas simply nodded in agreement.

Unaccustomed to the silence but insistent on making it a common trend, the trio turned and made their way back to the royal tent at the heart of the encampment.

When they reached there, a great pit had been devoured suddenly into the earth. Silas looked into it, uncertain of what to expect but partially assuming monsters might well be there scrambling to get out. To mild disappointment it was empty.

It took him a beat longer to realise its purpose, a grave for the fallen Adria.

"It's a great pity he can't be buried at sea," a voice sounded, pulling the wolf from his contemplation of the little grave, to see Niamh approaching at a steady pace. "It is a resting place a warrior like him truly deserves, but I imagine his spirit will understand that this is the best we can offer."

Levi softened as he watched her, "I'm sure he will," he affirmed. Niamh's returning smile was its usual all-encompassing affection, but the sadness in her eyes was enough to break the hearts of even the stoniest hearted Gods.

Steeling herself with a sharp inhale, she turned away from the grave and looked to the trio. Her gaze studied the wolf briefly, Silas didn't cower away from the watchful gaze. He could see hundreds of questions running through her wise gaze, and he stiffened in preparation to be bombarded with prying queries.

In the end all she said was, "Are you guys ready to get going?"

Relaxing somewhat at this, he allowed Mason to respond instead. "We are, hoping to reach Stedda by the time night falls again, that's why we're so early," he added with a playful resentment in his voice, lifting a hand to block a yawn from interrupting his words.

"I understand," Niamh answered, though her gaze didn't quite pull free from the wolf's muscled form. "I wish you the safest of journeys, and that whatever you are searching for at Stedda you are able to find." She explained.

Silas couldn't help but be struck with the sensation that there was something more to her wording, but Silas knew she wasn't likely to delve those answers, nor was the wolf willing to even begin to ask for further details.

"I'm sad our friendship was short," this woman of all people was the absolute least likely of them to see each other again. "But I did enjoy your company no matter brief," she added with a gentle chuckle, "And while I doubt it I hope we meet again sometime."

"We'll send word if we're ever going to sea," Levi promised solemnly. "And if you ever feel like becoming a land dweller for a day, let us know. It'd be nice to get to return your kindness."

Those wise eyes sparked with gentle amusement and kindness, "I will," and Silas knew she meant it. "Goodbye it is then, but not forever," she spoke it as an oath and Silas knew she intended to keep it.

The trio embraced with the queen, Silas held no ill against her and was willing to join in the farewells. Before the trio turned, and began making their way down the grassy knoll, Rehenney on the horizon, the rising sun framed by its towers.

Wordless, the wolf trudged ahead. He had the common sense in spite of his anger to keep his ears alert for any sounds that might go on in his wake; but nothing but quiet and uncomfortable chatter was heard from the pair behind him. He was content to take the lead, with Rehenney in their sights it seemed that at last their journey was going to be over.

Rather than be drowned out by oncoming storms as had been a recent trend, the sunlight remained bright overhead. Any clouds that threatened its rain were useless against its brightness, providing the trio with comfortable warmth with which to travel. The sodden ground underfoot, as well as his own still soaked clothes were quickly dried in its comfort.

Journeying comfortably through the grass, the long grass common to the area now thinned into moorland like expanses. The descent into the valley containing Rehenney was a gentle and meandering slope, interspersed with small woodlands.

They journeyed like that for a few miles, Rehenney originally but a spot on the horizon was quickly becoming larger with every few steps. Until the reigning city of the area came into full view in all its glory.

Whereas Brynde had relied on walls for its protection, this city believed so much in its own defensives that the walls were but more than a decoration. Small and pitiful compared to the beauty that had been Brynde, what felt like a lifetime ago. Silas could see not one entrance, but rather a handful dotted across the expansive walls, and even from a distance he could see that the walls were largely unprotected outside of the guards dotted about the foot of the walls.

It was when he spotted the foot of the walls that he noticed that everything wasn't as safe as it seemed.

But the foothills of the walls were the only true similarity that this city had with Brynde. For it was covered in people, intent to get inside with fear of the ensuing war.

Silas halted at the sight; the masses were easily double if not triple the size of those they had seen at the outskirts of Brynde. And their progression was even slower, Silas hesitated. Uncertain and unwilling to break his silence, but genuinely uncertain as to how in the name of the Gods they were going to be able to breach those walls.

Mason, fortunately, was more than willing to ask the questions that popped into Silas' head.

"How in the name of the Gods are we going to get through that?" The would-be Prince asked, it seemed that at every turn events were desperate to make sure the trio failed in their attempts. If they wanted this over by the end of the night, they were going to need to find another means of getting through those walls other than the customary means.

"Either of you any good at climbing?" The ex-King's guard asked uncertainly.

Both of the young men shook their heads, Silas persistently silent, but now out of shock as well as resent.

"Great," the older man considered, the trio came to a halt on the hillside just opposite the Rehenney's walls. Though smaller than Brynde, a drop from that height would be enough to kill the two more human companions and deliver a quite horrific blow to Silas. "We're going to need to figure something out," he stated the obvious.

Now his companions could only nod their heads, speechless and mildly panicked that yet again they were to be felled by an unforeseen obstacle.

Levi considered for a few moments further and offered. "I don't know if it'll work, and if it doesn't we will have to go through something pretty revolting and then go back all the same." He looked like he was trying to convince himself of any other option.

Silas regarded the guard, speaking for the first time in a low and blunt tone. "What is it?"

"Rehenney was one of the first cities to have sewers in Nekeldez," he explained lowly, "After the capital, of course. But they did it for cheap, the tunnels ended up crumbling and didn't take the waste out properly, so they had to spend a lot of money getting it redone." He explained lowly, his gaze dancing across Rehenney's forms. "But those tunnels still exist somewhere underground, if we can find one of the exits into a nearby river, we might just be able to get into the city using them."

Silas was made nauseous by the very idea, "How long have they been out of use?"

"Twenty years," Levi responded, swallowing hard. "And I doubt they even cleaned it well when it was in use, let alone now it is out of order."

Silas could imagine the smell already, and was desperate to find another way in. But it appeared their only options were those, especially if they wanted to do this with some inkling of speed. He simply nodded.

"Let's get searching then," Levi said with absolutely no enthusiasm to his tone of voice.

Relying largely on Silas' nose, the smell was faint at a distance but as they spanned out across the countryside it became almost unignorable. He was astonished his companions couldn't smell it, for to him the stench was nearly all consuming. He gestured, leading the way through the fields until they came across a small river. The followed its meandering paths a short while, until they came across a trio of pipes. Though they emptied nothing into the waters now, the area was still marked the pollution it had once pumped willingly into the waters.

The surrounding trees were long dead, a few fallen. The grasses along the banks dead and dry, it was a sad sight, but Silas wasn't here to comment on the scenery.

"Do you think we're going to fit?" Mason queried with some worry to his voice.

Levi regarded his companion with a withered grin, he was the… broadest by all of them by a longshot. "One way to find out."

Silas moved, wading through the shallow parts of the river until he was in front of the pipes. Knowing his luck it would be in that moment that the pipes decided to begin pumping again, but no sounds came from within. He elicited a shout, hearing it echo and trying to figure out its depth, but due to being a lycanthrope not a bat, struggled.

One way to find out, he mirrored Levi's begrudging statement.

Hooking his fingertips to the edge of the centre pipe, he dragged himself up, kicking off the ground he was in the pipe in the next second. He swivelled around with some difficulty, until he was peering his head out into the river again.

Trying not to concentrate too much on the smell he called, "Come one, I'll help you up." Silence was all very well and good but right now they needed to get into the city, he could continue his quiet streak once this obstacle was crossed.

Mason came to the front of the pipe, considered and lunged. Catching hold of the edge with outstretched fingers, he kicked like a madman at thin air. Silas grasped his hand and pulled him up. Allowing the would-be Prince to half clamber over him in order to get to the space behind. It was inelegant, but fortunately height wasn't the main problem, but width.

"Ready?" He muttered, trying not to cringe as the Prince delivered a kick to his kidneys by accident.

The ex-King's guard looked uncertain, but now was the time for none of that. "As I'll ever be," he launched upright. Silas caught hold of his hand, and with the other Levi was able to find leverage on the pipe and force himself through the opening.

Silas waited, worried that the pipe would snap beneath their weight, but after a moment it became apparent that they would be fine. It was a tight fit, and Levi would probably come out of this with a few scrapes and bruises from the ordeal, but he was in and alive.

Inhaling meekly, catching hold of the last breath of fresh air he could manage. Stuck between Mason's rear and the mountain that was Levi, it was an incredibly claustrophobic feeling. But they had little other choices than to trudge on now. It wasn't entirely possible to turn back, unless Silas felt like kicking Levi enough until he fell backwards out of the pipe.

The trio trudged on, staying on their bellies, dragging themselves through the what Silas hoped to be mud. It was dry and stank, only sticking to their clothes a little fortunately, thus allowing them something in the way of dignity, but given they were trudging through the sewers he didn't have great hopes in that regard.

It felt like they were moving for an eternity, but then due to the slow pace and minimal room to move they hadn't made much progression. Until suddenly from a few feet in front of him, Mason spoke up through the dark.

"The pipes have dropped off here," he spoke, worry apparent in his tone.

Levi shifted on the spot, uncomfortable, indignant and antsy. "That'll be where it opens up into where the water and… other substances should be, given none of us have drowned yet, it should be empty. Pull yourself out but be careful where you put your feet."

Scrabbling sounds lit the pipe, and then a thud of feet on concrete. "I'm okay!" His tone was triumphant in spite of it all.

Faster now, he dragged himself through the pipe and too was able to launch himself into the sewer works. It was dark and stank enough to rouse the dead from their sleep, but even he had to admit he felt triumphant at this minor victory. Levi followed a beat later, thankful to be out of the claustrophobic nature of the pipeline, even if here it was a little more grim.

"Which way now?" Mason's question was a frustrating one, namely due to the fact Silas had no idea how to answer it. He cast his gaze left and right, trying to catch any hint of fresh air in either direction but finding both annoyingly lacking. He shook his head – he had no idea.
"We should have enough time to get into Rehenney before nightfall, so it shouldn't matter too much that we get it right immediately," Levi offered hoping to keep morale up.

The wolf only nodded, following instinct and nothing else, praying it wouldn't fall for him now like everything else had done recently. He spanned right, following the concrete paths through the darkness, keeping his pace steady and careful. Though doubting that these sewers were home to anything other than rats, Silas had enough common sense to know there was reason enough to be careful in unknown territory, and from the looks of how many people were outside Rehenney's walls, he wondered if anyone else might try to take this route.

But aside from the occasional scrabble of tiny feet across hard concrete, and the occasional rattling as a misplaced foot sent cracked stone flying. It appeared they were the only ones in the sewers, that or someone nearby was a very talented hider.

The trio had been travelling at a reasonable pace for a period of time, the lack of light made their pace hesitant at first, but they soon gained confidence. Weaving down the tunnels until it felt like they had been going on for an eternity.

However, Silas slammed on the brakes out of the blue. Instincts rather than eyesight telling him the need to halt, at first he was uncertain. Muttering a warning sign for his companions to follow suit, he gestured in front of him. His hands colliding hard with the metallic bars, and whilst he wasn't tall enough to check, he assumed they reached the ceiling somewhere above them in the darkness.

Of course the Rehennians would have thought of this, Silas cringed. A groan pulling from his lips to demonstrate his frustration.

"At least we know we're on the right track?" Mason offered, but the attempt at a moral boost fell flat in the darkness of the tunnels.

He considered the bars carefully, remembering the situation in the Brynde dungeons briefly but that had been done by virtue of his wolf form only. And he didn't intend to shift in the darkness of the Rehenney sewers, knowing if he got lost here he would never be found. Plus if things went wrong and his companions ended up needing help from the wolf unleashed, no one was going to know it from the depths of these damp, dark cells.

"Silas you grab onto the one just left of the centre, me and Mason will try with the other." Levi's voice broke the silence, compliant the wolf took hold, and began pulling with all his might.

In their prime, the bars would have been a shining and brilliant form of protection. But now they were rusted and old, but still had some form of their former dignity, as despite Silas' best efforts it took a good few minutes for him to begin to feel the metal shift beneath his grip.

Kicking a leg against another bar, he forced himself almost horizontal as he pulled and dragged. Until slowly but surely a horrendous screeching sound echoed throughout the tunnels, and a few beats later the bar had been misshapen and bent.

Mason, the smallest of the trio was able to push through the gap and looked back with triumphant. But the wider Silas and Levi wouldn't stand a chance. Now with the teamwork of all three of them, they set to work once more, and it didn't take a few beats longer for that bar too to be forced out of shape and provided just about enough room for the remaining two to push through and onto the other side.

Silas moved to hurry through the tunnels again, but a grip affixed to his wrist and he looked back with surprise.

"Unfortunately boys, while I thank you for your help in getting me this far," it was Levi's voice, and he sounded genuinely apologetic as he spoke. "But this is as far as I'm going to let you go, as I have intentions for Rehenney, and unfortunately you too are quite in the way of what needs to be done.

Confusion ripped through Silas, he launched forward and tried to wrench his hand from the mountain of a man's massive grip. But by the time he had moved his feet the sound of clanging metal against metal sounded, and the wolf turned back to find his right hand in chains.

Mason panicked too, and lunged to try and intersect Levi, but he was simply knocked against the bars and handcuffed too without too much effort on the part of the massive gentleman.

"What in the name of the Gods?" Silas demanded, swiping out with his remaining hand but he found it impossible to reach the ex-King's guard, who now stood a few feet away. "I thought you wanted to help us!" Silas yelled, anger ricocheting through the tunnels as easily as any bullet.

"And I did, I didn't want two young boys to get themselves killed getting into Rehenney, but that doesn't mean I was ever with you, ever wanting you to help end this war," a frown etched into his barely visible expression. "I think you should have probably taken the time to ask exactly why I am an ex King's guard."

He'd said he was retired, but now the assumption he was being sincere seemed quite idiotic.

"I thought you were a friend," Mason's voice was heartbroken and terrified.

"I was," he replied with a frown and a shake of his head. "But that doesn't change things at all, I am here on a mission, and sadly I can't let you too get in the way of that."

"And what would this righteous plan be, so brilliant that you intend to stop some of the only people capable of stopping Nekeldez being thrust into war?" Silas demanded, the panic making it difficult for him to breathe, and despite the silver he pulled and yanked desperately against the silver cuff, but it rendered his wrist bloodied rather than free.

For a moment Levi hesitated, watching them uncertain but then deciding that they weren't going to be easily freed of those handcuffs, it didn't really matter too much. "I will tell the mayor here that the attack on Braxas is to go ahead, the breaking of the peace treaty will spark war. And the chaos that ensues will be utilised to overthrow that coward of a King and place a better suited person in his place." His answer was simple and easy, well-rehearsed and something their friend truly believed in.

"And you think Joseph will believe you?" Silas scoffed.

"He will," that voice harboured no doubt, "Mayor Joseph is my brother."

At first Silas assumed this was a lie, and then he remembered what the King had described the city's mayor as, *as big as a mountain*. That wasn't much of a description, but it was enough to assume there could be some truth in what the older gentleman said.

"Why?" Was all Silas could ask, his mother's terror of the idea that war might spark again had sparked his own motivations to ensure that it never happened. He was genuinely terrified as to why anyone would want otherwise. "And not just because that man is a coward, that is no proper reason to descend a kingdom into war," Silas snarled before Levi was able to use that as an excuse.

Levi shook his head, eyes saddened for a beat. "Because this kingdom deserves better than a man who would rather see it starved by taxes, ruined by invaders and used as little more than a footstool by the other kingdoms, than he would fight back to make Nekeldez something better than it currently is."

The ex-King's guard straightened and considered the two briefly. "It was good knowing you, and as a sign of that friendship I will be back in a day or two when all this is over to ensure you are freed and safe. But right now I need you out of the picture."

He gave neither of the young men the chance to answer, as he turned away and began trudging through the tunnels once more.

"Wait!" Mason's voice sounded uselessly through the tunnels, but the gentleman didn't turn back, the time for talking over it seemed. "I want to help."

Chapter Twenty-Nine.

Silas felt like he'd been hit by a brick wall, and Levi looked like he'd been struck by a train. A happy train; but the surprise lighting his expression was palpable.

He was initially certain that he'd heard things, that the young man had said nothing in the first place. After all they had been through it seemed impossible that his companion would want to change sides at the last moment.

Levi seemed equally confused, and when no further words followed he moved to continue through the tunnels. Which prompted the would-be Prince to speak again. "I mean it." He repeated, louder and more desperately this time.

"Mason, no." Was all he could manage, but the would-be Prince neither acknowledged that he had spoken or even turned to look at him. Those green eyes piercing through the dark, not wavering from where Levi now stood at a halt, unsure of whether to listen.

The ex-King's guard turned on his heel and returned at a slow pace. Considering the offer carefully, he watched the Prince for a moment, before asking with a gentle tone. "Why would you want to help me?" He asked lowly, before continuing with a tilt of his head, "And more importantly why should I believe you?"

Mason's weak laugh bounced of the tunnel walls; it was a broken sound. "You saw what the king did to Brynde, despite having every reason to believe that I was confined there with no hopes of escaping, he gave me up as a ward many days ago, that much is clear." His voice shook with emotion, but the young man remained steadfast and upright in spite of it. "And the last few days have taught me that isn't a man I want to follow or aid a day further; I believe dethroning him is the best thing that can happen for the Kingdom."

Despite having spent much of the morning avoiding the young man and not speaking as much as a word to him, Silas found his gaze hopelessly fixed to the young man's form. He shivered where he was tied upright, desperate to find words, but he found none.

The wolf was desperate to pick up on even a hint that his companion might have been lying, try to gain freedom from these bonds to do the exact opposite. But no matter how he tried he couldn't smell a lie within his words, and Silas bowed his head, broken.

Levi considered this and looked to be about to turn tail and continue through the tunnels in spite of this admission. But he was torn, gravity from either end pulling him in two directions and he seemed to find difficulty in deciding which to pick.

"Know if this turns out to be a trick you wont live to see another sunrise." The threat all but laced the older gentleman's tone of voice, and Silas had no doubt he was exaggerating even in the slightest.

"Understood, sir." Mason said quietly.

Levi approached at a careful pace, as though expecting some sort of trickery. He withdrew a key from his inner pocket and carefully prodded about at Mason's handcuff, until it could turn and was released. Mason stepped forward, wordless and his head bowed.

Silas could only watch, hate echoing through his very core, the betrayal of the last few days was a weight even the mountains would have quivered beneath. And now he was to be left here to rot for who knows how long, he might as well have not been freed of Brynde's dungeons, as it seemed that this was where he was always going to return.

Freed again, Mason turned and looked at Silas, the wolf could feel his gaze burning through his skin, but the young man didn't give his once friend the dignity of lifting his gaze to meet those green eyes. He watched the tunnel ground, unmoving, unspeaking, and all but writhing with anger.

"Sy, it doesn't need to end like this," he said lowly. His voice gentle and hopeful in spite of all of it, "You have to see that the Kingdom wants war."

Memories of his mother's terror when the prospect of war came up danced through his watery eyes, the number of people he had seen in his home time broken by their experiences of war. He knew that was a lie but said nothing.

Of course someone raised in the context of the King's court, and a gentleman who had only known war in small contexts of skirmishes and squabbles. Not the outright war so many of the older, less fortunate generations had experienced. This pair saw the prospect of war through rose tinted glasses, as the joys it might bring once over, not the pains it would wreak whilst ongoing.

"Sy?" Mason prodded, under some idiotic impression that it might be possible to convince him any further.

Silas growled lowly when the young man stepped forward, "Come any closer and you'll lose an eye, and I wont even have to shift." He warned, meaning every minute of it.

Mason recoiled, unused to being threatened by his once friend. He considered the chained wolf, trying to find the words with which he might convince him any further. But Levi simply rested a hand upon the would-be Prince's shoulder, shaking his head. "Its pointless, come on let's get going." Levi gestured, though the sadness was evident in his tone.

He moved to depart, but at the last moment seemed to think better of it. "Given this will go without use, it might not be silver, but one can never be too careful," his voice was matter of fact not taunting, but Silas hated it all the same.

Levi knelt down again, enough of a distance that the wolf couldn't lash out in order to hurt him. He set about cuffing the wolf's free hand, and tying that too to the bar behind up, until he was propped up by his muscled arms. With nothing to defend himself.

Silas growled low and loud. "Don't bother coming back for me, its safer for the both of you if you leave me down here to die."

The mountain of a man considered this briefly, eyes narrowed but otherwise seemingly unperturbed by what had been said. He turned once more and began departing through the darkness without a further word, Silas simply watched through broken eyes.

The young man watched as his companion departed, caught between choices. He looked back at Silas, hopeless and broken on the floor of the sewers. "We'll see you again soon Sy, please know we're doing this for the right reasons." He said quietly, but he too quickly departed through the midnight black of the sewers.

And in an all too familiar position, Silas was left alone, chained in the dark once more.

For a brief moment Silas remained there, watching and praying. Begging anything he thought would listen that all of this would turn out to be some cruel prank, that his companions would return to him laughing and joking, and they would continue on together. But no one appeared through the dark.

Silas doubted the Gods could even peer into a place as dark and hideous as this.

This was a place for rats, and dirt. Of course the wolf should have felt quite at home.

The wolf sat down with an inadvertent whimper. The chain didn't offer much room, and he could only just settle down on his bum, arm held rigid above his head where it was chained to the bars.

It was a familiar scenario, something a week ago he would have thought of as nothing more than a minor inconvenience. But now he had gone through the last week of adventure, fear and friendship, this was something that left him heartbroken. He had gained so much in the handful of a few days, and all of it had disappeared into nothing. He started where he had so often begun, but now every inkling of his hope had flooded free of his system.

Leaving nothing but a broken, hopeless young man, lost in the dark.

But in the dark and lonely tunnels, Silas couldn't help but consider the parting words of his once friends. The true belief that they could find a better life for those of Nekeldez, but that life was something that would be won through blood, tears and loss.

His eyes darkened with memories of the stories his mother would regale him with, that might it sound that the ones that were killed were the fortunate ones, and those who came back were never the same as they once were.

His mother had been among the fortunate few who had returned home alive, he hadn't been born in those days, but he could imagine what she would have been like before.

But one of the few times he had ever seen his mother scared was when faced with the possibility of the return of war to Nekeldez. Her true terror made the very idea of joining a group intending to help bring war back to the realm revolting too him.

For in the first war they had fought hard, with everything they'd had in order to win back a better life. And they had lost, and now people were starving, and the kingdom taxed to the point of destruction, things returned to the status quo if not worse.

Silas knew, if from stories alone that the idea of what came with victory was a beautiful and glorious concept. But at the end of all of it, there would be no certainty that they would triumph, and the chances that came with failure were all the worse.

But who are you to not even give them the chance to decide their own fate, a voice in his own head taunted him, and Silas shifted on the spot uncomfortable at the insistent prompting. His own ghosts teasing and laughing at him, the joys of the dark solitude of a broken young man. *Who are you to steal the chance of freedom from them, before they even know it's a possibility?*

The growl that tugged from Silas' throat was a violent and angry tone, but there was no one to be scared away in order to shut the voices up. They were all his own, stemming from guilt and uncertainty of all the choices he had made up until that point.

It didn't matter anymore, he told himself. Despite his best efforts it had all been in vain, and Mason and Levi were going to choose the Kingdom's fate, and that fate was to be war. Pain with the hopes of bringing the kingdom into enough chaos as to overthrow a coward King.

Silas buried his head into his knees in an attempt to stifle his cries. Even with no one around to hear him, the sound was as taunting as any of the voices he had been subjected to.

His mother would be so disappointed in him, the realisation struck him like bullet between the shoulder blades. Flick was young enough – she'd be drafted no doubt. His brother and sister, he would go free, no wolves would be permitted on the battlefield for fear of the dangers they might reap among their own ranks. But his family wasn't going to be so lucky.

He would be left to watch on the side lines, helpless as he ever was while his beloved family lost their lives for the sake of a losing cause.

The realisation that Rosie's funeral would have been and gone was like an unexpected freight train, in all the excitement he had so willingly pushed the tragedy to the back of his head. So intent to ensure that her death wouldn't be in vain, but now that was all for nothing.

The scream that wrenched from his lips was like nothing he'd ever made in his life, the echoing sound ricocheted about him, doubling tripling until it was all he could hear. He was certain that he was losing his mind in that moment, that even if he became free of these chains there would be nothing left of him worth being alive.

It hadn't been the feral parts of him that had gotten the worst of him, forced his humanity from his own body. But rather his own ability to trust too much, and now all he loved was going to suffer because of it.

The young wolf sat there, torturing himself with self-deprecating hatred, the echoing finished and through the dark he heard a voice.

It need not all be in vain, get yourself free and try one last time. The voice was a gentle song on the melody, kind despite its unfamiliarity, light in spite of the midnight black that flooded the tunnels and stole all hope from sight. *You cannot be felled at the final obstacle Silas.*

No face nor name came to mind at the sound of the voice, but somehow it was familiar to him. He had no idea where from. He was going mad, the wolf despaired to himself, rocking his head to the side in frustration, there were no other explanations for it.

But insane or not, he knew there was a truth in what had been said. But there was only one outcome he could see.

Please, please no. He begged anything that would listen, but he could see no other option.

He stood upright and began tugging with all his might. Desperate for the pole to break off without the need to shift and be more forceful. But the efforts rendered his restrained wrists bloodied, tears welled in his gaze as he fought on. Desperate to pull the silver free of his arm once and for all, but his best efforts seemed to make almost no difference.

Gulping hard, it seemed he had no other choice.

Silver was a strange substance, the amount of it differed the amount it effected the wolf. If consumed it was lethal, if it entered the bloodstream it was lethal. But when worn it would wear down the senses, weaken the strength and the speed of the wearer. And theoretically should have stopped the wolf from being able to shift outright.

The memory of what the Angofwen queen had said to him came in that moment. She had known creatures be able to fight against the restraints provided by silver, ignore its effects in order to use their full powers.

He had never asked what she had meant, only that she hadn't referred to lycans alone. For all he knew it could well have meant the unicorns, the trolls or maybe even the fairies. But for now, all he could hope was that the statement would be applicable to him.

He loosened his bloody hands, pulling the silver as far down until the restraints wouldn't budge an inch more. And using that leverage he carefully manoeuvred his hands, trying to make it so that no part of his skin was touching the silver itself, encapsulated but not in contact with it. A small space of a couple of centimetres around either wrist.

It was slow, agonisingly slow.

For the first time he could remember it was a choice, and he wasn't sure how to even ask. In the beginning it seemed that his efforts were for nought, then slowly but surely the prickle began to shake through his frame.

He felt every beat of it, every sprouting of fur across his arms legs and the rest of his body, the tail sprout from bare skin and ears relocate with a flourish. His muzzle lurched forward, dragging a cry of pain from him, as one by one the bones in his arms and legs broke and snapped, changing form.

In his transforming chest he could hear his heart thundering, and the thoughts flew through his head that this was a terrible idea and that he was going to get himself killed.

Yet he continued in spite of his worst fears.

Until finally he stood in the four-legged form of his wolf.

Forearms, or rather now forelegs caught in the cuffs, he jerked back. The pain was like nothing he had known, the silver trying to force him to shift back into human form, but he didn't permit it. Where once he would have fought with everything he had to return to human, now he refused to even let the idea cross his mind.

Until finally the handcuffs broke beneath the pressure he placed on them.

Grateful he had managed and terrified he might not be able to get back. He tried to return to human form, but he didn't – though not for lack of effort. He realised this might be the best form to keep up in, with a deep breath. The wolf took off running through the dark tunnels.

All he could do was try to follow the scents of his departed companions; above the even stronger stenches of the sewers they were only just noticeable. But he caught hold of them and followed. He had no idea as to how long he had been left in the darkness with his own thoughts, it might well have been anything between hours and minutes.

He followed the scents through the tunnels, but he had been travelling for maybe twenty minutes when the scent disappeared alltogether. He retraced his steps a few beats, but still it was gone, and Silas panicked desperately. Realising he might well have gotten himself hopelessly lost in the depths of the sewers.

Then he had the good fortune of looking up.

Above him and to the left a few metres, a small circle of light hovered in the ceiling by the wall. And careful prying brought him to the metal rungs of a ladder. A few of them were broken, and he could only hope that such was from a time before today, and that his once friends hadn't been hurt in their efforts to escape the tunnels.

Don't be so worried about them, they're traitors. The wolf told himself, but he couldn't help it.

Now he permitted the shift back to take place, initially terrified that his body wouldn't comply, but within minutes of painstaking waiting. He stood once more on two feet, and gratitude rocked through the core of his system.

Inhaling weakly, the wolf made his way up the metal ladder. Reaching the ceiling he had moved to shove it open but realised a beat later how terrible an idea that would be. He waited; the sound of footsteps so faint from this deep underground he wasn't sure he didn't hallucinate it.

But after a moment of silence, or what he could only hope was silence, Silas knew there was little other choice but to try. The wolf pushed upwards, hard. The manhole cover coming free with a metallic rattle. The wolf moved quickly, launching through the newly revealed opening and onto the rocky ground above once more.

He looked around, heart thundering. He was surprised when no one lunged to kill him for his efforts, but no one came.

And he found himself in the confines of Rehenney.

The manhole had allowed him entrance into the city from in a little back alley, and no one was about as far as he could see. He inhaled, trying to catch any signs of the direction that his companions might have gone in, but his nostrils were flooded with the new smells, as well as the lingering stenches of the disused sewers he had left behind.

Carefully he turned the corner and onto the main street, it was alive with the usual buzz of a midday city. People strolling in the now early afternoon sun, and no one paid him much attention, something he was very grateful for.

He tilted his head up, spotting not a palace but something more akin to a quite regal looking house, but nothing compared to some of the stories he heard. And given the central and quite isolated nature of it, atop a little hill, Silas could only hope that was the destination he was searching for.

Unnoticed, the people around him were oblivious to the lycan in their presence and continued about their lives. As the wolf meandered up the streets, trying to find a balance between a steady enough pace that no one would see him as hurrying and draw needless attention, but fast enough as the understanding was ever at the back of his mind that his companions had already made their entrance.

The great house was regal in short, it flew the mayor's colours on banners soaring high into the pale blue-sky overhead. A few guards patrolled the borders, but Silas approached as confidently as he could manage, until he came across an armed gentleman who he stopped.

All at once remembering the lost nature of the king's letters, the one thing that would ensure the mayor would believe what he had to say. Silas could only hope they would believe him at face value, for there was little other choices he had.

"Excuse me, I'm sorry but its quite urgent," he explained, grateful when the guard didn't tell him to get lost off the bat. "My name is Silas, and I am here on a mission from King Ezekiel, and I truly need to find the mayor and speak with him."

The guard regarded him with amusement, clearly assuming the wolf either to be highly intoxicated or simply mad, neither of which the wolf would have been offended by. "I didn't expect the King's ward to smell quite so much like weak old vomit." He responded.

Silas cringed at this but believed now of all times wasn't the time to explain his… unconventional means of entering the city. "But you have been expecting me?"

The stranger nodded, "Indeed, for a few days now, word came to us from Malowa that we should be expecting someone, forgive me if I didn't expect them to look like a drowned rat." Silas might have been offended had it not been for the kind laughter brimming in the guard's gaze. "Come, follow me." He said, gesturing, and the young man did as he was told without argument.

He couldn't begin to wonder where his companions had gotten too, nor what he would even begin to tell the mayor of this city when they met, nor how he would convince him that he was trying to tell the truth.

Either way, the choice he made that day would be the impossible choice, but in the absence of Levi and Mason, it was his choice to make.

Chapter Thirty.

As he was led through the great wooden entrance, Silas realised that the great house was far more regal on the outside than it was on the inside.

Much of the outside gave the insistence of elegance, demanded attention with just about its every aspect. From the extravagant flower gardens lacing the paths leading up to it, to the small statues littering the front lawn. It wanted to give the impression of extravagance and wealth.

Its innards, however, were bare and entirely fit for purpose. Ugly to an extent, its walls without the grandiose pictures he'd seen in Brynde, or any of the colour that had left him in awe in the context of the Angofwen wagon train, or really anything that made it a home for that matter.

The guard lead him wordlessly through the entrance hall, a small marble room, a handful of people scattered across it but those were largely the only inhabitants that could be seen.

He was led down a corridor and stopped abruptly at a small room, the guard knocked to ensure it was empty. Opened the door and lead the young man in, gesturing for him to take a seat on the chair.

"I'll go find him for you, it might take a short while but -" he didn't finish as he cast a narrowed gaze down at Silas' wrists, a glance downwards made Silas realise a beat too late that they were bloodied. No longer bleeding, but it was hard to tell from the amount lacing his limbs. "You're bleeding," the guard commented with the calm of someone who had seen far worse wounds in his life.

Flushing bright red at the comment, he nodded meekly. "Not anymore, I took a bad fall but it's not as bad as it looks, do you have somewhere I can wash off?" He begged to himself that his lie was believable enough, and he absent mindedly began wiping at the since fairly healed wounds, rather self-conscious that he was hardly coming across as a competent messenger.

The guard considered, wondering whether to permit the stranger to go roaming about the secure halls of the manor house. "No, but I'll see if I can organise to have someone bring you down a pail of water so you can make yourself a little more... presentable."

This gentleman was quite talented in making insults sound so pleasing to hear it was difficult to be offended by them. Though Silas would hardly have minded if he meant it as the utmost of insults, Silas could barely concentrate over the smell he carried.

Nodding his head appreciatively, "If you could I would be grateful," he said. Trying to force the colour from his cheeks, but the guard only regarded him with a genuinely kind smile, before departing from the room and leaving Silas to his thoughts.

It was hardly the brilliant start he would have wanted, coming across less the charismatic gentleman Mason usually conveyed himself as, and rather looking quite the insane idiot.

Here he caught not even the slightest indication that neither Mason nor Levi had been within a hundred miles of this place. None of their scent was even hinted at on the air no matter how he searched, and in spite of his common sense he couldn't help but be worried about what had happened to them.

But now wasn't the time to go searching for those idiots, he had to concentrate on getting the here and no done. Then he could go on the wild goose chase no doubt necessary in order to pinpoint the location of his friends.

Shifting on the spot, he was antsy and restless. The sensation of being deep within enemy territory was intrinsic in that moment, all too aware that he had lost the person who would normally have done all the talking, as well as the document they could use to demonstrate a single word he gave had even the slightest lick of authority behind it.

The little room he was settled in was a little more pleasant than the rest of the house he had seen so far, little sofas littered the room. Bookshelves and pots of plants lined the walls, and the smell was of ancient wood. He tried to feel at ease; but couldn't help but shake the sensation that he was a lone wolf over enemy lines.

It took a little while, but soon the great wooden door clicked again, and the guard returned carrying a great pail of water, which he set at the side of the room. Nodding to Silas, he said lowly, "Try to be quick, he will be with you as soon as possible, but wont even bother if you look like you've been dragged backwards through the sewers. "I'll be back as soon as I can, but right now I have other things to be concentrating on, don't get into trouble. Or it will be on my head."

Silas only grinned meekly and took his recommendations and set to work.

After a few moments he smelled a little fresher and looked a little neater. His clothes returned to his frame; he was grateful that much of the scent was masked from the air. He took a short while to run his fingers through his thick hair, trying to look more representable.

Mildly surprised that he was permitted to be alone in the depths of Rehenney, he found their composure and calmness bizarre in comparison to the strict carefulness that Brynde had demonstrated. Their almost lax attitude seemed out of place with war on the horizon.

Did they already know war was off? *How could they*? He scolded himself, annoyed.

But then he considered with some fear that they might not care what he had to say, if rebels had gotten into Brynde and brought Isaac onto their side; how did he know that plague of rebellion had spread here.

It couldn't there weren't enough people wanting this. But the truth of the matter was that Silas truly didn't know who he could believe.

He had moved to straighten his shirt, when the door opened once more. He looked up, praying to the Gods that he looked anywhere near presentable enough to be believed. But the face that looked at him belonged to mountain, nor did it belong to a man named Joseph.

Namely because the newcomer was a woman, though Silas wasn't one to judge unusual naming conventions he didn't believe Ezekiel would describe someone as short as the woman before him as anything near mountainous.

"Unless I'm grievously mistaken you're no the mayor?" He asked, tensed and uncertain. A single traumatic experience at Brynde had left him scarred to more of an extent than he cared to admit. His eyes watchful and dancing, aware of every place the stranger might have been hiding a weapon on her slender frame.

Despite her kind composure, Silas sensed something darker beneath the layers. Like this woman could tear open a neck or break bones or slit a neck with the same ease as she breathed and walked.

The wolf didn't know whether he was being over dramatic, overly cautious, fairly reasonable or something between the three. But an old wolf struggled to learn new tricks. And the bruises and wounds were still relatively fresh all across his muscled frame.

A shot of panic blinked through his veins that much like what had happened in Brynde, the previous mayor here had been killed too. But the relaxed and smiling composure of the woman demonstrated that either she was incredibly good at hiding her grief, or there was nothing to grieve at all.

Her smile was sardonic, observant and careful. Her chuckle humourless but steely, "You're clearly very smart," she said with a roll of her eyes. "No, I am not Joseph. I am his second hand; you may call me Lieutenant."

Whether a nickname, a careful means of ensuring Silas didn't know her real name, or some other reason he wasn't sure. Silas was happy to comply with her requests for the time being, but that didn't leave him without questions.

"And where would the Mayor be, Lieutenant?" He pried.

"Patience is a virtue you'd enjoy, young man," she replied, taking a seat on the sofa nearby though had enough common sense in not electing to share one. "He is in meetings, as I'm sure you saw from the massive crowds outside of the city – things are quite… uncertain at the moment, and he has a lot on his plate." Everything was matter of fact and calm, and Lieutenant looked like she wouldn't have been disturbed if a bomb went off.

"So, for the time being, what is it that I can do for you?" She asked with a tilt to her head, watching him as the starved vulture watches faltering prey. "What brings you to the wonderful city of Rehenney for today?"

For a moment Silas might well have given her the answers just to shake her intense gaze, but he remained steadfast.

"I'm sorry, Lieutenant, but I'm under strict orders to not tell anyone the information I have unless I'm in the presence of the mayor," he explained, cringing as the frown crossed her expression as deep as the blood in her veins. "Forgive me, but it would be my head on the chopping block if anything were to go wrong."

Lieutenant had the strict demeanour of someone who had never forgiven a person in her life. But she nodded, calmly stating. "Fair enough, but I did here there was meant to be more than one of you? Did your companion make the mistake of sharing too much?"

The wolf gulped, his gaze becoming affixed to the floor was he sought an alibi he thought he might get away with.

"Unfortunately, we were split up inside Brynde, there was some difficulties there and we weren't able to regroup," he decided upon the closest thing to the truth he could come up with. "There was some rebel trouble there and try as I might I couldn't find him. So I decided the best option would be to come here alone."

The woman considered this, and for several tense moments there was silence between the silence. From what the wolf had witnessed over the last few days, it was a believable enough lie, and like the best ones was built partially in the truth. But whether this stranger would see it like that, the young man had no idea.

Nekeldez was in chaos, and it wasn't that far out of the realm of possibility that two people – little more than ripples in the madness, had been split up in spite of their best efforts.

But Silas couldn't help but worry she wouldn't see it that way, that she would smell out the lie as easily as the wolf would be able to. He kept himself as calm as he could, hoping to mould himself as something inconspicuous and unassuming. But he couldn't shake the feeling that the lie would be as obvious as though he were holding a great sign above his head advertising that very fact.

"I heard about rebel action in Brynde," she admitted after a moment, her tone would have sounded kind but her composure and the light in her eyes was far from the magnanimous attitude she otherwise seemed to be trying to put across. "I'm sorry to hear you had to go through that, and I hope you are doing okay?" But her voice was neutral, the apology non-existent outside of the words she chose.

"Thank you," he replied quietly.

Her chuckle shook him, the sound seemed out of place on the woman's voice, as though it was a child's first attempt at copying a sound it had heard from parents. Not something stemming from a genuine or even humorous place.

Upon spotting his confusion, she shook her head. "The entire Kingdom is suffering with rebels you see," she explained, moving her hands to tighten the ponytail her long midnight black hair was swept meticulously back into. "In fact just today, some of my guards came across a pair of idiots; suspected rebels trying to break into the city, through the sewers of all places."

Silas laughed back, for fear if he didn't the terror in his frame would give away his connection to the idiots she described. "I can't begin to imagine," he responded with a weak smile. All at once the stench of the sewers returned to his nostrils, and he could only pray it was hallucinations playing games with him, and nothing quite as palpable as he believed.

The Lieutenant shrugged her shoulders, "Desperate times call for desperate measures, and they believe in the cause enough I suppose I must credit them that much at least." She shrugged, but no matter how much she devolved to Silas, the wolf couldn't shake the idea that there was so much more that she wasn't sharing.

But then the number of things he was keeping to himself couldn't be counted correctly on half a dozen pairs of hands. He smiled but felt no need to respond any further.

"And in times like these we need to keep our own safe before all others," her words brought the image of the desperate at the foot of the Rehenney walls. Couldn't help but feel that they were left there on purpose to some extent.

So far the wolf couldn't find any hint that this stranger aligned herself with a rebel, past experience had thus far demonstrated that such was enough of a reason for the King to send slaughter this way.

Don't let what happened to Brynde happen here. The innocents outside of Rehenney alone were greater in number than the people he had seen in Brynde, and he knew the fallout of an attack here would be all the worse.

But he wouldn't have to worry about that much more, he could call off the war, and none of this needed to continue a beat further.

Any further thoughts were stolen from him; however, as the door clicked open once more and a man much easier described as a mountain entered. The resemblance to Levi shook him at first, and for a moment he feared this would all be some terrible prank, or the gentleman wasn't mayor at all.

But a closer inspection brought to attention the details, whereas his once friend was scarred from years as a King's guard, this gentleman's features were flawless. Where Levi's features were hardened but humorous, this gentleman was soft but watchful.

Silas permitted himself to relax, even a bit.

Joseph approached, clasping hands around Silas' before he could react. He greeted the wolf kindly enough. "Its good to see you," he explained, but before the wolf had the chance to respond, a frown had already graced the Mayor's features. "It seems that the messengers sent to other cities haven't reached as much success, so I must admit I find a lot of joy in knowing that our city can harbour one of the few messengers able to make it."

"You believe me then?" He admitted in hindsight that was possibly the absolute stupidest thing he could have said in the moment.

"Is there a reason I shouldn't?" This mayor's voice turned to stone suddenly, his eyes narrowed and careful.

Hoping to play down his dumb moment, "I've spent the last few days terrified about the fact I lost the King's letter, so I'm thankful that it doesn't seem necessary to prove what I'm talking about," he answered, trying to keep a restraint on the hope bubbling from his chest.

The mayor seemed to consider this for a moment, elected what had been said was reasonable enough, and nodded his head. "Few people knew the king sent out messengers as far as I'm aware, so unless you happen to be psychic, I believe you are the real deal."

Thank the Gods. "I see," was all he said aloud.

"Now pray tell, I've been waiting on the edge of my seat for some days now as to what on earth the King has decided to do. We've been preparing for an oncoming war for some months now," he explained.

It was time to face the music.

Silas blinked at this understanding – he had known the journey would be dangerous for all parties involved, but to learn that almost if not none of the other parties had reached their destination was like being struck by lightning.

Had Ezekiel made it there alive? Surely he would have heard something about it had that been the case, but the last few weeks left the wolf genuinely uncertain.

He stiffened sharply, left only to pray that the decision he made was the right one.

"The King sent me here to tell you that the war with Braxas is over." He said at last, trying to keep the shake out of his tone of voice, his moon kissed gaze fixed to the towering mayor. "He wants you to remove your troops from the country, the King wants peace."

Whether that was what the Kingdom wanted… he wasn't sure, and time would only tell whether his decision was the right one.

Printed in Great Britain
by Amazon